THE DEADLY
INVITATION

By the same author:

No Accounting for Murder (The Book Guild, 1988)

THE DEADLY INVITATION

Derek Budden

The Book Guild Ltd
Sussex, England

The Book Guild Ltd
25 High Street,
Lewes, Sussex

First published 1997
© Derek Budden, 1997
Set in Baskerville
Typesetting by Keyboard Services, Luton, Beds.

Printed in Great Britain by
Bookcraft (Bath) Ltd, Avon.

A catalogue record for this book is
available from the British Library

ISBN 1 85776 180 4

With love
To my family and friends

Oft in the stilly night
Ere slumber's chain has bound me
Fond memory brings the light
of other days around me

Thomas Moore (1779–1852)

ACKNOWLEDGEMENTS

With sincere thanks to Angela Bishop for her
invaluable assistance.

My gratitude also to members of:

The Australian Federal Police
The Australian Customs Service
The Pearl Producers Association
and
Dr Ian Mertling-Blake

PROLOGUE

Moscow, April 1975

'So,' he murmured contentedly, 'the die is cast.'

A humourless smile settled on his scarred face, as he surveyed the four men and two women sitting opposite him at the conference table. It had been a long meeting.

'The die is cast,' he repeated slowly, 'or should I say ... the cast is dying? I rather like that. Rather droll, don't you think?' No one responded as they all watched him. 'The cast ... is all in place?' They nodded as one. 'Good. You are each sure of your man?' It was another rhetorical question. 'Remember you do nothing – nothing at all, until you are told. It may be soon, it may be next year or it may not be for ten years or even longer.'

'What if they talk afterwards?' It was a woman who spoke.

'You chose them. You know what to do. They are your responsibility.' The soft reply was intimidating. 'Just as you are mine. It is my responsibility that nobody talks – ever. I can rely on all of you. You can't rely on them.' His meaning was quite clear.

The oldest of the men said, 'You mentioned ten years. What happens if...'

'If you are no longer ... with us? You will never be alone.' Fingers drummed on the table. 'We will always know what is happening to you and the cast.'

His cold blue eyes looked up at the watery sun shining through the window, as he added, 'We have allowed for contingencies.'

A silence held for a second before he rose and nodded. 'We

will never meet again as a group.' He walked to the door and opened it wide. 'In fact, we have never met. You will receive your instructions when it is time. As of this afternoon, the fuse has been lit. Now, please leave this building by your designated doors. I wish you safe journeys back.'

They left, one by one. They made no attempt to shake his hand. They knew he never did. As the door closed he sat down and cracked the bones of his knuckles. It sounded like a salvo of small arms fire. Rather appropriate in the circumstances he thought.

2

1

'Wait a minute, wait a minute, I'm not sure about Tuscany. I think I'd like to go to Broome.' June Campbell rubbed her hand up David Price's crossed thighs, as she stood up and walked to the open wine bottle on the sideboard.

'But you've been on about Tuscany for months!' David was astonished. 'You said you wanted to wander around the olive groves and the tranquil villages up in the hills, visit Leonardo Da Vinci's birthplace...'

'Oh, my poor baby!' June smiled sweetly. 'Haven't you realised yet that women change their minds? No, I think Broome.' She refilled her glass. David shook his head in bewilderment.

'This Broome. Where the hell is it?' His eyes followed June's path back to the sofa. He admired the contours of her body and her long blonde hair as much as when he had first met her.

'It's in Australia. More specifically Western Australia and more specifically still, about two hours' flying time north of Perth.' She sat down next to David and sipped her Rosemount Chardonnay before placing the glass carefully on the coffee table, which was covered with multi-coloured brochures from every conceivable travel company.

David Price, tall, dark and mid-forties, was a partner in a West London firm of Chartered Accountants, married to an enthusiastic fashion buyer at a department store in London's

3

fashionable Knightsbridge, where, as she put it, the Sloane Rangers rode again and again. June had kept her maiden name for business reasons. She was frequently away on buying trips and, as David often worked late, so they enjoyed the rare luxury of a good dinner together at home in their 1920s house in a fashionable part of Chiswick.

'Well, I've never heard of it. It's not in any of these bloody brochures, anyway.' He threw the one he had been leafing through back on the table, but all it did was slide on to the floor and bring some others down with it. He bent over and slowly gathered them together.

'Are you sure there is such a place? You haven't had too much of that Australian vino?' As he said this, David frowned petulantly. His glass was empty again.

'Darling, don't be so rude and don't be so obtuse, you know it exists.' June rose and refilled David's glass, as the grandfather clock struck ten. 'Don't you remember that travelogue the other night on the television when you commented on the beautiful blue of the sea?'

'Oh, was that Broome?' David asked surprised. 'Yes, I remember that. I must say it looked quite good. Not that I saw any more than that. I only looked up from my papers at that moment. What else did the programme have to say?'

June smiled, warming to the subject. 'Well it's in the tropics; the best time to go is our summer i.e. June through September when it is not too hot, because, of course, it's their winter; the weather is one hundred per cent reliable at that time; after Puerto Rico it has the world's most prolific game-fishing grounds; the colourful birdlife is breathtaking, with over thirty species of migratory shore birds arriving every year...'

'Hey! You certainly watched that programme, didn't you!' David interrupted, with a quizzical raise of one eyebrow.

June continued with a ferocious glare, 'It has one of the world's most beautiful stretches of unspoilt sandy beaches; the earth is brick red and the sea, as you saw, is the bluest blue. And,' she tapped his knee, 'its still uncrowded, which can't be said of many places and it also happens to be one of the world's major centres of the cultured pearl industry.'

4

'Oh, God!' David closed his eyes. 'That sounds expensive! I knew there would be a drawback.'

Comfortable and warm as he was, in front of a blazing log fire, David agreed with June that London in February, with its short, grey days of cold winds and bleak rain, needed the escapism of travel brochures and holiday planning. He had visited Thomas Cook at lunch time and collected all their brochures for holidays in Europe. He hadn't thought of a trip farther afield, especially as June had been rattling on about Tuscany.

'I can't finish this cheese and biscuits, darling,' David sighed, as he looked at the remains on his plate which was perched precariously on his lap.

'You don't have to eat it, just because it's on your plate.' June smiled and took it from him. 'Coffee?'

'Please,' David looked into the fire. 'It's a long way to go, you know. Could be quite tiring.'

'Oh, I think I can just about manage it.' June's voice was soft as silk. 'Don't you worry your little head. It's only a question of dragging myself to the sink and putting the kettle on. I'll be careful.' She ducked, as a brochure flew across the room and disappeared with her into the kitchen. There was the rattle of crockery being fed into the dishwasher.

'It is the other side of the world, darling, but doesn't the thought excite you?' June's voice was masked by the half-closed door as she filled the kettle. 'Neither of us has been to Australia, the land of Oz and I'm told the natives almost speak our language and are supposed to be quite friendly.'

'Yes,' grimaced David, 'especially at the moment, considering they've just retained the Ashes! OK, I'll go into Thomas Cook tomorrow and see what I can find out.' He stifled a yawn. 'I think I've drunk enough for this evening, darling. How about an early night?'

June emerged from the kitchen with a coy smile and stood poised, with one hand stretched provocatively above her head holding the door frame, the other on her hip.

'Do you mean it's either coffee or me?' she asked.

David laughed in response as she came to him, 'Yes please,' she said and took his hand. As they reached the door, David heard a crackling sound behind him and looked over his shoulder.

'Oh, God,' he sighed. 'I'd better give that fire a good poke and quieten it down for the night,' and he moved back towards the burning logs glowing and spluttering in the grate.

June watched him thoughtfully and pushing back her hair, murmured to herself as she disappeared upstairs, 'There's no answer to that.'

2

'Ian Carlyle? Who the devil is Ian Carlyle? I've never heard of him.' Rita Hardy pushed the supper plate of three sausages, baked beans and chips towards her husband. Len Hardy didn't answer for a moment. He was too busy trying to undo the top of the bottle of tomato sauce. It was Friday night and he always had sausages in the kitchen on Friday nights.

Rita went to a whist drive on Friday afternoons and she could never face cooking a full meal after she arrived home. Rita didn't normally have more than one main meal a day, and usually she chose to have it round at her mother's house at lunch time.

She was pleased she had persuaded Len to buy the three-up, two-down, detached house just behind mother's road in Ealing. It had come on the market just when they were planning to get married. Poor mother had been a widow for a long time and Rita knew how much she appreciated visitors. She always sent the two boys round to keep mother company after school; it gave the poor dear a little interest in life. It also gave Rita a chance to sit down and put her feet up for a few minutes. Well, looking after a house and family was no easy job. Especially with the money Len brought home. When she had married Len he had just become a solicitor and the world had seemed to be his oyster. Instead he had toiled away in the same London West End firm where he had qualified, and although he was a partner he was never going to be a senior one. It wasn't as if he didn't work hard either. God, he was always ringing up saying he would be late as there were things to do. She had told him on many occasions there were things to do at home. She couldn't do everything.

'Well?'

'Sorry love, what did you say?'

The sausages, beans and chips were now liberally coated with tomato sauce, which was congealing with the fat on the edge of the plate.

'I said, who is Ian Carlyle? Why should he invite us, of all people, to his country house for the weekend?' With her elbows on the kitchen table, Rita pulled at her cigarette and stared belligerently at her husband.

'He's a client,' Len dropped a chip off the end of his fork on to his lap.

'For God's sake!' Rita flicked her ash unsuccessfully towards the ash tray, 'I didn't think he was the dustman! I hope that chip's gone on the serviette. I ran the mop over the floor today and I don't want grease all over it, thank you.'

Rita stubbed out her cigarette and reached for her cup of coffee. Len gave her a thoughtful glance, then his head and shoulders disappeared beneath the table. The chip had indeed finished up on the floor. He placed it carefully on the side of his plate and continued to eat.

Rita was an attractive brunette who wore her hair long to her shoulders. Her mouth was full but given to a suggestion of petulance and her dark-red lipstick accentuated this expression. She had long thick eyelashes that flashed over her brown eyes in her rare moments of animation. She had put on quite a few pounds since their second son had been born, but still had a good figure and she knew it. She bought good uplifting bras to keep her heavy breasts high, and deliberately wore blouses with the top few buttons undone. She enjoyed flaunting herself surreptitiously at the shopkeepers. Not for her the anodyne supermarkets. Pity short skirts were out now, but she still managed to knock a few pence off the bills at the butchers and fruiterers and the like, by letting them chat her up and getting an eyeful at the same time. She enjoyed being a tease. Nothing more. She had enough to do coping with the house, the kids, mum and Len. Anyway, although Len might not have progressed as well as she had hoped, he was still a satisfying husband in one sense.

'He's a new client, love. Only dealt with us for a few weeks.' Len sat back and smiled, knife and fork at rest. 'Enjoyed that.'

'Just as well,' Rita sniffed and stood up, taking his plate away. 'So why the invitation and what's it for?'

Len watched his wife's well-rounded buttocks as she leaned over and took a lemon yoghurt out of the fridge. She caught his gaze.

'Just get on with that and cool off,' she said knowingly, handing him a spoon. 'Now, if you haven't seen much of him, why the invitation?'

'Don't know, love.' Len tucked into his yoghurt with enthusiasm. His predilections in food had never greatly tested Rita's imagination, she was pleased to acknowledge. 'I've brought the invitation home. It's in my case.'

Rita surprised herself, and Len, by going into the hall and bringing in Len's briefcase. Sure enough, beside the morning papers and some all too familiar coloured files from the office, there was an impressive, typed envelope, addressed to Mr & Mrs L. Hardy at Len's office. Rita pulled out the invitation. It was extraordinarily worded.

> Mr. and the new Mrs. Ian Carlyle
> request the company of Mr. & Mrs. Hardy at
> The Manor House, Cordington, Sussex,
> for dinner on Saturday May 7th
> through to after lunch on Sunday May 8th.
> You are expected at 7.00 p.m. on May 7th.
> Please do not reply as Mr. and the new Mrs. Ian Carlyle
> are at present on holiday.
> Please bring this invitation with you.

'What a funny invitation,' Rita turned it over, as if looking for an explanation on the back. 'It sounds deadly. I'm not going.'

Len choked on his last mouthful of yoghurt. 'But, love, you must!' he protested.

Rita stared at him. 'Why, for Christ's sake?' she asked.

'Well, he's a client,' Len almost whined, 'this is a chance to persuade him to use the firm more, and if he does it could help my becoming senior partner. You know how much we both want that.'

Rita looked at her husband. She knew, in her heart of hearts, he would never be senior partner. Len was short, running to fat, balding and of very insignificant appearance. There was no personality, no character there. She had made a bad choice in trying to climb the social ladder with Len.

'OK. OK. I'm sure we're not doing anything that weekend,' Rita sighed reflectively, 'or any other weekend if it comes to that. Mother will have to come round and look after the kids. I hope she'll be able to cope.' She rose and filled the kettle. 'Coffee?'

'Yes please, love.'

Rita found some odd cups and saucers. 'What about this new Mrs Carlyle? What happened to the old one? Dead? Divorced?'

Len shrugged his shoulders as he lit a cigarette. 'Never met the old one. I've only met Carlyle once or twice to discuss some property contracts. Never met him socially. Not a particularly pleasant man, but worth a lot of money apparently and as is usual with such men he becomes very impatient. Most of his legal work is done by Linekers and Myers in the City.'

Rita brought over the coffee. She had lost interest in the discussion. 'Well, I'm not buying any new clothes for this funny weekend. He'll have to make do with what I've got. Now, I'm going into the sitting room to watch *Brookside*. Wash up when you've finished.'

As she disappeared, Len exhaled deeply. Nothing had been washed up all day.

*   *   *

'Well, you know how it was ... I mean Willie Whitelaw said ... can't understand it myself ... happened in Cape Town in '75 ...

well, where else would you have found Tuffy!' Malcolm Thatcher took another slug of his large whisky and water, his hand trembling as he dropped the glass on to the side table.

Maurice looked at his heavily built uncle, dressed in flannels and a blazer speckled with dandruff. He acknowledged, with irritation and unease, that each week that went by caused more friction between himself and his wife, Pat, over the prolonged stay of his only living relative, who showed no signs of leaving.

'Stuff 'n nonsense really ... well would be, wouldn't it – the cabinet was disunited and politics is ... Wilson smiling and that pipe – no one knew ... why should they? Happened at The Mount Nelson in Cape Town – splendid hotel ... only one to stay at – everyone stays ... Sundays in particular.'

'Uncle, what are you trying to tell me?' Maurice swallowed the last of his gin and tonic. They were both comfortably seated in the sitting room of Maurice's luxurious residence in Surbiton.

Malcolm gently spilled some of his whisky on to the surface of the table as he picked it up, and a little dribbled down his chin as he brought his glass to his thin, bluish lips.

'Why, South Africa ... good legs she had, I remember...'

'Who, for God's sake?' Maurice expostulated, his eyes glazed with frustration.

'Yes,' Malcolm nodded, 'your mother ... well ... splendid clear blue skies ... I ... well, February, would be. Went to ... for dinner ... yes.'

'Christ!' Maurice jumped up, as he saw his uncle's mottled face and vacant eyes staring at nothing in particular. He refilled his glass at the sideboard, as he heard a now familiar racking cough erupt behind him.

'Legalities were ... but like today, I suppose ... open to ... Scottish influence, shouldn't wonder. Nothing's changed ... good man, Heath ... couldn't last though ... Table Mountain usually in mist ... hot ... such a good sailor ... in fact, bloody hot.' The whisky was finished. 'I like Famous Grouse ... best of them at the time ... expensive ... useful in summer ... God, she was a good looking woman ... going out?'

11

Maurice had downed his refilled glass in exasperation and was making for the door. 'Yes, uncle, I told you.' He looked at Malcolm's perplexed and child-like expression. 'We're out this evening. You'll be all right. Martha will be more in than out, so don't worry.' He grimaced inwardly. His uncle was almost incapable of coherent worry.

'Fine,' Malcolm beamed, through bloodshot eyes. 'Have a good ... don't be ... silly really ... they all spoke Afrikaans ... couldn't understand a bloody word ... stupid language ... can't think why ... Good old Willie ... and Tuffy, of course.'

Maurice walked out into the hall, breathing heavily with stifled impatience. He found conversations like that almost unendurable. He ran up the stairs, dismissing his uncle from his thoughts as best he could. Learned solicitor Malcolm may have been once, but he was now just a sad old man, with hardening arteries. A widower. All he had was his club and Maurice. The future did not bode well for either haven, but he was damned if he was going to have more than his fair share of him.

'Pat, how much longer are you going to be?'

Maurice Thatcher stood in the bedroom doorway, glaring at the back of his wife's well-coiffured head of red hair. It rose an inch or two as she straightened her back, her eyes examining the reflection of her carefully made up face in the mirror.

'Not too long now, Maurice. Not too long.'

It was her standard reply at this juncture. It had no meaning. It could mean five minutes or half an hour. Pat Thatcher knew it angered her husband, but it didn't worry her. She had realised, after about a year of their marriage, that she didn't love Maurice. Oh, he had plenty of panache, style and, of course, money. He had swept her off her feet fifteen years ago, there was no doubt about that. She had been a young impressionable secretary in one of the world's favourite advertising agencies.

Maurice had been the boss' son, just down from Cambridge. He was tall, handsome in a craggy way, with jet-black wavy hair, and a thick moustache. She'd loved that moustache! When he

12

had kissed her it had literally made her tingle all over! It was inevitable that Maurice had found her attractive. Even her less charitable friends had to admit Pat was beautiful. At whatever age, she would inevitably be the one woman in the room the men would notice. She had an innate sense of poise and presence. She was nearly five feet nine inches tall, with an hourglass figure. The fact that they had no children helped, of course; as had the daily exercise class at the club in Surbiton. Her skin was flawless. Aided by careful creaming and beautician's wonder products she always looked like the honey and cream model on one of Maurice's TV commercials.

Maurice, being the only child of a loveless marriage, had inherited the company on his father's death five years before. In Pat's view, Maurice was in the same mould as his father; wedded to the business. This had been one of their problems. He was always out with clients. Coaxing, encouraging, bullying, pleading, challenging. Whatever was needed to develop the company. And the more it grew the more Maurice had to be at the helm.

She knew he had a very poor opinion of many of his clients. They were either arrogant, stupid, greedy or egotistical, or as Maurice often commented, all of those things and he was delighted to take them for as much as he could. His attitude sometimes frightened her, but at the end of the day, it was his affair, his business and so long as the money and attention lasted she would accept it.

However, Pat objected to being neglected. Only last evening after dinner when they had both drunk too much she had complained bitterly; but to no avail.

'It's my life's blood, and through me, yours,' Maurice had observed coldly.

'I want attention. I want to feel needed. I didn't marry the bloody agency,' Pat had screamed.

'Yes, you did,' Maurice had replied shortly. 'If you didn't realise that, well tough! I can't change. If you want to live your own life – fine! If you can't live it married to me and you want a divorce, so be it. I love you, but I won't crawl for you, you know that. It's your choice.'

13

At this point Pat had retreated. Divorce? Why a divorce? She had everything she needed. An elegant house in three acres of beautifully landscaped garden. A Mercedes sports car renewed on the company every year. Servants, even if they were Spanish. And suitors at the drop of a hat.

Pat played golf and badminton. She also played the men. She amused herself whenever she felt like it. No romance, just sex. Romance could be costly. Freeze the mind and enjoy the body. That way, she had all the pleasures of life. The prestige and glamour of being Maurice Thatcher's wife and the independence to enjoy her life with discretion. No, she would not upset the status quo. Not yet, anyway.

'Not too long now Maurice. Not too long,' Pat repeated, turning her head from side to side and adjusting the side mirrors. Pat loved dressing up and she usually had somewhere to go.

Maurice looked at his watch, frowning. Pat knew they were due at the charity premiere of the new British film in Leicester Square in an hour. He was chairman of the organising committee and the Queen and the Duke of Edinburgh would be there. He paced thick white carpet that complemented the ornate white and gold furnishings.

'Ready now, darling,' Pat turned and smiled. She was well aware she looked sensational. Her evening dress had been created especially for the evening, by a couturier who could boast royal patronage – and did, unremittingly.

'Come on then,' Maurice pleaded.

Pat swept up her fur wrap from the bed and gave him a perfunctory kiss on the tip of his nose, wiping off the faintest suggestion of lipstick.

'Don't get irritable,' she admonished, 'you know we've plenty of time.'

Maurice stood back and allowed Chanel No. 5 to waft over him as Pat made her way down the stairs. 'We haven't plenty of time, if there are any traffic hold-ups,' he muttered.

'Stop worrying,' Pat trotted purposefully down. 'Charles will get us there in good time.' Charles was the best chauffeur they had had for a long time. Courteous and a very good driver.

14

Neither of them thought of saying goodbye to Malcolm.

Pat smiled demurely at Charles as she climbed into the Rolls Royce. He was a very attractive man, and she liked his moustache. Why had Maurice shaved his moustache off so soon after they had married? She had never been able to talk him into growing it again. Oh, well. She sat back as Charles closed the door and started the engine.

They drove in silence for a few minutes, before Maurice gave a start and pulled out an envelope from his inside jacket pocket. 'Damn,' he said, 'I meant to check this with my diary while I was waiting.'

'What's that?' Pat looked at the envelope without curiosity.

'An invitation to Ian Carlyle's for the weekend.'

'Who?'

'Ian Carlyle. Potentially one of our bigger clients. Very wealthy man. I hope he'll use us exclusively, but he's also talking to Bannermans. Bloody annoying that. Keeps playing us off, one against the other. Always bitching about the costs and yet expects the earth. Impossible man.' Maurice tapped the envelope thoughtfully on his knee.

'Well, why don't you tell him to stuff himself?' Pat asked indelicately, as she watched a parade of shops flash by. Charles was certainly exceeding the speed limit.

'Because, my dear wife, if we said that to all our clients, we wouldn't have any left.'

'Agreed,' nodded Pat, turning to Maurice happily, 'but it would be fun telling them.'

Maurice sighed. 'Anyway, Carlyle's invited us down to his country house overnight. Here, read it.' He passed the envelope across.

'Us? Both of us?' Pat pulled out the invitation and read it in silence. She frowned at Maurice. 'I've never met him, have I? How extraordinary! "Please bring this invitation with you" Does it go in a lucky dip?' She turned it over. 'No number on it! "Mr & the new Mrs Ian Carlyle!" The new? What is she, number seven or something? Makes her sound like this year's model. Do you know anything about her, Maurice?'

'Not a thing.' Maurice shook his head. 'Never met him with a woman. Always been business only. Strange invitation, I agree. Better go though. I'm sure we're not doing anything that weekend.'

'Sounds intriguing.' Pat handed the envelope back. 'Does he have a moustache?'

*　　*　　*

'Evening, dear.' George Abbott leaned across and pecked Lesley, his wife, on the cheek. 'Thank you for meeting me.'

'Not at all, George. Had a good day?' Lesley stared straight ahead, as she let in the clutch.

'Not bad dear. Not bad. How's Peek-a-Boo?' George looked over his shoulder at the rear seat. Curled up, oblivious to the world around her, a Pekinese was lying on a tartan travelling rug.

'She's fine, George. Had all her food today. Must have lots. So much nourishment.'

Lesley turned the Volvo out of the station yard into the main road leading to the estate at the bottom of Amersham Hill. It was twenty-five minutes past seven. The same introspective conversation took place at twenty-five minutes past seven every evening of the working week. George Abbot was one of London's many bankers. In fact, a district manager of one of the big four to be precise. A stooping man in his forties, of lean build to the point of emaciation, exact in his dress and with metal-rimmed spectacles on his Roman nose, George managed to give the impression of a man who was sixty years behind the times. He was also a man who never wanted to take risks. His reputation amongst his colleagues was that of a man who, whilst a branch manager, had had very few serious bad debts against his name. His branch hadn't made the profits that other branches had either, but, as he had often pointed out to his district manager as well as to his staff, one can't have it both ways. 'Money is not to be played with', had been one of his favourite comments to new staff. The trouble was he had repeated it to them days, weeks and months after they had been at the branch. A man of irritating habits.

George looked at his wife. 'You look very pretty tonight, dear,' he commented dutifully.

'Thank you, George.' Lesley slowed down and put on her right-hand indicator. 'I had to go on the meals on wheels run today. Must wear something presentable. Bad enough being old and having a "charitable meal", without having to look at tired, middle-aged, women in tired, middle-aged, dresses. I try to look smart for them, George.' She turned into the drive of their mock Tudor three bedroom detached house, circling the small, precise lawn and neat, weed free, flower bed.

'And you do, my dear,' George responded vehemently. 'And you do.' He looked with surprise at the front hedge. 'You've cut it! I said I'd do it at the weekend. You really mustn't do too much.'

Lesley stopped the car and looking straight ahead, said irritably, 'George, I am perfectly capable of cutting out some of the old wood. I am perfectly capable of doing many things. Please don't fuss over me so.'

Without another word Lesley fetched Peek-a-Boo from the back seat of the car and led George up to the front door, where, as habit demanded, George opened it to let her and Peek-a-Boo in. Lesley carried the still-sleeping bundle through to the lounge, carefully placed it on the couch and sat down beside it, expectantly. Having removed his overcoat, George followed them in and headed for the drinks cabinet in the corner. The room was worthy of a *Homes* magazine photograph, except that it had no knick-knacks. Nothing out of place. Everything symmetrical. Clearly nothing was expected to be moved, except for dusting. There were no children to disturb things. The room didn't breathe. It endured.

'Sherry, dear?

'Yes, please, George. Anything exciting happen today?'

Lesley was a rather unattractive lump of a woman, who did her best, in an apparently uninformed way, to keep herself looking young. The results were not very successful. She kept her mousy hair short. It was easier to manage that way when she was gardening, helping the local community or indeed doing her studying and writing. At least it was always clean. She was

17

very short-sighted so had resorted to contact lenses, but unfortunately she had now discovered she needed corrective glasses for reading. Her nose had been broken at school playing hockey and her cheeks were extraordinarily hollow. Being almost flat-chested, with a very large bottom, she often felt God had looked the other way when she was born. Much as she tried, she exuded a certain masculinity.

Her father had sold his manufacturing business to a German conglomerate when she had been quite young and had retired to Switzerland, with his second wife. Father had never been paternal, but had made sure his daughter had had a good education, culminating in a First-class Honours degree at London University. He had then created a trust for her, which produced a sizeable income. This had enabled Lesley to become a research assistant at Conservative Central Office, where she still worked three mornings a week in a senior capacity. Many members of the Government discussed issues with her, acknowledging her in-depth knowledge of many subjects. There she'd met George at a seminar many years ago. Companionship rather than romance followed. She had had no hesitation in accepting George's suggestion, rather than proposal of marriage, although she was not in love. They both knew she was as strong as an ox and physically could accomplish so much more and keep going for so much longer than George ever could. She accepted that he didn't like his masculinity being brought into question, hence his petulance over the hedge.

However, all in all, theirs was a very comfortable existence. They had their own bedrooms and led very controlled and ordered lives. They didn't pry on each other. There was no need for lots of friends either, when there was contentment at home. Lesley had seen so many people locally surround themselves with supposed 'friends'. They were really only trying to submerge themselves due to their own inadequacies. She and George didn't need a continuous Sunday morning round of drinks, early evening cocktail parties, late dinner parties and all the ensuing slamming car doors and intoxicated guests falling into the rose bushes. They were contented enough.

'Sherry, dear.' George appeared at her elbow.

'Thank you. Do you have yours?' She smiled at George's easy chair as though encouraging it to invite George to sit down. George sank into it without further ado, as he did every night on returning from the office. Always with a dry sherry.

'God bless, dear.'

'God bless, George. Well, anything happen today?'

George smiled fleetingly, as he crossed his legs. 'Had to turn down a couple of large overdraft applications. People are extraordinary. Always expect banks to take risks they wouldn't take themselves. Seem to think bank money is a valueless commodity. Easy to come by and easy to lose. Afraid I had to give them the usual lecture on...'

'Yes, George.' Lesley had heard the lecture so often she was word perfect and she felt she really couldn't listen to it tonight. She had had a pretty exhausting day. 'Anything else? How is Mr Carpenter's wife?' Mr Carpenter was one of the corporate managers in the office.

'Oh, how nice of you to remember, my dear,' George smiled gratefully. 'As well as can be expected. Apparently there were no complications and she should be out very quickly. Nasty things, eye operations, though. Hate to have one myself.' George sipped his sherry contemplatively.

'You won't George, you won't.' Lesley leaned forward and patted him on the knee, as she would have had he been a small boy.

'Oh, yes...' George looked up brightly and searched in his jacket pocket, 'Look at this.' He passed Lesley an envelope.

Lesley placed her sherry glass carefully on the occasional table, took the envelope and extracted a card. Finding her glasses, she read it slowly.

'What strange terminology, George. The *new* Mrs Carlyle?' She looked up frowning. 'Has he already got a wife? Is he a Moslem?' She peered at the card again. 'Who is *Mr* Carlyle?'

'One of my newer clients,' George replied, proudly. 'Very wealthy man. Very successful businessman, I believe. Property, although I understand he also owns companies in other businesses. We only deal with a personal account as he normally uses the Midland, apparently. Don't know why he came to us, but some people believe in total privacy and I don't criticise them for that.' George nodded his head in agreement with his own statement and finished his sherry.

'Do we have to go, dear?' Lesley hated functions to be thrust on her out of the blue.

'Oh, I think so.' George looked concerned. 'I know you don't like these things, but it would be churlish not to go. It might even be interesting.' He smiled encouragingly. 'Never know who else might be there.'

'A weekend with strangers?' Lesley stared at the card, unhappily. 'What's he like? Do you know this new Mrs Carlyle?'

'Never met her,' George replied, shaking his head thoughtfully. He stared across at the card on Lesley's lap. 'Carlyle himself is around fifty, I should say. Not very tall, rather plump man with a dark, swarthy, complexion. Jewish, I shouldn't wonder. It is extraordinarily worded, isn't it? Can't think Carlyle worded it. Probably left it to some assistant.'

Lesley shivered and finished her sherry. 'Well, George, I can't say I rejoice at the thought, but if you think it's right we should go, we'll go. Now, dinner?.' She stood up, picked up the sherry glasses and bending over Peek-a-Boo, kissed the immovable creature on an ear. 'Go and change, George and then you can lay the table. Dinner won't be more than fifteen minutes. It's all in the oven.'

'Yes, dear.'

George stood up and followed Lesley out into the hall, just as the grandfather clock struck eight, as it did every evening as he went upstairs to change.

*　　*　　*

'Hi Kids! Dad's home!' Colin Gorman fended off Ben, the young Labrador, who jumped and barked a welcome as he climbed the stairs.

'Dad! Dad! Jimmy got in a fight at school today!'

'I didn't.'

'You did.'

'Liar.'

'You're the liar!'
'Hold it kids! Hold it!'
Colin Gorman stood in the doorway of the upstairs playroom. The dog, ignored, barked at everyone resignedly and slunk down the stairs. There were toys all over the floor and in the middle of the debris were two, fair-haired, eight-year-old boys. Identical twins – James and Christopher, who fought verbally and physically all the time.
'Hi there, honey.'
Colin swung round, startled. He hadn't heard his wife come up the stairs. Jenny aimed a kiss at him and just brushed his hair before she hurried on, into their bedroom.
'Dad, come and play trains with us!'
'Yes, come on. Mum says we haven't got to go to bed yet.'
'Oh, yes I did!, Jenny's exhausted, shrill voice called out as Colin followed her into the bedroom. The twins' interest faltered and they turned to each other and squabbled about who should have the blue engine.
Jenny sighed a deep sigh. The bedroom seemed to be the only oasis of peace in the house. She and the house always seemed to be at war. The house was clean; Jenny was very fussy about cleanliness, but it was still a shambles. Half darned socks, clothes waiting to be ironed, ingredients for food dishes yet to be made. Everything was everywhere! If they entertained, Jenny tried to insist on going to a restaurant. That way no blitz had to descend on the house to sort out the debris. The resultant clearing up was so quickly undone it simply wasn't worth the effort. They decorated one room every year. That way Jenny felt at least a little discipline was introduced. It was amazing, even to her, what they would find when they took a room apart. Needles, reels of cotton, pants waiting for new elastic, loose change, Christmas cards. Once, even an uncooked swede. Jenny sometimes felt she lived in a replica of an Oxfam shop, but it was only very occasionally that she felt she was losing her private battle. Like now.
'Christ, Colin! It's been quite a day.' Jenny was sitting at the dressing table, briskly brushing her short straight black hair. 'Went to see Mum and Dad this morning. I know I shouldn't say

it, but they wear me out! They fight verbally all the time – through me. Mum complains about Dad. You know the sort of thing. Doesn't wipe his shoes when he comes in from the garden. Never does the jobs she asks him to do – only interested in the greenhouse.'

'What's new?' Colin grinned, as he sat watching Jenny trying to bring life into her cheeks with some make-up.

Jenny continued, as if she hadn't heard the interruption. 'Then Dad complains to me, in front of Mum – about her moaning at him all the time and her always out at coffee mornings, just as she had been before he retired, and how he now wished he hadn't retired early. Then as soon as I got back Auntie May called in, just as I had to rush off and get the kids for lunch. So I told her to wait a few minutes and make herself at home, while I collected the children. As it happened the kids were late out, of course.'

'I told you the kids should have had school dinners,' Colin wagged his finger at Jenny's back.

'I want to be sure they have a decent meal, thank you,' she rejoined, pursing her lips as she perfunctorily ran some lipstick over them. 'Anyway she wanted to unburden herself about her arthritis. It doesn't sound very good, poor soul. Apparently she has it in both knees and the consultant suggests she has an operation on one of them pretty well straight away. I told her that we'd look after her budgie when she goes in and I'd keep an eye on the place. She's pretty marvellous, really.' She rose and went to the wash basin to wash her hands.

'Jenny, for Pete's sake you can't do any more,' Colin exploded.

Jenny knew the hurt in his voice. Her life was a continual roundabout. Round to school with the children; round to the Young Wives at the church; round to her seemingly endless supply of relatives in Sutton; lunch with the children; round to the local hospital to help with the visiting library; apart from all the obvious time-consuming, wearisome, activities of a young mother with boisterous twins and Ben the labrador to cope with. She was inevitably always worn out when Colin came home and by the time he had helped her bath the kids, persuaded

22

them to bed and eaten supper, she was finished. Too tired to converse, she would either watch television in an exhausted daze or fall asleep. She knew Colin tried hard to accept her busy way of life, but he found it difficult. Deep down she recognised that he was jealous of her lack of attention to him and that he felt that he was always coming second best. But she couldn't help herself. It was as though she had to fill every waking moment.

'Looking after a budgie won't exactly kill me, honey,' Jenny said as she dried her hands. 'Now, let me go and start supper before the bathing. Beef casserole?'

'Super.' Colin stood up and started to change out of his suit.

Jenny smiled, nodded, and straightening her dress she set off for the kitchen. Yells from the playroom stopped her at the head of the stairs.

'Any more noise and you won't have your party on Friday,' she called out.

The noise abated and Jenny could hear muffled laughter as she ran downstairs. Colin would moan about another party, poor thing! Her husband was a tall, red-faced, jolly-looking man who bristled a ginger moustache to match his ginger hair. He was the sales director of Caseys; the small, privately owned Sutton brewery. Correction; it had been privately owned until about a year ago. The family interests had been sold out to an entrepreneur who had offered a very good price. Apparently the argument had been that he would be able to introduce economies of scale, as he owned the large southern brewery Banters. Within a week of taking over Colin had apparently been summoned to Caseys boardroom to meet the new Managing Director. 'Increase sales by twenty-five per cent in the next year Colin, old chap or else we'll have to take drastic action. We're not sitting on our backsides in the Eighties you know. Get your chaps out to push up the sales. There doesn't have to be a brewery here at all. Good area for office development round here.'

That had been nine months ago and Jenny knew Colin had pushed himself very hard to try and increase sales. It wasn't proving at all easy in these hard competitive times. He had travelled everywhere; seeing old customers, visiting prospective

23

ones. He had been away more than at any time since they had been married.

Colin came into the kitchen, banging an envelope on his fist as he went to the letter rack. Jenny continued humming contentedly as she cut up the steak. Ben was noisily lapping water from his bowl. It appeared to be an unintentional unison of noise.

'Look what I received today, Jenny,' Colin held out the envelope.

Jenny rubbed her hands on her apron. Extracting the card, she quickly read it before putting it down. 'That's nice, honey,' she smiled and returned to her steak.

'You don't mind if we go?' Colin asked surprised.

'No dear, why should I? Make a nice change.' Jenny took hold of the frying pan and dropped in the steak and onions. 'Who is he, anyway?'

'Some wealthy fellow. Came round the place a couple of weeks ago. Professes he wants to export our beer to the continent. We gave him the red-carpet treatment as you can guess. He's phoned me several times since. Funny invitation.' Colin picked it up.

'What do you mean?' Jenny tipped the contents of the frying pan into a casserole dish.

'"Mr and the new Mrs" Odd wording?'

'Oh, I don't know.' Jenny added the beef stock and popped the dish into the oven. 'You could hardly expect him to talk about the old Mrs Carlyle, even if she was, could you? New, sounds exciting and attractive.'

'If she's anything like him she won't be,' grimaced Colin. 'Funny, I seem to be the only one in the company who's received an invitation. Reads less like an invitation and more like a directive. It doesn't say anything about requesting the pleasure. Ah well!' He looked out at the garden. 'Apparently it came down from Carlyle's office with a messenger. Wonder why me?'

But Jenny had lost interest. There had been a thump and a scream from upstairs, and she and Ben had rushed up the stairs to sort out victim and culprit.

*　　*　　*

'Look at it!'

'It's not that bad.'

'Of course it is! It's absolutely dreadful. Look at that photo the other day! You looked pregnant!'

'Well, if I am, I could sell my story to the Sunday newspapers and retire!'

'David. It's not funny. You'll have to do something about it.

David Price sighed. It was Sunday afternoon and really he didn't need a lecture. He knew he had been gaining weight. He had been having considerable difficulty in buttoning up his shirt collars in recent weeks and was beginning to cheat by tying his tie with a larger knot and leaving the shirt collar undone. His trouser zips were also taking the strain and he couldn't remember the last time he had buttoned a jacket.

June leaned towards him and kissed him gently on the nose. 'We'll start a diet in the morning.'

'Ah! Thank God!' David sighed contentedly. 'At least there are a few hours left, before purgatory begins.' He rose from the settee on which they had both been relaxing, reading the Sunday papers, and stretched hugely.

'That's what you need!' June nodded vehemently.

David turned, his arms falling to his sides. 'What?'

'Exercise. You don't get enough.'

He gazed at June, sitting with her legs curled underneath her as she thumbed through *The Sunday Times*. David didn't think he had ever known anyone more able to reduce a professionally printed and produced newspaper into such a crumpled, disorientated heap of newsprint. Admittedly it was normally limited to within a few feet of her, unless there was a breeze from the garden. Today was breeze-free, as the French windows were closed to keep the gentle rains of spring at bay. June, aware of his amused grin, looked up over the top of her spectacles.

'Well, it's true! Since you sprained your ankle last summer playing cricket, you really haven't had any exercise to speak of.'

David sat down and took off June's spectacles.

25

'David! I'm reading!'

'You were! But you can't without your glasses.'

'I'm well aware of that! It's not funny to suddenly reach that terrifying age when your arms aren't long enough to hold the newspaper.' June's mouth pouted slightly.

David grinned. 'Darling you are all of thirty-two. Think of all the other things that will start wearing out over the next thirty-two years. God! I hope I don't know you then. You're obviously falling to pieces at a rate of knots!'

June punched him on the knee. 'You're a beast!'

David sat back into the settee and without a word June lay her head on his shoulder and, as if programmed, they took each other's hands. David closed his eyes contentedly. He and June had been married for nearly a year and unbelievably life was still, as the song went, a bowl of cherries.

After a few moments he was brought back to the present by the increased intensity of the rain outside. It was hammering on the patio door. He squeezed her hand.

'Look at that damned rain.'

'Yes, darling,' June murmured.

'What do you mean "Yes, darling"?' David turned to look at her and in so doing moved his shoulder. Her head dropped sharply, before she brought it upright, and he realised she had been dozing.

'What?'

'Exactly! You're not listening to me. This must be the beginning of the end of our relationship! Where's that rapturous attention to my every word? You humour me now with "Yes, darling", without knowing what the hell I've said!'

June stared at him, blinking. 'What did you say?'

David leaned into her face until their noses touched. He looked her straight in the eyes. 'I love you.' He said, very slowly and deliberately.

June placed her hands round his neck. 'Call me a sucker, but I love you too,' she kissed him lightly on the nose.

'That's better!' David sat back.

'Can I doze now?' June snuggled in again.

'Yes, if you find my conversation so boring,' he replied lightly.

June was, in David's eyes, a beautiful girl. An intelligent fashion buyer, to boot. He had fallen in love with her at first sight, on an audit of all things! He had since maintained that as he was so short-sighted, and he didn't wear his spectacles all the time, he hadn't seen her properly and thought she was more attractive as a blur. June, quite rightly, hadn't believed him.

David's attention was caught by a movement through the french windows. A sparrow was jumping about in the bird bath. It splashed around for a few seconds and then jumped on to the edge to clean itself, raising and lowering its wings methodically. It was still raining miserably and David watched the sparrow finally look around, satisfied with its ablutions, but, instead of flying away, it dropped back into the bath and started the whole procedure again.

'Silly little perisher,' thought David, 'it doesn't even need to get into the bird bath. It's wet enough without!' Then he realised that the bird was enjoying the exercise for its own sake. It was like a man jumping in and out of a swimming pool. The name of the game was exercise. What had June said only moments ago? He didn't get enough exercise? God, how right she was! He looked down at his stomach bulging over his belt. Enough was enough!

'I'm going to Fawcett Manor!' David announced to a silent audience.

Nothing stirred. Even the sparrow had flown off.

He turned into June's hair and gently raised her head, causing a minute stirring of her being. 'I'm going to Fawcett Manor,' he murmured into her ear. The reaction was negligible. He stood up and carefully lowered her on to the settee where, stretched out, she continued to slumber.

Fawcett Manor was one of the audits that he visited yearly. All the checking and verification work was done by his junior colleagues, and his was a routine signing-off visit. It was in Hampshire, set amongst the most beautiful wooded country-side. The nearest town, Basingstoke, was ten miles away, by country lanes. He enjoyed his visit. It normally only lasted one day, walking round the house, chalets and grounds and discussing, before and over lunch, points of issue that had arisen from the audit. Surprisingly it had never occurred to him before to stay there as a guest. It was a privately owned health farm.

*   *   *

'They'll bring you back in a hearse!'

'You're bloody mad!'

'You must be joking!'

'We have a maniac amongst us! I always knew it! A maniac!'

It was Monday lunchtime in the firm's dining room. The partners didn't entertain clients to lunch on Mondays, so David Price was only amongst colleagues. Over a pre-lunch drink he had announced his thoughts about staying at Fawcett Manor. The reactions were predictable. No-one took him seriously, as they clustered round the drinks cabinet.

'You are joking, David, aren't you?' Baker, a thin, balding young man, leaned forward pushing his pebbled glasses back up his nose.

'No, I'm not! What's the matter with you all? I'm not the only one who would benefit from a stay there, either!' David refilled his glass with more gin and tonic.

'Now, don't start getting bloody personal, old sport!'

Douglas Price, David's heavily built and red-faced, lugubrious cousin helped himself to another large, undiluted, whisky. Known to all as DP, he was five years older than David. They had never really been friends. Apart from being partners in the same firm, they had no interests in common, and they saw very little of each other outside business. When David was really honest with himself he had to admit he didn't like DP very much. Most of the time however, he put such unchristian thoughts to the back of his mind.

'But David, what are you going to do there?' Baker looked very worried, his dishevelled, worn, pinstriped suit, hanging despondently on his thin frame.

'Lose weight, of course. Take some exercise. They have marvellous facilities,' David replied. 'Tennis, swimming pools, saunas, golf course, etc. I'll come back a new man.'

'Thank God,' muttered Scott, a white-haired partner who was

28

nearing retirement, 'this existing man is quite definitely going to put me off my lunch.'

'Well, David won't be having lunches, that's for sure,' commented DP, his chubby short fingers excavating the peanuts.

'When are you planning to explore this new world?' asked Scott, moving towards the dining table. The others taking his cue, followed him.

'Well,' replied David, pulling out his chair, 'I was thinking of going in the next week or so. If I don't go now I might think better of it!'

'Damn right, old sport,' commented DP, spilling his whisky, 'you might come to your bloody senses!'

Baker managed to get his feet inexplicably entwined round his chair and he collapsed into the seat. The table shook on impact. The anxious waitress placed the watercress soup in front of each of them, being very careful as she placed it in front of Baker.

The door burst open. It was Cox. Late again. A sandy-haired, sandy-suited, earnest young man. 'Oh, I say, I'm awfully sorry. Caught up. You know. Tax case. Awfully sorry. Capital Gains. Lot of money.' He slumped miserably into the nearest vacant seat and looked appealingly at the waitress.

'Soup, sir?' she smiled.

'Oh, yes. Thank you very much,' Cox nodded miserably.

'David's going to Fawcett Manor,' Baker announced to Cox, as the late soup arrived.

'Not on audit, but as a bloody customer!' added a now, more red-faced, DP.

Cox looked at Baker and then David, his soup spoon held high. 'Good Lord. I mean, really? Splendid, splendid. Yes, I say.'

'Bloody mad,' DP muttered, as he reached for the red wine. The roast beef was about to be served.

'I reckon I ought to lose seven pounds in a week,' David commented.

'How many pounds will you lose out of your pocket?' asked Scott, wryly.

'None,' replied David, 'I rang them this morning and they are delighted that I'm thinking of going and have offered me a complimentary stay.'

'Jammy bastard!' DP sipped his wine and pulled a face.

'Well done' rejoined Baker, 'It's normally about four hundred pounds a week, isn't it?'

David nodded, 'At least.'

'What does June have to say?' asked Cox, 'I mean, well, doesn't she mind?' He blushed, for some unexplained reason.

'Mind?' David laughed, as he helped himself to peas and carrots, 'She was the one who started it all! Telling me I needed to shed a few pounds and get some exercise. So last night I decided if I could re-organise my work schedule, I should get on with it!'

'Balls,' Scott nodded to himself, thoughtfully.

'Pardon?' Cox's fork hovered in front of his face, as he stared at Scott.

David laughed. 'A certain Ian Carlyle bought Fawcett Manor a couple of months ago and asked Scotty to join his Ball Committee for the Hyde Park Maternity Hospital, which has some obscure link with Fawcett Manor.'

'Yes,' added Scott, 'after he bought it, Carlyle came to us and said that he needed financial advice and assistance on the Hyde Park Maternity Hospital and bingo I was landed. Can't say I like him very much. Still if he brings us work, that's all that matters.'

'Never met the blighter,' shrugged DP.

'Nor me,' Cox acknowledged, 'but its good for the firm, as you say, Scotty.'

In silence the main course was cleared and the fruit bowl was passed round the table.

'Beats me,' said Baker pulling out a banana from the assortment and succeeding in spilling two apples on to the table, 'why people will pay that sort of money for a week of misery. They can exercise themselves for nothing.'

'True, but not true, you know,' responded David, picking up the apples. 'Firstly there is the question of discipline. It's so much easier to abide by the rules of self-discipline, if everyone around you is doing it as well. Secondly, not everyone has the equipment to get fit. Again, the encouragement of others all trying to achieve the same improvement in fitness is a tremendous psychological boost. And don't forget,' he added, 'that if you've paid a lot of money you make damned sure you get some benefit out of it!' He bit into one of the apples. 'I've never met Carlyle either.' David looked inquiringly at Scott. 'Since I've been involved with the audit I've only ever met the resident general manager.'

'You haven't missed anything.' Scott grimaced.

'Do they allow alcohol?' Baker went to scratch his ear, forgetting he was still halfway through his banana. The moment reminded David of the chimpanzee's tea party at the zoo.

'No,' David shook his head, 'but that won't be a hardship. None of us need drink. Healthy body can encourage a healthy mind – and a more active one!' He was sure as he bit into his apple he heard DP mutter 'Christ'.

The coffee was passed round and DP rose and brought the port to the table, where he proceeded to pour himself a large glassful. Nobody joined him. The phone on the table by the window rang, shrilly. Baker jumped up, managing to knock his thigh on the corner of the table as he did so. Wincing with pain, he reached for the receiver.

'Hallo? Yes, Yes, of course. Just a moment.' He turned and held the receiver out towards David. 'It's June. For you,' he added unnecessarily.

'Hallo, darling?' David looked out of the window at the tops of two buses meandering slowly down towards Kensington High Street.

'Darling, sorry to ring you at lunch,' said June, 'but I'm just off to the cleaners and I've just checked through the pockets of that suit you asked me to take. The one you were wearing Friday?'

'Yes?' David frowned.

'Yes,' June coughed, theatrically. 'I didn't find any handkerchiefs covered in lipstick, but I did find a letter!'

'Letter?' David frowned. 'What are you talking about?'

'It's all right, darling,' June tittered. 'I'm teasing. But there was a letter addressed to both of us in one of your pockets. Unopened.'

'Oh God, yes,' David nodded at the window. 'The post boy

gave it to me on Friday afternoon and I stuffed it in my pocket. I forgot all about it.'

'Well I've opened it and I think Fawcett Manor might have to wait!' David could hear the amusement in June's voice.

'Oh,' David watched as the buses stopped at the traffic lights. 'Why?'

'Well' ... There was a slight pause. 'We seem to have been invited to some weekend function in the country and it all sounds rather peculiar.'

The buses had started off again, with the sun breaking through and glinting on their roofs.

'A weekend function?' David couldn't think of anyone who would invite them for a peculiar weekend.

'Well, its an invitation from an Ian Carlyle,' June replied.

'Who?' David watched the buses disappear from view.

'Ian Carlyle.'

David stared at the dirty window. 'How odd,' he muttered.

'Well,' commented June, 'odd it may be, but let's go. It sounds exciting!'

3

London, May 1988

June snapped the suitcase shut with a contented sigh. 'That's it then. Everything in.' She turned to David, who was sitting at the foot of the bed watching her with a tolerant smile.

'Are you sure?' he asked, standing up.

'Yes,' June paused, her voice displaying the doubt that she obviously still felt. 'That is, I think so.' She looked along the dressing table, her hands to her lips, as though searching for divine confirmation.

'Darling, you have packed that suitcase full of God knows what, and we're only staying overnight. What else can there possibly be?' This was a rhetorical question, as David bent down to pick up both suitcases.

'Wait!'

He stood up with an impatient sigh. 'Oh, come on, darling. What now?'

'My rollers! I've forgotten my rollers!' June opened a dressing table drawer and pulled out a large plastic bag full of multi-coloured rollers.

David looked heavenwards. 'God forbid that I should escape a weekend without seeing you in those dreadful plastic sausages.'

June elbowed him to one side and knelt down to find room for the bag. 'You would be the first to say something, if my hair looked a mess,' she chided him.

David watched the case snap shut again. This time June had obviously decided that was it. She picked up her handbag and preceded him down to the hall and the front door.

'I suppose we ought to take raincoats and umbrellas?' she asked.

'What the hell for?' David stared at her. 'We're going to somewhere civilised I hope, or do you think the roof leaks?'

June smiled, as she foraged for their raincoats on the coat rack. 'I'm sure it is all terribly civilised, but even civilised people can be caught in spring showers, when they are out for a gentle stroll.'

'God, I hardly think we're expected to go for long, invigorating, walks!' He opened the front door and grimaced. It was spitting with rain. The grandfather clock chimed five.

'How long will it take?' asked June from amongst the coats.

'We should make Cordington by just about seven, unless there are any more hold-ups,' David replied shortly. He had been slightly irritated that she hadn't been ready when he'd arrived home. He had showered and changed and she still hadn't finished her packing.

'Here they are, David, and the brollies.'

June followed him out to the car. David packed the suitcases into the large boot of his Mercedes 420 SEL and whilst June settled herself into the car, he went back into the house and switched on the burglar alarm, before locking the front door.

'What do you mean, you hope you're not expected to go for long, invigorating, walks?' June looked at him as he fastened his seat belt. 'You could have been at the health farm now and you'd be walking there and thinking what a clever fellow you are!'

'Ah, that's different.' David said as he started the engine.

'Rubbish! And you know it.' June slapped his knee, as he swung the car out towards Kew Bridge. 'I wonder what sort of occasion it's going to be?'

'Dreadful, I expect.' David turned on the windscreen wipers as the raindrops became too insistent to be ignored.

'Well, why are we going?' June asked. 'We don't have to go.'

'You wanted to!' protested David. 'Anyway we've been over this before. Carlyle is a business contact and he obviously sent the invitation to me personally. None of my partners appear to have received one, so it seems he wanted me personally, though I can't think why.'

'Well,' June wriggled into her seat, 'it could be fun.'

Being a Saturday evening there were many cars on the road, but despite the fact that it was raining, David made good time through Kingston, across Hampton Court bridge and out on to the A24. The car was fast and powerful and David was extremely adept at overtaking whenever a safe opportunity presented itself. June watched the suburban houses grow larger and the grounds surrounding them more sumptuous. She couldn't help but reflect that they didn't need a large house and large mortgage to prove anything.

'I hope they are as happy as we are.'

'Who?' David's thoughts had been broken.

'The Carlyles. I wonder what she's like? A blonde model bombshell?' June mused. 'Or maybe a fat short-sighted heiress, whose only saving grace is her money!'

'Well, you will find out soon enough,' David smiled. 'I must say I shall be fascinated to meet Carlyle. I don't really know much about him as a person. Seems to be very successful in business, but doesn't have an awful lot of the old charm.'

David threaded his way through the winding, narrow, main street of Oxshott and on to the country road ahead. The rain began to fall more heavily and almost obliterated the green of the hedgerows and overhanging trees.

'Well, you can't have everything, I suppose,' muttered June as she watched a raincoated old lady, umbrella clutched closely, pulling a seemingly even older fox terrier along by his lead.

'I have,' remonstrated David. 'Money, good looks, youth and you ... what else is there?'

'Children?' smiled June.

'Yes, I must find out how you get them on the National Health. I don't know if I've paid enough contributions for our name to go forward for one yet.'

'We're not in that sort of world.' June punched him. 'It's much simpler than that!'

'So I've heard, darling, so I've heard.'

David eased off the A24 and began to wind his way down the B roads in the general direction of Cordington.

'Do you know the way?' June asked, stretching her long legs.

'Yes,' David nodded. 'I checked the route in the AA book. I must say it's a pretty outlandish place. It seems to be miles from anywhere. And from what I can tell, Cordington is only a pub, a few cottages and the odd country house in acres of land.'

'Oh well.' June commented, 'I'm sure The Manor House will be impressive. I hope so, anyway. I don't go away for weekends to just anywhere!'

They drove on in silence, the rain now prolonged and insistent. The sky was angrily heavy and grey. The windscreen wipers continued stubbornly in their efforts to clear away the depressing deluge. June watched the fields of dark shades of green zip past as David ploughed on, with little traffic to slow him down in his squelching drive through the meandering lanes.

There was little sign of life. It was too miserable to be out unless it was really necessary. Suddenly, however, a white mongrel shot out from behind a hut at the side of the hedgerow and darted across the road, just feet from the front of the Mercedes. David braked sharply and the car lurched violently before he corrected it and took his foot off the brake.

'Bloody idiot!' he cursed savagely.

June took a deep breath and exhaled. 'He was probably more scared than you were,' she said.

'He?' David looked at her wryly. 'Sure it wasn't a she? Be more understandable if it was! Impetuous, unguided, uncontrollable...'

'Oh, shut up, you male chauvinistic moron and just keep your mind on the road!'

They both relaxed, as David continued a little more cautiously through a sodden wood running along the brow of a hill. He knew that on a clear day there were magnificent views across the Downs as the road left the wood behind. Today was not one of them. He looked at June and ran his eyes over her suit. He hadn't really absorbed what she was wearing until now – a pleated skirt and jacket of heather-coloured mixture. It wasn't a suit he remembered seeing before.

'Is that suit new?' he asked.

June clapped her hands slowly, once, twice, three times.

'Well done,' she mocked. 'You can see a dog jump out and react superbly, but I've been with you now, for what, an hour and a half? And you've just noticed my new suit for the weekend! It's a good thing I love you. Some girls would have thrown a tantrum an hour and a half ago!'

David coughed loudly. 'You know where that would have got you, don't you?' he asked.

'Nowhere,' June nodded. She had discovered early on in their relationship that David would never rise to the bait of a feminine tantrum. He wouldn't row, wouldn't shout. He just considered uncontrolled emotion a sign of weakness and couldn't be bothered with it. There were times when he knew June was infuriated by his calm, but she had long since acknowledged that he might honour her and cherish her, but would never rage at her.

'It's nice,' David said quietly.

'Thank you, darling,' June smiled as David arrived at a junction and slowed down.

'Cordington, five miles.' June pointed excitedly, peering through the windscreen. It had, surprisingly, stopped raining and David switched off the wipers as he turned right following the direction of the sign.

'Cordington, here we come,' June sang out softly. He recognised nervousness in her voice.

'I love these country lanes,' he said. White blossom completely covered the hedges they passed and the roadside was flanked by a thick carpet of yarrow. 'You can imagine yourself in wonderland. In a land of fields and woods enjoyed exclusively by the birds and the animals of the countryside. The hedgerows bring you very close to nature.'

'Too close, darling,' cried June, ducking instinctively as her side of the car swept an overhanging branch sideways.

'Sorry,' David swerved outwards, 'but it's getting very narrow.'

'I'm glad you've realised,' June said drily, as she pushed her

37

hair back. 'I certainly haven't seen any double-decker buses for some time!'

David smiled as he slowed down and followed a sharp bend in the lane. Everything was wet and still as he reached a narrow grey stone bridge over a stream.

'Cordington! Here we are!' June pointed to the sign at the same time as David saw it.

'Now all we have to do is find The Manor House,' he commented, as he drove over the bridge and followed the lane.

He drove slowly. There was little to excite him. A thatched farmhouse with adjacent rundown-looking stables. On the nearside, about fifty feet back from the lane, ran a row of small, meagre, terraced cottages with unremarkable front gardens.

'Nothing very attractive about those,' commented June as they drove past. 'A good coat of paint on all of them wouldn't do any harm.'

Round the next bend they were confronted by a small public house, with badly peeling white-painted walls, leaded windows and a mangy thatched roof. The small colourful sign proclaimed it as The Lord Nelson.

'Looks as one-eyed as he finished up. Not an attractive sight.'

'No,' David agreed, 'Not the most prepossessing of villages. Where do you think The Manor House is?'

'Well, we can't have missed it,' observed June. 'There haven't been any roads off anywhere.'

They drove past a few isolated cottages and houses interspersed with meadowland. A small sawmill seemed to be the only sign of industry, as the meadows gave way to woods on both sides of the road.

'We must have missed it,' June speculated.

'We'll drive on a mile or so,' David replied. 'You don't normally get a manor house slap bang next to the journeymen's cottages.'

'Oh. We are erudite this merry, merry, month of May,' smiled June as she continued to watch out of the window for any promising sign.

The lane dropped down into a wooded valley and then

climbed steeply again. Near the top, an entrance half-hidden by the steep bank, revealed a five-bar gate half off its hinges with The Manor House in black paint on the peeling white structure.

'God, that's it!' June whispered. 'I hope the house isn't as decrepit as the pub and that gate!'

'Darling!' David remonstrated as he braked and swung up the drive, 'There aren't many places these days that worry about gates!'

'Well it would be better not there at all, than like that,' replied June firmly.

David drove slowly up the winding drive. Trees encroached and overhung – he identified beech and sycamore. The sky was almost shut out. The car crunched along the gravel as he swung the nose of the car through forty five degrees.

'Nothing straightforward here,' he said.

'Ha. Ha.' June wasn't laughing. 'Where's the damned house?'

The trees suddenly gave way to extensive lawns and the drive divided round an ornamental pond. The rain clouds were drifting away, leaving a watery evening sun to cast its pinkish-yellow glow on the face of The Manor House.

'My,' June sounded impressed, as indeed David was.

He guessed The Manor House was Tudor with its gabled roofs and mullioned windows. Ivy completely dominated the entrance, climbing nearly to the roof above the second floor. The house spread majestically in front of them with two bays either side of the entrance. The roughcast walls had darkened with age. Tall chimneys reached high above the eaves, as if at attention, to salute all comers. As David rounded the pond he noticed that the long garden sloped away beyond the house, giving views across to a nearby hillside, which was pockmarked with dead elm trees not yet felled. Beech trees lined a road disappearing over the hill. Mottled grey and brown farmhouses and sheds were scattered through the fields. It was all surprisingly open country after the dark journey through the trees to the house. David pulled up at the entrance, slightly skidding on the shingle.

'Well, here we are, darling,' he said as he turned off the engine.

'And here we stay for a couple of days,' remarked June, looking up at the house.

David smiled inwardly as he climbed stiffly out of the car. He had noticed an involuntary shiver run through June as she stared at the house. He had to admit that the idea of the weekend didn't exactly fill him with enthusiasm, but he was prepared to try and relax and enjoy it as much as possible. It was different from their normal weekend and if there was some good wine and good food to be had – free – who was he to complain? He slammed the driver's door at the same moment as June shut her's and the noise caused a number of pigeons to flutter off from the roof. June stepped back as she looked up and watched them fly into the nearby wood.

'They probably thought they were going into tomorrow's pigeon pie!'

David had walked round the back of the car, his feet crunching on the loose shingle and he slid his arm round June's waist.

'Ugh! This place gives me the creeps, already.' June shook her head, as though trying to rid her mind of an unwanted thought.

'Come on, let's see who's around.' David steered her to the front door.

The studded oak door had a large wrought-iron knocker that David enthusiastically pounded. He raised his eyebrows at June and smiled reassuringly. There was complete silence from within as they waited. Suddenly the door opened and a florid, middle-aged man stood confronting them. He had a mass of wiry grey hair, and was dressed in brown corduroys and a check country-style shirt, open at the neck.

'You are Mr and Mrs Price.' His English had a heavy mid-European accent, but his voice was soft as he stated a fact. He was not asking a question. He opened the door wide and with a halting gesture of the right hand, bade them enter. His eyes were searching. Actually David realised it was June that was really being looked at. Admired, almost ogled. Not one of those gropers under the table, please, he thought. He had learned of it more times than he cared to remember. He never did it to other women, why did men always seem to want to do it to June? He

40

knew the answer! He followed her into the hall as the door was shut behind them.

'I trust you had a good journey.' Again it was a statement, not anticipating a reply; the face expressionless. 'Follow please.'

David and June exchanged glances as they dutifully followed the slightly stooping, but swiftly moving, figure through the long hall. David couldn't help but notice the sumptuousness of the decoration and furniture. Thick, oriental rugs covered the already carpeted floors and a preponderance of old portraits fought for attention on the gold-papered walls. A central staircase divided the hall as they followed the man into a room to the left. Their host hadn't stood aside for them to enter first. As soon as they were all in the room however, David realised that the uncertainty that had been nagging at him since the front door had been opened, was justified. The man who had led them in was not their host, but some servant, untutored in the art of putting guests at their ease, or of establishing his status in the house. Their host was quite clearly the man who rose to meet them, hand extended.

'Mr and Mrs Price. How nice to meet you.' He shook their hands. 'I'm Ian Carlyle. I am not telepathic. My other guests have all arrived so you must be Mr and Mrs Price.'

This time David was aware that Carlyle's eyes were set fully on him and June had almost been ignored. No one could completely ignore her, but Carlyle's flicker in her direction had only been perfunctory.

David nodded. 'Very reasonable logic, Mr Carlyle!'

'Good, and please call me Ian. I hope perhaps that I ...' Carlyle hesitated, clearly waiting for David to pick up the cue.

'Please, June and David.'

David thought that Carlyle's smile seemed to falter momentarily, but he beamed over them both for a couple of seconds. 'June and David. What nice simple names to remember!' He paused for a moment and then banged his right fist into his left palm. 'Yes, well! Ross will get your bags out of the car and park it round the back out of the way. Did you leave the keys in it?'

'No,' David found them in his pocket and handed them to the

41

attentive, grey-haired Ross, who without further ado left them, closing the door with a bang as he went.

'Will you have a welcoming glass of champagne?' Carlyle walked towards a side table by the bay window. 'Please, do have a seat.'

'That would be very nice.' June eased herself into a Louis XV bergère.

Carlyle looked at her, as though surprised she had responded, but immediately smiled at her warmly. 'Good. Good.'

David watched their host pour out the champagne. Carlyle was a short, rotund figure of a man. His black hair was thinning noticeably, but he had a young boyish face and David wondered how old he was. Forty? Fifty? He was wearing a dark-blue blazer and grey flannels, and looked every bit the village squire. Except for his face. His eyes were black to the point of appearing to have no pupils. They were narrowed by the plump, spoilt-looking face and his mouth was equally thin and compressed. His complexion was swarthy and he clearly suffered from a growth of beard that was difficult to keep under control. David guessed he had to shave at least twice a day to be presentable.

Carlyle carried over two glasses of champagne, and then picked up his glass and raised it very slowly to June and David in turn, staring at David for some seconds before he smiled.

'Good health and I trust you will have an enjoyable stay.'

'Thank you,' David couldn't think of anything to add.

The champagne was vintage Dom Perignon. Carlyle greedily finished his glass and proceeded to refill it enthusiastically. The room was beautifully decorated with period furniture. One wall was completely filled with shelves of old books from floor to ceiling. David guessed they weren't the pound a foot variety. The bay windows looked out over the drive and, at the far end, leaded windows either side of a large stone fireplace gave views across a meadow to a large thicket. The focal point of the room was a grand piano open, ready for use. The music on the stand suggested it was used. Carlyle gestured David to another antique chair and himself dropped on to a chaise longue.

'Now,' Carlyle smiled stiffly at David, 'You must be wondering why I have invited you down here.' He paused, but neither

David nor June spoke. 'Well,' he continued, 'it is very simple, really. I have just bought The Manor House and I have also just completed some very successful business deals. I decided that I should find time on my return from holiday to develop acquaintances with people with whom I hope to have further business contacts. You see, people are business. Without the right relationships businesses can founder, or opportunities don't arise that could arise, and I'm in business. Any business that makes money. For that reason, I decided to have a weekend with hopefully five new important contacts, if you'll pardon the expression, and of course their wives. Hopefully you will leave here having enjoyed yourselves, and business, my business and all your businesses, will benefit in the future.'

For the first time Carlyle looked at June with interest as he paused to sip his champagne. David noticed that June had crossed her legs and her skirt was riding slightly above her knee. He also knew that June was aware that this was where Carlyle's eyes had focused. She did nothing but drink demurely and look round the room.

'Well,' said David quickly, 'it's a very nice idea. You are quite right. We haven't met, but, of course, we do hope to have business connections. I am sure I, and for that matter, our partnership, would be delighted if we could mutually extend our interests. It is a pity we haven't met before.'

Carlyle nodded, but his attention was elsewhere. On June's legs. David noticed beads of perspiration on Carlyle's forehead and on his upper lip as June smoothed her skirt down. Carlyle suddenly appeared to be aware of the silence that had overtaken them.

'Er ... yes, yes,' he brought his eyes reluctantly round to David. 'Will you have another glass, before I ask Mrs Ross to show you to your rooms?'

'I don't think so, thank you,' David looked questioningly at June, who smiled and shook her head.

'No, that was lovely though ... Ian,' she replied sweetly.

'All right, then,' Carlyle clambered to his feet and moving to the fireplace pressed a bell push. 'Mrs Ross will show you to your room. I hope you'll find it comfortable. It's the far room immediately over this one. I'm afraid it's quite a large house and people can get confused here, but I'm sure you won't have any trouble. It's been used recently as a private nursing home. Of the mental kind. Until very recently in fact.' He moved back to his champagne glass.

'I bought the house just before I went abroad. I had most things done while I was away. We chose all the furnishings, etc. and left Marbles – terribly good firm – to do everything ready for our return. One of the few things still to be done is removing all the dreadful bars from the windows. Sorry about that, but I completely overlooked instructing anyone to get rid of them.' Carlyle nodded at the bay window and David noticed, for the first time, the bars running vertically up all the windows in the room. 'Had to keep the patients in, you see.'

Carlyle smiled and looked at the door as it opened. 'Ah, Mrs Ross. Good. This is Mr and Mrs Price.' He waved his hand expansively. 'Would you show them up to Number One bedroom?' He turned to June and smiled. 'All the bedrooms were numbered when it was a nursing home and we've left the numbers on the doors. It's easy for reference!'

June smiled back and nodded.

Mrs Ross was about the same height as Carlyle but twice as fat. She had a bright-red, country face topped with hair as wiry and grey as her husband's. Not the most attractive of women, thought David. Her countenance was one of ill-tempered weariness. She nodded without animation and stood, holding the door open, implying that she had no intention of moving another step until the guests had preceded her out of the room.

'I hope you'll be comfortable,' Carlyle raised his glass in David's direction. He stopped suddenly and a frown crossed his brow. 'Oh, by the way, did you bring your invitation with you as requested? It is for a little game later,' he added by way of explanation.

'Why, yes.' David had made sure it was in his inside breast pocket, and he handed it over.

'Thank you.' Carlyle smiled, 'Now I look forward to seeing you both for dinner at eight.'

They were dismissed by the tone of his voice. David followed June past the stoical Mrs Ross, who banged the door behind them as ferociously as her husband had done a few minutes earlier.

'Follow me, please.' David wasn't surprised at the accent – it was the same as her husband's. She led them slowly up the staircase. Her weight clearly caused her a problem and her breathing was audible and strained. David idly looked upwards at a large skylight through which the mellow evening light shone and was mildly surprised to see that there were heavy metal bars here too. David wondered whose imagination had conceived that earlier residents might want to leave by such an exit! Mrs Ross led them down a wide, thickly carpeted corridor away from the landing. They passed two suits of armour on parade, a large old walnut chest and predictably, several portraits of sad staring aristocracy of past centuries. Mrs Ross had opened a door at the end of the corridor on their left. She held it open for them to enter.

'Your luggage will be brought to you in a moment.'

'What a lovely room,' June exclaimed, her hands clasped together as she walked in. Mrs Ross sniffed loudly. David smiled at Mrs Ross as he entered the room, but received no encouragement as she shut the door on him and disappeared.

David could understand June's exclamation. The room gave a sense of relaxed luxury with an underlying country atmosphere. An ornate wall-covering of wild flowers in cream and green with touches of blue and pink were matched by the curtains. Most of the furniture was solid antique pine. There was an attractive long dressing table with matching chest and bedside tables. The carpet, as well as the duvet on the kingsized bed, well matched the wall-covering. Two of the leaded windows were slightly open and the breeze was catching the curtains, causing them to tremble gently and bring the room alive. Two white bath robes lay over wicker chairs. In one corner by the windows was an open door leading to an en-suite bathroom. Everything in the bathroom was either white or pink.

'Well,' said June, turning on the taps of the bath, 'they work as well!'

'Hardly surprising, darling,' muttered David wryly.

'Just thought I'd check,' replied June. 'I think I might enjoy the luxury here, if nothing else.'

'Darling, there's no reason why you, we, shouldn't enjoy everything.'

June was clearly about to reply when there was knock at the door. She merely nodded at David and swept past him. 'Come in, come in,' she sang out brightly as she reached the door and opened it. A perspiring Ross brought in their suitcases, and placed them by the pine built-in wardrobes.

'Thank you,' said June, 'We were just admiring the room.'

Ross nodded slowly. 'Much money has been spent. It is now a good house.'

'Were you here in the earlier days?' asked June, surprised.

'Oh, no,' Ross frowned. 'My wife and I are new here. We live in the village. Others come in to help as necessary.' He went to the door, bowed his head to them and shut the door without waiting for any response.

'Not a very cheery couple,' commented June as she lifted her case on to the bed and opened it. She stared at the open case. 'That's funny.'

'What?' David had just thrown his case on the other side of the king-sized bed.

'Someone's opened this case.' June stood hands on hips, glaring at the contents.

'Rubbish, darling.' David started to take out his clothes.

'I tell you someone has not only opened this case but looked through my things.'

'How on earth do you know?' David asked. 'You pack in such a higgledy-piggledy way, how can you possibly tell?'

'Because,' June's voice was firm. 'I know. Yes, it looks chaotic, but I remember how it looked when I shut it. Remember my having to find room for my rollers? Well, I noticed that by sheer chance four blue rollers were at the top of the bag containing them and they half spilled out as I shut the lid. And next to them was my toilet bag. I always leave it about a quarter open so that my wet toothbrush doesn't get horrid. Now the zip is closed shut and there aren't four blue rollers spilling out of the bag!'

David came round and looked. He picked up the toilet bag. The zip was closed. The bag of rollers faced upwards and the open top showed one blue, one pink and two yellow rollers on top.

'You must have been mistaken,' he said comfortingly, but as June frowned at him he added quickly, 'or the movement of the car and then being brought up here jostled things around.'

'David,' June sounded angry, 'don't patronise me! Look how full the case is. Nothing can move in it when it is shut. You know me – there's never any space in my suitcases!'

'OK. OK.' David put up his hand as if to ward off the verbal assault. 'Maybe it came undone and things spilled out. They would be bound to go back differently.'

'And would someone zip up my toilet bag?' June asked sarcastically.

'Yes, quite possibly,' David nodded. 'Especially if your things fell out of it.'

'It wasn't for that reason,' June shook her head.

'What do you mean?'

'Nothing fell out of it. It was deliberately opened. I know it. Why didn't Ross say if it had come undone, anyway?'

'Oh, God. I don't know.' David returned to his side of the bed. 'What on earth would anyone be looking for in your suitcase.'

June stared at him, frowning for a moment, then her face lit up with a mischievous grin. 'Perhaps it's someone who likes looking at ladies' undies?' she giggled.

'Well,' David smiled, taking out some of his clothes and putting them in the wardrobe, 'I suppose as long as you're not inside them it doesn't matter too much! By the way, did you pack the camera? There could be some interesting shots to take round here, apart from you in your undies!'

'Yes, I did, and before you ask, there is a roll of film in it! I bought one this morning.'

The atmosphere relaxed, as they carried on with their unpacking. When David had finished, he stood at one of the barred but open windows and breathed in and out deeply several times. The air smelt so fresh, tinged with those

47

undefinable aromas of the country that are so very different from anything in London. He suddenly felt something tickle the back of his knee and as he swung round June kissed him on the tip of his nose.

'You haven't got time to stand and marvel at all you behold,' she chastised him. 'Go and shower, or whatever, so that I can follow you.'

David took her face in his hands and whispered, 'I know its not done in society, but I don't mind if you come in there with me.'

June put her arms round his neck and placing her cheek against his as David's hands enfolded her waist, she muttered in his ear, 'We certainly haven't time for anything like that. Now just be a good boy and get cracking!' With that, she playfully pushed him towards the bathroom.

'Hold it.' David stopped. 'Let me get my toilet things.'

As he went to the bed where he had left them, there was a knock at the door. He almost persuaded himself he had been mistaken. It had been very soft, more like a tap. June clearly hadn't heard it, as she was busying herself, humming quietly. The knock came again – a little louder – twice, and very tentative.

'Come in, come in,' David sang out rather loudly. It was almost a compulsive compensation for the quietness of the knock. June however, had also heard the knock this time. The door opened gently and a small balding man dressed in grey flannels and a dark-blue roll-collar sweater stood there.

'I'm terribly sorry to disturb you,' he looked very pained and apologetic, 'but I wonder if you could help?' He hesitated and then rushed on. 'My name's Len Hardy and we're staying here for the weekend ... Rita, my wife, and I. Actually we're in the room opposite and, well, there doesn't seem to be anyone to ask, and I...' he paused, and swallowed, as though he'd forgotten what he wanted, 'that is, Rita has just broken one of her finger nails. Isn't it silly? We didn't pack anything and it really is, you know, a bit of a mess.'

David noticed Hardy had yet to let go of the door handle. It was as though he was holding on for physical support.

'You'd like to borrow a pair of scissors?' June's voice sang out from behind David. 'That's easy. I always have a pair. Come in.'

Hardy let go of the door and stood, hands clasped in front of his chest as if in prayer, as June dived into her vanity case.

'My name's David Price,' David stepped forward and extended his hand. Hardy's grip was surprisingly strong, 'and this is,' he paused, 'my wife, June.'

June came up to them both and, smiling sweetly, handed Hardy a pair of scissors.

'Oh, that's marvellous.' Hardy smiled back with relief. 'I'm so sorry to worry you like this, but you know what women are.'

'Of course,' June replied, smiling reassuringly. 'There is nothing worse than a broken nail. It catches on everything.'

'Absolutely.' Hardy nodded gratefully. 'It's very kind of you. I'll bring them straight back.' He didn't seem to know how to leave the room.

'Don't worry,' June walked him back the two steps he had ventured into the room, 'I've got two pairs of scissors with me, so as long as I have them back by the time we go, that's fine.'

Hardy turned at the door and smiled apologetically at David and quickly at June, before, with a muttered 'That's very kind,' he disappeared.

June shut the door and leant back on it looking at David. 'What a funny little man,' she chuckled, as she held a hand to her mouth.

'God, he's going to be a bundle of fun,' muttered David, as he once again picked up his toilet bag. He looked at June pensively, 'Maybe his wife has big tits and long shapely legs, in which case, tough on you, darling.'

He dived into the bathroom as a cushion hit him on the back of the head.

* * *

'It's one minute to eight. How are you doing?' David stood up from tying his shoe laces and looked at June. She was standing at the foot of the bed, hands away from her sides ready for inspection.

49

'You look good enough,' David nodded, turning to the door.

'What do you mean, good enough?' June's voice was full of astonishment.

David turned. June hadn't moved, but her face was a mixture of despair and bewilderment. He looked at her very slowly, very deliberately, from head to toe – twice. She was dressed in a short, silk evening dress, finishing just below the knee. It was powder blue with light grey swirls, high at the neck, but with a plunge back. She had matching grey high-heeled shoes and evening bag. Her whole appearance was one of easy elegance.

'You look good enough ... to eat,' David smiled. 'You look gorgeous.'

'Beast!' June came over to him and linked her arm into his as he walked to the door. 'Teasing me like that.'

'Go on out!' David fondly patted her behind as she passed him and he turned, shutting the door.

'Aren't you going to lock it?' June asked, lowering her voice. 'There's a key in the lock.'

David looked at her, astonished. 'What on earth for? This isn't a hotel!'

'I don't know,' she shook her head and looked about her before continuing, 'I just think you should.'

David shook his head firmly. 'Don't be silly. Come on.' He took her elbow, guiding her along the corridor. Their feet made no sound on the thick carpet.

'I wonder what they'll all be like,' June said softly, as they descended the stairs.

'We'll soon know,' David stated the obvious.

As they reached the ground floor Ross appeared from the drawing room. He was now in a dark blue tuxedo. He smiled briefly, 'Ah, shall I show you the way? Please follow me.' He led them towards the back of the house, from where voices could be heard. 'I trust everything is all right in your room. Anything that you want?' His tone suggested that it was a rhetorical question, as he opened wide a door that had been ajar and the mumble-tumble of voices became all-pervading.

'Everything's fine,' David smiled.

'Ah! June and – ah – David!' Carlyle turned from the group of

50

people he had been with and bowed before moving towards them. 'Now,' he took June's arm, 'may I introduce you both to my other guests. We're all here now so no more names to remember!' He looked around the group he had left. 'This is ...' he paused as he smiled at June, 'June and David Price.' There was general murmur of 'Hallo', and 'Good Evening', with brittle smiles and a general movement of heads.

'The easiest thing is for me to just go from left to right – Rita and Len Hardy, Jenny and Colin Gorman, Lesley and George Abbott, Pat and Maurice Thatcher, and my wife, Tanya. Not my new wife as on the invitation. That was a stupid mistake. The "new" should have been referring to this house.' Carlyle smiled ruefully. 'Now! A glass of champagne before we eat. Good for the appetite!'

A rather surly-looking young man, also dressed in a dark-blue tuxedo, was immediately at their sides, with a tray of glasses of bubbling champagne. David smiled and took one. Dull, humourless eyes stared back at him. David thought of the suit of armour on the landing. The group seemed to unwittingly break in two and David found himself separated from June, by Carlyle leading her away. A rather plain woman in a long black evening dress, high at the neck spoke to him. She had been introduced as Lesley Abbott.

'David Price? No relation to Timothy Price, the poet? Lives near us at Amersham. Such a sweet man.' She paused for a moment. 'I've only met him once or twice at local readings you know, but terribly nice.'

David had never heard of him, but imagined Timothy as effeminate, wearing a smoking jacket, bright-red bow tie and sandals.

'No, I'm afraid not,' he smiled. 'Nothing poetic about me, I'm sorry to say.'

'What a shame,' responded Lesley Abbott, smiling awkwardly. David was not sure whether that was because he did not know Timothy, or because he wasn't poetic.

'Lesley is very keen on poetry.' The bespectacled gaunt figure to her right – now that was George Abbott wasn't it – smiled at Lesley adoringly as if his utterance had been that Lesley was the

Poet Laureate. David felt that she was irritated by this remark, as she sipped her champagne and ignored her husband.

'George is a bank manager, may I ask what line of business you are in?' She stared inquiringly at both David and the other man in their small group, Len Hardy. David guessed he'd have to wait all day for Hardy to speak – he looked only slightly less ill at ease than when he'd been standing in their bedroom. Whilst George Abbott was as unprepossessing as his wife to look at, they were both very well dressed and Abbott's black dinner suit was made of a very good cloth. This was in considerable contrast to Hardy's suit, which David guessed by its poor fit had been hired or bought off the peg, and not a terribly expensive peg at that.

David's gaze turned to Hardy's wife – what had been her name? Rita? Yes, she looked like a Rita. What did he mean by that? She was attractive, but in a coarse, suggestively sexual way. Her dark eyes were accentuated with layers of eye-shadow and were searching in their gaze. Her face was not altogether expertly made up, but enough attention had been given to emphasise the natural colouring of her pale skin and contrast it with her thick red, wet lips. She was wearing a short white silk dress with a plunging neckline that showed off the beginnings of her heavy uplifted breasts. The dress was very tight and, to David's mind, was probably a size too small.

'I'm afraid I'm a very dull chartered accountant,' he replied blithely. 'Nine to five man. Nothing exciting. How about you?' He turned to Hardy as he saw Lesley Abbott frown.

'Me? Oh . . .' Hardy had been surprised at the suddenness of David's attention. 'Well, actually, I'm a solicitor.' He sipped nervously at his champagne and then added, 'Yes, another nine to five man, I'm afraid.'

'Nine to five?' Rita Hardy's voice was throaty and David thought she even spoke lasciviously. 'When have you left the office at five? More like five to nine.' She turned her gaze on David and held his eyes. 'I'm sure you don't leave your wife all alone in the evenings.'

David dropped his gaze into his champagne glass, as he took a gulp. He tried hard to think that there had been nothing

52

suggestive in the question. He looked around the small group as he replied.

'Well, sometimes I'm afraid we all have to do what we have to do. Unfortunately life isn't always as easy to control as we would like.'

' "To learn and labour truly to get mine own living and to do my duty in that state of life unto which it shall please God to call me." So says the Catechism,' commented George Abbott, his eyes glinting eagerly from behind his spectacles.

David grinned inwardly, as he saw Rita Hardy's mouth open and close. She had clearly wanted to continue to complain about Hardy's hours of work, but introducing God into the discussion had torpedoed her for the moment.

'George knows his Bible,' commented Lesley Abbott off-handedly.

My God, thought David, they are two of a kind!

'How nice for him,' he replied, and quickly averted his eyes as he saw a glare begin to fill George Abbott's face.

'Now, how are you all getting on? More champagne.' Carlyle approached them, followed by the dour waiter. Glasses were refilled.

'I really shouldn't drink any more,' mewed Rita Hardy, halfheartedly. It was a token moral gesture.

'Nonsense, my dear.' Carlyle looked down her dress and back to her face. 'The weekend hasn't started yet. Dinner will only be a few more minutes and then we shall enjoy Mrs Ross's excellent cooking.'

As Carlyle commandeered the conversation for a few moments, David had a chance to look round the room. It was in fact an anteroom. A generous log fire burned brightly in the fire place. The wooden floor was covered with Persian rugs and, surprisingly, modern impressionist paintings adorned the sunflower-coloured walls.

'I'd give them eight out of ten for this room, wouldn't you? Not bad at all.'

David turned his head and stood looking into the smiling eyes of Pat Thatcher. He had remembered her name more easily than the others. After all Mrs Thatcher was the name of our governess. This Mrs Thatcher looked anything but a governess, however. She was strikingly beautiful, with incredible sapphire eyes. Her long rainbow-coloured dress showed enough of her body to cause even the most vehement misogynist to have second thoughts. Her bare shoulders were honeyed from many hours of gentle sunbathing and her face had been meticulously made up. David smiled back. It seemed the most obvious and natural response to someone who had managed to break any pretension of formality by that opening sentence.

'No, it's not,' he replied. 'I was admiring the paintings. I see they're all by the same artist. Can't say I know him.'

'I'm not surprised,' Pat Thatcher sipped her champagne. 'I think they're awful. That's why its only eight out of ten. I suppose I should have said that if it wasn't for the paintings the room would be utterly delightful. The closer I look at those paintings though, the more I'm convinced I must have bad eyes!'

'Oh, they're not that bad,' commented David, as he looked directly into Pat Thatcher's eyes. The word 'bad' was certainly the last word that he would have associated with them. Sapphire blue with specks of green.

'You do mean the paintings?' she asked with undisguised amusement in her voice. David felt himself blushing and the more he tried to suppress it the redder he knew his face became, exacerbated by the immediate rapport between them, which was excluding the rest of the gathering. He found it excitingly suggestive.

'You're blushing.'

'Don't you think I know!' David muttered. 'I've never felt so ridiculous.'

'Oh, I hope you have,' Pat Thatcher replied, her eyebrows raised in feigned horror, 'Otherwise you can't be the interesting, fascinating, person I have already decided you are. You see I am the eternal optimist.'

David smiled. 'The optimist proclaims that we live in the best of all possible worlds and the pessimist fears this is true.'

She laughed. 'I like that. Who...' She was about to continue, but was stopped by Carlyle who came up to her side. He gestured to the still unsmiling, but nevertheless attentive waiter to replenish her glass.

The moment of banter had disappeared as quickly as it had come, as they both succumbed to Carlyle's monologue on art appreciation. Suddenly, however, he appeared to do a double-take as he was extolling the virtues of Sydney Nolan and looked again at both David and Pat Thatcher. He laid his hand on David's arm.

'I don't believe either of you have had a chance to really meet my dear wife. Come over and have a word.' And without more ado he led them over to the other small group.

'Tanya, my dear, I've interrupted Pat and David to make them circulate.' Carlyle smiled and disappeared back from whence he had come.

'Hallo ... again.' Tanya Carlyle smiled stoically, without overwhelming warmth.

She was a thick-set, tall woman, certainly taller than Carlyle, with black hair showing signs of greying, held back in a bun. Her face had little make-up but heavy black eyebrows accentuated her brown eyes. Her thick lips parted to reveal beautiful white teeth. It was a face that had so much character in it that make-up would have done it a disservice. She was wearing a simple but very well-cut black silk dress, with no jewellery. Everything about her was simple, but she also portrayed total self-assurance. David hadn't the remotest idea whether Carlyle had been married for long, but as he looked at the Mrs Carlyle he decided she was definitely not his idea of a femme fatale. She looked a very daunting lady.

'We were just learning about Mr Gorman's fascinating job as sales director at Caseys Brewery. I must say if I was a man I can't think of anything more enjoyable than being involved in a brewery.' Tanya Carlyle's controlled smile turned to Colin Gorman, who grinned back.

'Well, I must say there are worse jobs,' he replied, but his face straightened as he added, 'although with the economic situation at the moment people are quite definitely cutting back on their spare cash. I think they're frightened to spend, in case times get worse or they lose their jobs, or whatever.'

'Surely it's during times like these that people tend to look for solace in drink?' murmured Pat.

'Depends where you live,' replied Gorman. 'In the north of England that's true because they've always spent money. In the south we worry more about mortgages, schools, appearances, and that means being more careful when times are hard. Even if we're not personally affected.'

'Rubbish, surely.'

David and everyone else in the group turned to the tall, handsome man dressed in a white dinner suit. David thought that he looked like an ad-man's dream. Maurice Thatcher stroked the back of his head, as Gorman flushed.

'If people are worried and apprehensive they tend to imbibe that little drop more. On your argument alcoholics would only be the rich people with no money worries. In fact many alcoholics have turned to drink for the simple reason that they couldn't cope, as often as not, with their financial problems.'

'Well, that's not been our experience over the last year or so,' responded Gorman, drinking his champagne.

'Perhaps you should try a better advertising agency, old boy,' commented Thatcher smoothly.

'Oh, do you work for an advertising agency?' The rather slight woman in a polka-dot red dress at Gorman's side looked up, her eyes wide open with interest. She appeared to be oblivious to the atmosphere becoming strained. 'When you came down from university you were thinking of trying to get into one, weren't you, Colin?' She looked up at Gorman and then back to Thatcher.

'I own an agency,' Thatcher smiled fulsomely at Jenny Gorman.

'That must be terribly exciting ... glamorous, I guess.' Jenny Gorman nodded her agreement at her own words. 'I've always thought it must be so exhilarating trying to capture the public's attention. All the colourful interplay and, I guess, bad tempers that go with such superficial and supposedly artistic, people.'

'You paint a somewhat simple, lurid picture of us,' Thatcher bridled, but held on to his smile.

'Oh?' Jenny Gorman looked uncomfortable. 'Really? Lurid?

56

Yes, well perhaps that is a good description in itself. Doesn't it mean extravagantly coloured?' She had now regained her composure and smiled happily at Thatcher.

Bingo! thought David. This could be an interesting weekend after all. He caught June's glance and she winked at him, as she masked her face with her right hand. Thatcher stared at Jenny Gorman searching for the underlying taunt, but her face was lit with such an openness it was impossible to believe that her words held any hidden derision.

'And are you in business?' Thatcher threw a question back.

'Oh, no!' Jenny Gorman laughed. 'I used to be a nurse before I had the children, but I'm afraid they take up most of my life now. Mind you, talking as we were just now, about glamour, there was nothing glamorous about being a nurse. It was all bed pans and bed baths. How it ever got the image of a glamorous occupation I'll never understand. Perhaps it was the black stockings.'

They all laughed and Tanya Carlyle commented dryly, 'Well, you wouldn't notice on a lot of nurses today, would you?'

'No,' Thatcher nodded vehemently. 'Do you know, before I was married and I was at university, we phoned the local nurses home one night for some girls to come to a dance and six came and they were all coloured! How about that! Not a white girl amongst them!'

'Must have been quite a shock to the old system,' replied Gorman, stroking his moustache and nodding sympathetically. 'I guess the only beds with which you felt they should have been associated were the hospital ones.'

'Colin!' Jenny looked at her husband, horrified. It was, however, Thatcher's turn to go red and David and June's eyes locked in happy acknowledgement of the riposte by Gorman. Fortunately at that moment the double doors were opened by another young man suitably attired, who half bowed in the general direction of Carlyle.

'Excellent,' Carlyle expansively gestured to everyone. 'Ladies and gentlemen, dinner is served!' He led the way into the dining room as the guests put down their glasses and followed.

'What a lovely room,' sang out Pat Thatcher. The others

mumbled their agreement in varying degrees of audibility. Another log fire burned in the grate and the walls were oak-panelled, cased by a beautifully ornate beaded ceiling. The furniture was period oak and an abundance of silverware included several candelabra, all casting their shadows round the room.

'There are place names,' Carlyle called out, as he headed for the top of the table. After a few moments of lighthearted searching they were all seated, and David found himself at one end, opposite Abbott, with Tanya Carlyle between them facing down the table towards her husband. A humming Jenny Gorman sat next to him on his left.

The dinner that followed could only be described as superb. The two young men waited at table, quietly and efficiently. David wondered who had trained them, because they were certainly not country bumpkins in the art of service. He felt that whoever it had been had missed out on one point – he had not taught them to smile. With the wine flowing and good food – very high marks to the cook – David felt totally relaxed. The conversation on the whole had been very enjoyable. After the initial reserve had been attacked surreptitiously by the wine, everyone had relaxed and conversation had become that much more interesting, as it often was amongst strangers. The views expressed may have been straight from *The Times* or the Sunday newspaper supplements, but they came from companions of only an hour or two and therefore were certainly more refreshing than usual.

Conversation was buzzing all round him, like bees on the return to the hive and David reflected on the menu – *Crème de Concombre, Sole à la Colbert, Roti de Porc, Mousse au Chocolat* – all helped down with beautiful French wines. Pouilly-Fuisse, Saint Emilion and now as he enjoyed the last of his cheese, a very pleasant Tokay d'Alsace. He felt replete. Most of the guests were more flushed than he had remembered them when they had sat down.

'Don't you think so, David?'

David started from his reverie, as he realised Abbott and Tanya Carlyle were hanging on his reply.

'I'm sorry,' he said, 'I missed that. It coincided with my water biscuit!'

Tanya Carlyle smiled. 'I was saying that one has to discount an awful lot of what people say at the end of a good meal that includes plenty of wine. It is one of those wonderful times of freeing of one's thoughts, the process not held back by the fear of saying something that might appear provocative or ill-advised. The touch of alcohol allows that relaxation from deep thought, so that easy words flow from an easy mind. Nothing is said that matters particularly.' Abbott was nodding like one of the toy dogs seen on the back shelf of some cars.

'On the contrary,' David replied, 'I think you have to pay more than a passing interest to the conversation.' He saw Tanya Carlyle frown momentarily, before the smile returned. Abbott had recoiled six inches and busily ate some of his hardly touched cheese.

'Oh, why do you say that?'

David turned, surprised, not having realised that Jenny Gorman had also been listening. 'Well,' he paused, 'many people certainly say things more easily when they are relaxed, but in many cases, if opportunity permits, their real thoughts and beliefs come out, which otherwise would be kept bottled up. Especially when there is an audience! Of course, there is an awful lot of superficial chat that goes on, but it isn't too difficult to appreciate when a person is talking about something which is really important to him – or her. He added dryly, '*In Vino Veritas*. I'm a great believer in that.'

There was silence as David looked at Tanya Carlyle.

'How very fascinating.'

David flushed, as he felt mentally slapped down. He remembered his maths master at school making the same comment, with the same inflexion, when during one of their first geometry lessons he had asked if anyone had heard of Pythagoras. David had put his hand up and suggested it was a snake. It was surprising that he had done as well at maths as he had, considering that inauspicious start.

'I trust you mean interesting and not amusing,' David commented wryly.

Tanya Carlyle looked at him thoughtfully as she played with the stem of her wine glass. 'I'm sorry,' she replied sweetly, 'that was very rude of me. So condescending. I didn't mean it to be. I did mean – thought-provoking.'

Before David could think what to say, he was aware that a silence had descended on the table and that the last few words had been listened to by everybody. There had been one of those unplanned pauses in other conversations that had allowed Tanya Carlyle's words to be projected right round the table.

'Hallo, Hallo,' called out Carlyle inquisitively from the far end. 'What's going on up there that you're having to apologise, Tanya? Upsetting our guests wasn't the order of the day!'

'It was nothing,' laughed David, 'and I'm certainly not upset!'

'I'm pleased about that,' replied Carlyle. 'We can't have our guests' feathers ruffled on their first evening.'

'You heard what David said. It was nothing!' Tanya's words were like a whiplash. They were said quietly but quickly, with a tenseness that was freezing in its intensity. David was suddenly aware of the crackling of the logs on the fire.

'Yes, sorry, my dear. I should have minded my own business. I didn't mean to go on about it.' Carlyle was like a dog that had just been chastised for putting its paws up on someone's dress. David caught June's glance. Her eyes were flashing messages and he was sure she was rather enjoying it all.

'Well,' the relaxed voice of Thatcher broke an awkward silence. 'That was a splendid meal. My compliments to the cook!'

'Yes.'

'Absolutely.'

'First class.'

Everyone was obviously relieved to contribute a word or two to drown the awkwardness that had developed and they were back to something with which they could cope.

'Excellent,' Carlyle had recovered his poise as the door opened and the two young men came in with coffee. 'Now June, please, what liqueur would you care for? We have most of them.'

'Oh, I don't know that I can,' June placed her hands over her breasts accentuating her protestion. Others round the table murmured their understanding of her reluctance.

'Nonsense, nonsense. I insist.' Carlyle leaned forward and held her elbow. 'We're going to have a little game over coffee, and a liqueur will help you enjoy the last few minutes of the evening.'

'Oh, dear,' June smiled at him anxiously, 'All right, I'll have contreau on ice then. But only a small one, please.' She turned and looked at the young waiter at her side, who nodded and moved to Gorman.

'Oh, I'll have brandy, please.' There was no hesitation.

Carlyle nodded and smiled. 'An armagnac, Colin? As you're what I suppose could be described as "in the trade", no doubt you'll appreciate it.'

'Absolutely,' Gorman's ginger hair bobbed up and down as he nodded.

Everybody, with varying degrees of reluctance, chose a liqueur and relaxed as the coffee and liqueurs were served quietly and efficiently by the two young men, who then withdrew.

'Apart from the splendid food I feel I must congratulate you on the splendid service.' Thatcher chose a cigar from the box Carlyle held out, as he spoke. 'How on earth do you find fellows like that down here in the back of be ... Oh, look, sorry, I didn't mean...'

'Don't worry, Maurice,' Carlyle smiled. 'we chose this place because it is the back of beyond! We wanted a country place away from everything and indeed away from everyone we know. Tanya and I wanted to start afresh, as it were, so that's exactly what this place is. The back of beyond. With its recent history too, of course, it seems even more appropriate!'

David saw Jenny Gorman shudder involuntarily. 'I'm not sure I'd want to live in a place that had been an ... an ...'

'An asylum?' Carlyle nodded. 'Why not? It's all in the mind!' He laughed at his own wit. 'There's really nothing here now to associate with the past. He paused thoughtfully. 'Well, there won't be when we've had all those bars removed from the windows. Sorry about that, but I'm afraid they were just overlooked.'

David looked across at Abbott who was fondling his liqueur glass as though it was a most treasured possession. He wondered if Abbott had drunk as much in his whole unexciting life as he had tonight. He appeared decidedly inebriated. David searched the table's guests. He doubted if anyone could pass a breathalyser test. Thank God no-one was going anywhere. In fact, David thought, between us we could probably change a police car from blue to red by blowing up its exhaust. He chortled inwardly. He felt quite drunk. The logs on the fire suddenly spat as he watched them. Drunk too?

'How can you overlook something as obvious as bars at the windows? Not exactly prepossessing.' Thatcher's words were slightly slurred as he raised his glass to his lips and drained it dry.

David sensed, rather than saw, Tanya Carlyle's head rise in response to Thatcher's forthright comment and as he glanced at her she was staring at her husband. Just for a second. Then she laughed and laid her hand on David's arm.

'Well, I'm not sure if that proves David's or my point just now about alcohol and people speaking their mind! You must forgive us Maurice. You're absolutely right of course, but we did have a lot on our minds trying to get the place done up quickly.' She squeezed David's arm playfully.

'Oh, dear,' Thatcher almost looked embarrassed, as his face tightened. 'How rude – I mean, of course ... oh ... do forgive me ... wasn't thinking.'

'Ah, but you were!' David turned, surprised, as he felt Jenny Gorman pat him on the hand. What was all this touching him, he wondered. Do most nurses have such unattractive hands, he asked himself.

'This does take us back to what David was saying a few minutes ago.' Jenny looked triumphant. 'You *were* thinking Mr Thatcher, but the difference is that normally you wouldn't have said it. So you've helped David prove his point!'

Before anyone else spoke, Lesley Abbott was leaning over the table, arm outstretched, in a vain attempt to reach her husband, who seemed to be dozing off.

'George! I think you've had slightly too much to drink,' her voice was full of anxiety.

'Nonsense, Lesley.' Carlyle rebuked her lightheartedly. 'You're now all just relaxed at the end of a long journey; after a meal in different surroundings; mixing with hopefully new friends. What better way to be able to relax than over the after-dinner drinks.'

Lesley Abbott looked decidedly unconvinced, but smiled weakly at Carlyle before glancing back to her George.

'What was this about a game?' Thatcher's cigar smoke rose imperiously towards the ceiling, as he blew it away, head thrown back.

'Oh, yes! I love games!' June clapped her hands.

'I hope its nothing too difficult.' Len Hardy looked worried.

'Don't worry, Len,' Rita rubbed the end of her nose with her knuckles, as her eyes dwelt on Carlyle. 'If it's too difficult for you, I'll ask Ian to send you to bed early, so as not to wear your brains out. I will soldier on alone – as a woman – without you.'

Everyone laughed, including Hardy, but David was not convinced it was really meant as an innocent joke. Was she really letting it be known that she was prepared to set herself aside from her husband, if the opportunity arose? He stared at his empty glass, feeling glad it was empty.

The door opened at the far end of the room and the waiters, with many protestations, refilled the glasses as well as the coffee cups, whilst Carlyle threw some more logs on the fire. The table was cleared, except for nuts, fruit and delicate chocolates and as Carlyle sat down again he switched on a speaker system that produced a soft, quadraphonic, orchestral piece that David didn't recognise. Beautifully melodic, muted strings.

'Now,' said Carlyle, smiling happily at everyone in turn, 'before we retire, just a little game?,

Pat Thatcher picked up a chocolate and commented in dulcet tones, 'I'm always ready for a little game.' David couldn't imagine why June grinned.

'Right,' continued Carlyle, 'its very simple. All someone has to do is say an imaginary sentence that could have been said by someone famous or well-known and we've got to guess who it is.

The originator has to write down who he or she thinks could have said it, as they say it, so that there's no changing minds if someone guesses it easily! Then the person who guesses correctly thinks of one, and so on, and so forth. Here's a pad and pencil,' Carlyle picked up a silver boxed notepad and pencil from a table by the fire and put it in front of Thatcher. 'Any questions?'

'Never played this before,' Thatcher's words came out as though their meaning was 'Never heard of anything so ridiculous'.

'Sounds fun,' laughed June, 'Go on Maurice, you start!' She turned and nudged his arm. Everyone was clearly relieved that they hadn't been asked to start and all joined in supporting June's encouragement. Thatcher frowned, but obviously decided that it would be unseemly to be too churlish and shrugged his shoulders in a defeated manner.

'Does it matter if they are dead or alive?' he asked Carlyle unenthusiastically.

'Only to themselves!' Colin Gorman grinned from ear to ear.

'No, no, not at all,' replied Carlyle as he leaned back in his chair, relaxed.

Thatcher stared ahead for a few moments whilst everyone watched him in anticipation. He finally wrote something on the pad. 'OK,' he muttered reluctantly, 'When you're ready.'

'Right,' asked Carlyle, 'what's the sentence?'

'He must be around here somewhere.'

There was silence as they all thought of an answer, whilst the logs crackled encouragingly.

'Sherlock Holmes,' sang out June brightly. 'Looking for Moriarty!'

'No,' Thatcher shook his head apathetically.

'Good try, June,' encouraged Carlyle. 'Come on, who else?'

'Montgomery looking for Rommel.' suggested Gorman.

'No.'

'Whoever was looking for the rabbit who was always late for a very important date,' said Pat Thatcher, 'in *Alice in Wonderland* or was it *Through the Looking Glass*, darling? You know!'

Thatcher looked at her slightly condescendingly and replied,

'My dear, if you don't know who was looking for the rabbit isn't that the point of this game? Anyway, no!'

'Jack Benny looking for Rochester?' asked Colin Gorman doubtfully.

'No.'

'My, this is difficult.' Pat Thatcher shook her head.

'Hardly, darling,' her husband replied. 'It just needs a little grey matter, that's all.'

'Oh, God, and I have so little,' she whimpered mockingly.

'Robinson Crusoe looking for Friday?' a very apologetic Len Hardy interposed, pulling an ear nervously.

'Well done!' June clapped her hands, nodding vehemently.

'No.' Thatcher was now clearly warming to his being able to dismiss every suggestion put forward, and he began to smile smugly.

'Abbott looking for Costello or Costello for Abbott?' mooted an intoxicated-sounding Abbott. 'Can't remember which is which, but the straight man looking for the little fat fellow?'

Pat Thatcher gave a little yelp, 'Of course, you'd think of them! I say,' she paused theatrically, 'You're not related are you?'

Abbott looked puzzled for a moment and stared at her. 'Oh, I see what you mean. No. Good heavens.' The full impact of the suggestion that he could even be possibly considered as being related to a comedian clearly hit him hard. 'Definitely not.'

'Anyway,' Thatcher looked skywards, 'the answer is no.'

'Could it be Stanley looking for Livingstone?' asked Jenny Gorman thoughtfully.

'Why, yes,' replied Thatcher, almost reluctantly, 'it is.'

'Well done, old girl,' congratulated her husband and every-one joined in to Jenny Gorman's acute embarrassment.

'Your turn!' called out Carlyle, enthusiastically.

David noticed that everyone was watching Jenny Gorman in varying degrees of animated anticipation, except Tanya Carlyle who hadn't, as yet, participated in the game. She was sitting, chin resting on her hands, elbows on the table with a set half-smile on her lips. But she was looking straight down the table at her rather flushed, perspiring husband. In contrast, David thought, she looked ice cool, almost cold and in total control of herself. He had only just realised how little she had drunk during the evening. The glass of brandy in front of her was untouched from the first round of after-dinner drinks. She turned and gazed at David at that moment and he realised he must have been staring at her, for she slightly inclined her head towards him smiling enigmatically and asked, 'Penny for your thoughts?'

David quickly returned the smile and replied, 'I was just trying to think up a sentence in case I have to do one.'

'Quite right,' Tanya Carlyle appeared to support the idea totally, 'and so you should.' She passed her attention easily on to David's neighbour, 'Have you one?' Jenny nodded doubtfully as she wrote on the pad that had been passed to her.

'I'm sick of the word "steps".'

There was silence, as the music wafted gently across the room.

'I'm sick of the word "steps"?' was then repeated by Thatcher and echoed by Gorman who was gazing at his wife, as if he had never heard her say anything quite so extraordinary in his whole life.

'What do you mean, 'I'm sick of the word "steps"?' Gorman insisted.

Jenny Gorman ruffled her hair irritably. 'What do you mean, "What do you mean"?' she retorted. 'Just get on with the game.'

'Right.' Lesley Abbott nodded knowingly. 'How about the hero in John Buchan's *The Thirty Nine Steps*. I can't remember his name.'

'Then you don't know who it is,' Jenny tapped the table firmly, as though she were addressing a child.

Lesley Abbott flushed slightly and retorted, 'Then I'm right! Hold on a moment and I'll think of his name.'

'It's Richard Hannay,' said her husband quietly.

'George!' Her face was now slightly mottled.

'Well it is!' he protested.

'Look. Damn it! I'm not arguing!' snapped Lesley Abbott furiously.

'It doesn't matter as it happens,' chortled Jenny, 'because it isn't he.'

66

'Oh, how ridiculous!' Lesley Abbott slumped back, chewing a chocolate.

'Napoleon?' enquired David cautiously.

'Napoleon,' echoed Jenny. She stared at him and from the distance of no more than two feet David stared back into her quizzical big brown eyes. She had that well-scrubbed look that Matron would have fervently approved of. There was no eye make-up at all and only a hint of lipstick. Nevertheless her candour and apparent total lack of guile attracted him to her. His father would have described her as 'a good sort'.

'Yes,' he smiled. 'When he was invading Russia, he must have been sick of the steppes.'

Jenny chuckled, 'Not that sort of step, you clot,' she replied and laid a hand on his arm.

'How about John Kennedy?' asked June, looking severely at David.

'John Kennedy?' David frowned back at her.

'Yes, when he had to climb up to look over the Berlin Wall, that time.'

'Not bad, not bad,' smiled Jenny, 'but sorry, no.'

'Ah,' mused Carlyle, 'How about Neil Armstrong after his walk on the moon? Everyone must have talked to him about his first steps on the moon.'

Jenny nodded happily, 'Absolutely right.'

'Well done, darling,' Tanya shook her head slowly in mock disbelief at her husband's success.

'Right, let me think while I relight my cigar.' Carlyle slowly pulled on his cigar, as he carefully used a gold lighter. He turned the cigar and stared at the smoking tip. Apparently satisfied he took a strong pull. He allowed the hazy smoke to escape from his rounded lips very, very, slowly. He stretched his right arm out as Jenny pushed the pad and pencil towards him, looked round the waiting participants and then silently wrote on the pad.

'We're ready,' sang June eagerly.

Carlyle smiled at her. 'All right,' he said. 'We were young, we were merry, we were very, very wise.'

There was a pregnant silence, that seemed to last a lifetime.

'Pardon?' asked Pat Thatcher.

'We were young, we were merry, we were very, very wise.'

'My word that could be anybody,' June's eyebrows had risen spectacularly.

David had been half listening to Carlyle as Carlyle had started to read the sentence out, but his gaze had drifted sideways to Thatcher as Carlyle finished speaking. Thatcher's reaction had been extraordinary. His head had jerked round to look at Carlyle as his mouth had fallen open, and total disbelief was clearly written all over a face that had drained of all colour. He had recovered quickly and was now sucking on his cigar, like a baby with its bottle. David looked round the table. Bewilderment was the word that immediately sprang to mind to describe the reaction he was witnessing. With the exception of Abbott.

Abbott's head was slumped down on his chest and David was unable to see the reaction on his face. He did notice that Abbott's hands were clenched, one inside the other, and the knuckles were white. Drink was having its effect.

'What an unhelpful sentence,' Jenny Gorman now looked very puzzled, as she clearly tried hard to come up with a suggestion.

'Churchill,' a very disenchanted Lesley Abbott sounded petulant.

Carlyle shook his head, smiling enigmatically.

'Henry VIII or one of the Three Wise Men,' suggested Pat Thatcher, more in hope than belief.

'Alice – of Wonderland fame?' David queried, but a smiling Carlyle again shook his head.

'Wendy or Peter Pan?' offered Rita Hardy without success. 'Well, I've no idea,' she grimaced, looking down at her breasts.

'Neither have I,' smiled David. 'I guess I've drunk too much or else my grey cells have disintegrated.' He noticed that Gorman had a smile of extraordinary contentment on his face, as he sat gazing at the ceiling, almost it seemed, oblivious of his surroundings. Thatcher was totally in control of himself again and was actually strumming his fingers on the table, apparently deep in thought.

'I think it must be some politician,' said Jenny Gorman, 'but as

June said, it really could be anybody.' She rubbed the back of her head as she ruminated. 'Is it President Reagan?'

Carlyle had his eyes shut as he answered simply, 'No.'

Thatcher gently pushed his chair back. 'I wonder Ian, whether we shouldn't call it a day? I – um – I'm sure we've all had a very busy day – and – well – after a superb meal and a – a – thought-provoking game, I think it is leaving us all a little tired.' The brightness of his eyes somehow, belied the comments.

Carlyle looked at Thatcher and slowly licked his lips, as though they were sore, as he nodded, 'Of course, Maurice, of course. My apologies for having prevailed upon you like this. I shouldn't have prolonged the evening. I'm sure you're all very tired.'

Thatcher's brow was moist as he stood up and David was vaguely surprised. He had begun to think that the temperature in the room had been dropping fast, as the logs had burned down to greying ashes.

'I'm sure that you're right, darling.' Tanya rose and everyone else began to do likewise. 'You shouldn't have started silly games.' She walked round to David and slid her arm into his as he felt himself guided gently, but firmly, towards the door.

'No, the game was fun,' protested Jenny Gorman, 'but I must say I am quite tired.' They all moved slowly through to the anteroom.

'Well, it's been a wonderful evening,' murmured Rita Hardy as she stood by Carlyle, 'but before we retire for our beauty sleep what was the answer to your sentence, Ian?'

Everyone was now in the anteroom as Carlyle stopped and took hold of her hands. David wondered if she was enjoying the way Carlyle's thumbs were stroking them.

'I'm afraid it was a bit of a catch on my part,' he smiled.

'Catch?' asked Rita Hardy.

'Yes. It wasn't really a fictitious imagined statement. It was the first line of a verse Mary Coleridge wrote.'

'Who?' Rita frowned, shaking her head.

'Rita. Stop worrying about it. You've never heard of her,' Hardy sounded impatient and cross.

His wife turned on him. 'I'm not worrying about it. How do

you know whether I've heard of her or not? I may not be the world's most educated woman, but that doesn't mean I don't know anything.' Her voice had risen as she had replied. 'Anyway,' she looked back at Carlyle and continued softly, 'I'm sure Ian won't mind if I ask him what the whole verse is.'

'Rita, for God's sake, let's go to bed,' Hardy walked slowly towards her.

Carlyle extended an arm, arresting Hardy's advance, laid the other against his brow in a mock theatrical, oratorical, stance and in measured tones recited:

We were young, we were merry, we were very, very wise,
And the door stood open at our feast.
When there passed us a woman with the West in her eyes,
And a man with his back to the East.

'Mary Coleridge?' Rita Hardy mused – clearly out of her depth.

'Yes.' Carlyle turned to David. 'I believe she was a grand niece of Samuel Taylor Coleridge, who was at Cambridge, your old university David, but Mary studied at home as most girls did in the eighteenth century. Great pity, but fortunately times have changed. Did you know,' he continued to address David, 'her first novel published in 1893 was *The Seven Sleepers of Ephesus*?'

David frowned. He couldn't follow the thread of this conversation at all. It was obviously too late for him. 'No,' he shook his head, 'I didn't and I didn't go to Cambridge, Ian.'

Carlyle's mouth half opened and he swallowed before repeating. 'No? Oh, I thought ... No, of course...'

'No,' David smiled, 'none of the Oxbridge Universities for me, I'm sorry to say. Goodnight Ian. He took June's arm, 'and thank you for a splendid evening.' He started to lead June up the stairs, but swung round as he heard a heavy thud followed by a stifled scream.

Abbott had passed out at the foot of the stairs.

* * *

'Well, I must say one could describe this evening as a very

70

interesting one.' June switched off the bedside lamp and slid under the duvet to nuzzle into David.

'One could certainly call it that,' David replied firmly. He was thinking of Abbott. Having watched Jenny Gorman calmly and efficiently bring Abbott back to what he supposed was life, he thought that Abbott had still looked nearer to death than many people he'd seen alive in hospitals. Everyone bade each other goodnight in a somewhat subdued manner, and he and June had made nothing but small talk as they had prepared for bed. His brain, however, had been formulating anything but trivial thoughts.

'Food was superb,' enthused June as she wriggled close.

'Yes.'

'Wine was excellent.'

'Very.'

'Company was stimulating – well, some of it was,' June added wryly.

'Yes. But for God's sake, darling, what was it all about?'

'What do you mean, David? I'm not with you.' She kissed his cheek.

'Oh, yes, you are!' He put his arm round her shoulders and she moved her head on to his chest. David started to caress her hair with his lips, then stopped and shook his head. 'I don't know. It's just that I felt we were taking part in a play. Everyone was in it, even the bloody waiters! They all had parts, knowingly or otherwise, including us. Our roles were unexplained, but we were certainly taking part. It was all so...' he struggled for words and finished lamely, 'weird. This is the first time since we arrived here that I've felt in any way in command of what's happening to us.'

June pulled David's face towards her and kissed him warmly. She clung to him, as her hands slid down his stomach between his legs.

'But now, of course,' he whispered, 'I'm again not sure I'm in command of what's happening.'

June pulled her hand back and playfully slapped his chest. 'Behave yourself! You're just a randy old man! What do you mean, "weird"?'

71

David lay back and stroked her hair, as he gazed out of the window. The stars were bright in the evening sky and the only noise that interrupted the stillness was the insistent call of an owl. Perhaps the affection and love for the country was more stark in the minds of those who lived, as they did, in suburbia. Affection, however, was not an apt description of his reaction to this evening in the country. The blackness outside reflected the blackness of his innermost thoughts.

'Weird, odd, strange,' he replied.

'I know what "weird" means, darling,' June yawned.

David stared straight ahead, 'Yes, well, let me give you some specifics.' He paused as he assembled his points. 'One. None of the guests had ever met Carlyle socially before. OK. Not odd in itself, but ... Two. Carlyle must know many people. Wouldn't you expect him to invite, say one couple along he knows reasonably well, to ease such an occasion? Three. Why over-night? Surely a dinner party, which is certainly more normal, would have been sufficient. Four. Look at the way he ogled you when we arrived and the way he reacted positively towards Rita, "all boobs" Hardy. Is that the way a man just back from holiday behaves, with people he has never met before?'

'Oh, come on, David,' June lifted her head off his chest and lay back on the pillow. 'That's rubbish. He just likes looking at women. Most men do you know. He's obviously one of the more blatant types that's all.'

'And yet when his wife wants to shut him up or say something she considers important, he behaves like a lamb,' David replied. 'Wouldn't you think such a lamb would be a little more circumspect?'

'Oh, I don't know,' yawned June, 'I'm not sure I care either.'

'All right,' David was determined to finish now he'd started, 'let me go on. Five. The Ross couple and those waiters. They gave me the creeps. The waiters didn't speak or smile all evening. Wouldn't you expect local village girls to be servants?'

'Oh, for pity's sake!' June sounded irritable now.

'All right,' David continued. 'Six. That game that we played. It was fine until Carlyle played his sentence. He didn't even obey his own rules. He admitted that. It wasn't imaginary at all. It was a line from a damned poem that made no sense. We still don't know if it was supposed to have been said by someone, in his game, or not.'

'Yes,' June yawned again, 'that was all a bit peculiar.'

'It was, if you noticed how the sentence affected Thatcher. He almost had a seizure when Carlyle said it.'

'Oh, I didn't see him.'

'If Carlyle had hit him he couldn't have been more poleaxed.'

'Well, well,' said June, 'and then Abbott faints. I'd put that down to drink.'

'Good Lord. So had I,' David turned to her, 'You could be right. Abbott could also have been reacting to the verse!'

'But it's just as likely he was reacting to all the drink, darling.' She paused. 'It's a funny thing though,' she said slowly, 'if you think back, none of the men took part in trying to guess Carlyle's sentence and when Rita tried to get to the bottom of it, Hardy did his best to shut her up!'

'Hardy actually tried to shut his wife up.' David pondered slowly. 'That was unimaginable, up to that point. What made him change character so? He shook his head, 'It must have been that sentence.'

June turned to him. 'It didn't mean anything to you?'

'No,' he shook his head again, 'not a thing.'

'Can you remember it?' June asked, but continued, 'We were young, we were merry, we were wise.'

'Very, very wise,' corrected David, 'Not that that makes much difference. And then it went on,

And the door stood open at our feast,
When there passed us a woman with the West in her eyes,
And a man with his back to the East.'

'Well done!' June yawned again, 'word perfect! How come? This is a hidden talent I'd not been aware of.'

David chuckled. 'Some people can remember phone numbers or faces or routes. I can, amongst my many gifts, remember words.'

'And I didn't realise you had so many gifts,' whispered June,

73

as she began to caress his body again. 'Can we leave all the oddities for tomorrow, now, darling and just shut everything else out till the morning?'

David's response was to pull her naked body to him and begin kissing her nipples. They hardened under his lips and June arched her body as she began to moan. Her hand reached for and held his hardness. They kissed ardently as they made love intensely, satiating each other's pent-up desires as they both knew how. Later, as they lay exhausted, David wound his arm round June's breasts as she backed into him ready for sleep.

'Darling?' she whispered.

'Go to sleep,' David mumbled. He was drifting off already.

'Darling. I can give you numbers seven and eight.'

'Mmm?'

June merely went on, 'Seven, Ian thought you had been to Cambridge for some reason, and eight, someone did go through my suitcase.'

'Yes, dear,' David felt himself drifting off into the blackening, beckoning, land of nod. He really couldn't wake up now.

4

London, June 1988

'Mr Hardy?'

Hardy's eyes shot open and he jerked his head round.

'Sorry, sir. I didn't mean to startle you.' The very blonde stewardess was smiling at him. 'Can I give you your complimentary toilet bag and head-set for the journey?'

Hardy nodded and took them from her as he wiped his glistening forehead with his other hand.

'The cabin temperature will cool down as soon as we're airborne,' the stewardess said reassuringly, as she moved on to the seats in front.

'Going all the way?'

Hardy turned to the man seated next to him. Piercing blue eyes stared at him through rimless spectacles. The eyes were tired and bloodshot, but they were sharp. Hardy felt he had been expertly examined and assessed by this fellow traveller, a large unattractive man in his forties. Len doubted if he was less than six feet tall, his coarsened grey face with bushy eyebrows topped by a thick head of wavy white hair.

'Er, yes,' Hardy nodded nervously.

'First trip down under?' The man grabbed a handful of nuts off the plate between them.

'Yes.'

The man nodded, as though Hardy was merely confirming what he already knew. 'Sydney?'

'Er, yes.' Hardy sipped his drink.

'Ah, you'll like Sydney. Great city. One of the most attractive in the world.' The man half smiled at Hardy. 'The name's Ron Carter.'

'Len Hardy.'

'Yes, I know.'

It was as if hands had gripped Hardy's intestines and tied a knot in them. He couldn't raise his eyes to look at the man's face. They reached the chest and stopped. 'You know?' His voice sounded hoarse. How could the man know? Unless ... no, stop imagining things. The stewardess had addressed him as Mr Hardy.

Carter looked beyond Hardy and out of the window. 'Ah, we're off!'

The noise and bustle all round became muffled, as the cabin door was slammed and the outside world sealed from the passengers. Hardy leaned back in his seat and shut his eyes. What would happen in Sydney? The purr of the engines sounded very reassuring as the majestic plane lumbered backwards to enable it to swing round and begin the approach to the runway. Watching through the cabin window, Hardy marvelled at the variety of parked aircraft and the number of different airlines represented – Air France, Lufthansa, PanAm, TWA, Qantas, Singapore Airlines, MAS, Air India, Iran-Air. He lost count. The world was encapsulated into an area of a few acres. It was a fine afternoon and the sun shone brightly, reflecting off the window of the last terminal building as they moved past.

One of the stewardesses was demonstrating the use of the life jacket. Hardy was not at all convinced he'd be able to follow the instructions. He had never been very good at following the simplest procedures. He prayed it wouldn't be necessary for his aptitude, or lack of it, to be put to the test. His thoughts were interrupted as the Captain introduced himself over the audio system. It appeared that the weather en route to Bahrain was expected to be fine.

The engines roared into life, and then they were rolling along the less than smooth runway, picking up speed until suddenly the wheels had clearly lost contact with terra firma. Hardy felt the adjustment of angles as his shoulders were pressed into the soft, sumptuous seat back. An indefinable tension remained amongst the passengers for some minutes until the seat belt sign was switched off, by which time the smooth quiet ambassador of the American aviation industry had levelled out above the clouds. Deep breaths were drawn, seat belts unbuckled and one or two pairs of legs were being stretched in the aisle.

Len Hardy had been on a plane only twice before in his life. That had been when he and Rita had had a holiday in Majorca a couple of years back. A package tour from Luton Airport. Majorca had been all right. Rita had loved the sun and a holiday doing nothing was her cup of tea. Mother-in-law, albeit reluctantly, had looked after the boys for the week. Rita had said it wouldn't be a holiday if she had to worry about funny Spanish food being digested by their young stomachs. There were always newspaper stories about food poisoning and people even dying from it. Hardy hadn't argued too much. Four people going away was more expensive than two.

The plane journey hadn't been one of his greatest experiences, however. Luton Airport had been bulging with bad-tempered parents dealing with bawling, fractious, kids. Some go-slow by air traffic controllers in Spain or somewhere, had caused a three-hour delay. Luton hadn't been built for that sort of problem. There hadn't been enough seats and people had sprawled on the floor, their backs to pillars and the walls. Going anywhere meant stepping round or over bodies with 'Excuse me' and 'Sorry' becoming less frequent as the delay lengthened. Finally they had been called, and Hardy's heart had raced as they had walked to the plane. He hadn't known whether it was fear or excitement. Rita hadn't stopped telling him how she knew she was going to be sick, because she always was on boats. He had had to clench his fists at one point to stop himself shouting at her to let him concentrate on trying to enjoy his first flight, if he could.

The plane had been packed. Not a spare seat anywhere and everyone had got very hot in the airport building. It was one of the summer's hottest days and body odour was something to which Hardy was very averse. The seats were terribly narrow and the room for his knees had seemed totally inadequate. The plastic food had been awful and Rita hadn't eaten hers, which had proved to be a blessing as the flight turned out to be very bumpy. It seemed inevitable that Rita should be sick – the only one on the whole plane. Hardy had been singularly unimpressed with the whole experience.

The return journey had been a replica of the outward crossing, except that they had been five hours late coming into Luton. That had made it four o'clock in the morning when they'd arrived. Neither of them had enthused at the idea of suffering the ordeal again, even for the sun of Majorca. Especially with the kids, who had stated unequivocally that any more jaunts like that could only be done if they came too. They and Grandma had not seen eye to eye on anything while they'd been with her.

Hardy closed his eyes and wondered what the kids would say if they could see him now. Sitting in first-class on a 747, holding a glass of champagne. But this trip was to be no holiday. God, no.

'What's your line of business?'

Hardy turned to look at his companion, who was busily taking his tie off. More questions? 'Er, I'm a lawyer.'

'Really?' The tie disappeared into a brief case, in exchange for a paperback. 'Your trip business or pleasure?'

The idea of his travelling first class to Australia for pleasure caused Hardy to grimace inwardly. 'Oh, business,' he replied, nodding.

'Going for long?'

Hardy looked out at the dark-blue sky. The clouds had been left far behind. He clenched his fists. 'Oh, a week or two. Depends.' He turned slowly to his neighbour who was eyeing him contemplatively. 'How long are you going for Mr ... er, Carter?'

'Me?' Carter laughed. 'Oh, I live in Sydney. Have done since 1960.'

'Oh, I see,' Hardy commented automatically, 'you've been to England on business?'

'No,' Carter opened his book and looked for his bookmark. 'I've been to Eastern Europe.'

Hardy's brain buzzed and filled with questions, but Carter appeared unaware of the interest he had awakened, as he settled into his book.

The champagne glass was replenished often in the next hour. Hardy tried to read the magazines he had bought, but he couldn't concentrate. He fitted the head-set, having fought to open the plastic wrapping and flicked through classical, jazz, western and light music. After a few inattentive minutes he pulled the pads from his ears, wearily. The smell of food was filling the cabin and he decided it would be sensible to make himself comfortable before dinner. As Hardy wandered up the aisle he looked at the other first-class passengers. He was surprised to realise that clothes clearly didn't make the man on a plane, even in first class. Every seat was taken and he reckoned all the men would have done more justice to the Fulham Road than to Pall Mall. Jeans and loose T-shirts were much in evidence. He seemed to be the only one who was travelling in a suit. Well, he'd learn for the next time. If there was ever to be a next time.

When Hardy emerged from the toilet, he found that one of the stewards had started laying starched white tablecloths ready for dinner. The blonde stewardess was following, wheeling a trolley down the aisle and arranging cutlery and wine glasses on each person's table. She smiled a toothpaste smile at him, as he eased passed her and went to sit down. There was a piece of paper on his seat. He idly picked it up, looking at it as he sat down. Scrawled on it were the words ENJOY THE FEAST. The paper slid out of his fingers on to the floor before he recovered from the surprise, picked it up and stuffed it in his pocket.

Hardy looked at Carter, who still seemed to be totally engrossed in his novel. He hadn't even raised his head as Hardy had returned. The steward leaned over and pulled Hardy's table out and Carter reluctantly put his book down and allowed the stewardess to spread his complement of dinner paraphernalia in front of him.

'You didn't happen to notice the person who dropped a note on my seat, I suppose?' Hardy asked Carter.

'Sorry?' Carter sounded lost. 'Note? What note?'

79

'Oh, I've torn it up now. It doesn't matter.' Hardy shrugged his shoulders.

'No, I didn't see anyone,' replied a very bored Carter.

Hardy twiddled his wine glass. So he was not alone. The food was good. A choice for each course and some good cheese at the end. Hardy liked cheese and surprised the stewardess by asking for a little of each on the trolley. The glass of port with it crowned his glasses of Australian Rhine Reisling and Cabernet Sauvignon. Not that he knew anything about wine, but Carter told him they were good ones and they certainly tasted very pleasant. Extraordinarily enough, considering everything, he almost felt contented and relaxed. Almost. As the coffee cups and napkins were removed he pressed the arm button and eased his seat back to a more reclining angle. A pretty little brunette stewardess leaned over him and pulled down his window blind.

'Ready for the film?' she smiled. Hardy caught a whiff of her perfume as she straightened up and he noticed her heavy breasts swelling under the dress. He thought of Rita and wondered how she was. The cabin lights were dimmed, the screen pulled down from the ceiling and the projector flickered into action. The film was the latest James Bond. Hardy hadn't seen a film other than on the television for years. He settled back to enjoy it.

He awoke just as the film ended. Minutes later as the cabin came back to life, hot towels were offered. They looked like blue asparagus rolls. It was steaming hot as he undid it, but he found it quickly cooled down and he gratefully soothed his face.

'Well, Bahrain soon.' Carter seemed to be trying to immerse his whole head in his towel.

'Er, yes. I suppose so,' Hardy agreed.

Carter's assured statement was confirmed as the Captain announced that their descent into Bahrain had commenced. Hardy was interested in the way Bahrain was pronounced – 'Bach Rain'. Perhaps Handel hadn't been the only one to compose water music? He sniggered inwardly. He had drunk a considerable quantity.

Tables were being folded away, seats pressed to attention,

glasses removed, and seat belts buckled around their occupants. The plane's wheels were lowered and locked into place as Hardy watched the green-blue sea rise to meet them. He couldn't see land, and for a moment controlled panic set in as he wondered if everything was all right. Then suddenly land appeared ahead, and almost immediately the wheels touched down smoothly in the early morning middle-eastern sun. A pale golden welcome.

'Good duty free here,' Carter ran his hands through his hair. 'Airport's a dump, but most airports are. Good idea to get off and stretch the old legs.'

Hardy felt it was almost a directive. 'How long are we here?'

'Oh, about an hour. They refuel and bring on fresh food, etc. The usual.'

The plane was taxiing towards the terminal, where a group of men in white overalls stood ready to carry out varying tasks. Another 747 was next to them. Qantas. Hardy followed Carter, who didn't appear to be inclined to be companionable, and they joined the throng of transit passengers from the economy section jostling their way to the lounge. Sure enough, many people strode off purposefully to the duty-free shops.

Hardy wandered around, idly looking in various windows and then finally out of a relaxed interest, made his way to the main duty-free store with no intent to buy. The range of cigarettes and spirits was impressive and the prices even more so. Carter had been right. At that moment he noticed Carter apparently trying to make a decision as he moved from the Gordon's gin shelf to the Beefeater and back again. People were milling everywhere. Carter appeared to come to a decision and reached forward to pick up a carton of Gordon's gin. At that moment another man, tall, balding, safari-suited, sauntered up, reached out and grasped the same carton. They both turned to each other and became engrossed in conversation, but their backs were turned away from Hardy and he couldn't tell whether they were arguing or merely chatting.

'I'm sorry! Oh, I am so sorry!'

A young woman had her arms round Hardy and he stared into a lively, grinning, face, studded with freckles. Her jet-black hair was long, styled into short curls, and she wore a cobalt-blue,

81

sleeveless dress. Her body was boyish, not given to the female contours of provocation. She stepped back and brought her hands flat to her cheeks, with obvious embarrassment.

'That's all right,' Hardy smiled, as he realised that the young woman had been looking at the shelves and not looking where she was going.

'I spend my life walking into people and lamp posts.' She shook her head in disbelief that she had done it again. 'I know, I know,' her hands again came up to her face, 'why don't I look where I'm going? I'm not aware that I'm not, that's the trouble.'

Hardy gave her a friendly smile. Her Australian accent was unmistakeable.

'Please don't worry. The pleasure's mine.' Her openness was really rather enchanting. 'Have you found what you want?'

'Oh, yes,' she nodded vehemently. 'This Teacher's whisky is what I want. Now, how much can I take in? I think it's a litre.' She had picked a carton off the shelf and it seemed to Hardy that she had addressed her question to the carton and was expecting it to reply. Momentarily, Hardy thought of a ventriloquist act.

'Er, I'm afraid I can't help you,' he replied. 'Where are you going?'

'Oh, Sydney,' she answered, still staring at the carton. 'I'm sure it's a litre. Come on then,' Hardy stared at her retreating head as she made for the cash desk. Come on then? Had she been addressing him? He didn't know her from Adam ... well, Eve. He looked round. Carter had disappeared. Come on? OK. He followed her and watched her sort out some notes, pay and collect a plastic bag to put her carton in. She turned round, saw Hardy and grinned happily.

They walked out of the shop with a group of gesticulating, shouting Arabs dressed in what could only be loosely described as Western attire. Hardy had never before seen anyone dressed in an open-necked dark blue shirt, a brown pinstriped suit, no socks and open sandals. As he and his carefree companion wandered slowly back towards the departure gates Hardy noticed a number of bare-footed Arabs sprawled out on seats,

82

fast asleep. He wondered if they were waiting for planes or had adopted the airport in the way certain Londoners had adopted main railway terminals. Logic told him that they must have come through controls, so they must be travellers. But how did they know when their planes were due to leave? Perhaps it was a matter of days, not hours.

'Do you come here often?' asked his companion, laughing at her own question.

Hardy smiled, 'No, in fact this is the first time.'

'Oh, how exciting.' A mouth of uneven white teeth shone at him.

'Well, yes. In a way. Business trip though.'

'Oh. It can still be exciting. Work hard, play hard. You know.'

Hardy wasn't sure he did. An announcement was being made that their British Airways flight was ready for boarding.

'Here we go again,' sighed his companion as they joined the other passengers at their gate.

'Sounds as though you travel a lot,' Hardy commented.

'Oh yes, from time to time. Well, see you in Singapore I expect.' She bade him farewell and he followed the first-class arrow, as the girl followed the economy one.

Carter was already back in his seat with a glass of champagne.

'Did you get your duty free?' asked Hardy as he sat down.

Carter's unexpressive eyes stared at him. 'Yes. You didn't buy anything?'

'No,' Hardy replied. 'I'll get some going home.'

Carter nodded, taking a large gulp of his drink. 'Long way to go yet. Plenty of food and films before Sydney. Next stop Singapore.'

Hardy drank less alcohol on the next sector. He slept intermittently and for a while did actually pick up the thread of the novel he had bought at Heathrow. It was the normal mixture of explicit sex, gory murders and car chases.

Carter made no move to get off when they arrived in Singapore. He was engrossed in his very thick paperback, which he had turned back on itself, so that he could hold it in one hand. Hardy thought this a very undisciplined and destructive way of reading. He decided to stretch his legs and made his way to the terminal, which was refreshingly cold – the air-conditioned atmosphere enveloped him. Singapore airport was a world apart from Bahrain in purposefulness, sophistication and size. Travelators transported people everywhere, smoothly, quietly and efficiently. He remembered, as a boy, reading a comic that talked about wonders of the future. One of them had been moving pavements. Here they were and here he was – in the future.

The terminal was spotless. Hardy couldn't see a piece of litter anywhere. Thick carpets and potted plants abounded. Chinese, with identity cards on their shirts and blouses, busily went about their business, many quietly jabbering into walkie-talkies.

'Just think what China could be like today if they had developed as Singapore has.'

Hardy was standing watching a group of little Japanese men helping one of their number choose a watch at a duty-free shop. An arm had gone through his and was hugging it. He turned, recognising the voice of the girl at Bahrain.

'Hi.' She grinned at him.

'Hi,' he responded, surprised, but rather pleased.

'Isn't it a great airport? Just great!' she'd answered herself, as she looked around her.

'Yes,' he agreed. 'I'm very impressed.'

'We've an hour's wait again. How about a drink?' There was a pause, punctured by a child's scream, as some family discord within a couple of feet of them reached its inevitable conclusion and smack. 'My name's Patti, by the way. Patti Cross.' The family moved on. The airport was a subdued hubbub of noise. All colours, races, creeds, were on the move. Some anxiously, some happily, some bored.

'Er, Len. Len Hardy.'

'Hi – again!' Patti rubbed the end of her nose, and pointed, 'There's a bar.' Hardy wasn't sure if he led her, or she led him, but they climbed on to two stools at the bar and he ordered two beers. Australian, at Patti's insistence.

'You've got to start drinking the real stuff now,' she said. 'First trip and all that!' Hardy liked his pint of bitter at room temperature. This 'stuff' was ice cold and very fizzy. He said so.

84

'Australia's a hot country, Len.' Patti searched in her large handbag and finally took out a cigarette packet and lighter. 'We need cold beer. You wait and see.' She lit a cigarette without offering him one. 'You'll soon appreciate it.'

He doubted that, but there was no point in labouring the subject.

'Where have you been?' he asked. 'Away on holiday?'

'No. Well, not really.' She shook her head. 'I'm a travel agent. Well, sort of. I work for a large company and head the department that runs all our travel and hotel organising. I've been in London on what is euphemistically called a fact-finding tour. If I have to be honest it was a bit of a rave-up! I was looked after by one of the airlines with whom we do a lot of business.'

'Sounds good,' Hardy tried some more of the beer. It hadn't improved with age.

'Oh, I had a good time. Re-negotiated some hotel discount rates, saw a few shows, had some good dinners and got laid a couple of times.' The flicked ash missed the ashtray. Hardy blinked mentally. He was sure he'd heard right, but Patti was unconcernedly quaffing her beer. He felt silence was golden.

'You work in Sydney?' he asked lamely.

'Yes. Just off Macquarie Street. Good city address. We have a travel agency on the ground floor for the public and my office is up on the twenty-first floor of our building. Superb views over the harbour. You'll love Sydney. Beautiful city.'

'So I believe.' He doubted if he'd love it.

'Let me buy you one,' Patti had already attracted the attention of the alert waiter. 'What's your line of business? Let me think. You look like an accountant.'

'No,' Hardy forced down the rest of his beer as the next one appeared at his elbow. 'Lawyer.' Was she going to start interrogating him, as well?

Patti shrugged her shoulders. 'Near enough,' she commented. 'I could tell you weren't a pop star. You are clearly one of the professional classes.'

'By my suit?' Hardy nodded. 'I guess it sticks out a mile.'

'Does it ever!' exclaimed Patti, scratching her nose. 'Are you going to close some exciting gold-mining deal, or buy some land to build an hotel or office block?'

'No.' Hardy shook his head. 'Nothing like that. Just a very ordinary business deal for a client.'

'Boring. Boring,' was the response, with the wide grin belying any real criticism.

The group of Japanese who had been looking at watches wandered by and stopped by the cascading waterfall in the central area. Cameras were suddenly in evidence and everyone was photographing everybody else in front of the waterfall.

'Biggest con game of all, photography.' Patti commented as they watched. 'What the hell does the world do with all the photographs cluttering up everyone's houses? Every man who takes them probably only looks at them once. No-one else ever does and when he dies they die with him. Stupid pastime if you ask me.'

'I take it you don't have a camera?' Hardy asked amused.

'Oh, I've a camera, all right,' Patti replied, dismissively. 'But I don't use it. Look at that lot, still at it!'

Hardy followed her gaze and as he did so he caught sight of the now familiar face of Carter, sitting watching Singaporean television, just beyond the waterfall. That wasn't, in itself, very interesting, but in the seat immediately with its back to Carter's was the bald-headed man in the safari suit from Bahrain. Hardy could have sworn they were holding a conversation, but physically they didn't appear to acknowledge each other's existence, for as he watched, Carter's lips appeared to move and then the other's. Carter suddenly rose and walked off, with no apparent reaction from the safari suit. Perhaps he'd been wrong. But Hardy was still thinking of that note left on his seat.

'How long will you be in Sydney?'

'Er ... I don't know,' Hardy mentally returned to his companion. 'Probably just a few days.'

'You'll have to have a good look round while you're there.' Patti smiled encouragingly. 'Go down to Circular Quay and see the old pubs in the Rocks. We don't get many ocean-going liners in the harbour any more, it's all container ships and tankers, but its worth keeping your eyes open. There's a lot to see; the

Botanical Gardens with its avenues of trees and plants is an oasis of tranquillity – I spend hours in there. Then there's the Sydney cricket ground, home of Test matches – not that I go there! Go out to Paddington and see the lovely old terraced houses with their wrought-iron balconies. Then there's The Opera House, a mind-blowing building – talk about white sails in the sunset. They have great music there and plays, it...'

Hardy held up his hand in mock horror. 'Stop! Stop! I've forgotten half of that already!'

'Ah, well,' Patti smiled and nodded, 'you'll have to do it all. Chance of a lifetime.'

She paused for a moment. 'What a terrible thought! It may be your only visit to Sydney!'

Hardy stared downwards – seeing nothing. 'Yes, it might,' he said.

'We can't have that,' Patti placed her hand over his and Hardy felt a tingle down his spine he hadn't felt for years. For more years than he liked to think. Abruptly, however, the hand had gone and was waving nonchalantly at a very fat woman in a mauve tracksuit walking by.

'Looks as though it's time for re-boarding. Ann's on her way.' Patti knocked back the rest of her lager and checked her face in her handbag mirror. She obviously decided no repairs were needed.

'Ann?' Hardy tried hard to consume the rest of his fizz, but gave up the attempt.

'She's sitting next to me,' Patti replied. 'Been on a three-month tour of Europe. Hitch-hiking. Not for me! That tracksuit she's wearing hasn't been washed very often either!'

Hardy unhitched himself from the bar stool and they walked back along the travelators to the gate.

'Well, see you in Sydney, Mr First Class!' Patti showed Hardy her teeth again and without waiting for a reply disappeared down the economy passageway.

Hardy had beaten Carter back this time and watched as the new passengers were shown to their seats and their baggage stowed. He felt he'd been on the plane for months.

'Well, what did you think of Singapore's answer to Heathrow?'

A surprisingly affable Carter sighed into his seat and flicked his shoes off.

'Very impressive,' Hardy replied. 'So clean and efficient. Very impressive.'

'Right!' Carter nodded emphatically, 'everybody's impressed. The airport is a reflection of the way Singapore is run. Lee Kwan Yew is the nearest thing to a benevolent dictator there is. Problem is from a visitor's viewpoint it's not an interesting place any more. All the back-street squalor and old Chinatown is being, or has been, razed to the ground and its all new high-rise buildings. Good for Singaporeans, but uninteresting to overseas visitors. It's too hygienic and just like home to them these days.'

Hardy nodded agreement. He had no reason to argue.

Soon airborne again, a new, eager young steward beamed an enquiry as to what they would like to drink. As he gulped more champagne, Hardy felt as though any moment Eddie Cantor would appear, singing:

Another crew, another meal,
Another drink, another reel,
It's in the price, folks,
It's all the way, folks,
We're making whoopee!

His lightheartedness, or maybe, he accepted, his lightheadedness, didn't last very long. The plane began to shudder and lurch like an autumn leaf caught in the wind, torn from its umbilical branch.

The Fasten Seat Belts sign was illuminated and a reassuring female voice asked everyone to observe the sign whilst they passed through 'this area of turbulence'. Hardy's head jerked back instinctively as a vivid flash of lightning lit up the sky outside. Glasses tinkled behind him and something heavy fell in the galley. His stomach began to feel as though his seat belt was being drawn tighter and tighter. His hands were clammy. He leaned back, shut his eyes and prayed. Suddenly all was smoothness again.

'Often get storms round here,' Carter unbuckled his seat belt. 'Had a good flight so far. Hope it stays that way. Where are you staying in Sydney?'

'Er, the Inter-Continental.' Hardy's throat was dry and he cleared his throat hard. Should he have told Carter this?

'Ah, about the best pub in town,' Carter nodded.

'Pub?' Hardy voiced his surprise.

'Oh, don't worry.' Carter scratched his chin, 'We tend to call all hotels, pubs. No, it's good there. Only opened recently. There are other new ones coming, but at the moment it's regarded by most people as the best one and certainly well placed for business.'

The Captain came on the intercom and apologised for the unfriendly start, but promised a smooth flight for the rest of the journey and hoped they'd enjoy the meal, the film and a sleep. He wouldn't speak to them again until they reached Sydney.

'I guess,' Carter took a stiff gulp, 'your business will be in or around the CBD?'

'CBD?' Hardy looked puzzled.

'Central Business District,' Carter explained.

'Oh, yes,' Hardy sighed inwardly, 'I believe the address is George Street.'

'Don't need taxis from the Inter-Continental then. Most offices along there are easy walking distance. Know the number?' Carter was pulling his paperback out again. Alarm bells began to sound louder in Hardy's brain. Enough was enough.

'No. Er, I'm afraid I can't remember. Papers are in my suitcase.'

'Ah, well,' the paperback was folded over, 'won't be far.'

Hardy made his way to the toilet. Every first-class seat was taken. There were some new faces on this sector. Sector! He'd even begun to think the lingo. No-one he recognised. Some of the passengers looked at him without interest; most didn't even look. Sluicing his face and cleaning his teeth with a complimentary brush and individual tube of paste – how could they make them this small? – he returned feeling calmer and fresher. There were no messages on his seat this time. Who had put it there?

Were they still on the plane? He guessed so. Food came, was played with, and went. The cabin was darkened and another film was heralded. Hardy pulled out his foot-rest, accepted a blanket and easing his back-rest down, closed his eyes.

'Well, ladies and gentlemen, boys and girls, I hope you had a good rest. We're now two hundred kilometres from Sydney and we should have you on the ground at half past six.' Hardy awoke abruptly to the voice of the Captain. A soft and relaxed voice. 'I hope you've enjoyed the flight and would like to thank you for flying British Airways.'

Activity heightened. Blankets were folded and stored, headsets removed, lingering glasses and coasters whisked away. Orderliness for landing. Hardy was aware of a quickening of his pulse, a measured breathlessness as the landing wheels locked into place. He could see the outline of the city, as the plane banked and began to almost labour its descent to the tarmac. Wheels screeched, the squeal of rubber was drowned by the change in engine noise and then they were taxiing. All so easy, Hardy thought. All in a day's work. Less than a day. How long had it taken in the days of sail? He couldn't remember.

The cabin was sprayed with a sickly sweet aerosol, apparently to prevent new diseases entering Australia and then everyone was up collecting their paraphernalia.

'Well, good luck,' Carter nodded, half smiled and moved to the doorway without waiting for a response.

'Thanks,' Hardy reached for his case.

Customs and immigration were efficiently handled and in less than twenty minutes Hardy was wheeling his luggage out to a sea of expectant faces and jabbering mouths. Families whooped as a friend or relative emerged from the Customs Hall. Those waiting were a mixture of Orientals and Caucasians and English didn't seem to be the prevalent language. Hardy had to remind himself that Australia now had a very mixed population. No-one moved to greet him as he looked for the taxi sign.

'Len! Hi! Len!' He turned and there, wheeling her trolley through the turbulent throng, was Patti. 'I know! I always turn up! Like a bad penny! Only its cents here now! Dollars and cents!' Her big uneven white teeth were still smiling at him. 'God, I'm glad that's over! Not so good down the back with the other slaves!' She ran a hand through her hair and shook her head. 'There might not be many taxis. Can we share one? You'll be going to the city and I live in Woollahra, so you're on the way.'

'Of course,' Hardy was quietly pleased.

There were plenty of taxis, but they still took one together. The driver started the engine. 'Where are you staying?' Patti turned to Hardy quizzically.

'Er, the Inter-Continental?' Hardy made it sound like a question.

'Fine. Driver, the Inter-Continental and then Marco Polo Road, Woollahra.

Hardy said little during the drive. Weariness was catching up with him, but Patti chatted away amiably. He didn't take in a great deal. Neon lights, houses, offices, sped by. He could have been in Ealing, until he saw some of the towering office blocks come into view. Nothing like those in Ealing.

'Wait till you see the Sydney Harbour Bridge,' Patti had followed his gaze. 'By the way, here's my card. You might need some travel help while you're here.'

Hardy took it with thanks, as the taxi swung up the ramp and he saw the warm welcoming glow of the vestibule of the Inter-Continental Hotel.

'Well,' Hardy turned and smiled as a doorman opened his door, 'I've enjoyed your company. I hope we meet again.' They shook hands.

He had arrived.

5

'Now, Mr Carpenter, I shall only be away for two days. I don't think there should be any problems. Certainly no foreseeable ones at any rate.' Abbott was slowly and systematically polishing his spectacles in his rather austere office. No pictures on the wall, no potted plants – much as his secretary had tried to introduce them – just the regulation bank furniture.

'I'm sure I can cope, Mr Abbott,' replied Carpenter, a young polytechnic graduate who found his boss's pedantic style very irritating, but disguised the fact as much as he could.

'Well done,' Abbott replaced his spectacles carefully. 'Now, if there's nothing else?'

Carpenter happily took the hint and wishing Abbott a pleasant journey left him in peace. Abbott rang the buzzer for his secretary. Mrs Humphreys had been in the bank's employ all her working life. She was coming up to retirement and as far as Abbott was concerned could teach all the youngsters a thing or two. She was smart, alert, sensitive to his every whim, and very, very efficient.

'You rang, sir?' The short, stout, grey-haired lady came in and shut the door.

'Yes, I shall leave,' Abbott checked his watch, 'in ten minutes from now. I'd better have my tickets and papers. Is there a taxi coming?'

'Yes, sir.' Mrs Humphreys nodded emphatically. 'I ordered it for exactly five o'clock. I'll get your briefcase. Everything's in it.' And she disappeared.

Ten minutes later Abbott left the bank, nodding perfunctorily to the security guard. The taxi was waiting as
promised.

'Kings Cross,' ordered Abbott as he closed the door.

'Kings Cross it shall be, Guv,' called out the young driver, who
had Radio One blaring out. Abbott firmly closed the sliding
window between them.

The day had been cloudy and airless, very unlike a normal
June day. Glum-faced early evening commuters were making
their way to bus stops and underground stations. The bill
boards for the *Evening Standard* proclaimed a rail-strike threat
and a Wimbledon tennis sex scandal. Abbott guessed the latter
was more likely to sell the paper than the former. Traffic lights
and pedestrian crossings all seemed to be against them as the
taxi slowly edged its way through Piccadilly, round the remains
of the Circus and up Shaftesbury Avenue. Abbott thought the
new buildings looked as unattractive as the old. He wondered
why London was always so dirty? There was no inbuilt pride in
cleanliness and order. He shuddered inwardly as they drove
round Cambridge Circus, the periphery of Soho, and up into
Tottenham Court Road. The mecca for shoppers looking for
tape recorders and all things electronic. Abbott began to check
his watch every few seconds as their progress continued to be
laboured. He really should have allowed more time. He musn't
miss this train! Suddenly, for no obvious reason, the traffic
cleared and they swung easily into the Euston Road and arrived
at Kings Cross without any further difficulty. He gave the taxi
driver the exact fare and thoughtfully added ten pence tip as he
picked up his two bags.

The driver leaned out as Abbott made his way under the main
arch. 'Sure you can afford it, mate?' he shouted, and drove off to
a hail of laughter from the half dozen porters leaning idly on
their trolleys, waiting for rich pickings. Angrily, Abbott passed
them. He did not accept that people should be paid extra for
merely doing their job. Tipping was antediluvian and should be
made illegal. It was demeaning. It was just unfortunate that
there had been an audience.

Kings Cross was busy; a scurrying mass of humanity. An

93

unintelligible announcement was coming over the public address system about some cancellation. He sincerely hoped it wasn't his train. He hadn't thought of cancellations. He felt somehow inadequate looking for departure details. Everyone else seemed to know where to go. No, not quite. A large elderly woman in a severely cut tweed suit and brogue shoes was also peering at the departure details, on a notice board by the cafeteria.

'Dear me. Dear me.' She was rummaging about in a voluminous leather handbag. 'I can't find my spectacles.'

She looked up at Abbott, realising that she had an audience. 'Can you tell me, young man, what platform I need for the Newcastle train? I think it leaves at five forty-five.' She wore no make up and had just a suggestion of a fuzzy moustache.

'It does indeed,' nodded Abbott. 'I am on it, or I hope to be on it, as well. Let me see what it says.' He was mildly pleased to be addressed as 'young man'.

'Oh, thank goodness,' came the relieved response, 'Stations aren't what they used to be. No nice caring porters any more. They're all...' she looked around her, 'foreign ... if y'know what I mean. They don't have the same sense of duty as the old pre-war porters had. Nobody knows anything. They just point as though they haven't a tongue in their heads. Not that I'd understand them, anyway.' She exhaled deeply as though getting that off her ample chest had been a physical, but rewarding, exercise.

'I see it's platform one,' Abbot turned to her and smiled.

'Thank you so much,' she beamed and picked up a well-travelled suitcase. It seemed natural to her that she should accompany him towards the platform they both wanted. Her strides were the same length as his.

'Going to see my niece in Newcastle. Well, Whitley Bay, actually. Nice time of the year for a visit,' she paused, looking straight ahead, 'if one has to go there at all. Can't stand the place personally. Do you know, you can actually see the coal dust being washed up on the beach there? And they call it a holiday resort! Well, I suppose it is a holiday resort for some poor devils.' They approached the silent locomotive. 'Not even a nice old Flying Scotsman to take us there, with that lovely smoke smell and sense of excitement.' It was almost as if she had been reading Abbott's thoughts.

'No, but much cleaner and faster.' He tried to mollify her, as they walked up the platform. She merely sniffed.

'I guess this non-smoking carriage will do me.' She stopped and contemplated an open door.

'Well, if you'll excuse me,' Abbott nodded and whilst she stared expressionless at him, he hastily strode on to find his reserved, first-class seat. The thought of listening to her nostalgia all the way to Newcastle was unattractive. The train was remarkably full, but he was pleased to find nobody near his seat. He settled down, and almost at once the train silently eased itself away and began the three-hundred-mile journey north.

The grey back-to-back humourless houses, the junk yards, the small nineteenth-century factories, the occasional dash of green provided by some long-departed planner, gradually gave way to red-brick houses with well cared-for gardens of the outer suburbs. The clouds were drifting eastwards and a watery evening sun broke through, shining now on the increasing numbers of fields and woodlands as they sped on into the countryside.

'Anyone sitting here?'

Abbott jumped. He had been mesmerised by the telegraph poles rushing by and his mind had been dwelling on very superficial thoughts of his garden and how well Lesley kept it.

'No. Er, no.'

'I just managed to catch the train as it was ready to leave and I've been working my way through the carriages.'

'Oh, yes,' Abbott was not best pleased. He didn't like the threat of company. The interrupter of his solitude was a lean, smiling young man in a blue pinstriped suit carrying a holdall. He slumped down opposite Abbott and spread his feet wide. He had long blonde hair swept straight back from a high forehead. Abbott instinctively disliked blonde men and even more so if they had a moustache to match. This young man had.

'Train's pretty crowded.'

'Yes,' Abbott was pleased he had been holding *The Economist* when the young man had spoken to him. It made it easier for him to start reading it.

'Newcastle?'

'Sorry?' Abbott painstakingly looked across at his companion.

'Going to Newcastle?'

'Yes.' His low-profile journey could be going awry.

'Me too. Giving a talk at the university.'

Abbott regarded him, surprised. 'Really?' The man didn't seem old enough to be able to talk on anything worthwhile.

The man laughed. 'Don't look so astonished. I'm not a lecturer or anything learned. I travelled from Australia to England last year by land and a friend asked me to give a talk on it. I've a few days off, so I agreed. Why not?'

Abbott was reluctantly impressed. 'Very interesting.' As an afterthought he added, 'how long did it take you? You don't sound very Australian.'

'Oh, I'm not.' The young man stood up, took off his jacket and placed it on the rack with his holdall. Abbott realised he had company, like it or not.

'I flew out to Australia on a six-month working visa and when it was nearing the time to come home I decided it would be interesting, and hopefully fun, to come back over land.' The young man moved slightly to avoid the evening sun shining into his eyes and Abbott noticed that he had no top joint on the little finger of his left hand.

'And it sure was. By the way my name's Ray Anderson.'

'Oh. Er – George Abbott.'

'Nice to meet you.'

Anderson immediately appeared to lose interest in continuing his life story and leaned back and closed his eyes. Thankfully, Abbott raised *The Economist.* Silence reigned, apart from the insistent clattering of the wheels.

'First sitting for dinner.' The dining car attendant, a large bald man with a very prominent bulbous nose, passed through. The colour of his face and nose gave conclusive evidence of his off-duty drinking habits. Anderson opened his eyes, yawned and stretched. Abbott decided that he did not want to risk

96

having to sit and suffer this garrulous young man and that he would have dinner.

'Yes, I think I will too,' Anderson had watched Abbott rise and he reached up for his jacket. The carriage suddenly lurched, as the brakes were applied quickly and Abbott lost his balance and fell against Anderson. He straightened immediately.

'So sorry.'

'Forget it. No problem,' Anderson smiled widely and with a grand flourish waved his hand. 'Shall we go?'

The train had eased down to a crawl as they made their way to the dining car. It was passing through Peterborough station as they were shown to a table for four.

'Sorry, sir. No tables for two left.' A tall, spotty young waiter, with unkempt hair, addressed Abbott. Annoyed, Abbott eased himself down carefully, over to the window seat. He'd wanted to stay alone and concentrate on the reason for his journey.

'I hope we're not going to be late,' the young man commented as he looked out at the streets of houses.

'Oh, no sir,' replied the waiter, reassuringly, 'just some track repairs here. We'll pick up speed again in a mile or so.' The young waiter turned, 'Would you care to sit here?' he asked someone behind Abbott.

'Why not?'

Abbott looked up, realising that he knew the voice. The beaming face of the walking tweed suit was looking down at him. His heart sank as he forced a smile. Surrounded! The ample body collapsed beside him, dragging the tablecloth and half the cutlery forward, almost onto her lap.

'Always think British Rail meals are jolly good value for money,' she commented, as she looked around.

The train had begun to pick up speed again, as Abbott watched shafts of sunlight pick out the varying shades of green in the undulating fields.

'One more,' the spotty lad was gesturing the one remaining seat at their table. It was going to be a full sitting. Not good, not good at all.

'Thank you.' A deep resonant voice boomed out and Abbot watched a tall, upright man with a military bearing, seat himself.

'Good evening,' the man looked around at his dinner companions, as though inspecting them on a parade ground. He had penetrating, almost black eyes, sallow complexion and grey hair that matched his suit. He was immaculately dressed and Abbott couldn't help but admire the grey silk tie and the plain cherry-coloured shirt with white collar. Not that he would ever wear a shirt like that. Not the image for a bank manager, in his opinion. Everyone muttered in reply and Anderson remarked on the fact that every seat in the restaurant car appeared to be taken.

'You from Australia,' Abbott wasn't sure if the man was asking, or telling, Anderson.

'Well, half and half,' Anderson smiled. 'Been there recently, but I'm very English.'

'Picked up their terrible accent,' was the condemning response.

'Oh, how wonderful,' the tweed suit enthused. 'I've always wanted to go there. Did you enjoy it? Where did you go?'

Abbott picked up the menu and deliberately distanced himself from the ensuing conversation. Soup. He'd have that. He liked soup, always had. Ever since school days. God! He'd hated school days, the latin, chemistry, physics, games, physical training – the bullying, the taunting. Private-school idealism. Why had his parents wasted what little money they had on such a preposterously costly education?

'A drink before dinner, sir?' The others looked at him. He'd been oblivious of the waiter's presence.

'Er – sherry, please.'

'Amontillado?'

'Thank you,' Abbott nodded.

'And what's your line of business?' Anderson turned his face towards the man next to him. The others had obviously all relaxed, good humouredly, over the last few minutes.

'Insurance broker,' came the resonant reply. 'Not a bad business. My own business.' He pulled out his wallet and handed round business cards. 'Goode by name and good by nature!' he laughed. 'Came out of the Army in 1950 and my father taught me the family business and hey presto! Took to it like a duck to water! Enables me to travel round the country a

98

bit. Can't stand being shut up in an office all day. That must be terrible.'

Abbott felt personally affronted. He'd never thought it terrible. He positively enjoyed the situation. He was not, however, going to argue the point with this overbearing ignoramus. The drinks arrived and miniatures were opened and poured.

'Good health!' Anderson grinned at everyone.

The other two enthusiastically raised their glasses, as Abbott nodded. It turned out that the tweed suit was named Dr Asquith. Dinner orders followed and the staff efficiently set about the business of serving up their entrees. Wine had been introduced to the table by Goode who, to the delight of Dr Asquith, had insisted it would be a pleasure to buy the wine.

'It's so nice to eat in civilised company.' Dr Asquith was becoming slightly pink in the face. 'People are in such a hurry these days. No-one has time to relax and talk. Do you know I was outside the local library the other day and was just chatting quietly to a dear old friend of mine, whom I'd not seen for an absolute age, when this young man in jeans – I think that's what they call those washed-out blue things – knocked into me – I mean I was standing still, not him – and he said, "Why don't you move woman, you're not in the cemetery yet?" I think the world's getting very unpleasant.' She took a large helping of butter and mashed it into her roll.

'Standards. We don't knock them into children at school, any more,' barked Goode. 'Half the teachers are Commies. They're out to deliberately lower standards so that anarchy is easier to spawn. Bloody disgrace our school system.' He glared at Abbott. Abbott was not used to arguing over dinner. He found it rather distasteful. He contributed a 'Quite' and scraped his soup plate. The soup had been good. Finding no encouragement from Abbott, Goode focused his attention on Anderson.

'You're a young man. What do you think of this country of ours? Eh?'

Anderson smiled, 'I don't think it's as bad as all that. You'll always find the louts, the malcontents in any society. But there are plenty of others who are working hard, who are trying to

99

achieve something. Look at the continual breakthroughs in medicine, in science and technology. It's all being achieved by people who were young once – ten years ago or even five years ago. No! I reject your generalisation, sir.'

Surprising Abbott, Goode guffawed. 'Well said! I drink to that!' and raised his glass in Anderson's direction.

Plates were cleared and replaced by piping hot empty ones, soon filled with roast beef and all the trimmings. The train entered a tunnel and Abbott was surprised that there were no lights in the carriage as they thundered on for at least a minute in total darkness. The beat of the train echoed off the walls of the tunnel and a strong smell of diesel fumes assailed Abbott's nostrils. He took out his handkerchief and held it over his nose. Suddenly they were in the open again and the welcoming sight of sheep grazing close to the fenced embankment in the evening light, encouraged him to concentrate on what turned out to be a splendid main course. Sherry trifle and coffee completed his dinner and he watched as Anderson tucked into a large portion of biscuits and cheese. Perhaps food had been in short supply across Asia and the Middle East.

Abbott had never been abroad, unless one included Scotland. That had been an idyllic holiday with Lesley about four years ago. They had toured without any pre-booking of hotels and had, surprisingly enough, not had any trouble finding accommodation. It had been June and the weather had been superb. Lesley had enjoyed Edinburgh and Glasgow; the latter surprisingly clean with impressive pedestrian malls and attractively austere squares of nineteenth-century stone houses. He had enjoyed the rural scene much more; the glens and the small villages and ports strung out around the coast. Lesley had grown homesick for Peek-a-Boo, which had ruined the relaxation of the last few days. She had made it clear that a week away was all she was prepared to have in future. They hadn't been away since, but he was thinking that perhaps later this summer they'd drive to Wales and stay at a nice farmhouse. This summer? Maybe, maybe. So much to be done first.

'Yes, so I shall be staying at the Station Hotel.' Goode was draining his cognac glass dry, and Abbott realised he had been day dreaming for quite a few minutes. 'So jolly convenient for business. Much improved from the old steam days, too. It's now as good as anything in Newcastle.'

Dr Asquith had plonked her handbag down on the table between them and was busily rummaging for something. 'I've heard the Gosforth Park Hotel is very good?' she asked, head almost buried in the bag.

'Top hotel,' replied Goode, 'but such a deuce of a way out. Need a car, or a girlfriend with one!' Anderson was cracked in the ribs by his neighbour's elbow and he grinned back to the accompaniment of a gale of laughter. At that moment the large bald waiter who had heralded dinner, but hadn't been much in evidence during the meal, arrived to write out their bills.

'The wine is on me,' beamed Goode.

'How kind.'

'Very kind of you.'

Abbott added, 'Yes.' He had, after all, consumed a glass.

The bills came round the table and money was passed and changed and pocketed. The handbag was snapped shut. 'Well, gentlemen, that was a good meal and I thank you for your company.'

Abbott felt he should rise as Dr Asquith eased her way out, but she had gone without another look and he waited until the other two had risen.

'Goodbye, my dear chap. And good luck with your career.' Goode extended a hand and Anderson smilingly thanked him. No farewell was offered to Abbott, other than a perfunctory indication of the head, which didn't either surprise or worry him. He followed Anderson back towards their carriage, but kept a good distance between them. He needed to be alone for a few moments, to clear his mind. To think.

Evening had drawn in over dinner and as Abbott arrived back and sank into his seat, he could only just determine the shapes of the trees and the farm buildings as they journeyed on north, now at great speed. The train shot across some other tracks before it sped through a station, white with neon, too fast to read anything. No idea where he was. Anderson had closed his eyes. Abbott closed his.

101

He awoke with a choking cry. Anderson was tapping his leg and smiling urbanely.

'We're just pulling into Newcastle.'

'Good gracious. Are we there already?' It was a rhetorical question as Anderson was reaching for his holdall and the train was jerking slowly into Newcastle Station. Abbott blinked and settled his spectacles before rising.

'Well, nice to meet you. Have a good evening,' Anderson beamed down.

'Oh, yes, thank you,' Abbott smiled faintly. 'I hope your talk goes well.'

A good evening? Abbott looked at his watch. Half past nine. He supposed Anderson would still think it early enough to have a good evening.

He joined the other passengers alighting. A vicar and his wife, with a mountain of luggage, found a delighted porter's welcoming arms. Abbott made his way slowly along the platform. He was in no hurry. Mail sacks were being tossed into a guard's van by a black porter. He hadn't expected a black porter up here. He even spoke with a Geordie accent! A young couple ran past him laughing their way to the exit. They looked carefree and very happy. Abbott arrived at the barrier and felt in his pocket for his ticket. He pulled it out, and handed it over.

'Thank you, sir. You'll want it for the return journey.' He'd forgotten that and had picked up his briefcase again. 'And I guess this is yours, sir?.' The ticket collector had bent down and picked up a piece of paper.

'Mine?' Abbott frowned. People were queuing behind him.

'It fell out of your pocket when you got your ticket.' The porter gave him the paper and his ticket and moved to the next passenger as Abbott, bemused, moved sideways out of the way. He put the ticket in his pocket. The piece of paper was a dinner receipt from the train. Not his, he had torn his up and left it in the ashtray on the table in the restaurant car. He turned it over. On it in capitals was scrawled GLAD YOU DIDN'T GET TOO MERRY.

He shivered involuntarily. His jaw tightened. He didn't like being made to feel a fool. So, he was not alone. He picked up his

102

case again, on second thoughts slightly mollified. Whoever was expert enough to put that in his pocket was clearly expert enough to be around, if help was needed. He couldn't think that any help would be needed, but it was nevertheless comforting. He walked along the concourse and through the swing doors to the Station Hotel. A haven from the smell of fumes and beer. He'd forgotten about Newcastle's brown ale and how it seemed to hang in the air over the city. As he walked up to the reception desk he noticed both Anderson and Dr Asquith in animated conversation, walking to the lift with a porter. So all three of his dinner companions were staying here. The world was certainly full of surprises.

Well, he had arrived.

6

'Now, behave yourself while I'm gone,' Maurice Thatcher ran his hand down Pat's back, as he kissed her warmly on the lips.

'Darling! What a thing to say,' Pat pouted and pulled her head back in mock horror. 'I've got the hairdressers this afternoon, bridge at the tennis club, tonight. Tomorrow I've got a round of golf with Ann...'

'OK! OK!' Thatcher smacked her behind lightly. 'I know you are always so busy.'

Pat took his hand, as they walked down the front steps of their house. Charles opened the door of the car. Thatcher churned up the gravel on the drive, as he spun on the soles of his feet and gave Pat a final peck on the cheek before climbing into the Rolls. She stood, waving spasmodically, until the Rolls pulled out into the main road.

'Right, Charles, Heathrow as fast as you can. I've cut it a bit fine, but I think we'll be all right.' Thatcher picked up *The Times* on the back seat.

'Don't worry, sir. I'll get you there in plenty of time,' Charles's confident reply rose above the soft purr of the engine.

Thatcher didn't really have any doubt, and he sat back and relaxed, reading the paper. Charles pulled the Rolls up outside the terminal, with fifteen minutes to spare. He quickly took Thatcher's bag from the boot, opened the passenger door and followed his employer to the check-in desk.

'All right, Charles. I'm fine from here.' Thatcher nodded without looking at the chauffeur, 'Mrs Thatcher will tell you

104

what plane I shall be coming back on, in due course.' He took out his ticket and placed it on the counter.

'Very good, sir. Have a good flight,' and Charles had disappeared into the scurrying crowd.

'Your passport, sir?' The ground stewardess, unconscious of Thatcher's impatience as he found it in his briefcase, gazed around her.

'Here, here!' Thatcher waved it in her face.

The smile didn't leave her lips, as the stewardess took it, looking him straight in the eyes, and said 'Thank you, sir,' very softly.

Baggage dealt with, boarding pass issued, Thatcher was directed to the Concorde lounge. His face took on a slightly pained expression, as he queued behind several Africans, happy and laughing, unhurriedly moving through the personal luggage checks. He picked up his briefcase as quickly as he could and strode purposefully through, aware of the noise and bustle all round him. The quiet of the lounge was a welcoming oasis. Passengers were relaxing in comfortable chairs, reading, drinking, or talking quietly. Coats were being collected, to save the passengers having to worry about dealing with them.

Thatcher found a seat, then went and poured himself a large gin and tonic. He filled in the immigration and customs forms ready for New York. He smiled inwardly – nothing to declare. Nothing, in any way, whatsoever! As Thatcher put his pen back in his inside pocket, he became aware of a pair of high-heeled, black patent-leather shoes topped by black tights and as his eyes rose, he appreciated very shapely legs disappearing into a black leather skirt. His eyes quickly moved to the face, as the body hadn't moved and was clearly standing facing him. Thatcher's heart missed a beat as he leapt to his feet.

'Elaine!'

'Maurice! How are you? How absolutely wonderful to see you here! You must be going to New York, too!' Perfume assailed his nostrils, as a perfectly made-up cheek was offered to him to kiss.

105

Elaine Gable was a very well-known English actress. Well known for her considerable acting ability, her beautiful features and her four marriages. Thatcher and his wife had met Elaine for the first time with her third husband, Eric, at a cocktail party given by a mutual friend, who had backed her in a new West End play. It had flopped badly. A friendship had developed between the couples, however, and they had seen each other occasionally, until Elaine had moved to New York with her future fourth husband, Frank Sorretto, three years ago.

'Darling, this is so thrilling! Do you know I've never been on Concorde before and I'm just a wee bit scared?' Elaine put her finger to her ruby lips, conspiratorially. She acknowledged the glass of champagne that had appeared on the table behind her and smoothed her skirt, 'I'll make sure I'm sitting next to you and then you can hold my hand, when it rattles.'

Thatcher was finding it difficult to collect his wits, but he forced a laugh. 'It doesn't rattle, Elaine. It's not an old steam engine! It's Concorde!'

'So, what's in a name?' Elaine strode over to the reception desk and strode straight back again. 'What's your seat number, darling?'

'6B.'

With a little coquettishness, aided by her being a celebrity, Elaine wound up with 6A and returned to Thatcher in triumph. 'Oh, isn't that marvellous!' She dropped into the seat beside him and drank the champagne enthusiastically.

Thatcher noticed how many of the passengers were covertly watching them, or rather, Elaine. Her vivacious manner, beautifully sculptured face and the red hair cascading to her shoulders was enough. There could hardly be anyone who hadn't recognised her.

'Good morning, ladies and gentlemen. British Airways are pleased to announce that Flight 193 to New York is now ready for boarding. We would ask that those with seats between rows...'

Thatcher had heard it several times before. He knew he, and now Elaine, would be called last. Wonderful plane, Concorde. Another British invention – well, with just a little help from the

106

French. No doubt the next generation of supersonic aircraft would be American though. They'd make the real money out of supersonic travel. Ah, well. He noticed that the lounge was almost empty. Scattered cups and saucers, half-empty glasses, newspapers in disarray, told their own story. The last few rows in the front of the plane were being called.

'Come on, darling! Isn't it exciting!' Elaine had jumped to her feet, grabbing her snakeskin bag. Boarding cards were smilingly accepted and they lowered their heads to enter the plane.

'My!' exclaimed Elaine, as she stared open-mouthed up the aisle, 'it is like being inside a bullet, isn't it? Thank goodness I don't suffer from claustrophobia.' She eased herself into her seat and peered out of the window. 'It's so small! I can't see a thing out of it!'

'There's not a lot to see, Elaine,' commented Thatcher, as he slipped out of his jacket and handed it to the smiling stewardess. 'You'll be up higher than you've ever been before and all there is, is a dark blue sky, full of nothing.'

'Oh, darling, you make it sound so unexciting!' Elaine shook her red hair, as though freeing it from some invisible hairnet. She placed long red talons on his arm. 'Where are you staying in New York? You are staying there, aren't you? Not going to some miserable place like Chicago?' Thatcher laughed and patted her hand, which turned palm upward and closed over his, squeezing warmly.

'No, I am staying in New York. At The Waldorf.'

'Oh, that's marvellous! We have an apartment on 68th and 3rd. You must come and dine with us. How long will you be in town?' Elaine's hand was still holding his.

'Not quite sure, actually,' Thatcher frowned and was saved from further comment as the Captain welcomed everybody on board in a very quiet, reassuring manner, explaining that the flying time to New York would be three hours and fifty-five minutes; that they would be flying at 55,000 feet and once they were over the Atlantic they would be travelling at Mach 2, twice the speed of sound.

'Isn't it wonderful!' Elaine clapped her hands and peered out of the small window as they began to taxi for take-off. For

Thatcher, Concorde had become merely the quickest way of getting from A to B. He guessed it was wonderful for Elaine.

It was a beautiful morning and clear blue skies heralded a smooth crossing, soon confirmed by the Captain, after they had levelled out and were heading westward. Canapes and drinks were solicitously served, as Elaine explained that she had been to London to check over their house in Chelsea and see her dear mother.

'Lives in Hurlingham on her own now, since poor daddy died. Tried to persuade her to come back and stay with us. She wouldn't. I don't think she likes Frank very much. She's only been to New York once and hated it. She says its all noise and squalor. I said to her, where isn't? I'm opening in this new Neil Simon play on Broadway quite soon, so I shan't be able to see her for a while. Now,' Elaine's large brown eyes took in his whole face, 'enough of me! What are you over for? Who are you persuading to spend a massive advertising budget, this time?' She smiled wickedly.

Thatcher thought how absolutely beautiful she was when she smiled. 'Now, Elaine,' he smiled back, 'You know I can't talk business! Not done and all that.'

'Oh, rubbish,' she pouted light-heartedly. 'Everyone does all the time. I bet most of the people on this plane finish up talking business as the drinks flow.'

'Maybe, maybe not. Anyway it's not very exciting business.' He nodded to the steward for a refill of champagne.

The Captain came on the intercom to announce that they were about to accelerate through the sound barrier, which they would know when the indicator at the front of the cabin reached Mach 1. Thatcher closed his eyes as the Captain went on about afterburners and the colour of the sky and then, as the voice fell silent, he felt the usual thrust in the small of the back as the plane accelerated, effortlessly. Lunch came and went. It was good, but Thatcher only picked at it, as Elaine tucked in enthusiastically.

'Frank's out of town, at the moment. Some deal in Fort Lauderdale. Did you know he's into industrial catering?' Thatcher couldn't remember. He knew the tycoon owned

108

amongst other things, a TV company, a baseball team and a European newspaper. 'Won't be back till the weekend, so I guess I won't bother with any proper meals until he's back. Hate eating on my own.'

Thatcher's pulse quickened slightly, 'Would you like to have dinner with me, say, tonight?' he asked, as he watched the coffee being poured.

'Maurice, I'd love it!' Elaine clutched his arm. 'I know Frank wouldn't mind! We are old friends!'

'Not so much of the old!' Thatcher smiled.

'Brandy or liqueur with your coffee, sir?'

'Er, no.' Thatcher shook his head, irritated at the interruption.

'Madam?'

'Yes, please! Cointreau on ice? Good, thanks.' Elaine was smiling. 'Let's fix it now, before you meet someone else to while away your evenings!'

'Fine,' Thatcher agreed. 'You're on.'

'Lovely!' Elaine nodded. 'May I come to The Waldorf at, say, seven thirty? I'd love to have a drink there first.' She didn't anticipate a negative response and didn't get one. Thatcher was thrown by this unanticipated alteration to his plans, which was nevertheless of his own making. He quietly watched the passengers begin to squeeze their way up and down the aisle to the toilets. There certainly wasn't a great deal of room to pass. As soon as he could, he rose and made his way forward. The two toilets were engaged and one man was waiting, a very large American with smoke-coloured glasses and a ginger crewcut. He was chewing gum as if he was trying to kill it. He gave Thatcher a perfunctory stare, as one of the toilets became free and Thatcher stepped back to let him in and the erstwhile incumbent pass. He hadn't realised someone else had come up behind him, and tripped over a foot and stumbled backwards. Fortunately he was saved by a strong arm, steady as a rock, and he managed to haul himself upright.

It was all over in a matter of seconds. The tall, gaunt, fair-haired young man in jeans who had left the toilet squeezed past him smiling, as Thatcher turned and thanked the man who had put out his arm. He was a thick-set man, florid and overweight with jet-black hair and an unpleasant scattering of dandruff over his jacket.

Fortunately, Thatcher was saved from further embarrassment by the other toilet becoming free and an elderly lady emerged to filter past him. When he returned to his seat, Elaine was flicking through *Vogue* magazine.

'Didn't realise you became drunk so easily, darling,' she commented as he fastened his seat belt. 'Falling all over the plane. There wasn't even any turbulence!'

Thatcher was not amused. Elaine's theatrical background enabled her to throw her voice very adequately. He didn't enjoy being mocked. He muttered about having a snooze, which only brought forth an equally loud comment from Elaine that sleeping it off would be a good idea. Her first supersonic flight didn't appear to be affecting her adversely in any way.

Thatcher awoke whilst the passengers were being addressed by the Captain, as they were making their final approach into Kennedy Airport. He could see a few white cumulus clouds around, but generally it looked a good morning in New York. He looked at his watch and adjusted it to New York time. They were landing an hour earlier than they had left London. He felt stiff and slightly crumpled. Elaine was checking her face and, satisfied, snapped her bag shut, holding out a card to Thatcher.

'Our address and phone number, darling. It's not in the phone book.'

He thanked her and as his coat was still with the stewards he placed the card in the breast pocket of his shirt. Funny. There was something in it already. He normally never used such a pocket. He certainly hadn't used it this morning.

He pulled out what appeared to be a visiting card. It was plain on one side, so he turned it over and stared. Nothing was printed on it, but written in rough letters was YOU ARE THE MAN WITH HIS BACK TO THE EAST, REMEMBER.

Anger engulfed him as he roughly stuffed it back, together with Elaine's card. He knew what he had to do. He didn't need reminding. Who had put it in his pocket and how? It must have been when he stumbled, as he went to the toilet! But which man?

The young man in jeans? The dandruff man? Or maybe the elderly woman – she had squeezed by him and could have done it. I'm not likely to forget, Thatcher thought, angrily. Who is following me on Concorde? The wheels hit the runway with a bump and a screech and he heard an Oxbridge voice in the seat behind him, 'Well, I've never landed in New York twice on the same day before.' Normally he would have found such a remark mildly amusing, as Elaine clearly did – she had turned round and laughed – but his mind was back to the reason for the trip. Not Elaine. Not enjoyment. A mission. A very important mission.

Coats were handed out and as the plane came to a halt, the experienced travellers were already on their feet, anxious to be at the head of the tiresome immigration queue and away as soon as possible. As he escorted Elaine down the ramp into immigration, Thatcher looked back but didn't see any of the people he had encountered on the plane.

U.S. immigration and customs were happy and efficient for once and they emerged within twenty minutes.

'Are you being met, darling?' Elaine asked, putting on a pair of large sunglasses.

'Er, no.'

'Well, let me drop you at the hotel. Jackson will be here. Yes, there he is.'

A tall elderly negro in a dark-blue suit and cap moved out of the crowd.

'Good morning, Jackson.'

'Morning, ma'am.' His voice was husky and polite, as he took Elaine's two holdalls.

'We are going to drop this gentleman off at The Waldorf.'

'Yes, ma'am.' Jackson nodded unsurprised, as he led the way outside to a black Cadillac. As they climbed in and Jackson stowed the luggage, Thatcher's heart jumped. Out through the airport's sliding doors came the thick-set man over whose foot he'd tripped. He looked angry and frustrated. He was looking expectantly around, but not seeing what, or who, he was seeking, he ran back inside.

The windows of the Cadillac were dark. Thatcher doubted if

111

he could be seen from the outside, even up close. Had the man been looking for him? Or had the man lost his luggage? He hadn't been carrying any. The Cadillac eased away from the terminal, the engine almost silent, as they joined the traffic leaving the airport. The traffic was heavy, but there were no breakdowns, so it kept going into the city at an even pace. Four lanes in each direction, each one as busy as the next. The massive advertising hoardings screamed their absurdly low air fares to Florida, as each airline tried to send its rivals into liquidation. Unsuccessfully, the hoardings tried to hide old, ramshackle apartments and squalid timber houses from the eyes of the freeway. Jackson was a good steady driver, not bothering to move from lane to lane, as other drivers were doing.

'Well, I must say that's a damned better way of crossing the Atlantic,' Elaine had startled him out of his reverie. 'Cuts the time by half and none of that utter boredom. It's all over so quickly and it really isn't all that more expensive. I think British Airways could charge more than they do, to fly people supersonic.'

Thatcher idly watched a plane taking off from La Guardia, as they wound round the freeway. 'Yes,' he agreed. 'It is a good way to travel. I have flown over, held a couple of meetings and caught an overnight plane back, to arrive in London first thing the next morning. Mind you,' he added, 'I don't recommend it. It hits you later.'

'I should think so, darling,' Elaine protested. She crossed her legs elegantly. Under the pretence of looking out of the nearside passenger window he watched her sitting there contentedly, also looking out of the same window. She was a wonderful actress and, he thought, one hell of a woman.

Jackson paid the toll and the car drove down under the Hudson river through the midtown tunnel. Brake lights glowed on and off intermittently, as the traffic uneasily flowed ahead of them. Thatcher hated this route. That nauseating smell of diesel and petrol fumes. He looked ahead waiting for the first sign of daylight to appear.

'Could be a train coming,' Elaine said.

112

'Sorry?'

'That light at the end of the tunnel,' she laughed.

'God, was it obvious?' Thatcher grinned sheepishly.

'Only to me, darling, because I'm the same.' Elaine touched his arm. 'I sometimes feel I've held my breath the whole time we've been in the tunnel, although I know that's physically impossible. Anyway we're out now!'

Sure enough they had emerged and hit the first traffic light of Manhattan. Jackson, with consummate ease, threaded the Cadillac left and right, over the elevated section, round Grand Central Station and the now equally famous Pan Am Building, to come down again along Park Avenue. They drew up outside The Waldorf-Astoria.

'I'll be in the main foyer by the theatre booking agency tonight at seven thirty,' Elaine leaned forward as Thatcher kissed her cheek.

'Many thanks, Elaine.'

'Think nothing of it,' she said. 'Thank you for your company, even if you can't stay sober and upright all the time!' She laughed as Thatcher climbed out. The doorman already had his bags and he followed them into the check-in desk. Christ! He had just left one problem – was this another? In front of him at the desk, signing in, was the young man in jeans who had been on Concorde.

Oh, well, he had arrived.

7

'Bye kids. Now be good and do as you're told. Don't give Mummy any trouble.' Colin Gorman hugged and kissed the twins and patted Ben on the head, as he barked and tried to join in, tail wagging furiously.

'You are joking, of course,' Jenny stood smiling at him, arms folded, as Gorman stood up and put his arms round her waist.

'Shan't be long, honey. Just a few days. I'll let you know when I shall be coming back.' He kissed her on the end of her nose.

'I should hope so,' she retorted. 'Not taking me to Paris is one thing, not communicating either, is another!' She kissed him back and they walked to the car.

'Dad, bring me back a present!' James yanked Gorman's jacket to gain attention.

'And me, and me,' cried Christopher, running ahead and opening the car door.

'Christopher out of there! Daddy's late already!'

Gorman looked at his watch. 'Yes, I'd better get going. See you, honey.'

They kissed fondly, amidst the shouting and the barking, before Gorman slammed the door and started the engine. He wound down the window and with a wave let off the brake.

'Bye, Dad!'

'Be good!' Jenny waved, and he was out of the drive on his way.

He should make Dover in good time for the mid-morning hovercraft. It was a lovely morning. The sky was clear, a very pale blue, with just a few wisps of pure white clouds on the horizon away to the south. There was a heavy dew glistening in the sunshine, as he threaded his way through the leafy Surrey suburbs. Heavy commuter traffic headed for London but it didn't affect him, as he meandered purposefully across the arterial roads, heading south-east.

Gorman switched on the radio and listened for the traffic news. He had to satisfy himself, as best he could, that he wasn't heading for any overturned lorries or ones that had shed their load. He didn't want any unforeseen hold-ups. Nothing was reported along his route, although with great urbanity the announcer said that a lorry had shed its load on the elevated section of the M4 into London, and there must be many motorists who were now shedding a few tears, as it had closed the road completely. The queue was already back to the Heathrow turn-off! Gorman was hardly surprised to hear that information, it was almost a daily ritual on that elevated section. The weather forecast followed. Light winds and temperature in the low seventies sounded very promising. Happily there was even a statement that Channel crossings should be good! He switched over to F.M. and Radio Two and relaxed to some middle-of-the-road music.

Gorman was approaching a roundabout and as he slowed down he glanced at his fuel gauge. The indicator was resting on empty. How long it had been there he had no idea. How stupid. He had meant to fill up at the local garage the night before. He threaded his way through the narrow streets of Ashford, avoiding early morning delivery vans parked indiscriminately on yellow lines. There weren't many pedestrians about; too early for shoppers. He had better pull into the first garage. He glanced in his rear mirror. Nothing close behind, if he had to brake and turn into a forecourt round the approaching bend in the road. The nearest car, a white Mercedes with a badly dented nearside wing, was at least fifty yards back. As he followed the curve in the road, he saw a garage a half a mile ahead, luckily on his side of the road. He turned into it and pulled up.

'Yes, sir?' Gorman looked up surprised, as he was climbing out of the car.

A grey-haired, elderly man, in a blue overall, was standing over him.

115

'Oh, fill her up, will you? I expected it to be self-service. Most garages are these days.'

'Too true, sir,' the attendant had already neatly inserted the hose into the tank. He started the pump. 'Days of service are going everywhere, I'm afraid, sir. The boss has told us that he is thinking of changing the pumps here and going self-service. To think I've been filling cars for twenty-five years since I came out of the merchant navy. It's an open-air life, and I meet some interesting people. I have plenty of time for my garden and allotment. Don't know what I'll do. My wife says give up work. Only a couple of years off sixty-five, but I hate the idea of doing nothing. Terrible.' The attendant shook his head, as the tank filled and the pump stopped. He replaced the petrol cap and the hose. 'That's twenty pounds thirty-eight pence, sir.'

Gorman handed over his credit card and followed him into the forecourt office. He watched as a steady stream of cars and lorries followed behind a very lumbering farm tractor. He supposed he would be joining the back of that queue in the next few minutes. Still, better that than running out of petrol in the middle of nowhere. With a muttered goodbye and good luck for the future, he strode back to his car and restarted his journey. The road was invitingly clear as he swung out, but he knew it was an illusion as he passed the remaining outlying houses of the town and sped out into the countryside of pasture and woodland. Sure enough, now, he could see the rear of the procession and as the road wound round and up the hill ahead he could guess that there were probably about twenty vehicles behind the tractor. There seemed little chance of anybody passing it either. There was a solid white line indicating the dangerous blind bends. He joined the procession and noticed his speed was down to twenty miles an hour. It seemed like two miles an hour. He looked idly in his rear mirror to see if he was still at the rear.

Behind him was a white Mercedes, about two hundred yards back. There were plenty of white Mercedes around. A very popular car and a very popular colour. But not many had badly dented nearside wings. If it was the same car that had been behind him before Ashford however, it should have been well ahead of him by now. Unless – it was tailing him? Rubbish! Nevertheless, Gorman felt perspiration gather on his forehead.

He leaned forward and turned on the fresh-air fan. All he received was the smell of the exhaust of the car in front of him. Unfortunately, it was belching blue smoke and he should have known better. He switched the fan off and wound down the windows. A little better, but not much. As he glanced in his rearview mirror, a blue Ford overtook the Mercedes and drew up behind him, at which point the Mercedes accelerated sufficiently to ensure nobody else came between them and the blue Ford. Was he being tailed? Surely not. Thankfully, a long section of dual carriageway arrived and all the cars and lorries overtook the tractor and at their varying speeds settled into their normal rhythm.

Gorman pushed his foot down hard and accelerated past most of them and finally eased into the inside lane, behind a BMW doing about ninety miles per hour. They left everyone behind. Except the Mercedes. It was holding back from approaching him, but it was steadily holding his speed. Gorman frowned. Surely whoever it was would realise that he could be aware of the tail by now? If it was a tail.

The road signs were now specifically for Dover and again Gorman joined a convoy of cars and lorries, this time converging on the route to the docks and the harbour. He glanced at his watch. Plenty of time. He would go through the town. Slowly, he passed the terraced houses and corner shops of the outskirts of the town. A few hopeful Vacancy, Bed and Breakfast, signs were apparent as zebra crossings and traffic lights reduced the speed again to a crawl, and he had time to look around him. He turned off the radio and immediately heard the shrieking cries of the gulls as they wheeled around overhead. Progress was slow and he began to kick himself for not taking the direct route.

He had a container lorry behind him totally blocking the view in his rear mirror. The Hoverport sign at the next roundabout pointed left and he followed it away from the main ferry terminal. As he checked his mirror neither the lorry nor the white Mercedes had followed him. In fact nothing was following him. He must have been mistaken. There was no time for contemplation, as he drew up at the Hoverport entrance. Tickets and passports were checked and he was asked to join the queue through the gates on the right. There weren't more than a dozen cars in the queue. He turned off the engine. All was peace and quiet, except for the persistently crying gulls as they glided round in apparently meaningless arcs. White and feathered flotsam. He climbed out, stretched his arms and legs to the utmost and drew in a deep breath of fresh sea air. The breeze caught his hair and blew it over his face. He turned round to let the wind blow it back again and took a good look at the next few cars straggling into the holding area. There was no white Mercedes. In fact no Mercedes of any colour. His imagination had been working overtime.

As he turned back to look at the sea he became aware of a hum on the horizon and focused his attention on the incoming hovercraft. He watched fascinated as the hum became a buzz then a roar, as it grew closer; the whirring propellers like gigantic moving windmills. The extraordinary invention climbed the beach effortlessly and came to a standstill on the tarmac ahead of him. The air cushion sagged and the boat – was it called a boat? – gently sank and the propellers gradually came to a standstill.

Peace again. Gorman had never been on a hovercraft before, and he watched as great doors opened at the rear and cars and vans drove off, guided by wildly gesticulating seamen. A steady stream of foot passengers also descended like a troop of soldiers instructed to walk in single file. The whole business took no more than ten minutes and then he saw the drivers of the cars in front of him climb back in and start their engines. He followed suit and soon he was driving up a ramp and being signalled by the same seamen where to put his Rover. It was all done with speed and efficiency.

'Leave your keys in and the car unlocked, sir,' he was instructed by a white-overalled attendant, his face covered in streaks of oil and grease. Gorman couldn't imagine how anyone's face could have got like that. He took out his attaché case and followed the signs to the passengers' cabin. It was fitted

118

out like an aircraft economy section and he found a seat next to a window.

His few fellow passengers were a motley crowd. Some boisterous French schoolchildren, several couples of varying ages – including what looked like a honeymoon couple – two or three families with young children and several elderly ladies, clearly on a day trip.

A stewardess spoke to them about the length of the journey to Calais, weather conditions and duty-free shopping. The engines thundered into action with the inevitable smell of oil and diesel. The noise became associated with a rumbling movement and they were under way. The movement reminded Gorman of the first time he had been in a bumper-car at an Easter fun fair. Only this time the whole bumper-car arena was on the move as well! He soon realised that sitting by the window was a pretty pointless exercise, as the sea spray totally precluded any enjoyment of watching other shipping movements, or the sight of the white cliffs of Dover. He pulled out of his case the red thermos that Jenny had thoughtfully filled with coffee and drained a couple of cupfuls before replacing it and taking out *The Daily Telegraph*. He became absorbed in the crossword. Today it was one of the more difficult ones.

Half an hour had passed very quickly, when the stewardess announced their imminent arrival in Calais. He tucked his paper away and watched the outline of the French docks appear as the hovercraft homed into its berth. The drivers were asked to rejoin their cars and as he climbed into his seat the giant doors were opened and car engines all around were started. Within two or three minutes he was driving slowly down the ramp following the car in front to the customs area. A disinterested customs official waved him through with only a perfunctory look at his face and he felt his passport could have been a building-society passbook for all the attention it received. Not that he wanted any attention paid to him. None at all. He grimaced with intense private thoughts as he slowly followed the diffident drivers from the hovercraft. He noted the signs reminding drivers to drive on the right and followed the first signpost to Arras.

'Paris,' he said out loud, 'here I come and may God help us.'
He sighed deeply and shook his head.

The signposts were more than adequate and Gorman didn't take long to join the autoroute. The weather was exactly the same as he had left behind in England. Clear skies and a warm summer's day. He settled back and kept the speedometer at a steady 110 kilometres an hour. He had no wish to have any brushes with the French police. The countryside was undulating and unremarkable and there was little traffic on the autoroute. He looked in his rear-view mirror and smiled. No white Mercedes. In fact the only vehicle within a half mile behind him was a blue Citroen van. He overtook a petrol tanker and pulled into the inside lane. It was a very boring drive. Gorman couldn't help thinking that the earlier days of travelling on *routes nationales* with the villages and lines of plane trees were much more interesting. But, of course, speed demanded long boring autoroutes. One couldn't have everything. Not everything. Just a toilet! Ahead were signs of an impending layby.

He pulled off the autoroute into a pleasantly landscaped area, with vacant picnic benches and tables set amongst young fir trees. At the end of the layby were toilets and refuse bins. He stopped by the toilets and as he opened his door he heard and then saw the petrol tanker roar by. Gorman relieved himself, and on coming out, checked the contents of the boot of the car. He, stupidly, hadn't checked it on leaving the hovercraft. Everything was as he had packed it early in the morning. No light fingers at work on the hovercraft.

He walked back and opened his door, and as he did so his eye caught sight of an unfamiliar object on the back seat. He slid his hand round, pulled up the lock of the rear door and opened it. On the seat was a card. He picked it up and stood staring at it. It was a birthday card. A woman throwing a kiss with her hands. The words inside were from a wife to her husband on his birthday. It wasn't his birthday until October. Anyway it wasn't signed. In capitals, however, was scrawled A WOMAN WITH THE WEST IN HER EYES. He tore the card up very slowly, walked over to the refuse bins and threw it in, his hands trembling uncontrollably. How had it got there? It must have been on the hovercraft. He hadn't left the car at any other time. Except at the petrol station and the car had been in view the whole time there. No-one had been near it whilst he'd paid.

He slowly climbed back into the car and started it up. He understood the message perfectly. So they were not leaving him alone. But they weren't showing themselves either. He rejoined the autoroute, checking his mirror. Pulled up on the hard shoulder before the layby, was a blue Citroen van. It was now moving out into the inside lane. Gorman smiled grimly. So near and yet so far. Or should it be, so far and yet so near. First a white Mercedes and now a blue Citroen van.

The outskirts of Paris began to invade the countryside about an hour later and the traffic thickened as the factories intensified. He didn't bother checking his tail any more. If the van wasn't there another car would have taken over. Why should he try to lose them? Gorman joined the *periphérique*, concentrating hard. He knew from past experience that if he missed the turnoff, he could go round Paris and get totally lost. The traffic was heavy and travelling fast. He saw his turn-off ahead, pulled across to the inside lane and swung off the *periphérique*. Immediately he had to stop for traffic lights. He wound down the window and breathed in some air. Noise enveloped him. The sound of a police siren, the chatter and shouting from some children outside a patisserie, and the inevitable screech of brakes as a van almost side-swiped another one coming out of a side road. Paris! He loved it – normally. The lights changed and he drove on.

Ten minutes later Gorman pulled up outside The Grand Hotel at Place de L'Opéra. A porter was at his door opening it before he had switched off the engine.

'Can you park it for me?'

'Of course, monsieur.'

Another porter was hovering, 'You have baggage, monsieur?'

'Yes, in the boot.' He didn't bother with French. They were talking to him in English. His car was already being driven off as he walked up the red-carpeted steps and through the doors. The beautiful interior of the hotel was just as he remembered it. Elegantly dressed customers were sipping drinks and for the first time that day Gorman thought of food and drink. He felt hungry. He walked along the plush carpet to the reception desk. He had arrived.

8

Sydney, June 1988

Hardy awoke feeling surprisingly fresh. The sun was shining vividly into his room. He had set his alarm for two p.m. and it was buzzing persistently.

An orange juice later, he showered and dressed. The local *Sydney Morning Herald* seemed preoccupied with a local upheaval in the Liberal Party. Hardy found there was little world news of interest, but his mind was preoccupied with his imminent appointment, anyway. He wondered how it would go. It mattered a great deal that he controlled himself. The only way to be sure of success was to appear to be in total command. It wasn't going to be easy. At precisely two forty-five Hardy left the Inter-Continental and turned up the slight hill where he reached the traffic lights and paused to look around him. The blue sky was totally clear and the sun was blazing down on to the numerous high-rise office blocks around Phillip Street. Single-decker dark green buses hustled along with the cars, whilst the wide pavements were busy with purposefully striding pedestrians. The concierge had assured him he would have no difficulty in finding Martin Place. Hardy hoped he was right.

As he made his way along Phillip Street, he admired the extraordinarily attractive buildings. Varying heights and colour, red brick, green glass, grey aluminium. They were all adamantly individualistic and yet blended into an acceptable overall pattern. Somehow the planners had allowed freedom of expression, but had retained a city format that impressed. Male couriers, dressed in a uniform of blue shorts, shirt and white knee-length socks, headed for varying destinations, carrying envelopes and parcels. A couple of sad-looking Aborigines sat at a bus stop. He had never seen any before – they were so black and their features coarse by Caucasian standards. The sun was hot, although he understood this was supposedly not yet summer. No wonder all building workers on a new construction site he passed were in shorts and stripped to the waist.

Pedestrians clearly did not cross until the lights showed 'Walk' and he had a moment to marvel at an old colonial building resplendent with its wrought ironwork in Pitt Street. As the lights changed, pedestrians criss-crossed quickly in front of the idling traffic. Hardy soon found Martin Place ahead. There was DCC Tower, a glass and sandstone fronted building set back from the pedestrianised area, with an attractive piazza containing a large waterfall feature.

An incurious commissionaire told Hardy the DCC office was on the twenty-fifth floor. A more lively, indeed pert, frizzy blonde-headed receptionist, smiled at him as he stepped out of the lift.

'Good morning, sir.' The smile displayed white buck teeth.

'Er, good morning. I have an appointment with Mr D.C. Charrington. My name is Hardy. Len Hardy.' His voice sounded croaky and he gripped his briefcase hard.

'Yes, sir. Would you take a seat?' He was gestured into a sumptuous leather chair. The decor suggested that David Charrington, the head of the DCC Corporation, or someone in his trust, believed in spending money on the surroundings. Why shouldn't they, though? DCC was one of Australia's largest corporations. A conglomerate involved in advertising, telecommunications, newspapers ... Inaudible conversation on the phone by the receptionist, brought forth another, older, angular woman, dressed in an impressively cut, grey suit.

'Mr Hardy?,' Another polite smile, this time from a deep measured voice. 'I am Mr Charrington's secretary. Would you care to come this way?'

He followed the secretary across carpet, seemingly three feet thick, and was led into a conference room, with panoramic views over Sydney and its suburbs.

'Mr Charrington won't be a moment. Would you care for tea or coffee?'

'No, thank you.' Hardy placed his case on the walnut table.

The secretary smiled, nodded and withdrew. Hardy walked round the long table and stood gazing out at the impressive harbour view running away towards the ocean in the distance. A green and yellow ferry was slowly ploughing its way across the shimmering water being easily overtaken by a catamaran. Several dinghies were bobbing about in the breeze, their white sails taut with endeavour.

'Breathtaking view, isn't it?'

Hardy hadn't heard the door open behind him. The man walking towards him was tall and powerfully built, with a lean, bronzed face. His hair was thick and black. Long, thin eyebrows accentuated the eyes, which were pale blue and piercing. Hardy found his hand in a grip of iron.

'Charrington.' He made Hardy feel physically insignificant.

'Shall we sit down and get on with it?' Charrington made it a statement, not a question. Hardy found himself seated with his back to the window, facing Charrington.

'Well?' Charrington was drumming his fingers on the table. Hardy cleared his throat.

'I believe you received my fax?'

'Of course,' Charrington was irritated. 'We wouldn't be here talking, otherwise.'

'Well,' Hardy felt his face flush, 'My client is prepared to sell to you his Liechtenstein-based trading business for a very reasonable figure.'

'So your fax said,' Charrington was looking out of the window. He clasped his hands together and leaned forward. 'Mr Hardy. I don't know, and indeed I don't care, who your client is, but I don't buy any business without due diligence investigations that take weeks, and that is only if I want it.' He paused and then said quietly. 'I don't know anything about and certainly don't want, your client's bloody business! So far, you've wasted five minutes of my very valuable time. You have one more minute.'

Hardy's heart was pounding heavily. His mouth felt horrible. This was the moment he had known would happen.

'Mr Hardy!' He was sharply brought back to focus on the man sitting opposite, who was glaring at him. 'Well?' It sounded like his old army sergeant major.

'Mr Charrington.' Hardy tried to sound in control of the situation, 'The payment is ten million dollars. The money is to be transferred tomorrow by bank transfer to Banque D'Or in Basle, Switzerland. You will set it up straight away. The account the money is to be transferred to is detailed on this piece of paper.' He pushed it across the table, 'You will, of course, destroy this as soon as possible in your own interest and it will all be done before midday tomorrow, Australian time. I am a lawyer...

'I don't care if you're a bloody magician,' roared Charrington. 'Unless you are also a damned hypnotist, there's no way I am in any way remotely interested in your "deal". Ten million dollars? For what? You've just wasted my time, your time and your clients' time and money, Mr Hardy. You must be stark raving mad!'

Charrington stood up. He seemed to Hardy to have grown six inches since he had sat down. 'G-day, Mr Hardy.'

Hardy swallowed hard. 'Er, I think, Mr Charrington, I should explain.'

'Mr Hardy,' Charrington sounded bored, but sat down again. 'What is there to explain? I'm not interested in buying anything.'

'Oh, I think you will be. Only fools don't change their mind.' Hardy was rather pleased with that response.

Charrington stared at him for a moment, frowned and nodded. 'Well?' His ill-temper was overwhelmingly evident.

'Mr Charrington,' Hardy tried to smile, but failed. 'I acknowledge there is no business to buy. That was merely a subterfuge to get the appointment. But I do have something you will buy and it will cost you ten million. Your love letters to Peter Melville and Roger Way and certain other, I understand the word is ...

evidence? There is no point in saying you don't know what I'm talking about.'

There was a very long silence. Hardy watched Charrington's face drain of all colour. The man who had seemed so dark and threatening, now seemed suddenly vulnerable and gaunt. It was an incredible transformation. Hardy could hear a typewriter somewhere, the only noise that broke the silence. Seconds, minutes, dragged by – or so it seemed. Hardy knew it was for Charrington to break the silence.

'You rotten, stinking bastard.' The words were squeezed out. No more. Charrington just sat and stared, then he scratched his upper lip intensely as if trying to rub it off.

'What proof do I have that you have these ... letters and that anyway they have not been photocopied?' Charrington's voice was less authoritative than five minutes ago and Hardy almost felt sorry for the man. Almost.

'None,' replied Hardy, 'none at all. In fact, I haven't got them. I don't know anything about them. Nor do I want to. Once the money has been transferred they will be made available here, in Sydney, and be part of the concluding documentation.'

'What concluding documentation?' Charrington frowned. 'You realise this is blackmail, Hardy. I could have you arrested.' Charrington slowly ran his tongue over his top lip.

'Your word against mine at the moment, Charrington.' Hardy had never addressed anybody without the Mr in his life before. It had come out, unhesitatingly, on this occasion. He pressed on, 'The only time there will be any evidence is after the meeting tomorrow and I don't believe you will risk that evidence being made public. Anyway, there will be nothing to prove a link between the money and the letters etc. after the deal has been concluded. And please,' he continued, 'don't think you can attempt to get hold of them from me beforehand, because I will never have them. They will be delivered to you, by courier, as soon as the deal has been concluded. There is nothing you can do, Mr Charrington.'

Perspiration began to glisten on Charrington's forehead. He closed his eyes as if in deep thought. 'How did your clients get hold of all this?'

'I'm told,' Hardy replied, 'that Melville gave his letters and photos to Way, sometime after you had all left Cambridge. Melville apparently knew he had cancer and only a short time to live, and they had agreed that the evidence might prove useful to Way one day. You were, after all, apparently going far and already making a lot of money.'

'Bastards. Rotten bastards,' Charrington snarled.

Hardy said nothing. There was nothing to say.

'Then what happened?'

'Way, some years later, fell on hard times. He needed some money and talked to my client about contacting you, but he was persuaded to sell his "investment" to my client instead.'

'Why didn't he come to me?'

'I don't know, Mr Charrington. It doesn't matter, why. My client has what he is sure you would like. Way died last year in a motor accident, by the way, so there is no one else involved.'

'Accident?' Charrington's eyes narrowed. 'Convenient?'

Hardy reddened. 'That's all I was told.' He didn't like the implication. It hadn't occurred to him. 'Anyway, your transgressions with two undergraduates can be forgotten for ever tomorrow.'

Charrington shook his head. 'How can I get that sort of money that quickly? It's impossible, it's ridiculous.'

Hardy had been well briefed. 'We know what you have in Switzerland alone Mr Charrington. More than enough to cope with this slight inconvenience. Never mind your accounts in Cayman and the Netherland Antilles, where we happen to know...'

'All right, all right. Shut up.' Charrington actually spat spittle on to the table. He stood up and walked to the window.

Hardy watched this impressive figure of a man standing, shoulders haunched, staring out at the city. He doubted if Charrington was taking in anything he saw.

'It's the photos,' muttered Charrington, almost to himself. 'The letters are unfortunate, but the photos are damning.' He turned and walked towards Hardy, who stood up. 'You haven't actually mentioned photos.' Charrington rasped.

128

Hardy nodded. 'The photos are damning, I understand. They are included and I'm to emphasise there will be no copies retained – of anything. I can also assure you that this will be the end of our association. We have no wish to cause you to do anything silly. We want only this sum which you can afford and you can then get on with the rest of your life.'

Charrington clenched and unclenched his fists. 'I'd often wondered what happened to those photos,' he mused and then swinging his right arm he dug his fingers into Hardy's chest. 'I'd kill you here and now if I thought it would do any good. Believe me, I mean it.'

Hardy didn't doubt it for one second. He watched Charrington move to the table, pick up the paper Hardy had pushed across and turn, saying, 'I'll see about the money. I'll see you here at five tomorrow.' Charrington narrowed his eyes. 'Come back, then.'

Without a glance Charrington strode out, slamming the door behind him.

He had done it! It had been almost easy. Fleetingly Hardy thought of the phrase, 'too easy,' but dismissed it. Charrington couldn't fight this battle and hope to win. His career, his public standing as a foremost Australian entrepreneur, probably his marriage into an English aristocratic family, everything, would have collapsed around him, if he had fought. The door opened and Charrington's secretary stood there, looking rather bewildered and flushed. 'I've been asked to show you out, Mr Hardy,' she explained, 'at once.'

Hardy smiled. He could afford to. 'Of course,' he acknowledged and followed her to the lifts. As he stepped out on the ground floor he collided with a man about to enter. They both muttered 'Sorry,' and then both stopped.

'Well, well.' Ron Carter smiled affably. 'How are you finding Sydney – warm?'

'Yes,' nodded Hardy. 'Fancy seeing you.'

'Oh, It's a small place, really,' smiled Carter. 'Never have an affair in Sydney, somebody will see you. Didn't tell you that on the plane, did I? Still, I'm sure that advice is unnecessary for you. You don't know anybody in Sydney do you?'

'About three people,' Hardy replied, 'and you're one of them. And here we are bumping into each other. Quite a coincidence.'

As he made the thoughtless comment, Hardy was looking Carter in the eyes. Did he imagine there was a flicker of unease?

Carter laughed brusquely. 'Yes, indeed. Well, see you around,' and with that he stepped into the lift and the doors closed.

Hardy stayed and watched the lift indicator. It stopped at the twenty-fourth floor. Almost coincidence? The euphoria was ebbing from Hardy fast. He walked thoughtfully out into the bright sunlight.

'You don't look as though you know where you're going!'

Dressed in a blue and white striped summer dress and sitting on the white marble round the waterfall was a smiling Patti Cross. Hardy frowned uneasily. He didn't seem to be able to move without coming across about the only two people he knew in the whole of Australia.

Patti stood up. 'Here, what's the miserable face for?' She linked her arm in his. 'It's not every man in a foreign city who is accosted by a friendly girl who is not after his money!' As an afterthought she added, 'My office is in the DCC Tower. Am I going to see you around here often?'

'Well,' Hardy replied, hesitantly, 'I really don't think so.'

'Oh, what a shame,' Patti pouted lightly. 'Are you sure?'

'Well,' Hardy shook his head, 'I'm coming back tomorrow, but I think that will probably be the last time. Other things to do and all that,' he added, studiously.

'You're not getting away from me that easily,' Patti responded and Hardy found himself being propelled across to a coffee shop on the far side of the piazza. 'Let me buy you a coffee.' Patti had already sat down at an outside table.

'I can't have a lady buy me coffee,' Hardy protested, joining her.

'My dear Mr Hardy, this is Australia.' The middle 'a' pierced Hardy's ears as an 'i'. 'It's all different here.' A young alert waitress took their orders and disappeared inside.

'I'm beginning to realise that,' Hardy nodded, looking skywards. 'I'm roasting already.'

'Oh, move your chair. You're right in the sun! Come round

this side.' Patti patted the table firmly, 'it's in the shade. We can't have any red raw Poms.'

Hardy moved round, and sitting next to Patti, could see the whole piazza from the shade of the corner building. The clear sky was a piercing blue and the sun was rampant. Coffee came, as hot as the sun, which irritated Hardy, as he found it impossible to drink it hurriedly. He really wanted to be on his own and reflect on his meeting with Charrington. His every thought was shattered before it became measured, by the continual burbling of this excitable, not unattractive, young girl. At least Rita didn't interrupt his thoughts when he was busy. He then felt rather mean. How should Patti know he wanted to be alone, if he didn't say so. She was trying to be friendly to a first-time visitor. As though sensing his frustration she commented. 'I'm sorry I keep rattling on. I guess I'm a little nervous, not just for myself, but also for Sydney. I want you to like it here. We're very proud of our city and state and I guess I've gone overboard a little. Forgive me, please?' She held his arm.

'Of course, of course,' Hardy squeezed her hand. 'You're being very kind. If the weather stays like this and everyone is as friendly, I don't think you need worry about my impressions.'

She really was attractive when she smiled. 'Oh good.' She hadn't tried to remove the hand resting on his arm, although Hardy had only momentarily squeezed it.

'Another coffee?'

Patti raised her eyelashes at him and then suddenly sat upright and looked at her watch. '... Oh! I've just remembered! I have a meeting with a client down at Potts Point. I am so sorry, I'd forgotten all about it!' She quickly rummaged in her handbag and put a two dollar note on the table as she smiled ruefully. 'Sorry, but I must fly. I'll catch up later – bye.' She touched his shoulder, rose and hurriedly made her way through the people in the piazza.

'I'll have another coffee,' Hardy nodded to the waitress. He chewed his lower lip as he lost sight of Patti in the crowd. He couldn't help but wonder if the suddenness of her departure had anything to do with the emergence of Carter from the DCC Tower. She had gone off in the same direction and thinking about it she had always, from the moment Hardy had seen her, had the entrance to the office building in her sights. Coincidence? Hardy didn't know. If Patti Cross had her office in the DCC Tower why hadn't she been in it?

He ordered a cream bun.

*   *   *

At five o'clock the next afternoon Hardy was shown into the same conference room by the same, now rather frosty, secretary.

'Mr Charrington will be with you shortly,' she said severely, as she shut the door on him.

Hardy was not overly surprised that her manner had changed. No doubt she had picked up Charrington's animosity towards him, but Charrington was hardly likely to have told her why. His thoughts were interrupted as the door opened and Charrington came in. He looked more haggard than Hardy expected. He nodded, his eyes not leaving Hardy's face and sat down. Hardy inwardly shrugged. He guessed he could hardly expect normal courtesies. He sat down, as before, with his back to the window.

'How do we proceed, Hardy?' Charrington's voice was deep, and clipped.

'Did you destroy the piece of paper?' asked Hardy.

Charrington nodded. 'Of course,' he replied irritatedly. 'In my own interest, as you so kindly put it.'

'I have a statement already prepared,' Hardy pulled it out of his briefcase and passed it across the table. There was total silence as Charrington read it.

'What's this for? It merely says the money I have already transferred is not a loan, nor part of any business transaction and is a gift made not under duress. So what?'

'So it is really – ah – a simple, case of signing it, Mr Charrington and then we can proceed. Thank you, we acknowledge the money has been received.'

'Simple he says!' Charrington laughed, without humour.

There was silence as he signed the statement and almost threw it across at Hardy.

'Right, you bastard. Where are the letters and photos?'

Hardy shook his head. 'I've told you, I don't know. They will be passed to you as soon as I confirm you have signed.'

'Well, bloody well confirm it!' Charrington jumped up angrily.

'I can't. I don't know how to,' Hardy watched warily, as Charrington came round the table.

'What?'

'I will be contacted,' Hardy tried to sound reassuring. 'I told you the arrangements. Please trust me.'

'Trust you?' Charrington towered over him. 'You snivelling little runt! You despicable little sod!'

Before Hardy could think of a reply the phone rang. Charrington snatched it up. 'I thought I said no interruptions, Miss Appleby,' he fumed. There was a pause. 'What?' 'Oh!' he looked at Hardy, his eyes narrowing as he thrust the phone towards him. 'It's for you.'

Hardy was as surprised as Charrington. He took it. 'Hallo?'

'Is it signed?' Hardy closed his eyes to shut out the picture of Charrington glaring at him.

'Yes.'

'Stay there. Give me Mr Charrington.' Hardy's brain was spinning. He recognised the voice. But who was it? He couldn't think. He handed the phone to Charrington and walked unsteadily to the window. He couldn't get his mind to function. He stared out, unseeing.

Hardy heard Charrington rasp 'Yes' and slam the phone down. The man's heavy breathing moved away. Hardy turned and watched him open the door and stand in the doorway. After what seemed a lifetime of inaction, there was movement and noise outside and Charrington stood aside as Patti Cross came in carrying a briefcase. Patti Cross – that was the voice! Her face was set, unsmiling, as she turned to Charrington.

'I suggest you shut the door and then we'll get on with everything.'

Charrington shut the door slowly and belligerently.

'Mr Hardy,' she turned, 'Where is the statement?'

Hardy picked it up and she took it quickly, checking it through.

'Right. That's that done,' she seemed satisfied, as she pushed it into her briefcase.

'Patti, you work for me! What the hell are you doing involved in ... this?' Charrington was almost shouting.

Patti turned to him brusquely. 'Shall we get on? I take it you want your part of the deal?' Without waiting for a reply, she waved at the patio doors. Let's go on the balcony where there is total privacy.' She added firmly, 'Outside.'

Charrington, still obviously nonplussed by her involvement, moved past her, opened the windows and led the way. Patti ignored Hardy and followed Charrington. Hardy stepped outside in a daze, but he was very conscious of the afternoon heat after the air-conditioned office. He had been perspiring in the room and he didn't need any encouragement now he was outside.

Patti sat on the parapet and slowly opened her briefcase. She pulled out two large sealed manilla envelopes and held one out to Hardy. 'Put this in your case, Mr Hardy,' she ordered, and then turning to Charrington she gave him the other. He snatched it from her and tore it open.

Hardy stood looking down at the pedestrians far below, slowly moving along like ants, whilst the sun burned the back of his neck. He heard Charrington snarl, 'OK, these are photocopies of the letters, and there aren't any negatives with the photos. You said I'd have all the originals.'

Hardy turned, as he saw Charrington advance towards Patti who was only a foot from him. He expected Charrington to grab her in his anger. It was Patti however, who moved and pushed, not Charrington, but Hardy, hard. Very hard. He screamed piercingly, as he toppled over the parapet and realised there was nothing to stop his fall. His terror was agonising, as he accelerated towards the piazza. Hardy's briefcase burst open as it hit the ground at the same time as he did, but he was no longer interested.

9

Newcastle, June 1988

Abbott was not in a good mood. Below his bedroom window, engines seemed to have been trundling along with endless coaches and wagons all night. He was sure he had not had one hour's uninterrupted sleep. Now, lying in his bed all he could hear was gurgling in the wash basin. Other people were obviously up and about.

He looked at his watch, which had been neatly lined up with his change, his comb, his wallet and his spectacle case. It was ten minutes to seven. Normally, he never woke before seven. He had set his travelling alarm for that hour. Why didn't hotels ask whether their guests wished for hard or soft mattresses? It made all the difference to a good night's sleep.

The breakfast scene in the dining room did not improve Abbott's humour. The hotel was obviously very busy and he had to wait for a table. After a few interminable minutes he was seated at a table next to a large bald man who had finished his breakfast and was about to light up a cigarette. Abbott stopped that from happening with a few sharp words; and the man rose without acknowledging Abbott's existence, lighting up as he went. After a few more frustrating minutes, Abbott managed to catch the waiter's eye to give his order.

'I'll have fresh orange juice, a soft boiled egg – just two minutes – and some brown wholewheat toast – lightly toasted – and china tea.'

The waiter irritatingly moved on to another table to take two more orders before strolling through to the kitchen. Abbott noticed that most of the guests having breakfast were men and nearly all of them were trying to read their newspapers whilst they ate. Abbott never read a paper at the table. It was not acceptable behaviour.

'I say how marvellous! I wondered if I might see you down here. I asked if I could join you. I hope you don't mind?'

Abbott was brought out of his reverie by Dr Asquith taking the seat opposite him. Today, she was wearing a different colour blouse under her jacket, but it was the same tweed suit. He forced himself to smile and half rise, 'Good morning. I trust you slept well?'

'Oh, I did! I did!' She clasped her hands together, leaning forward. 'I'm up so many nights normally, that it was heaven! Such a comfortable bed! And so quiet! I live on a very busy road at home, but I didn't hear anything this morning until my alarm call came through!'

'Good,' Abbott just managed to keep a smile on his face. 'Er – are you a medical doctor may I ask?'

The response was withheld, as the lugubrious waiter slid Abbott's orange juice in front of him and took Dr Asquith's order. Then she nodded, 'Yes. Father was a doctor, you see. Good start. Helped me. Wanted a son, but mother couldn't have any more children. I didn't have a chance really. No mind of my own in those days. Accepted my father's encouragement and made the grade.' She raised a hand as if to ward off a blow, 'Not that I'm complaining. Very good life as a small town GP. No complaints, really.'

Abbott nodded, but didn't reply. He was quietly impressed with the self-assured woman and drank his orange juice, thoughtfully.

'A British Rail reunion?'

Abbott recognised the voice before he looked up and confirmed the presence of Goode from the night before. His heart sank. What was it that was attracting everyone to him? Could it be...?

'Hallo there,' sang Dr Asquith, beaming happily. 'Do join us.' She tapped the next table, which was now set up and free.

'Very kind,' the booming voice softened slightly.

'I'm sorry to see there's been another hijacking in the Middle East,' remarked Goode, waving *The Daily Telegraph* around. 'Bomb the bloody place; only language they understand. When I was in the Eighth Army, we knew how to deal with the trouble makers.'

Breakfasts were served and although Abbott resented the fact that everybody's breakfast arrived with his, he was surprised and pleased that his boiled egg was almost as good as Lesley's would have been. Dr Asquith was happy to pick up the Middle East hijacking as a topic of conversation. Abbott wished he could have eaten in silence.

'Do you really think punitive measures would work?' asked Dr Asquith through a mouthful of scrambled egg.

'Absolutely, absolutely,' nodded Goode. 'None of these people have any backbone. They only commit these atrocities because they believe no one will retaliate. Retaliate once, just once – hard, that's all that's needed.'

'And then?' asked Abbott mildly.

Goode's hand stopped on its way to depositing bacon and egg in his mouth, as he stared at Abbott for a moment, before contemplating the completion of the exercise. 'Aid,' he replied, and carried on eating.

'Aid?' repeated Abbott.

'Stick and carrot, old son,' Abbott mentally winced at the familiarity. 'Afraid of us one moment, grateful to us the next. That approach will tear them apart. Soft option. Governments will see the sense in abandoning the terrorists they've turned a blind eye to and sanity will prevail.'

Dr Asquith, scrambled egg finished, nodded. 'Sounds sensible.'

'Far too easy,' commented Abbott, as he reached for the marmalade.

'Why?' The response from Goode was angry and Dr Asquith smiled.

'It's a simplistic, unreal, view, that's why.' Abbott concentrated on his toast. He was saved from expanding his views as a figure appeared in front of them. The latest arrival was young Anderson.

'Sit down, sit down,' Dr Asquith patted the table next to her as though she was instructing a young pupil. 'Now, Mr Abbott, do carry on . . .'

'I'd rather not, if you don't mind.' Abbott had resolved that he was not prepared to worsen this unseemly breakfast, by inviting further unnecessary argument.

'Aha!' boomed Goode, who had managed to clear his plate by this stage and was moving on to the toast, 'no stomach for a good argument! No facts to back you up!'

'My stomach,' retorted Abbott, 'is only fit for acid digestion at this time of the morning, not acid discussion.'

'Oh, very good,' Goode's heavy sarcasm was not lost on Abbott, but fortunately everyone else laughed, diffusing the sting.

'If you'll excuse me,' Abbott rose, smiling weakly at Dr Asquith. He felt that his unintentional witticism was a good exit line and without a further word strode towards the door. He returned to his room, cleaned his teeth and gargled, before he methodically packed his overnight bag. He looked out of his window and was surprised and pleased to see a weak sun straining through the watery clouds. He placed his bag by the door. The meeting would allow him to be back before twelve and he would pick it up before checking out. He checked in his briefcase that all the papers were in the order he wanted them and casting a final glance at himself in the mirror, opened the bedroom door.

'Hey, ho, and off to work we go,' Goode, striding towards the lift, was just passing Abbott's room. Pressing the lift-call button he turned and smiled. 'Now I guess we're going to compete for a taxi!'

'Not at all,' replied Abbott, following Goode into the red-carpeted lift. 'It's a fine morning and a short walk is good for one.'

Goode patted his bulging briefcase. 'Too much paper to carry. Afraid I can't face walking with this lot.'

Reaching the ground floor, Abbott felt it unnecessary to reply, as he followed Goode's heavy figure through the revolving doors.

'Aha,' boomed Goode. 'so much for your fine morning.'

It had started to drizzle, with that fine rain that is almost invisible, but can drench a coat in a few seconds. The sky was now darkening to a uniform grey.

'Typical bloody Newcastle,' commented Goode to the world at large. 'Thank God, there's a taxi.' He waved his free arm vehemently to the only cab driver on the rank. 'Where are you going, old boy?' he turned to Abbott. 'I can drop you off.'

Abbott bristled again at the familiarity and his instinctive reaction was to take evasive action, but he knew that would be foolish. Now that it was raining insistently there would probably be a dearth of taxis and he certainly didn't want to get wet.

'Er, that's very kind,' he muttered as Goode opened the taxi door and stood back to let him in. 'I'm going to Barford House by the Tyne bridge.'

'No problem,' returned Goode as he eased his bulk in, 'I'm just going over the bridge into Gateshead, so that's absolutely fine. Barford House? Isn't that the tall, impressive tower? The headquarters of *Northern News?*'

'Yes,' Abbott nodded, as the smoke-ridden taxi lurched off into the traffic.

The yellow double decker buses were full of office and shop workers, who were alighting at city stops and the taxi had to follow, unavoidably slowly, in the morning crawl. Abbott had hardly been able to push *Northern News* out of his mind for one moment during the last week. He chewed his lower lip as he gazed unseeing out of the window.

'Here we are, old boy,' Goode pointed across Abbott as the taxi driver circumvented the busy roundabout and pulled up outside Barford House.

'Er...' Abbott searched for his wallet.

'Don't worry,' Goode stayed his arm, 'I was going past anyway. Hasn't cost me any more.'

'Thank you,' Abbott nodded and smiled weakly. He reached over and opened the door.

'Tell that egocentric old bugger Hawkins to print more photos of pretty girls in his newspapers and that'll be the best

139

reward I can have,' Goode roared with laughter, as Abbott climbed out. The taxi pulled smoothly out into the traffic again almost before Abbott had shut the door. Certainly before Abbott had digested Goode's comment enough to think of a response. It was the surprise of hearing Hawkins' name that had really caught Abbott unprepared. He should have expected it, of course. After all Hawkins did own *Northern News* and, in fact, many regional newspapers north of Birmingham right through Scotland, together with a countrywide daily tabloid, *The National.* It was this paper that Smith had been referring to, of course. Not a paper that Abbott had ever bought or read – until the last few days. Little that was printed in it could be termed news. In his opinion it only pandered to the semiliterate members of society, with gossip concerning film and TV stars, considerable sports coverage and plenty of pin-ups.

His appointment was with Hans Hawkins and Abbott presented himself to the large, pasty-faced commissionaire. After a phone call, the commissionaire gave Abbott a sticky label to plant on his lapel with VISITOR in large letters, underneath which the commissionaire had written the date.

'Sorry about all this, sir,' he said as he opened the lift door, 'but security is the name of the game here.' He inserted a key in the lift and turned it. 'It will go straight to the twentieth floor, sir.' The commissionaire smiled, as the doors closed. Abbott noticed there were only nineteen floors indicated. Security.

As the doors opened he was greeted by another, younger, commissionaire who, without a word led the way to a large mahogany door, knocked and opened it, standing aside for Abbott to pass. Abbott heard the door close softly behind him as his hand was grasped strongly by Hans Hawkins.

Hawkins would have been recognised by millions who had never met him. Apart from reports and articles in the press, his continual presence on television when it covered his many spectacular business forays and romantic attachments gave a clear indication as to how much he enjoyed the limelight. He had the build of a sumo wrestler – small, squat, but fat and round with a condensed, red face and receding white hair. His face stretched into a big smile. He was Jewish and shorter than

Abbott had supposed, but the girth was as wide as he had anticipated. A real dumpling.

'Do come in, my friend. It is good to meet you,' the smile widened to show uneven yellowing teeth. His accent unmistakably reflected his German birth.

'Now do sit down, Mr Abbott. Here, here.' Hawkins gestured to an upright red chair in front of a glass-topped, chrome-legged table that obviously served as a desk. The whole room had a modern house magazine look about it. All chrome, plastic and stark colours. The walls were covered with expressionist paintings, full of colour and fury signifying nothing to Abbott, who thought it all in execrable taste. Hawkins picked a cigar out of an onyx box and sitting down the other side of the table, began to perform baptismal rites on the cigar, his eyes never leaving Abbott.

'I must say I think you've wasted your time coming all the way from London. As I told you on the phone, I have always had bankers who have supported me since I came to England and there is no reason why I should think of any changes at present. However,' he lit the cigar and pulled deeply, 'I'm always prepared to listen if someone believes there is a deal to be done. You said on the phone that your bank knew of a newsprint company that would be available for a price I couldn't refuse – so fire away.'

Abbott took a deep breath. 'I said also that it would have to be understood that you didn't talk to anyone about my visit, including anyone in my own bank, before I arrived and that you should have five million pounds available today in a bankers' draft should you wish to proceed.'

Hawkins nodded emphatically. 'I understood. To humour you I haven't spoken to a soul and the bankers' draft is in my desk made out as you requested. However, I don't let money go that easily. If this company is a bargain, of course I want it, when I've checked it out. Otherwise, forget it.'

Abbott breathed a sigh of relief and smiled involuntarily, 'Good,' he opened his briefcase. 'In that case, I think we can do business. May I see the draft?'

Hawkins shrugged his shoulders, rose and went to a drawer in a side cabinet. He returned with the bankers' draft and sitting down, handed it to Abbott, who studied it before putting it in his case.

'Hey! What are you doing?' Hawkins half rose, glaring at the briefcase.

Abbott put up a hand, pulled out a sheaf of papers and placed them in front of Hawkins. Surprised, Hawkins looked at Abbott and leaning forward gave them a quick glance. 'What are these?' He moved them around. 'They look like photocopies of bank statements.'

'They are indeed, Mr Hawkins,' Abbott's hands were moist and he wiped them on his trousers. '*The Newcastle Courier*'s bank statements, dated 1950.'

'When?' Hawkins showed total surprise.

'1950. You remember? The year you bought your first newspaper, *The Newcastle Courier*. They aren't the only bank statements here, though.'

Hawkins drew slowly and deliberately on his cigar. He had recovered his composure and his eyes had narrowed to a slit. There was no smile now. 'So?' It was very softly asked.

'So, Mr Hawkins, one statement there, yours, shows a receipt of seventy thousand pounds on the first of April 1950 and a payment of one hundred thousand pounds a few days later.'

As it was clear Hawkins had no intention of speaking, Abbott continued in carefully rehearsed, measured tones. 'You will also see there, if you care to look, photocopies of Lawsons' account at a different bank showing seventy thousand pounds in and out just before that first of April. Let me remind you, Mr Hawkins, in case you have forgotten.'

Hawkins continued to gaze masklike at Abbott, his cigar ash glowing a dull red.

Abbott continued, '*The Newcastle Courier* was an old established family business, not doing particularly well after the war and with the only heir killed in a bombing raid over Germany. It was run by a sick owner in his seventies, who had become a recluse and who had no immediate family, other than his, also frail, wife. He had entrusted the day-to-day running to his faithful general manager and sole executive director, John Carr. Carr, however, was a betting man. Newcastle races, any races. Horses, greyhounds, anything. It was compulsive and he owed thousands. You met him and befriended him. After a while, he took you into his confidence and he told you he had thought of a way of getting his hands on the ownership of the paper. He didn't really want the paper, he just needed money to pay off his debts and carry on gambling. With a little money and plenty of ambition, it was a heaven-sent opportunity for you. No doubt you had befriended him in the first place because of his position at the paper.'

Abbott paused for breath. He wasn't used to lengthy monologues. It was just as well he had been over and over the story, otherwise he felt sure he would have dried up by now and lost the thread. Hawkins was watching him, as a cat watches a bird.

'Carr,' Abbott continued, 'drew a number of cheques for the normal settlement of monthly *Courier* creditors, but he exceeded the overdraft limit and the bank started returning cheques. The company had been going through difficult times for long enough. It was a matter of hours to a receiver being appointed, or worse. The old man was desperate and Carr told him of a certain Hans Heneker he knew, a splendid friend and business contact, who would lend them one hundred thousand pounds without wanting interest on it, just for a seat on the Board. This was, unsurprisingly, jumped at. The money was used to settle creditors and then within days Heneker demanded his money back. *The Courier* had no means of paying it and Heneker threatened liquidation. The old man was too ill to fight. The paper had become a nightmare to him and he signed over all his shares to prevent a public debacle that he couldn't bear to face. The little money he had left wouldn't have saved the paper and he was not prepared to jeopardise financially the remaining years of either his, or his wife's, life.'

Hawkins carefully knocked the grey ash off his cigar into an ashtray, for the first time taking his eyes off Abbott. A ship's siren sounded on the Tyne below them and a plane could be heard in the distance as it approached Newcastle Airport. There was no sound from Hawkins.

'You now had control of *The Courier*,' Abbott continued, 'and

143

your business acumen and ruthlessness were enough to see it out of its difficulties, as well as its sister papers in York and Leeds. You were on your way to the influential position you hold today. The interesting facts don't stop there, however. One of the cheques Carr had drawn creating the original crisis was for seventy thousand pounds for newsprint from Lawsons, a company that had managed to acquire a supply at a bargain price. However, because of *The Courier*'s financial situation Lawsons demanded payment before delivery. Lawsons, was, in fact, a small import–export subsidiary company of yours, Mr Hawkins. That seventy thousand pounds was most of the money you found and loaned to *The Courier*. Its own money! Carr paid Lawsons the money they were really owed which was only ten thousand pounds, with the other creditors in the fullness of time. Meanwhile, you issued a credit note for the seventy thousand pounds because the quality of the newsprint was not up to standard. Not that *The Courier* said so – you did, as Lawsons. The newsprint, of course, had never existed.

The earlier transaction was settled when you, of course, repaid the money a few weeks later, but only after you had ensured that you had received your loan back from *The Courier* in time. That was after *The Courier* had sold a property the company owned, which you and Carr had identified earlier as easily saleable and surplus to requirements. You then changed bankers. The circle had been closed. No-one ever suspected. You looked after Carr's debts and then he began to drink and he had an unfortunate accident, a verdict, confirmed by the authorities, of course. But, then no-one knew of the previous events that I have just related.'

Abbott wiped the moisture from his upper lip. His hand wasn't quite as steady as it should have been. He had rehearsed the words but not the atmosphere. It seemed stiflingly hot in the room. Hawkins leaned forward, a cruel smile playing on his lips.

'And now what, Mr Abbott?' He spat the question out. Abbott winced as saliva hit him in the face.

'Now, Mr Hawkins,' he replied, wiping his face with his handkerchief, 'all this will be made public. These are not the only copies of the bank statements, as I am sure you realise and

144

circumstantial though the evidence might seem, it is good enough to finish your credibility – especially as it's true. It's all there. *The Courier*'s, yours and Lawson's bank statements.'

Hawkins pulled on his cigar. 'Who's behind this? What do you want? Clearly not to publish all this or you would have done that already. Someone wants something. What?'

'Well,' Abbott replied, 'apparently your John Carr was not as discreet at the time as you might have assumed. Back in 1950 the story found its way to people who were very interested, and Carr recorded his version of events in one of his more sober moments, for which he was well rewarded. Some banking staff can be more co-operative than their reputation suggests. Even bankers can be bought and with help it was all pieced together. It has been a case of biding time. I am, of course, only a messenger. As you rightly say, something is wanted for silence.'

Hawkins rose and stood looking out over the grey, uneven rooftops of Newcastle.

'Five million pounds.'

Abbott's hands were gripping the briefcase resting on his lap. 'No, in addition I want two cheques – payable to me – each for half a million pounds. One dated the end of this month and one dated the end of next month.'

Hawkins turned round slowly, surprising Abbott with his broad smile. 'Cheques? I can stop cheques! Surely you want cash in old notes? Isn't that what they ask for in the movies? Old fashioned blackmail. But that's too simple. Am I to be bled till I die? I'm worth much more than six million. Why not all of it straight away?' Hawkins leaned on the table and mashed his cigar into the ashtray. 'I shall call your damned bluff – you publish! I've been in tough situations all my life. I'll come through. Go to fucking hell!'

Abbott was feeling very warm and very uncomfortable. He hated overheated offices. He rose and began to collect the papers. 'Have you forgotten your son's forthcoming marriage to the Duke of Belmont's daughter? Do you really want publicity at this time? When you are about to become accepted in the blue-blooded circles of society? What about your daughter?'

Hawkins glowered at him and his face, reddening even more

harshly, was full of hatred as he fought to speak. 'You little shit; you filthy, fucking bastard! I'll take you with me!' He moved forward, as Abbott, frightened of the very idea of violence, took a step back.

'Please,' Abbott almost shouted, 'nothing will be gained by brutality. Nothing.' He hoped the words sounded confident. He had never experienced anything like this and violence was something he hadn't really considered as likely. Momentarily, he wondered if he had been wrong.

Hawkins stopped and frowned. His eyes pierced Abbott. The silence hung in the air, then slowly, 'Is this all that's wanted? Six million?'

Abbott nodded. 'I can assure you that that is all that's wanted. The photocopies and the tape will then be destroyed or you can have them.'

There was another long silence, as Abbott realised Hawkins was wrestling with the enormity of the decision. Finally, as if to herald action, another ship's siren sounded. Hawkins turned and slumped down into his chair. 'All right,' he murmured, almost to himself, 'nothing will spoil my son's wedding. Nothing.'

He pressed a buzzer on the table. The door opened behind Abbott. 'Bring me my personal cheque book,' he spoke over Abbott's shoulder.

There was no reply, but within seconds a nervous, large middle-aged woman placed a cheque book in front of Hawkins and quickly withdrew.

Hawkins wrote out the two cheques and whilst he did so, Abbott inserted the bankers' draft in a pre-addressed envelope and sealed it before putting it back in his case. Hawkins put the cheques on the table as he stood up. 'You've only given me a few days to arrange the first half million, so bugger off. I've got things to do. If I ever see you again, I'll mince you into a thousand pieces.'

He glared at Abbott, his forehead glistening with perspiration. Abbott quickly shuffled the papers back into his case, next to a copy of the tape still sealed in its envelope.

'You won't see me again,' he assured Hawkins. Hesitating at

146

the door, he added, 'The last instruction is very important – whatever happens from now on, don't even think of going back on the deal.'

Pulling the door to quickly behind him, Abbott found his way to the lift without another word. The commissionaire downstairs took the visitor's pass and saluted him, as Abbott passed through the doors on to the Tyne bridge. The rain had stopped, but the air was moist and fresh, as Abbott thankfully breathed deeply and made his way along to Pilgrim Street. He found a post box and taking out the pre-addressed envelope, posted it. It had all worked according to plan! No hitches. Back to normality! He mentally relaxed for the first time and he sauntered his way towards a busy pedestrian crossing outside Binn's department store in Market Street.

'Yoo hoo! Mr Abbott!' A strong female voice from behind stopped him, just as he was about to cross the road.

'Why, Doctor, fancy seeing you.'

Dr Asquith beamed. 'Isn't it a small world! I feel I keep meeting an old friend!'

Abbott forbore to reply. He was more irritated than surprised. He wanted to be alone.

'I've had a wonderful little shop round Binns. Such a nice store.'

People were congregating ready to cross at the next change of lights. The streets were crowded now.

'I'm just going to have a look round Eldon Square and then I'm on my way out to Whitley Bay. Have you had a successful morning?' She smiled eagerly.

'Oh, Yes,' Abbott replied. 'Yes, thank you. Very.'

'Oh, good,' Dr Asquith enthused, as the lights changed and they joined the throng crossing the road. They only had a few seconds before the traffic would start moving impatiently forward again. Abbott half turned, albeit reluctantly, to stay with her and in so doing noticed – what was the young man's name? – Anderson, in his blue pinstriped suit, walking behind her, head turned away as though looking for something or somebody farther back. It's incredible how we all keep meeting, Abbott thought. Or was it? He brought his head round to listen to Dr Asquith talking about the weather, as they stepped on to the pavement, he on the outside next to the kerb. The traffic started to move off. Suddenly Abbott felt a hand push him in the small of the back as Dr Asquith also stumbled into him, and he fell uncontrollably, losing all his sense of balance.

He didn't stand a chance. His neck broke on impact with the bus which was passing close to the kerb. Dr Asquith was quickly on her knees, as other passers-by ran up. She only needed seconds to know the worst, as a crowd quickly gathered. 'I stumbled into him,' she cried out agonisingly. 'I killed him!'

'Nonsense hinney, dinna ya talk daft,' a small, white-haired old man waved his stick as he bent and held her shoulder. 'Some fella knocked ya both over, as he barged through the crowd. He didna stop as he nearly knocked me over as well. He's the guilty one really hinney, whoever he is.'

10

Maurice Thatcher had spent the day at his New York office on Park Avenue, discussing some of their high-profile accounts. Everything seemed to be progressing well and money was flowing in. It had been a lovely warm day and the vibrancy of the New Yorkers, hurrying, scurrying, shouting, in the office had helped him to stay alert. He couldn't carry out the real reason for his visit just yet, however. Towards the end of a satisfying afternoon, he returned to The Waldorf-Astoria.

He was finishing drying his hair. The mirror was steamed over following his soak in the bath and he wiped it with the towel. He hummed contentedly, as he tossed a little cologne on his hair and searched for his comb, on the shelf over the washbasin. The television was blaring out in the bedroom, but Thatcher suddenly realised that the insistent shrill tone of a telephone was genuine and not coming from the screen. He turned and banged his funny bone on the open door. 'Shit.' It was not a word Thatcher used anywhere but in the States. Everyone seemed to use it here and extraordinarily the more he heard it, the less offensive it became.

'Hallo?'

'Maurice, darling. It's Elaine,' the soft tones purred down the phone.

'Well, hallo there.'

'What are you doing?'

'Standing naked chatting up a telephone.'

149

'My word,' a giggle was half stifled, 'I know telephones have a receiver, but little did I guess ... How about coming round for a late afternoon snifter?'

Thatcher picked up his watch from the bedside table. It showed ten o'clock. Less five UK hours. Five o'clock. He nodded mentally to himself. Why not?

'I'd love to,' he responded. 'I've finished all my work for the day.'

'Splendid,' Elaine exclaimed, 'remember the address? 68th and 3rd, Bellway Towers, Apartment 1202.'

'Hold it, hold it,' Maurice grabbed a pen, 'it sounds like a clue to a treasure hunt.'

Elaine breathed heavily down the phone, 'You never know your luck!' She repeated the address. 'Come when you're ready,' she whispered and rang off.

Thatcher replaced the receiver slowly. He inhaled deeply, pursing his lips. Was his imagination running riot or was there really a hint of invitation to more than a drink in Elaine's voice? He acknowledged that she was very attractive, but he was vaguely surprised to realise that he had never, before today, thought of her in a personal, sexual way.

He dressed, to the clamour of the late-afternoon movie and satisfied with his appearance, left the air-conditioned room for the hot corridor and elevator. The reception area was full of early evening guests checking in, and the hubbub of people meeting round the lobby banquette seating area was drowning the delicate tones of the cocktail lounge pianist. The whole area was crowded and noisy. He strode out and nodded to the doorman for a cab.

The negro driver showed no sign of interest as Thatcher gave him the address, but eased away, immediately sounding his horn at another yellow cab for not pulling away at the lights quickly enough. Along 48th Street to 3rd Avenue, bowling across noisy manhole covers and lurching through dreadful holes in the road, a left turn almost on two wheels, then a straight race with every other cab and car to 68th. Easing himself out with the difficulty he always found with American cabs, and dollars lighter, he strode purposefully down 68th Street. On the right-hand side was a white-brick modern apartment block on its way to 2nd Avenue. On every floor and at nearly every window, air-conditioning units protruded like space-age gargoyles. Bellway Towers was the second block. The smiling, large-framed, negro doorman showed two rows of gleaming white teeth as Thatcher entered.

'Sah?'

'Elaine Gable?' Thatcher enquired, 'or Mrs Frank Sorretto, I guess?'

'Sure thing!' the teeth remained exposed, as the doorman gesticulated towards the elevator. 'Twelfth floor, first apartment on your left.'

Ringing the door bell a few moments later, Thatcher was surprised that Elaine opened the door almost immediately.

'Darling! Come in! Come in!' She stood aside, beckoning him to enter. The apartment was beautifully furnished as, of course, he should have expected. Fine Caucasian rugs, antique walnut furniture, a baby grand piano and some very impressive Picassos on the white walls, were all breathtakingly arranged to be admired. Elaine, however, had other ideas.

'Come on out on to the balcony!' she sang, linking her arm in his. 'The champagne's on ice and its marvellous outside!'

'What happened to your seven thirty?' Thatcher smiled.

'Couldn't wait, darling,' Elaine pinched his arm, leading him outside. Thatcher couldn't believe his ears. The noise was deafening! 'Don't go away.' Elaine disappeared inside, calling over her shoulder, 'take your jacket off and relax.'

Thatcher looked over the balcony and realised he was at the back of the apartment block. Contractors were drilling the foundations of a new apartment block over on the corner of 3rd Avenue and 67th, and along on the corner of 2nd Avenue and 67th another block was at ground-floor level, with steel erectors creating the most terrible din. The traffic, as always, was a cacophony of car horns and screeching brakes. Added to all this was Elaine's stereo braying out jazz. Thatcher shook his head in disbelief. She must surely have only meant the weather, when she had said it was marvellous outside!

151

'Here we are!' Elaine reappeared with two glasses and a bottle of Moet. She placed the glasses on the small table and handed Thatcher the bottle. 'Yours to open, Maurice,' she smiled. He noticed that she had to raise her voice a few decibels to make herself heard. He guessed she probably didn't realise it. She would be used to it. As Thatcher popped the cork from the bottle, the noise was almost masked by the din of a steam-hammer opposite. He poured the champagne as Elaine stepped forward, holding the glasses. His nostrils were assailed by the pleasant fragrance of her perfume. A different one to that on Concorde.

'Good luck!' Elaine looked into Thatcher's eyes, as she raised her glass. Her eyes suggested to him that this wasn't her first drink of the afternoon. Thatcher clinked glasses, smiled and took a gulp. He breathed in at the wrong moment and half choked, quickly putting down his glass, as he spluttered for a few seconds.

'Goodness gracious,' Elaine rested her hand on his back, 'are you all right?'

'Sorry about that.' He nodded as he regained his breath.

Elaine smiled and as Thatcher picked up his glass again, she refilled the glasses and linking his arm turned them both to look over the balcony. 'I didn't know being alone with me would make you so nervous,' she said, gazing out over the rooftops of Manhattan.

Thatcher looked at her with surprise. 'Nervous?' he asked, 'I'm not nervous. The thought of being alone with you fills me with nothing but pleasure, I do assure you. Certainly not nerves.'

Elaine rested her chin on Thatcher's arm and looking at him from under her eyelids, whispered, 'Good.'

'When did you say Frank would be back in town?' Thatcher watched the cable car rising gently from its 2nd Avenue station on its short journey over to Roosevelt Island. The sun glinted on its roof.

'At the weekend. He flies in two o'clock, Saturday. I'm all yours, until then.'

Thatcher could hear the lightness in Elaine's voice, but it was contradicted by the firm pressure of her shoulder as she held his arm. 'Isn't it lovely out here?'

'Elaine!' Thatcher laughed, involuntarily. 'It's terrible!'

She swung round and stared at him, open-mouthed. 'Terrible?' Thatcher realised he would not be able to explain his meaning without upsetting her and smiled blandly.

'I was teasing! I was teasing! It's absolutely splendid,' he assured her.

'Good,' Elaine turned and gulping her champagne, refilled their glasses.

'Here,' Thatcher pretended to withdraw his glass, 'that's enough!'

'Rubbish!' Elaine leaned on the balcony rail. 'I drink a bottle on my own easily, so we can certainly drink one between us.'

'A bottle on your own?' Thatcher frowned at her, pointedly.

'Sure,' she laughed at him. 'Often.'

The ear-piercing sound of several car-horns interrupted the conversation, as they both involuntarily watched impatient vehicles on 2nd Avenue try and circumvent a traffic-blocking queue on the corner of 67th Street. The sun was now throwing lengthy shadows across the streets.

'Why does it matter to you what I drink, anyway?' Elaine's voice was flat and portrayed petulance.

Thatcher looked down at his glass. He felt he didn't need to reply.

'Are you happily married, Maurice?'

The question caught him unawares. He felt his cheeks begin to burn. 'Of course,' he replied.

'Of course,' Elaine mimicked him, 'Of course. I guess I shouldn't have expected any other reply. The terribly British parry of a response! True or untrue, one shouldn't expect any other response, should one?' Her voice was now sounding shrill.

'But it's true.' Thatcher replied quietly.

'Is it? Is it really?' Elaine mocked. 'Don't you have affairs? Doesn't Pat "play around" while you're away? Are you trying to tell me you're both faithful, till death us do part? Neither of you give me that impression.'

Thatcher stared at the brown brick building opposite.

'Whether we are or not, doesn't in itself prove that we're not happily married.'

Elaine turned back for the champagne. 'That's true,' she nodded quietly, 'Accommodation of each other and travelling the world alone some of the time, could keep you happily married. Gives you both – space.'

'What's the problem, Elaine?' Thatcher could feel the champagne relaxing him. There was a long pause.

'Just that, Maurice, that's all,' Elaine replied dully. 'I'm not.'

'Oh, come on!' he protested, waving his arm dismissively, 'You haven't been married to Frank for longer than...'

'What the hell's time got to do with it?' Elaine interrupted. 'Anyway, three years is a long time, for me!' Her shoulders slumped over the balcony. 'What's the matter with me, Maurice? Married four times and I've still not found the right man. Money, career, travel, fame if you like, but happiness? Forget it! I guess I'm just bad at choosing and I don't learn from my mistakes. One a drunk; one jealous of my success; one as queer as an eight-cent piece, and now, Frank.' She threw her hair back.

Thatcher turned and put his glass down. A police siren erupted below them, moving south. 'Now Frank?' he repeated.

Elaine nodded, without looking at him. 'He beats me.'

'He what?'

'He beats me! He beats me! He beats me!' She began to sob, quietly.

Thatcher instinctively put a hand round her shoulder and she turned, burying her face in his chest. Her body shook gently and he could feel her warm tears soak his shirt.

'Elaine. Oh, Elaine,' he whispered. 'I'm so sorry.'

She shook her head and pulling herself together, dried her eyes. 'Most of the time he's fine,' she blinked tears away. 'He runs his worldwide chain of companies extremely efficiently. You know all about them in your line of business. He can be charming, amusing, exhilarating, fascinating. But...' she paused, twisting the stem of her glass, 'he has this frightful, uncontrollable temper. And he only seems to lose it with me! Obviously I don't see him all the time, but I've never seen it displayed with anyone else. Ruthless in business, yes, but that's

154

different. With me he ... he just goes bananas! Over trivial things – if his clothes haven't been to the cleaners; if I've forgotten to buy something he wants; if the flowers haven't been thrown out when they're dying. Maurice, I'm so frightened of him!'

Elaine's strained face looked up, the tears glistening in her eyes.

'What happens?' Thatcher led her over to a chair and sat her down and then dropped into the one the other side of the table. 'What happens?' he repeated.

'He just lets fly,' Elaine replied simply. 'Back of the hand, clenched fist. Always hard enough to knock me down. Then the blows keep raining down until its out of his system.'

'But,' Thatcher stared at her, horrified, 'doesn't he realise what he's doing? Doesn't he realise he could injure you or that you could leave him?'

Elaine nodded glumly, 'Oh he's always very contrite afterwards. It's no good though, Maurice, I can't take it any more. It's a living hell when we're alone. I spend all my time wondering when it's going to happen again. It's awful. Awful.'

She thumbed away some tears on her cheeks, causing mascara runs to become smudges.

Thatcher rose and coming round the table dropped on his haunches in front of her. He pulled her head towards him in an attempt to stem any more tears, but as he did so Elaine blushed and smiling weakly, reversed the action and took Thatcher's head between her beautifully manicured hands and kissed him long and warmly on the lips. With difficulty, and a little reluctance, he forced her away.

'Oh, Maurice,' she whispered, 'You're such a nice person. So full of warmth. I need someone like you.'

'Now come on, Elaine,' Thatcher's voice sounded parched as he wrestled with the situation, which was rapidly becoming beyond his control.

'What's the matter, Maurice?' Elaine asked woefully, stroking his hair. 'Don't you find me attractive? Am I only attractive to the second-rate men in the world? The ones who can't love me as I want to be loved? Is it me, Maurice?' she sighed. 'Is it me?'

'Of course it isn't you!' Thatcher instinctively put a hand round her shoulders and her head came forward, so that they were held together cheek to cheek. Suddenly Thatcher found himself hauled to his feet as Elaine stood up and threw back the hair that had fallen over her face. The mood was broken.

'I'm sorry. Forget it. Let's have another bottle.' Without waiting for a response Elaine disappeared through the open door.

Thatcher took a deep breath and mentally shook himself. This was such a bizarre, unexpected turn of events that he couldn't help but think if he wasn't careful he could become involved in something rather messy. And he didn't need it at the moment. Certainly not at the moment. To be the confidant of one party of an unhappy marriage was one thing, but the woman normally confides in another woman, surely not a man who is not really much more than a passing acquaintance. He had done nothing to start that outburst, had he? Why saddle me with it, he thought angrily. I only came round for a bloody drink! He calmed down almost immediately. Elaine was frightened. She was tired from the journey, a little tipsy ... and very beautiful.

She really was very beautiful. Her make-up – not at all exaggerating her features – had been impeccable. Until the tears. A well-groomed lady. A well-groomed, beautiful, lady.

'There, that's better!' Elaine reappeared. She had repaired her make-up and, Thatcher guessed, had quickly brushed her hair and by the brightness of her eyes quickly bathed them too. No-one would have guessed the scene of a few minutes ago. Thatcher couldn't fail but remind himself that she was a renowned actress. Had it all been an act? Preposterous! Why? For his benefit? There was no point.

He realised that Elaine was standing coquettishly in front of him, hands held behind her back, smiling roguishly. He frowned as he realised that she was waiting for his move and he didn't know what it was.

'The bottle, Maurice. The bottle.' Elaine held another bottle of champagne up above her head in triumph.

'Oh, no,' Thatcher balked, 'I don't think so. We've had

156

enough.' He took it from her and put it on the table next to the empty one. A repeat performance of a few minutes ago had no appeal to him.

'Rubbish,' Elaine shook her head firmly. 'I haven't started yet.'

'Well, I've finished,' Thatcher replied resolutely. 'You carry on if you wish, but not with me. I'm happy to open it for you.'

'Maurice, you're a pain in the arse!' Elaine suddenly seemed to lose all of her newly found vivacity and dropped heavily into the nearest chair. 'I want to get drunk!' she complained. 'Don't you understand, I want to get drunk!'

Thatcher momentarily thought of Pat. Was she getting drunk somewhere? Who was she with at this moment? He brought himself back to New York with some difficulty. He looked down at Elaine who was staring unblinking straight ahead, elbows on her knees. 'Look,' he gently touched her shoulder, 'We arranged to have dinner tonight. Why don't I leave you for an hour or so, pick you up at say...' He checked his watch, it showed a quarter past six, 'seven forty-five? I'll book a restaurant, I know one or two, and we'll take it from there?.'

Elaine looked up at him flatly. Her face showed no expression. 'Fine,' she replied, standing up. 'I'll see you out and perhaps you'll pick me up later.' Thatcher was surprised at the way her mood had changed again. Calm, subservient. No argument, no enthusiasm, no nothing. Was this another scene from another play? He kissed her on the cheek, as she watched him let himself out, without another word. Downstairs the black doorman waved him farewell.

'Now youse have a good evenin', sah,' he waved in a half salute as he hurried to open the door. Thatcher stepped out into the fading light. Pedestrians were scurrying by. Rabbits returning to their burrows? A young negro on roller skates flashed by, carrying a blazing radio. He ducked and dived across the road through the slow-moving traffic, overtaking it with the ease he had overtaken Thatcher. Thatcher watched him mount the opposite pavement, almost bump into a man looking in the window of a large furniture store and then disappear round the corner.

157

Thatcher's attention went back to the man looking in the store's window. The man interested Thatcher. It was the young man in jeans from the Concorde flight. Thatcher walked on. As he looked back on reaching the corner of 3rd Avenue the young man was leisurely making his way in Thatcher's general direction. Thatcher's head began to pound slightly. Was this a coincidence, or was he being tailed? He had never been tailed in his life before and if this was the first time he certainly wasn't going to make it easy. He hailed a passing cab.

'Grand Central Station.'

Thatcher had no wish to go to Grand Central Station, but couldn't think of anywhere else near enough to his hotel where he would stand a chance of losing someone. If, of course, there was anyone to lose. He looked back over his shoulder, but it was impossible to tell whether the young man had followed him. There were yellow cabs behind him as far as his eye could see.

Thatcher paid off the black driver, who hadn't opened his mouth, except to chew his gum, and joined the throng of commuters making their way into the bowels of the station concourse. The atmosphere was almost reverential. Like Sacre Coeur in Paris or Westminster Cathedral in London. There was a general hush as people weaved their way forward. No voices were raised, no undignified speed of movement, as platforms were sought, companions found. Thatcher couldn't help but feel that an array of candles wouldn't have been out of place. Maybe to Saint Christopher?

In a controlled, measured way, he made his way through the concourse and along the seedy alley of shops out into 42nd Street. He stood in the doorway of a nearby record shop, waiting to see if the young man followed him out. He stared at the advertisements proclaiming the latest records of Lionel Ritchie and Shirley Bassey until he knew the blurbs by heart. No one he knew appeared. Slowly, he wound his way back to the hotel, occasionally stopping to look in windows and surreptitiously looking behind him, but nothing untoward disturbed him. The doorman saluted him at the hotel, with no smile, no sign of recognition. Thatcher pushed through the heavy, reluctant, revolving doors.

The young man in jeans was sitting in the foyer reading a newspaper.

Thatcher realised at once that that would have been the obvious move, if it was known where he was staying and the tail had lost him. Irritated, because he didn't know whether to be worried or not, he made his way to his room. The young man hadn't moved by the time the lift doors had closed. Why was he worried about being followed anyway? It was presumably for his own good. It was just that it was all so different from his normal existence. His thoughts were interrupted as he noticed the message light flashing on his bedside telephone. The operator, in a very bored voice, informed him that Mrs Thatcher had rung.

He threw off his jacket and tie and in the bathroom sluiced his face and gargled. Feeling slightly refreshed he sat on the bed and pushbuttoned his way home.

'Hallo?' Pat's voice sounded unusually strained.

'Darling, it's Maurice.'

'Oh, you got my message? Did you have a good flight?' Her voice had relaxed slightly.

'Yes, fine thanks.' Pat didn't normally phone to learn if he'd had a good flight. 'Everything all right?'

'Yes,' the reply was not convincing. 'It's a lovely day here. Went over to see Mother this morning and she seems better this week, thank goodness.' Then it came, 'Maurice, I think I'm being followed! I know it sounds crazy, but I'm sure I am!'

The temperature in Thatcher's room seemed suddenly to rise, although he could still hear the air-conditioning working.

'What?'

'I know. I know,' Pat sounded impatient. 'I knew you'd think I was mad. But it's true! I did some shopping after I'd been to Mother's and called in to the golf club before dropping in to Kay and each time I've been followed by a blue Corolla.'

'A blue Corolla?' Thatcher laughed uneasily. 'Darling, there must be thousands of blue Corollas.'

'Yes,' replied Pat, 'But they don't all have the number 747 in their registration. I noticed it parked up the road as I passed it early on and you know I've always been interested in registration numbers. I noticed the 747 and thought how inappropriate it was that this time you weren't going by Jumbo. That's all. As simple as that. And 747,' she added agitatedly, 'has been with me ever since.'

Thatcher's brain was in a whirl. Pat tailed? A tail on him he could understand – just – but why Pat? Surely she was mistaken, but he feared – God, he feared – she wasn't.

'Well,' he tried to sound lighthearted, 'if anyone is trying to find out when the house is empty to burgle it, they'll be surprised by our sophisticated burglar alarms. Don't worry darling, if you are right I'm sure it's not you personally they're interested in. Just go about your business as normal and keep Charles around you, but,' he added thoughtfully, 'don't tell him about it. It's better he's just around, without getting that limited brainpower of his overworked. Just get him to drive you, although, I know, you prefer to drive yourself.'

There was a pause at the other end. 'Yes, all right,' Pat sounded slightly mollified, 'at least you're not laughing.'

'No,' Thatcher assured her, sounding as cheerful as he could, 'I'm not laughing, but don't worry about it. I think you're mistaken, but you keep people around you and leave the house to our sophisticated devices. Just make sure they're switched on if the house is empty and when you go to bed.'

'God, it's not empty. Malcolm's still here for a start! Don't you think I should tell the police?' Pat asked.

'No way!' Thatcher realised he had overreacted and tried to sound confident. 'Not at this stage. Leave it in my hands. I'll have a word with the office security officer. Leave it to me and don't worry.'

'All right,' Pat replied. 'Everything all right with you?'

'Yes, fine,' Thatcher assured her. 'Nothing to report.'

'OK darling,' Pat sounded slightly more at ease, 'keep in touch. Love you. See you soon.'

'Bye.' As he replaced the receiver, Thatcher realised he hadn't mentioned meeting Elaine. Just as well. His mind was trying to absorb and deal with an awful lot of unusual happenings. Thatcher pulled back the bed cover and taking his shoes off lay down. The pillow felt crisp and cool at the back of his neck. He closed his eyes. Control. What was needed was control. He breathed in and out deeply several times and then tried to let his whole body relax. What a time he was having. Time! Thatcher suddenly looked at his watch. He hadn't booked a restaurant! The Dove Cote had one table left. It was nearly time to leave again after his absurd detour to Grand Central Station. He quickly ran his razor over his face, splashed on some after shave and prepared to leave. He hesitated at the door and looked back round the room. He mentally took note of where everything was. Just in case the room had an uninvited visitor, he placed several small grapes from his fruit bowl in the deep-pile carpet inside the door. As he left the room he hung the Do Not Disturb sign outside.

Elaine had changed in every sense. There was no sign of the earlier upset or the subdued Elaine. She was back to the vivacious, vital girl. She was now wearing a classic cream silk blouse with a large deep-red bow matching her calf-length flared red skirt. Thatcher smiled at her appreciatively. 'You look gorgeous,' he commented as she picked up her wrap and locked the apartment.

'Of course,' Elaine sang over her shoulder, 'I'm going out with the best-looking man in town. I have to look gorgeous.'

With superficial banter they strolled their way to the restaurant. It was only two blocks away. The night was mild and it was a pleasant walk. Elaine had tucked her arm in Thatcher's and began telling him all about the rehearsals for the new play she was in. She hoped it would be a Broadway hit, of course. As they crossed Lexington Avenue, Thatcher relaxed for the first time in the last two hours. He liked New York and he was with a beautiful woman. He was decidedly going to do his best to enjoy himself. For now.

At the restaurant they were greeted by a suave young man, somehow incongruously dressed in a light fawn suit who, having checked the name, led them upstairs and handed them over with a 'Have a good evening' to a more formally dressed head waiter. The restaurant was only half full. The walls of open brickwork were partly adorned with hanging baskets of ferns and ceiling-high mirrors, cleverly suggesting alcoves that didn't exist. The atmosphere was relaxed gentility. The immediately attendant wine waiter was despatched to deal with two champagne cocktails, at Thatcher's request.

'This is more like it,' Thatcher smiled as the menus were presented to them.

There was a mirror immediately behind Elaine and he could thus, by merely swivelling his eyes, look at her from a front view or a back view. He decided she looked delicious from either angle and devoured the view in the mirror.

'Stop eyeing my bumsy daisy,' Elaine reproached him mockingly, after the drinks had been served.

'What an extraordinary description.' Thatcher raised his glass.

'My mother's,' Elaine replied simply. 'She tries to be with it, but can't say bum or arse. I guess she's just behind the times.' She raised her glass and chuckled. 'That's a rather clever pun!'

Dinner was chosen, wine was chosen, but the flower-seller threading her way through the tables was not so lucky.

'Definitely not, Maurice. Sweet as you are. Thank you, but a waste of money. At the end of the meal I'll forget them and they'll probably be half dead anyway.'

'Like us?' Thatcher smiled.

'I sincerely hope not!' Elaine retorted, as four elderly people were shown to the next table.

'The evening's young and you'd better be.'

'Is that a promise?' Thatcher grinned.

Elaine looked searchingly into his eyes, a smile playing her lips.

'That's for you to find out later.'

'A tingling sensation ran down Thatcher's spine. 'I see,' he said, knowing that he didn't.

The restaurant filled and waiters hovering discreetly, ensured a smooth transference from smoked salmon to roast best end of lamb to mango pavlova fragrantly enhanced with a Californian chardonnay. Soft laughter abounded and Thatcher relaxed in a way he would not have believed possible an hour earlier. Elaine laughed and joked, amusing him with theatrical anecdotes that

162

he had never heard before. He noticed her surreptitiously look at the Cartier watch on her slim wrist, and before raising her coffee cup, she commented on the late hour.

'Maurice, this has been a wonderful evening,' she smiled happily. 'Come back for a nightcap.'

'No...' Thatcher began to protest.

'I insist.' Elaine laid a hand on his. 'It's the least I can do. Now, while I disappear for a moment, I will allow you the doubtful pleasure of settling the bill.'

Thatcher rose as Elaine, acknowledging the waiter's help in pulling the table forward, swept away. The bill was a little breathtaking, as Thatcher proffered one of his credit cards, but such an enjoyable evening could not be too expensive.

'All right?' Elaine had returned, refreshed and perfumed.

With smiling pleasantries they were shown out, to a still, warm evening. They strolled back. New York was still very much alive. Busy pizza and hamburger joints; delicatessens; shops were open everywhere, with their neon lights colouring the night sky. Street-corner flower stalls, and news-stands, lit by bare lightbulbs, were surprisingly busy. Cars hadn't disappeared either nor had their horns become muted. Above, the blackness was intensified by the strips of office lights, where they were still burning in skyscrapers lost in the night sky.

'I love it here,' Elaine remarked as they reached her apartment. 'It never sleeps. London dies. London can be killing. It hasn't the propensity to live that New York has.'

Elaine threw her jacket over a chair and turned on the radio to a Cole Porter melody.

'Great,' she remarked, as she disappeared into the kitchen. 'Sit on the settee. I won't be a moment.'

Thatcher sank into the luxurious cushions as Elaine came out with a tray.

'Now, what will be your pleasure?'

'Oh, Elaine, I really don't think I want anything,' Thatcher protested vainly.

'Nonsense, have a bourbon on the rocks,' she replied and proceeded to pour one without more ado, pushing one shoe off, followed by the other.

'OK, plenty of ice then, please,' Thatcher sighed, shaking his head.

Seconds later they clinked glasses and Thatcher felt the warm strength of the liquor envelop him. Elaine sighed contentedly and leaning back, managed to pull her skirt above her knees, displaying an elegantly hosed thigh.

Thatcher stirred uneasily as he looked up at her face. She was running the glass along her cheek watching him with an amused smile.

'Do you fancy me, Maurice?' she asked softly. Her left hand began to stroke his thigh gently as she leaned into him. He could feel her warmth and her perfume was captivating.

'Now, Elaine!' Thatcher leaned forward putting down his drink with the intention of remonstrating, but Elaine, who had also put her glass down, caught him unawares, as he turned to her. Her hands slid round his neck and she kissed him long and hard, working her head from side to side with intensity. Passion overcame Thatcher as she relaxed for a moment and leaned her forehead against his. The fire in him had been stirred and the moment of fighting had come and gone. He slid one arm round her shoulders and cupped a breast with the other. There was no resistance as he pulled her towards him. Elaine's face fell back, eyes closed as he kissed her. Her free hand ran through his hair and then caressed his cheek, whilst the other dug into his back. He slowly undid the top of her blouse and slid his hand inside. He found the top of her bra and easing a breast out, kneaded it gently.

'Oh, Maurice,' she whispered, 'Please, please, come to bed.'

Thatcher stared at her beautiful face. 'Elaine, this is not good news,' but he knew it was a false protest. He was already lost. She rose and led him by the hand to the bedroom. A shaft of light from the sitting room was enough illumination as she quickly pulled down the coverlet. She stroked Thatcher's hands as she walked round the bed and opened the patio door to the balcony. Manhattan's sounds immediately intruded. However, Elaine was by now undoing her skirt, letting it fall to the floor. Thatcher undressed, his heart thumping, as his desire heightened at the sight of red silk bra and panties being removed.

164

For a few seconds, Elaine stood proudly naked, except for her stockings and suspender belt, before sliding sensuously between the silk sheets.

'Hurry,' she whispered.

As Thatcher slid in beside her he noticed Elaine look at the glowing digital clock on the bedside table.

'It's not midnight, so Cinderella is safe at the moment,' he remarked.

She looked round at him surprised and then laughed gently as she moved to him. 'This Cinders has found her Prince Charming,' she whispered 'And it's control she's lost, not a shoe!' But wait a minute,' she stroked his chest, 'would you like a Kir Royale? There's some champagne open.'

'I couldn't drink any more,' Thatcher kissed her hair.

'Oh, you don't have to drink it, darling,' Elaine sat up and slid out of bed, throwing back the sheet. 'Just hold on, if you can,' she whispered.

Thatcher lay back conscious of his erect member caught in all its glory by the shaft of light.

'Aha!' Elaine returned with a bottle in each hand and looked down before kneeling on the bed at his side. 'Now first a little cassis,' she murmured and to Thatcher's astonishment, poured the cassis over his pubic region. He couldn't begin to control what was happening.

'What ... ?'

'Ssh, darling,' she chided him, 'Kir Royale, remember?' She then put down the cassis bottle and turning back slowly poured champagne over him. He could feel it running between his thighs as he heard the fizz of the bubbles on his groin. Elaine dropped the bottle as she went down on him, and whispered, 'This drink is on you, darling.' He gasped and moaned, not believing what he was experiencing. Certainly not with Elaine.

Suddenly Thatcher found her legs entwining him and they feverishly explored and caressed each other. He kissed her neck moving slowly down to her breasts. Her nipples were enlarged and proud as he moved from one to the other. He moaned as her nails raked his back and finally she climbed on top of him and guided him in. They made magical, overwhelming love,

165

perspiration becoming a moist bond between them. They climaxed in unison and lay locked together, no words passing.

Finally Thatcher fell back on the pillow as Elaine turned over and kissed his chest.

'That was wonderful, my darling,' she whispered softly. 'Wonderful.'

Thatcher smiled and closed his eyes. He felt Elaine moving and easing herself out of the bed. He turned and watched her pull on a silk robe, tying a bow at the waist. At that moment they both heard the front door open and then close loudly.

'Honey? Are you there?' A melodious, deep southern voice called out gently.

'Christ, it's Frank!' Elaine whispered. 'He wasn't supposed to be back tonight! Get dressed and get out on the balcony! I'll tell him we're just back from dinner and having a drink outside.' She pointed to the patio door. 'The glasses are there from earlier! Hi, darling!' She raised her voice, as she went out closing the bedroom door firmly behind her.

Thatcher, his heart hammering against his chest, dressed in record time, fumbling with his tie as, in the half light, he checked himself in the mirror and then quickly combed his hair. Quietly he let himself out on to the balcony. Finding a glass, he leaned over the rail and tried to appear normal. He felt anything but normal!

Elaine had clearly managed to delay Frank somehow. Voices were muted. She came out from the sitting room. 'Frank's in the bathroom – I've told him I've changed because I spilled some food over my skirt and blouse and I'm going to bed while you two have a chat.' Loudly she called, 'Frank, darling, out here!' She held out her hand theatrically to him as Frank emerged.

Frank was a tall, overweight, man with thick blonde hair. His rimless glasses were resting uneasily on a bulbous roman nose. He came forward and shook Thatcher's hand enthusiastically.

'Maurice, how great to see you! How's yer been?' He closed his left hand over the top of Maurice's arm.

'Fine, Frank, thank you. Busy, of course, but that's nothing to complain about.' Thatcher tried hard to appear relaxed.

166

'Sure thing,' Frank Sorretto beamed.

'Well, boys,' Elaine placed a hand on each of their chests, 'forgive me, I've got a little bit of a headache and I'm going to bed. Maurice, thank you for a lovely evening. Do keep in touch, and Frank, darling, don't be long.' She kissed Thatcher on the cheek and disappeared through the glass door that Thatcher had had the sense to close, as the men made their polite responses.

'Lovely lady,' Thatcher turned to the balcony.

'And mine,' Sorretto lit up a cigarette without offering one.

'Absolutely,' Thatcher nodded, continuing to sweep the Manhattan skyline.

'So forgive me, Maurice, but what brings you to town so urgently, apart from bedding my wife?' Sorretto stood leaning against the wall of the apartment.

Thatcher turned and stared at him, 'What do you mean, Frank?'

'You stink of her fuckin' perfume and she's got nothin' on under her goddamn robe! That's what I mean!'

'Frank,' Thatcher stood up from the balcony and put his glass down, 'you received a message to be here tomorrow?'

'There was a silence, before, 'What's that to you?'

Thatcher breathed deeply, as he looked at a very belligerent face. 'What was the message, Frank? Was it to return home and someone would call you about a matter of life and death?'

Again, as well as the glare, a pause before, 'Yup,' came the spit of a reply.

'Well, I'm the caller, Frank. My instructions were to call on you tomorrow, but I hadn't allowed for meeting Elaine at Heathrow. I know it doesn't help, but this was all unplanned.' Thatcher walked passed Sorretto into the sitting room.

'Hoo-fuckin' ray.' Sorretto followed him in. 'Well, speak up or shut up and get the hell out of here.'

Thatcher sat down to gather his wits. Sorretto stood over him, dragging on his cigarette belligerently.

'In the wall safe behind that Picasso, Frank, you have bearer bonds worth a few million dollars. I want them now and in exchange you will be able to lock away, or destroy I shouldn't wonder, the video of you and little Annie. The little Annie in that downtown "house" here in New York which you frequented a few years ago, Frank. The little Annie you killed, Frank.'

There was an eerie silence that hung in the room. The silence was not echoed in the busy streets below. It made it seem even more telling.

'What?' Finally Sorretto stubbed out his cigarette at the mantelpiece and sat down heavily. Thatcher allowed the silence to take hold again for a few seconds.

'Well, I'm sure this is a great shock to you, Frank,' Thatcher paused. 'Your little escapades years ago with young girls might not have been all that remarkable, but you did occasionally hit them very hard and I'm sure you remember poor little Annie.'

'What the hell do you know about it all?' Sorretto spat out.

'All that is necessary,' Thatcher smiled. 'All that is necessary.'

There was further silence, that Thatcher would not break, before Sorretto's shoulders sagged forward towards his knees. Arms crossed his chest, his head was addressing the floor. 'It was a fuckin' accident. I didn't mean to kill her.' It was almost a plea.

'But you did kill her, Frank,' Thatcher replied. 'You smashed her with those lovely fists of yours – you beat her senseless and then you realised your manic compulsion to hurt had gone too far. You exterminated her.'

'I paid hugely for the cover-up,' Sorretto muttered, shaking his head.

'Oh, you did, Frank,' Thatcher nodded. 'To the police she was just another fifteen-year-old, conveniently found on the street. No money, no papers, no life – a death statistic. Forgotten inside a couple of hours.'

'So?' Sorretto lit another cigarette.

'The house – a very up-market place, I understand – went out of business, but not before business interests from elsewhere had bought the video recording of the episode. You didn't know the room was set up for filming, Frank?' When there was no reply, Thatcher continued, 'A little naive, but people can be very blind sometimes, can't they? Anyway, never mind all that. Your past is secure if I leave here with the bearer bonds. The video

168

original and the only copy I'm told – will be delivered by messenger, soon after.'

'How do I know all of this isn't just bullshit?' Sorretto rasped, his nostrils flaring.

'A still from the video, which I must add, I haven't enjoyed carrying, might impress you?' Thatcher pulled out his wallet and handed over a print.

One look appeared to be enough for Sorretto. 'How do I know that this isn't the beginning of a bleed to death – that I'll get the tape?' he asked, as he set the print alight with his lighter.

'You don't,' Thatcher replied, 'but I'm told to assure you this is a one-off deal and it will then all be over. I'm to point out that my clients could have done this at any time in the past, but now is the time it suits them. Now – not before, nor later.'

Sorretto rose unsteadily, and walking slowly across the room, he slid the Piccasso to one side and with his back firmly to Thatcher, played with the combination until the small steel door of the safe swung open. After a few moments the safe disappeared again behind the painting.

'How did anyone know these were here?' Sorretto asked as he handed over a thick manilla envelope.

'I know next to nothing about this,' said Thatcher, 'but it has been a long well-thought-out operation. Time uncovers a lot.'

'Why are you involved? No! Forget it! I don't give a shit about you. Just get the hell outa here before I throw up at the sight of you!'

Thatcher went without another word, holding the envelope closely to his chest. The night doorman, standing on the sidewalk, watched as Thatcher came out, crossed the street and passed a darkened doorway. As he told the New York police a short while later, it was all over in a flash. A Caucasian had stepped out and appeared to start a conversation and then must have knifed the visitor to the apartments, who fell forward and slumped down the legs of the attacker. The assassin seemed to wrench a package from the dying man's hands, with difficulty. He then ran off. He couldn't give chase. No, sir. Not with his artificial leg from Nam. He'd just called the police and gone to see if he could help the poor son of a bitch. He couldn't, of course, and had just picked up the video by the man's body, when the patrol car appeared with its sirens blazing. Another New York mugging. Another murder. Another crime statistic. What the hell, buddy. What's new?

11

Paris, June 1988

Gorman enjoyed the luxury of The Grand. It was not his everyday hotel experience. The bottle of champagne and the basket of fruit that had greeted him in his room had been very acceptable. He grimaced. Jenny would have raved about the marble bathroom and all the complimentary toiletries – even a man couldn't fail to be impressed by the sumptuousness of it all. He had been told that during the Second World War, nearby buildings had been used as the Paris headquarters of the Gestapo. It was hard to imagine now. Bejewelled, rasping American widows; bowing and respectful Japanese business-men, and even a few wealthy-looking English, roamed the laby-rinth of thickly carpeted corridors.

The previous evening Gorman had wandered through the Place Vendôme, admiring the elegant shops and buildings as he made his way through to the strolling Parisians along the Rue St Honoré. Later he had dined at Café L'Opéra where he had relaxed and enjoyed a superb meal. Determined to make the most of the time he had to himself, he had then hailed a taxi and gone up to Montmartre to see the interesting, seamy side of Paris. Neon lights had beckoned everywhere. Strip clubs, book shops, burlesque shows, had all been touting for business. Bored men had called out to him from each establishment and he had finally followed two laughing American couples into one of the more respectable-looking clubs. Photos of large bare-breasted women in G-strings had adorned the foyer, as he had

171

paid his hundred francs entrance fee. He had stayed for an hour, quietly drinking, watching the strip show and refusing the occasionally offered attentions of the hostesses. No-one had really bothered him and it had all been very inoffensive. He had been to far worse, or better, places, depending on the point of view. But the evening was not for getting drunk or whoring – it was for enduring – until the next day's assignment. Gorman was back in his room, asleep, before midnight.

Gorman picked up a *Herald Tribune* and had breakfast in the beautiful lobby area. He was surprised at the number of French people who seemed to have come in for breakfast, but then realised that most of them were meeting people staying in the hotel and having business meetings at the same time. At least, thank the Lord, he was spared that! He checked his watch. Only nine-fifteen. His meeting wasn't until ten. He wandered slowly round the ground floor, and aimlessly looked in the windows of the expensive hotel shops. The opulence reminded Gorman of books he had read on bygone eras.

It seemed easier to reflect on the glories of past centuries in Paris than London. Gorman guessed the Blitz during the Second World War had changed the face of London in a way that Paris had escaped. Paris had suffered in other ways. The foyer was buzzing with guests arranging tours, using their safe deposit boxes, making internal house calls and exchanging currencies. He stood for a moment by the lifts waiting for one to come and smiled at a very pretty redhead getting out. She didn't smile back. Gorman was pleased to find his room had already been serviced and he ordered coffee and biscuits for two. He didn't have long to wait before the phone rang.

'Mr Gorman? My name is Schmidt.' The voice had a strong Afrikaans accent. 'I believe you are expecting me.'

'Yes, please come up. I am in room 312,' Gorman replied. Replacing the receiver he went and sluiced his face with cold water and checked himself in the mirror. He looked totally relaxed and assured, and he felt it. A few minutes later there was a peremptory knock on the door. Gorman opened it to see an elderly, heavy, thick-set man with a grey crewcut standing there. He was all of six feet six inches tall. He was wearing an

172

immaculate grey suit and Gorman imagined everything that Schmidt wore was custom made. He exhibited self-assurance and wealth as he passed Gorman and strode to the ornate marble fireplace.

'Do please have a seat,' Gorman gestured towards the settee.

'Thank you,' Schmidt lowered himself into the seat, but had still to smile. There had been no attempt to shake hands.

'It was good of you to come,' Gorman sat down opposite. 'I have ordered some coffee.'

'Mr Gorman, I am not here for coffee, but because I am intrigued. You appear to know that I am often in Paris on business and therefore I was prepared to meet you, following your fax to me in Johannesburg.'

Gorman had never met an Afrikaaner before. He couldn't remember meeting any kind of South African come to that and he was fascinated by the way the words came out clipped and guttural.

'What exactly do you want, Mr Gorman?' The voice was relaxed, but slightly impatient, as if Schmidt was dealing with a recalcitrant employee.

Gorman nodded, 'Well Mr Schmidt, as I said in my fax, I am in the brewery business too and I thought the opportunity of our meeting in Paris shouldn't be missed. We can do business together.'

At that moment coffee arrived and it was a couple of minutes before Gorman returned to his seat. Schmidt smiled at him humourlessly, 'What you say is perhaps interesting, but I don't want to sell or buy any brewery, Mr Gorman. I have enough on my plate, apart from my brewery, with my mines and my English newspaper. Why should we meet? What business can we possibly do together?'

'There is a price at which everything is for sale.' Gorman replied easily. 'Everything and everybody.'

Schmidt didn't miss the cue. 'Everybody, Mr Gorman? Why everybody?'

Gorman picked up his coffee and sipped it. 'Well,' he responded, 'Apart from the obvious, when something is sold at a price that has been found to be too good to be refused, the person selling it has, to a lesser extent, of course, been bought at the same time, wouldn't you say?'

'No, I wouldn't,' Schmidt took out a gold cigarette case and lit up a cigarette without offering Gorman one. 'Anyway, I'm not here for philosophical discussions. Do you have anything else to say before I leave for an important appointment?' He had emphasised the word 'important'.

'Yes,' Gorman put down his coffee, and his eyes rested for a moment on the tape recorder on the top of the television. 'The business we can do together, Mr Schmidt, has nothing to do with your breweries, vineyards, mines or newspaper interests. It has to do with you personally. A book – a biography – has been written and I thought you might like to buy it from me before I try and get it published.' Gorman waved his arms expansively. 'It will be a must for the first publisher I choose. No-one but a fool would turn it down.'

'Mr Gorman, I am not a book publisher.' Schmidt slapped his hands on his knees and began to rise. 'I am not interested in anyone's literary achievements. If it is as good as you say, I wish you well. Now I must go.'

'Herr Meinen. It is your life story.'

The reaction was limited to Schmidt subsiding slowly back into his seat, but Gorman was content with that.

'I am sorry Mr Gorman? Who is this "Meinen"?' The reply was flat and calm.

'I wouldn't expect you to jump into my arms, acknowledging yourself, Herr Meinen, or should I say SS Oberführer Meinen, or even Mr Schmidt?'

Gorman smiled. There was no response. Schmidt just stared back, unblinking.

'I suggest you just listen, for a few moments, to what I have to say and then we can discuss your interest in the purchase.' Gorman tossed a key on the table.

'This is the key to my safe deposit box and it is worth fifteen million Swiss francs. Inside the box is the microfilm of the typescript, which has now been destroyed. It was too bulky for confidentiality. You have no choice, but to believe that, I'm afraid.'

174

Schmidt studiously crossed his legs, very slowly.

'The biography traces your early childhood in Bavaria, where you were born in 1918, the son of a maidservant and a carpenter. That's ironic, isn't it? Your father, however, was not a very good man – he drank too much. You, however, were surprisingly bright, scholastically. Surprising, because you didn't seem to have to study hard. You had plenty of time for physical activities, sports and terrorising the weaker village children. Oh and of course, the Hitler youth! How you loved the Hitler Youth – the parades, the marching, the uniform. It gave you something you didn't have at home – dignity. Dignity of purpose.

'The systematic training in Nazi ideology and soldiering, led you to know very early on that with your enthusiasm, drive and intelligence, the Nazi party was for you. Why should you accept your poor background as a limit to progress and influence? Why should privileged academics, financiers, businessmen be able to dictate the fortunes of others? A lot of them were Jews, anyway. Miserable creatures that were beneath contempt. You tried, successfully, to join the SS, and when the time came with the advance into Poland, you followed the Wehrmacht and helped set up houses of horror, which together with "house cleaning" of Jews and the intelligentsia, gave you plenty to do. Administering the new German justice for transgressors of the grotesque new order.'

Gorman paused for a moment, but there was no movement from Schmidt. He was as though cast in stone, except for the occasional – very occasional – blink of his expressionless eyes. Gorman continued.

'The world was to see many vile men like you. Never fighting the good fight. Never risking your life. Leave that to the soldiers. Your operations moved into occupied countries, unremittingly. As night followed day, you followed the army. Torturing, terrorising, humiliating, degrading, ordinary men and women. Oh and naturally, if they were unfortunate enough to be Jewish, exterminating them locally, if there were only a few. If there were too many, you arranged the despatching to the camps. You were not only very good at your job, you enjoyed it.' Gorman's voice was cold and controlled.

'Incorporated into the book are statements from former receivers of your earnest attentions, describing how you would smile and laugh at their every agony. Your masters were well pleased with your dedication and you moved ever onward and upward. An SS Obersturmführer rising to be a very young Oberführer. Through Poland, Czechoslovakia, Holland, back to Germany. A success story. The only problem of course was that Germany began to lose the war. It became clear that there was little chance of the reversals being satisfactorily repulsed and the earlier offensives being repeated. Time for a reassessment of the future.'

Their eyes were now locked with antipathy, as Gorman continued.

'It became clear in early 1945 that the war would soon be over and plans were made to help a considerable number of hand-chosen SS officers to disappear. Many went to South America where new identities, new lives, were created for them. Some, however, went to South Africa, to a country that had many German sympathisers. Many who had hated Smuts taking their country into the war on the Allied side and couldn't wait to help people like you disappear into their society. Especially with the fortune that came with you. Gradually, your good business ability brought you ascendancy and here you are today, a very successful businessman. With a past that no-one suspects and one that not even the Israelis have uncovered. Oberführer Meinen disappeared in the rubble of Nazi Germany.'

Schmidt made his first move for several minutes. He took out another cigarette and calmly lit it, watching the smoke drift upwards. 'So?' he replied softly, 'there is a book of fiction. Be careful of the laws of libel, my friend.'

Gorman laughed easily. 'Your South African wife and your children will, I'm sure, be outraged and support you in any action, but,' he leaned forward, 'my dear Herr Meinen, remember we have truth, supported by depositions and photographs, on our side.'

'Depositions? Photographs?' Schmidt sneered, 'Of whom? Some long dead German? What on earth has this man to do with me?'

176

Gorman watched a fly settle fussily on the edge of his chair. Flies in The Grand Hotel? He grinned at Schmidt, but his eyes were cold.

'The evidence is all in the book, my friend. You'll find it fascinating. Your records in the SS were never destroyed, as intended. Everything happened too fast. The records in themselves, of course, didn't indicate your whereabouts. That was much more difficult, but it has been very painstaking work. Your whereabouts have been known for some years, but it hasn't been appropriate to do anything about it until now.'

'Why now?' the words were uttered slowly and deliberately.

'Also,' continued Gorman, ignoring the interruption, 'you have that unfortunate scar on your wrist from the Alsatian dog that turned on you at Krakow when you were rounding up some Jews. Alsatians can be very treacherous animals, can't they? Maybe this one had had a stomachful. Tired of tearing off women's breasts and men's genitals? Who could have blamed it.' Gorman saw Schmidt's right hand instinctively draw back into the sleeve of his jacket.

'And what about my background in South Africa?' Schmidt asked softly.

Gorman nodded, 'Ah, that was very clever. You supposedly came over from South America in 1946, where you had been travelling extensively and conveniently, all during the war. Your parents had been killed there in the twenties and you had been brought up by foster parents in Uruguay, also unfortunately dead. Your "inheritance" inevitably came from Switzerland, the path expertly and confusingly leading backwards, into an apparent void. Filling the void took a lot of hard work. But the work has been done. Read all about it. It's yours for the buying.'

Schmidt pulled on his cigarette and then rolled it between his fingers. A full minute passed. 'Fifteen million Swiss francs?' his eyes bore into Gorman. 'That is quite a lot of money, my friend. Why, and how, did this get pieced together? Who are you representing? You couldn't have done this. You, yourself, said even the Israelis haven't uncovered anything. How could anyone?'

177

A police siren blared its way around the Place de L'Opéra below, as Gorman beamed the smile of the victor.

'Don't worry about all that. I have the story, I have the book and its yours for non publication. If you want it to go ahead, the microfilm will sell for a reasonable sum – maybe not millions, but certainly a sum, which together with the satisfaction of seeing a miserable end to a miserable bastard, will be acceptable. The choice is yours.'

Gorman watched the thin line of cigarette smoke climb upwards, as Schmidt sat, not smoking, in fact seemingly unaware of the cigarette until the ash fell on his trousers and he angrily knocked it on the floor. The action seemed to bring him to a decision. He stubbed out the cigarette and rose to his feet.

'It would appear I have little choice.' His voice purred softly.

Gorman looked up at Schmidt who suddenly seemed to him a colossus of a man, albeit ageing. 'Please don't get any funny peculiar ideas, Mr Schmidt,' he commented. 'The microfilm is downstairs, as I said, but I wasn't quite truthful earlier. There is one other copy. My life insurance, as it were. It will only see the light of day if anything unfortunate happens to me. So you see, you'd better help me stay alive by not dreaming up any retribution after you've paid me. You are going to pay me, aren't you?'

Schmidt's cheeks appeared to become inflamed, as he ran his tongue over his lips. His Adam's apple jumped like a table-tennis ball.

'You had better talk on, Gorman.'

'You are in Europe for a week, I believe,' Gorman rose and wandered over to the French windows, handing Schmidt a piece of paper as he went. 'As soon as you leave here, go and transfer the fifteen million to this account at Banque Credit in Geneva. You can do it. You have more than that on deposit with the same bank here in Paris. It will be known when you have carried out the instructions. Then tomorrow the microfilm will be delivered to you at your hotel.'

'Fifteen million is not going to ruin me, Gorman. Why not more?' Schmidt frowned, 'Why not more?'

Gorman shook his head. 'That is one of the differences

between us,' he replied. 'For us enough is enough. You won't be bothered to try retribution later for that sum and you'll never really know about the second copy, will you?'

Gorman stood, hands in his pockets, as he watched Schmidt open his mouth to speak, but he obviously thought better of it and without a word, buttoned up his jacket and turned and walked slowly from the room. The door did not close behind him and Gorman slowly closed and locked it. With a smile of satisfaction, he stopped the tape recorder and began the rewind. He felt good and finding the pot of coffee still hot, he poured himself another cup and walked back to the window. He undid the brass catch and opened it wide. A blast of noise and warm air hit him. Standing by the very narrow balcony, he could smell the fumes from the traffic, immediately under his window.

Traffic lights and whistling gendarmes were seemingly at odds as to which traffic should be moving. The Paris morning was beautifully hot and sunny. Women and children were strolling along the steps around the opera house. Gorman breathed in deeply. Thank God that was over. No snags. No problems. All according to plan. A gust of wind caught his hair and blew it in his eyes. As he stepped back into the room to put down his coffee, the phone rang shrilly on the desk.

'Hallo?'

'How did it go?' He did not recognise the woman's voice with a French accent.

'Who is that? Gorman frowned at the mirror. His hair was a mess.

'Please!' The voice was sharp now, 'Don't waste precious time. Did he agree?'

'Yes,' Gorman replied carefully. 'Absolutely.'

'Good,' the voice relaxed measurably, 'and the tape? You recorded it all?'

'Yes. The whole meeting.'

'Let me hear it, please. Play me the beginning of it.'

Gorman rested the telephone and checking the recorder as he collected it, he placed it on the desk. He switched the recorder on and placed the telephone next to it. Gorman turned and looked at the open windows, but realised that the

179

throbbing noise down below would not interfere with the tape, due to its proximity to the phone. He idly heard the voice of Schmidt saying, 'I am often in Paris...' and after a few seconds switched it off. Putting the phone to his ear again, he asked, 'Satisfactory?'

'Very,' came the confident reply, 'you know what to do now.'

'Don't put the tape in the safety deposit box,' Gorman replied. 'Seems rather odd to me.'

'Please don't worry yourself.' The voice was soothing now. 'Just carry the tape with you at all times and we will collect it from you in your room at five o'clock tonight. We will then edit it for our purposes. Now you can relax – perhaps go to the Louvre.'

The click told him the conversation was over, and he replaced the receiver. The tape and the key safely in his inside pocket, Gorman wandered out into the hubbub that was Paris. It hadn't been too difficult to get some holiday. He was due a considerable amount and Jenny thought the rest and change would do him good. Gorman decided that in case it was all over very quickly, the first thing should be to go and buy some presents to take home. He knew the boys loved those enormous French lollipops and Jenny, glacé fruits, so the first treat would be of a sugary kind. It was mid-morning and Paris was wide awake. Tourists and Parisians were shop-gazing, strolling in the sun, or earnestly threading their way to meetings, intrigues or pavement cafés. Gorman, his job done, smiled at all the elegantly dressed, pale-faced, beautiful women, but they all ignored him. He mentally shrugged his shoulders. *C'est la vie*, or more appropriately, he thought, *c'est le mort*! He meandered purposefully, though circuitously, past the mouthwatering Fouchards, around La Madeleine and numerous elegant expensive boutiques, until he arrived at Les Printemps in Boulevard Houssman. It was very busy. There was no quarter given. The French, and the Parisian in particular, stood on ceremony for no-one.

Gorman was pushed and jostled as he found and bought the sweets. Satisfied, he turned to make his way out, when he caught the foot of a young woman, who fell to the floor with a startled cry. Several people, including Gorman, stopped to pick her up.

She was about twenty-five, slim, dressed in a blue jersey suit, white stockings and blue shoes, but what really caught his attention was her long auburn hair. It was luxuriously groomed and her perfume knocked him sideways, as he held her by her elbow while she regained her feet.

'*Excusez-moi,*' he stammered in his schoolboy French accent.

She looked at him with her wide blue eyes and hesitatingly smiled, revealing large, even, white teeth.

'Oh, you are English?' She spoke English with that attractive accent that has Englishmen drooling.

'Yes,' he smiled back easily. 'I am so sorry.'

'Please,' she replied, 'It was my fault. I was not looking.'

The other customers, realising no harm had been done, had melted away. Gorman felt as if it were he who had been knocked or maybe bowled over. He had never seen anyone quite so breathtakingly attractive.

'May I buy you a coffee?' he asked impetuously and was delighted when she thanked him and said, yes, she would like that.

'There is a little café I know in Rue Trenchet,' she smiled. 'It is a little less busy there than in here. Shall I lead the way?'

'Please,' Gorman happily fell in next to her, as she made her way out of the store. The mass of people precluded him from talking further, but he was just happy to be in her presence. They crossed at the traffic lights and luckily found a table on the pavement just vacated by a cigar-smoking negro.

'I think this will do.' She smoothed out her skirt as she sat down, smiling up at him. Gorman found it difficult to man-oeuvre his chair to sit down, as ummoving customers seemed to be all round him. The young lady laughed and pulled the table towards her and he managed to squeeze in, rather unceremon-iously, beside her.

'Thanks,' he puffed. 'Not very easy. What will you have?' He placed his packages thankfully on the table.

'Espresso, thank you.'

Gorman nodded, grinning happily. 'My name is Colin Gorman and again, I am sorry for the accident, but I guess in a way I'm not, because otherwise we wouldn't be sitting here.'

181

'Michelle Blot,' she smiled. 'Not quite true for me, as I was coming here, when I fell over.'

The waiter arrived and hovered. 'Two – sorry, *deux espressos, s'il vous plait*'. Gorman watched him move to the next table and shrugged his shoulders.

'I expect he speaks English, too. Thank God nearly everyone does these days.'

Michelle Blot had pulled her skirt up to examine her knees. Gorman didn't fail to examine them either.

'Good,' she exclaimed happily, 'I just wondered if I had...' there was a pause as she searched for the words 'torn my stockings.'

'I would be pleased to buy you some more.' Gorman wondered what Jenny would make of this conversation. Good old Jenny – it wouldn't bother her in the slightest, he thought wryly, too busy peeling spuds or cleaning out hamster cages.

The small cups of coffee arrived and they both peeled the paper off their sugar lumps as Gorman brought himself back to Paris and Michelle Blot.

'Do you work around here?' he asked.

'Oh, no,' she smiled, shaking her head, 'I work in Neuilly, but this week is a week of holiday for me.'

Gorman's pulse quickened as he picked up his cup and proffered it as a gesture of a toast. 'Well, I am pleased to meet you, Madam, Mam'selle?'

'Mam'selle,' was the reply as she smilingly reciprocated, 'and what are you doing here in our lovely city?'

'I am on holiday, too,' Gorman replied and quickly added, 'alone.'

The traffic was heavy now, almost, but not quite, at a standstill, as pedestrians stood impatiently waiting to cross the roads at any opportunity. Some took their lives in their hands and Gorman watched one rather elderly lady, with her Pekinese under her arm, uncompromisingly set out against the red 'No walking' sign at the junction, as the traffic eased slowly forward. A gendarme whistled and gesticulated at her, but she clearly returned his rebuke with a harangue that lasted until she disappeared into the crowd on the other side.

'It would be wonderful if you could show me a little of this beautiful city of yours.' Gorman watched the pedestrians congregate at the roadside once more. 'You wouldn't be free for an hour or two? I hope you don't mind me asking, but I'm a total stranger in town.'

He felt he sounded like a cowboy in a Western movie and he was lying into the bargain. Michelle Blot scrutinised him, as she sipped her coffee. Apparently satisfied, she nodded.

'All right – I am free for a little while,' she nodded. Then she threw back her hair and undoing her handbag examined her face in a small mirror from every angle. Satisfied no action was needed, other than a little deep-red lipstick, she snapped it shut. A delighted Gorman could have told her she looked ravishing, but contented himself with peeling off three ten-franc notes and slipping them under his saucer.

'All right. What would you like to see?' she asked, her bag resting on the table.

'Anything,' Gorman replied, 'it is all new to me. Anywhere convenient to you.'

There was a pause, as she looked straight ahead, contemplatively. Then turning to Gorman, she raised her eyebrows to emphasise the question and asked, 'Shall we go?'

Gorman rose and forgetting his tight predicament, went to push his chair back with the back of his calves but it didn't move and he sat down again knocking the heavy man behind him.

'*Pardon, M'sieur. Pardon.*' Gorman received a frozen stare, as he then more carefully eased himself out, picking up his packages.

'You appear to be a little dangerous,' Michelle Blot remarked lightly, as they extricated themselves from the tables and headed slowly along Rue Tranchet.

Gorman laughed. 'I'm not normally clumsy. It must be Paris.'

'Clumsy?' she frowned. 'What is this "clumsy"? I am afraid I do not know the word.'

'Sorry. Careless? Not careful?'

'Ah, yes.' Changing the subject abruptly, she pointed ahead, 'Perhaps we walk through to Place de la Concorde and along Les Champs Elysées? It is a nice day – not too hot?'

'Fine,' Gorman agreed happily. They talked and strolled past more atrociously expensive shops; several hotels with smoked-glass and marble façades; inconsequential doorways, hiding as Gorman well knew, ornate courtyards of beautifully furnished apartments. Their conversation was light and friendly, and Gorman discovered Michelle had worked and lived in London for a short while, two years ago.

'I am afraid my English is a little,' she paused, 'rusty,' she smiled deprecatingly.

'It is very good,' Gorman assured her, as he took her arm to cross to the Champs Elysées. The traffic here was roaring past, being one of the few places where cars could show their real speed. The cafés were busy and small groups of tourists stood turning maps all ways, searching occasionally at street corners for a recognisable name.

'Perhaps we walk up to L'Arc de Triomphe?' Michelle looked over her shoulder and eased herself towards the kerb, 'or maybe we get a taxi?'

Gorman moved with her. 'I don't mind. I'm happy to walk.'

'I think a taxi. It is quite a long way.' She waved her hand, not looking at him.

'OK.' Gorman watched as a dark-blue Mercedes drew up and she opened the door and quickly climbed in.

'But,' Gorman leaned in, 'this isn't a taxi.' As he looked in, he saw an overalled negro passenger in the front seat jump out, and the next thing he knew there was a tremendous thump as a knee hit him on the behind and he was pushed head-first on to the floor, unceremoniously. He recognised the negro as the one who had vacated the table at the café. Bewildered, he heard doors slam and a screech of tyres, as the car swung out into the traffic.

He tried to rise, but felt a sickening thump on the back of his head, as something came crashing down. It didn't knock him out, but dazed him into submission, as he gasped for breath. Winded, he gradually realised that, incredibly, Michelle was now talking quietly and confidently to the other occupants of the car.

Someone had his foot on Gorman's neck, pressing his face

184

down and all he could see was Michelle's feet and ankles. She suddenly reverted to English.

'Be quiet, Gorman, and nothing will happen to you.' Her voice was cold.

'What...' he couldn't speak as the foot rammed painfully into his neck, forcing his face into the carpet. He wanted to tell her he recognised her voice now. She was the woman who had phoned him.

'Be quiet, I said,' she hissed.

His brain wouldn't function.

Gorman could tell that the car, after the early acceleration, had now eased into a normal traffic speed and pattern. He realised that they were probably now travelling as inconspicuously as possible, having lost anybody that might have been following, or thinking of following them. After what seemed an age, he felt the car slow down and drive over cobbles, its wheels pounding the surface until it stopped abruptly. Gorman sensed, rather than saw, that they were inside a building. He guessed a garage – yes, here was the usual foul smell of a mixture of oil, petrol fumes and rubber, as the doors were opened and he was hauled out. He was dragged uncaringly upright and pushed against a cold wall, his head banging against it. The doors of the garage were being closed as Gorman looked round.

Before he had time to think or say anything, the negro, who must have been the one whose foot had been on him in the car, kneed him viciously in the groin. As Gorman screamed and doubled up, a fist burst into his solar plexus and he vomited as he fell to the concrete floor. Lying sprawled in a pool of oil, the kicks came raining in. He had never known hurt like it, as he slipped agonisingly into unconsciousness. Without a word, the negro pulled a small box from his pocket and taking out a syringe, bent down and pushed up Gorman's sleeve with some difficulty. He plunged the syringe in and emptied the contents into Gorman's arm. There had been a quick change of number plates. Nobody spoke until it was done.

'Leave this to us,' the negro looked sharply at Michelle Blot, who had stood quietly throughout smoking a cigarette, arms folded, away from the action. 'Disappear. Like now.'

185

She eased the heavy doors open and without a glance, strode out through the courtyard, into the street. A few moments later, she was passed by the Mercedes, as it made its way carefully and slowly down through Suresnes, back towards Paris and away from the block of luxury flats. Underneath them were numbered garages for the occupants. Most were empty, as husbands had taken their cars to work, but number 26 had been rented for a month and Gorman's now dead body had been abandoned on the garage floor. No one noticed them come or go. Mercedes were quite normal cars in that area. It was a very upset janitor who telephoned the police the next day when he found the body. It was quickly determined that rigor mortis had set in, and the approximate time of death established. No-one had seen or heard anything. The police found nothing of real interest on the body, except a microfilm that had been taped inside a breast pocket. Gorman hadn't thought of doing that.

12

The general hubbub in the restaurant was stilled as there was a terrible screech of brakes followed by a resounding crunch. The tall, amply proportioned owner looked through the window and then turning back, smiled and addressing everyone within hearing distance, commented, 'One taxi that didn't get away with it!'

There was an immediate resumption of conversation, as parties lost interest in the interruption to their own flow of words.

David Price looked at his watch. Ten past one. It was unlike Donald Havers to be late. Ever since their university days together he had had a reputation for punctuality. Havers had been David's closest friend at university. It had begun on the playing fields, where they had both enjoyed their rugby. Cold seeping mud, lashing rain, tremendous physical effort and great camaraderie. Their friendship grew quickly as they found, not necessarily that all their interests were in common, but that there was a bond of understanding and enjoyment in their exchange of ideas on wide-ranging, and in those days, ephemeral matters. They had maintained this relaxed association intermittently over many years. When they came together it was always as if they were picking up from the day before.

David wondered if Donald was caught up in the office, but as he thought wryly, what did Donald do? He knew he worked for the Government. He was pretty sure it was in MI5 or MI6 or

187

something similar, but didn't really know. Donald had certainly been very guarded over the years about his work. 'Looking after you all', was as far as he would ever go in referring to his occupation. David realised that several of the tables were still unoccupied. Probably problems with the London traffic. Charlotte Street was a little way from the City and also from the West End, where he knew Donald worked. Anyway, Donald appreciated good food in an amenable atmosphere, which was why David had suggested L'Etoile. At that moment the door opened and Donald Havers was silhouetted by the sun's faint rays. He quickly handed over his trenchcoat and was escorted to David's table. Havers was a tall, slender man, elegantly dressed. His features were soft and rounded, but his blue eyes were very alert.

'David! I'm so sorry.' Havers shook hands.

'Forget it!' David smiled. 'Sit yourself down and have a drink.'

Wine waiter and hors d'oeuvres trolley later, they had both relaxed into their usual tempo of friendly conversation.

'We really must get together for dinner,' Havers commented. 'It must be nearly six months and that's unforgivable. It's in our court, I know.'

David finished a mouthful of delicious dressed crab. 'Life is hectic for all of us.' He sipped his Chablis. 'But it would be nice. How is Phyllis?'

'Fine, fine,' Havers smiled. 'We had a long weekend in Rome a couple of weeks ago which was splendid. Just walking around the Pincio and the Piazza del Popolo in the sun; window shopping along the Via Del Corso and eating at good noisy restaurants like Nino's.'

'Sounds good,' David commented.

'It was.' Havers finished his paté. 'A wind down. Much appreciated by both of us.'

'How about you and June? Been anywhere interesting?'

'Well,' David smiled, 'We had a wind down of sorts a few weeks ago as a matter of fact. We were down in the village of Cordington in Sussex. Stayed with Ian Carlyle.'

'Ian Carlyle?' Havers' hand hovered over his wine glass. 'I didn't know you knew him?'

David shrugged his shoulders. 'Don't actually. It was a case of trying to get to know him really.'

'And did you succeed?' Havers acknowledged the grilled sole being set out in front of him.

The noise of the restaurant appeared momentarily to grow as David tried to assemble his thoughts. He frowned and played with the stem of his wine glass, as his escalope of veal with a garnish of vegetables was served.

'This is really why I've invited you to lunch, Donald. Can I tell you about it?'

'Of course.' Havers reached for the salt whilst the pepper grinder was expertly whisked in front of him and away.

'Well,' David placed his elbows on the table and stared at the tablecloth, 'Let me take you back to the evening it all started...'

*   *   *

'...so you see, Donald, we had an interesting time, to say the least. Ian Carlyle, however, we knew no better at the end than we did at the beginning.' David looked up at Havers and eased himself back in his chair.

'But that sounds contrary to the purpose of the weekend?' Havers drank his coffee.

'Yes it was,' David nodded. 'Clearly the circumstances were such that all parties should have been able to get to know each other quite well. However, I must say in retrospect, Carlyle was more successful casting his eyes over us than vice versa.' He paused, 'Do you know Donald, both June and I haven't been so relieved to get home from somewhere for a long time, if ever. But the extraordinary thing is we don't know why.'

'Doesn't sound much of a relaxation,' commented Havers wryly. David caught the wine waiter's attention and asked for some Perrier water.

'Well it was and it wasn't,' David laughed, 'we didn't have to do anything. We were waited on hand and foot and the weather was pleasant. But there was just a sense of an omnipresence. Inexplicable.'

Havers looked at David quizzically.

'On the Sunday morning,' David reflected, 'we were phoned

through in our room and asked what we would like for breakfast, as it would be brought to us! Fine, but no suggestion of the straight forward alternative of eating downstairs in the dining room. At the time we just put it down to an awareness of the possible early-morning condition of some of the guests! Anyway, that was OK. Sunday papers came as well, so we were clearly not expected to hurry to do anything. After a while, however, June thought it would be rather pleasant to go for a walk, as it was a clear sunny morning. When we went to leave the room we found the door was locked! You can imagine our disbelief! We thought that the door had stuck, or that the carpet was rucked up or something, but no, it was definitely locked. We were conscious, of course, after the first few seconds, that we couldn't get out of the room at all, because of the iron bars on the windows! So at that point. I rang down and asked what the hell was going on. After a few moments Carlyle appeared at the door, full of profuse apologies. Apparently before we had arrived, the door-catch had proved faulty and the door had kept banging when the window was open to air the room, and Ross, the man-servant, had without thinking just locked it again after serving us our breakfast.'

'A little odd, but plausible,' mused Havers, scratching his cheek.

'Well, there was no harm done,' David replied. 'We then decided to go for our walk and Carlyle asked if we minded if his wife joined us, as she had been thinking of going out. We said no, of course not, but what about the other guests? Apparently he had spoken to the others who had all decided to stay in until lunch.'

'Did you see any of the them?'

'Oh yes,' David nodded. 'A very wan, unhappy-looking Abbott, who had fainted after dinner the night before, was downstairs in the sitting room studiously reading a paper. Jenny Gorman was sitting playing scrabble with her husband Colin in the next room and she invited us to join them, but at that moment Tanya Carlyle joined us, explaining to them that we were just off for a short walk, and Carlyle went in to join Abbott.'

'So,' Havers smiled, 'all sounds very relaxed, really.'

190

'Yes,' David scratched his chin, 'but, and I know it sounds very melodramatic and ridiculous, but Donald, it was only afterwards when June and I discussed it that we realised that that episode was typical.'

'Typical? Typical of what?' Havers watched two elderly ladies get up and leave, to the obvious chagrin of the bowing waiters.

'Typical of the fact,' David looked doubtful, 'that strange as it may seem, we were never really left on our own the whole time we were there, other than in our room. And by that I also mean we were never able to talk to any of the other guests, alone.'

'Oh, come on!' Havers laughed.

'No, it's true,' protested David. 'Our walk with Tanya was pleasant enough. We seemed to go for miles following footpaths and winding country lanes. We stopped at the village of Parsonbridge and had a drink and arrived back just in time for lunch. Carlyle and Thatcher, the advertising agency fellow, were standing talking together at a window as we came up the drive and Carlyle came out of the room to greet us at the foot of the stairs and told us lunch would be in five minutes. We shot up to our rooms and, yes,' David hurried on, as he saw Havers about to interrupt him, 'the door was unlocked! But,' he paused as their water glasses were refilled, 'when we came out, Ross was waiting for us at the top of the stairs to escort us down to lunch!

'Lunch was very good, but the conversation, unlike the previous evening, was very stilted and as June said, if it hadn't been for the girls it would have been hard going. Thatcher, Abbott, Hardy and Gorman seemed to find it hard to communicate, to keep up with the conversation. Not patently so, and if it had been one of them on their own we probably wouldn't have noticed, but it was all four of them as we realised, when we discussed it going home. Maybe we imagined it, or allowed the idea to blossom unreasonably, but,' he shrugged his shoulders resignedly, 'why would we, if it wasn't correct?'

David immediately continued, implying that his question had been rhetorical. 'After lunch Ross or Carlyle or Tanya was with us the whole time, until we left. Again not obviously, but nevertheless, that's how it was.'

L'Etoile's other customers were beginning to leave and the noise was abating measurably.

'It seems,' Havers tapped his coffee spoon on the tablecloth, 'that you just had very attentive, very cordial hosts, who were out to make the acquaintanceship as pleasurable as possible, admittedly for their own self-interest, and the other male guests relaxed, letting their wives do all the talking. That's not unknown, you know, David.'

David toyed with his coffee cup. 'It seems like that Donald, doesn't it? And I would go along with it, but for one thing...'

Havers looked at David and raised his eyebrows.

David was watching a very attractive brunette at the next table light up a cigarette. 'When we left it was at the same time as the Hardys – he was the solicitor with a quite attractive wife – in fact all the wives were attractive in their own way...'

'Now we know why you were all invited,' chuckled Havers.

'...and I heard Rita Hardy say to her husband, as she was shutting her door before he started the engine. "Why did each of you men have a session with Ian on your own this morning?" and he replied something about, "Getting better acquainted for business".'

'So?' Their coffee cups were finally removed, as David waved them away.

'I didn't have "a session",' remarked David, 'but obviously Hardy did and we saw Abbott with Carlyle on the way out and with Thatcher on our way back. It would make sense as a follow-up to the previous night's dinner, being the supposed reason for us being there. But there was no attempt to talk to me at all. It now looks in retrospect, more and more, as though ... as though ... we were there by mistake.'

13

The phone rang and rang – insistently; it would not die. Sighing mentally, Lesley Abbott pulled herself together and unhurriedly left the garden chair in which she had been lost to the world – not asleep and yet not really awake. She crossed the paved courtyard, her shadow edging across the lawn as she kicked off her garden shoes and entered the kitchen. She picked up the still ringing white telephone.

'Hallo.'

'Lesley Abbott?' Lesley frowned. She didn't recognise the voice. 'This is Rita Hardy – you know – from . . . ?' The voice was hurried and anxious.

'Yes,' Lesley's attention was caught by two magpies landing on the lawn. What was the saying – one magpie for sorrow, two for joy? Joy? Maybe these two represented two lots of sorrow.

'Hallo?' Her thoughts were interrupted by the enquiring voice.

'Yes,' Lesley addressed the phone sharply. 'Yes, of course. I remember.'

There was a pause, as though Rita Hardy was wrestling to find the right words. 'Did you agree?' The question was almost wailed and Lesley held the phone away from her ear, involuntarily. She watched the magpies as they frightened away all the small sparrows and bluetits that had been happily pecking away at the stale bread she had thrown out earlier in the afternoon.

'Did you agree?' Rita repeated the question. 'Did you agree?'

Lesley frowned. 'Of course,' she replied abruptly. 'Now, I think we should leave it there. And I don't think you should phone me again. Goodbye.'

She replaced the phone firmly, before listening for any response, and looked up to see the magpies lazily fly off, as though satisfied with her response to the telephone call.

*   *   *

Rita Hardy proceeded to ring Pat Thatcher and just caught her as she was about to have a shower, before going out to dinner.

'How did you find me?' Pat was not amused.

'You're in the phone book,' Rita replied, 'but never mind that. Did you agree?'

Pat bit her lip. 'You mean, did I accept, don't you?'

'Yes,' Rita replied, 'you're right. That's a better question.' She added bitterly, 'everything's a question.'

'Well, let's just say, it was agreed, and now good night – forever!' Pat put down the receiver as firmly as Lesley had done moments before.

*   *   *

A busy Jenny Gorman answered the phone.

'Yes? Hallo?'

'Jenny Gorman – This is Rita Hardy – you remember?'

There was a long silence as Rita gazed at the kitchen curtains. They needed cleaning.

'Yes, but...' Jenny closed her eyes, as if in prayer, bowing her head.

'I won't keep you,' Rita interrupted, 'just tell me if you agreed. That's all I want to know.'

'Of course,' Jenny snorted. 'Have you rung anybody else?'

'Yes,' Rita replied truculently, sensing the annoyance in Jenny's voice, 'Lesley Abbott and Pat Thatcher.'

'Well, why don't you stop ringing people? Certainly me. There's no point.' Jenny slammed down the phone and picked up the socks for darning.

14

David Price was searching through *The Daily Telegraph* intently at the breakfast table, as June came in with the milk, which had just been delivered. She put the milk in the fridge and came and sat at the pine table.

'David, what's the matter?' she asked quietly as he looked up. The false smile that he had beamed at her disappeared and he coloured slightly. The kettle had begun to hiss and June, frowning, rose and made a pot of tea, as silence prevailed.

'Are you in some sort of trouble?' she asked quietly, with her back to him.

David laughed bitterly, as he put down the paper, and for a moment there was only the sound of next door's cat meowing.

'No, darling. Not the kind that you'd ever dream of, anyway.'

June swung round and asked sharply, 'Well, what sort? For God's sake, something is clearly the matter! For the last week you have hardly spoken and when you have it's been in monosyllables!'

David scratched the back of his neck slowly, wearily, looking at her. She could tell by his tired face, even if she hadn't known, that sleep had been avoiding him recently.

'Come and sit down, darling,' David indicated the vacant chair, 'but maybe a cup of tea first?'

He said no more until she had placed the cups on the table. As she stirred her cup, elbows resting on the table, David took a deep breath.

'This probably sounds utterly ridiculous, but I think I could be in some sort of danger.' His face was very straight.

'What sort of danger?' June stared at him, bewildered.

He sighed and sipped his tea thoughtfully, before replying. 'You haven't seen the papers for the last few days I know, because you've been so busy, but the other day, for example, there was a report of an Englishman being found dead in mysterious circumstances in Paris.'

June looked at him, her face creased in puzzlement.

'So?' She reached for her cup of tea and stirred it vigorously, unnecessarily.

'The name of the dead man,' David's voice was as cold as ice, 'was Colin Gorman.'

June just stared blankly and David repeated quietly, 'Colin Gorman' and again, 'his name was Colin Gorman.'

June shook her head 'So?'

'Colin Gorman.' David's voice was now slow and soft, 'was in the party at Ian Carlyle's house.'

There was total silence as June stared at him and blinked hard. 'So he was. He was the nice man with an even more pleasant wife. J ... Jane ... Janice ... no Jenny, Jenny Gorman.' June smiled, pleased with her powers of recall. She then realised what David had said.

'Oh dear, how terrible.' She looked at him inquiringly. 'Maybe it's not him? There must be many Colin Gormans around.'

'It's the Ian Carlyle one all right.' David pushed his chair back and crossed his legs.

'How on earth can you be sure?' June protested, sipping her tea.

'Because' David paused, unintentionally dramatically, 'in the last week or so, all the other men who were there as guests have died in extraordinary circumstances. That's why!' He rose and walked to the window looking at the garden but not seeing it. 'I know you've been tied up and haven't had much time for news, but believe me, it's true! Their deaths have all been in the papers. That fellow Hardy who borrowed the scissors on the first evening, he died in Australia. Abbott that pious bank manager type, died in Newcastle. Thatcher the advertising agency director died in New York, and now Gorman has died in Paris!'

'Jesus Christ!' June whispered, as her hands flew to her cheeks. Her eyes were locked into David's. 'What ... why ... I mean ... Hell, I don't know what I mean!' She shook her head. 'How did they die? What have the newspapers reported?'

David shook his head and collapsed back into his chair, running his hands through his hair as he rested his elbows on the table. 'It would appear that none of them have died from natural causes,' he muttered. 'Hardy fell to his death from the top of some skyscraper; Abbott fell in front of a lorry; Thatcher was mugged and killed on a New York street and Gorman's body was found dumped in an underground car park in Paris!'

There was a deafening silence as June took it in. David rose and went to pour out another cup of tea.

June finally spoke, very slowly and quietly. 'And you are the only other man who was there. Is that it?'

David nodded, as he turned and came back to the table.

'But, OK, they've all been unlucky, David. Why should they have anything to do with us?' June rubbed her nose, mystified.

'Think about it for a minute,' David took both her hands in his. 'I assure you I'm not being melodramatic. Don't you think it odd to the point of absurdity, that all four were the guests at that very peculiar weekend in Sussex with us? There quite clearly must be a link between them. There must be. But I don't have the remotest idea what the link is!'

June jumped, as the front door rattled and they heard the postman feed some letters through the letter box.

'God,' she muttered, smiling wryly and taking a deep breath, 'they may not have died of natural causes, David, but surely all could have just been coincidental, unfortunate accidents?'

David shook his head. 'No, darling. Each death appears to have been surrounded by controversy. In Australia David Charrington has been arrested for Hardy's murder. You know – the magnate. In New York, Frank Sorretto has been charged with murder.'

'Another big-shot,' commented June.

'Yes,' continued David, nodding, 'and Hans Hawkins is

helping the police with their enquiries in Newcastle, about Abbott's death.'

'But you said Abbott fell in front of something – a lorry,' June protested.

'He could have been pushed, couldn't he?' asked David quietly.

'This is ridiculous!' June complained, and sat silently staring at her tea leaves.

'Oh, God! And now Gorman?' June stood up and collected the cups and saucers. As she put them in the sink, she said, 'But it doesn't make sense. No sense at all!' She turned and pointed a wet finger at David, 'They are hardly likely to have connived at their own deaths!'

'I know. I know,' David came up behind her and encircled her waist with his arms, 'but the connection must be that weekend. Coincidences like that just don't happen in real life. The important thing is that we were the only other guests and we can't just sit around to see what happens to us – to me!'

'Maybe nothing will – why should it?' June turned and nestled her cheek against his. 'They'd all gone away somewhere when they were killed – you haven't!'

'An interesting point, darling,' David acknowledged, thoughtfully, 'but it doesn't change my belief that I could be in some sort of danger. Apart from being number five, there's also the fact that I – we – can link these deaths together.'

'But, how? Nothing happened there! It was actually a bloody awful weekend.' June paused and looked up at David, eyebrows raised fearfully. 'What are we going to do?'

'*We* are going to do nothing. *You*, my love,' he replied, 'are going on holiday for a few days. Immediately. Like now. Go and visit your parents. You'll be away from everything in Bucks. Say your doctor has told you to have a rest. The business can cope without you. I shall just do a little investigating, but away from here. The less you know at this stage the better. Anyway, you'll be all right. It's the men that have been killed. God, that sounds terrible doesn't it? But there haven't been any reports about the wives being hurt in any way. I'll keep in touch by phone, so don't worry.'

'Don't be ridiculous,' June looked close to tears, as she replied angrily. 'Don't worry?'

David stroked her hair. 'Darling, please don't misunderstand me. I'm trying to keep you out of something. I don't know what it is, but I know we're better apart. I'm not having you involved any more than you are already.'

June shook her head fiercely. 'If you're involved, I'm involved!'

'No,' David held her head still, 'No. Think about it. As you say, these men have all died in different countries, in fact, in varying ways. We're not dealing with one or two people. Whatever it is, must be worldwide. It must be! But all we know is that "it" is lethal. And that means an organisation, a network. I'll keep in touch, I promise. And if I think it is safe and sensible to involve you, I will.' He let his hand slide down June's arm. 'Now go and pack a suitcase. Please.'

Half an hour later in the warm early-morning sun, presaging a fine day, they kissed fiercely before June, face torn with anxiety, settled into her car and without a backward glance drove off to Bucks. Hopefully to countryside and safety.

David slowly shut the front door, leaned back against it and shut his eyes. He had formulated no real plan, no constructive first steps. All he had were some intuitive ideas. What was it all about? He had the fleeting ludicrous wish to sing 'What's it all about, Alfie?' the haunting song of years ago. Alfie! Michael Caine – what would he do in this predicament in one of his films? Not many people would know, David thought wryly.

He picked up the letters and went to put them on the hall table. A gas bill, a circular from his stock brokers, but wait, an envelope addressed to him in black capitals? He frowned, as he found the envelope tightly sealed and irritatingly difficult to open. When he finally opened it there was just one piece of paper inside. He went cold as he stared at it. It was a plain piece of paper with just the word FORGET written in capitals in thick red ink. There was nothing else. The postmark was W1. That was all. FORGET.

Forget what? David walked into the kitchen and sat at the table staring at the piece of paper. Forget? The weekend! It had to be connected with that! The newspaper stories, the accidents, murders, deaths. Everything led back to that weekend. Forget! The message was simple and dire. Or else! And it was clever. If he had no idea what it meant, no-one had shown their hand – just a crank, a crackpot and the letter thrown away and forgotten. What would happen after that was anyone's guess. However, if he had understood it – he was warned. Suddenly the house seemed too small for him – claustrophobic. He had to get out and away.

David rose and stood contemplating the remains of breakfast, untouched after his conversation with June. If they, whoever 'they' were, were telling him to forget, they could well be watching him to see what he did next. If anything.

Heart pounding, he stupidly almost tip-toed into the front dining room and carefully went to the bay window, covered, at June's insistence, with net curtains. Without touching them he looked up and down the road. The usual busy road and the inevitable parked cars. Nothing extraordinary. Except? Except, about two hundred yards down, parked by the Methodist Church, was a blue Ford transit van that looked vaguely familiar. It was the dented off-side door that he remembered. Only last time he had seen it, it had been parked beyond their house the other way. When was that? Yesterday. It was certainly not a resident's van. God, David chastised himself, I shall be a nervous wreck in half an hour at this rate. Why the hell shouldn't the van be there? Deliveries; estimators for central heating; it could be there for one of any number of reasons.

He watched as his mind turned somersaults. Nobody came or went to it. But that didn't mean anything. Necessarily. The office. He must go to work as usual. Give no indication of anything amiss. Once there, he could decide what to do next. He packed a few overnight things in a holdall, so that basically he could be self-sufficient for a while, and locked up the house. The notes for the papers and milkman? He could hardly leave them outside for anyone to read. That would show last-minute unplanned intentions and invite burglars, if no-one else! David wrote a note to Mrs Phillips, the widow next door, referring to a family bereavement and asked her to stop the milk for him, until

200

he contacted her. He cancelled the papers by phone. Fortunately the garage could be approached through the house and he dropped his holdall in the car before wandering apparently unconcerned next door, and dropped the note in Mrs Phillips's letter box. He knew she was never up and about before nine in the morning.

As he returned to the garage, he looked up the road. A few commuters were leaving in their cars, but the blue van was still there. David reversed his Mercedes out and pressed the control in the car to lower the garage doors. Satisfied, he continued out into the road and drove gently off, passing the van. There were two men in it, apparently deeply engrossed in something below the windscreen. As he reached the main road he had to wait for a break in the busy rush-hour traffic. It always took a few minutes and he glanced in his rear-view mirror. The van was doing a three-point turn. His heart began to race, but he took advantage of a sudden gap in the stream of cars and joined the flow of traffic on its way to the Hogarth roundabout, into London. His hands were moist on the steering wheel. It was a sunny morning, but not that hot. David found it very difficult to concentrate on the traffic ahead and nearly rammed two cars in the first two or three hundred yards. His attention was focused on the van. After that however, he relaxed. It followed him, always with several vehicles between them. It never tried to get close and David soon decided that the occupants, who, he was sure were trailing him, had guessed where he was heading.

The heavy commuter traffic was the same as every other weekday – crawling along. He would lose the van at one set of lights but it would catch up with him by the next set. Hammersmith, Kensington High Street – the usual route. Had they been following him on other days? For how long? God, what was it all about? He arrived at his office block, a 1980s glass, pseudo classical edifice. As he drove down into the garage he glimpsed the van drive past the entrance without stopping. Were they satisfied in the knowledge of where he was? David's reaction was positive. He drove straight down the ramp, round the concrete columns in the basement and after waiting a few moments, drove straight back up out again. There was no sign of any blue van. He grinned humourlessly and headed for Westminster Bridge.

'Beth, afraid I shan't be in for a day or two. An elderly aunt has been taken ill and I have to give her a little of my time.' David was in a phone box at a garage in Dorking, watching a stream of mid-morning delivery vans and cars with lady shopper drivers.

'Oh, I'm sorry, Mr Price.' His secretary's concern was genuine and breathless. June maintained that Beth Edmunds was in love with her boss, but David always responded by ridiculing the idea, although he secretly suspected June was right. 'Is there anything I can do to help?'

'No,' David replied reassuringly, 'it's her heart, but I think she'll be all right. I just have to act as her crutch for the moment. Give any urgent work to Paul Oliver and I'll ring in as and when.'

'Have you a phone number where...'

'Bye,' David hung up. He had no elderly relatives. The last one died long before Beth had started working for him. She might wonder why he had never mentioned his aunt, but hopefully she would accept that she didn't know everything about him. Any enquiries as to his whereabouts could be dealt with very satisfactorily by the protective Beth. No-one, but no-one, would learn anything worthwhile. Certainly not an outsider, hoping to find out why he hadn't gone home, nor appeared in the office, as usual.

*   *.   *

Cordington was as picturesque and unruffled as it had been when he had seen it before, but now a strong sun blazed down from a cloudless sky. Few people were about – two men in orange donkey jackets were mending a hole in the lane; an elderly lady was bending lovingly over her front-garden pond and a young lad was delivering milk. That seemed to be the sum total of Cordington activity. David drove slowly up the hill through the streaks of sunlight breaking through the arched trees and slowed as he approached the remains of the five-bar gate. What was he going to do? He knew he had to come back to where it had all seemingly started, but his line of action had veered in his mind from knocking on the front door and taking

202

it from there, to reconnoitering the house and surroundings to see if anything at all gave a clue as to what had been happening.

It was only a couple of weeks since his lunch with Donald Havers and David had tried to speak to him on the telephone, but had been told he was abroad. It was not known when he would be back. He certainly wasn't going to talk to anyone else. He was far from sure he wouldn't be considered a fool, or an alarmist, or both.

David drove on past the entrance and followed the lane as it swung left down the hill, the vista changing to meadows of varying shades of green. Only a few hundred yards on, the hedges fell back, leaving a grass verge easily wide enough to allow a car to pull off the road safely. David eased on to the grass and shut off the engine. There wasn't a sound. He looked back. He couldn't see any houses due to the heavy woods on the crest of the hill. He locked the car and retraced his route to the gate. The direct or indirect approach – he was still undecided as he stood staring up the winding drive. His concentration was startlingly interrupted by a toot of a car-horn right behind him. David jumped to one side as a white Ford Granada drove into the beginning of the drive and stopped. A smiling, fair-haired, young man lowered his window.

'Can I help you at all?' he asked engagingly.

'Er, that's very kind of you,' David replied. 'I ... I stayed at The Manor House a few weeks ago and thought I might just call in and ... and ... say hallo,' he finished lamely.

The young man stared at him for a moment, as a tractor trundled noisily along the lane. 'At The Manor House? No, sir, you must be mistaken.' He shook his head with a smile.

'Oh?' David couldn't think why. This was definitely the place.

'No,' the young man wound down his window further, 'This house hasn't been lived in for about six months since Lady Cookson died. In fact I'm from the agents that have just been appointed to sell it.'

David stared and his heart began to pound. This didn't make any sense. What the hell was the young man talking about? 'But, I'm positive it was here.' He realised that the young man was beginning to lose his smile. 'Are you going up to the house –

perhaps I could come with you and have a look? Maybe it was another house nearby.'

'Yes, I don't see why not.' The car inched forward to allow David to walk round the back of it and climb into the front passenger seat.

'You say you've just been appointed?' David watched as the car drove up the quite definitely familiar drive.

'Yes, last week, actually.' The young man concentrated over the wheel. 'The executors decided to wait until all the furniture and other household goods had been properly catalogued for auction, before allowing people to look over the house. That's been completed now and the auction is on Friday, so we can get on with selling the house. There are no relatives apparently and all the money is going to some charity or other.'

The car swung round the front of the house and stopped. 'Would you like to come in and have a look round? It's quite a place.' The young man was climbing out of the car and appeared to have totally dismissed the idea that David could have been to the house recently. A pigeon called from the rooftop.

'Yes, thank you,' David followed him to the front door. His gaze followed the same arc over the gardens as it had when he had arrived before with June. Nothing had altered. 'The grounds look well cared for, in the circumstances,' he commented.

'Yes,' the door was now open as the young man turned back, 'I believe there have been some contract gardeners employed from time to time.' He held the door open for David to enter.

The first impression David had was that nothing, but nothing, had changed since their visit. The same thick rugs hugged the carpet and the same austere portraits stared down at him.

'By the way my name is Alan Russell,' the young man smiled, inquiringly.

'Er . . . Ron Smith,' David replied and hurried on. 'Which firm of agents are you with?'

'Smithers.' Russell walked into the drawing room where

Carlyle had greeted them. Nothing had changed in here either, except that the grand piano was closed.

'What a lovely room!' David had decided that he was not going to argue as to whether he had been here any more. There might be more to learn this way.

'Yes,' Russell nodded. 'Would you be interested in the house or the furniture, by any chance?'

David caressed the top of the piano, 'I might be interested in some of these splendid items. Yes, when did you say the auction was?'

'Friday,' responded Russell. 'Like to have a look at the other rooms?'

'Please.' David followed Russell around the ground floor of the house, making appropriate noises of impressed surprise as he felt necessary. Nothing had been removed. Not even the bars on the windows!

'I haven't seen a phone,' David remarked.

Russell shook his head. 'No, there isn't one.'

David couldn't remember any of the number on the invitation, anyway.

'Yes,' Russell nodded to David's comment, 'Poor old girl was frightened of living here with just an old housekeeper and a nurse and she had all the rooms protected. I guess the bars will come out pretty quickly under new ownership. Not very attractive, are they?' Russell led him up the stairs.

'I thought it might have been a mental home, with all the bars,' David commented.

Russell laughed. 'Not that I know of. I wouldn't have thought it big enough, nor really suitable, so far as the layout is concerned, would you?'

'No.' David realised how true those observations were.

They toured the upstairs; the bedroom June and he had used was very familiar. The beds were bare of linen and the room had an unused look about it – otherwise it could have been yesterday they had slept there.

'Jolly interesting,' David commented, as they meandered their way down and back to the front door. 'I might well come to the auction – if only out of curiosity.'

'Well, it starts at eleven in the morning,' Russell dived into the boot of his car. 'I have some catalogues here,' and he proffered one to David. 'Would you like a lift back? Just give me a few moments, while I pop back in.'

'No, thank you.' David smiled gratefully, 'You've been very kind. I'll make my way back to my car. The walk will do me good.'

Russell nodded, bade farewell and excusing himself, went back inside the house, leaving the door open.

David made his way slowly and thoughtfully down the gravel drive – the scrunch from his shoes violating the otherwise sylvan peace. His mind was finding the turn of events bewildering to say the least. No Carlyle. No occupier. No occupation by Carlyle at any time, according to Russell. But he had been there. Carlyle had been there, with his wife, with his staff ... his staff! The husband and wife ... what was their name? Rogers? Robb? Ross! That was it, Ross! Hadn't they said they lived in the village? He was sure he remembered Ross saying that. David breathed deeply and couldn't fail to appreciate the country fragrances, as he reached the end of the drive. He plunged his hands into his pockets as he made his way back to his car, wondering how he could find Mr and Mrs Ross. Start at the pub – the landlord is as likely to know all the village inhabitants as anybody. He could also do with a drink.

'Ross, you say? A few weeks ago.' The landlord of The Lord Nelson, a dour, thick-set man in his early fifties, scratched his head with one hand and wiped the bar needlessly with a cloth with the other. 'Can't say I've ever 'eard of 'em. Hey! Fred! Do you know a couple, name of Ross, who worked up at The Manor House recently?'

David turned in the direction that the landlord was addressing. There was no-one else in the saloon bar, except an elderly, red-faced, white-haired farmhand in the window seat, stroking a sandy-coloured Labrador.

'Ross?' Fred shook his head slowly and in tremulous tones added, 'name means nowt to me. Certainly don't come from round 'ere. I reckon you and I knows everyone in these parts, Tom.'

'Aye,' the landlord nodded, scowling, 'that's as I reckon.' He turned to David, 'Nope, afraid you're on a loser there, my friend. Sure you've got the name right?'

'Yes,' David sighed as he ordered another gin and tonic, 'I'm sure.'

'Hell,' Fred gave the dog some nuts off the table, 'that Manor House hasn't been occupied for a while, anyway. Old Smithers' estate office has been looking after it I 'eard.'

'Smithers?' David looked round inquiringly.

'Aye,' the landlord interjected, 'has an office off down Pritchetts Lane, behind the pub 'ere. 'E looks after all local properties. Sales, estate management and the like. Should be there now.' As a big office in Horsham with about twenty staff, but always comes out to this small one on Tuesdays. It's only part of someone's 'ouse, really.'

David tried hard to remain calm. This was a lucky break. If Smithers had been 'looking after' The Manor House, rather than having just been appointed to sell, who better to answer questions about Carlyle, Mr and Mrs Ross, the weekend? He downed his gin and tonic in one final gulp and bade the landlord, Fred and the dog, farewell.

He drove out of the car park and turned into the narrow Pritchetts Lane. He hadn't really noticed it before. It was very narrow and overhung with beech trees on either side. After no more than a few hundred yards David came to a bend where the land dipped away into a small valley, revealing a surprising number of cottages, several with picturesque thatched roofs. He drove down and passed some on his left, before he pulled up outside an old cottage with the name Smithers proclaimed above a bay window. It was the first one on the right-hand side.

'Morning?' The voice suggested surprise, as David closed the door of the cottage, come estate agents.

'Good morning,' David smiled at the young brunette, who was busily typing at a small desk by the window. The front door opened into what had been the front parlour and now passed as an office, with brochures for a building society on a low table and a rack with a few particulars of properties for sale running along one wall. David wondered how it survived as a business.

'Can I help you?' the young girl reluctantly stopped typing, and looked up.

David caught a whiff of cheap perfume as he advanced a few steps across the bare wooden floor. 'Er ... yes, that is, I hope so,' he smiled. 'I believe Mr Smithers is here this morning?'

She looked at him with a little more interest. Her thoughts were transparent. He couldn't be an idle time-waster, if he knew Mr Smithers was there. She smiled, from ear to ear. 'Why – yes. He's in his office.' She made it sound very important. 'Would you like to see him?'

'Please,' David nodded.

'May I have your name?' The girl rose, expectantly.

'Smith – Ron Smith.' David didn't know why he had lied about his name to Russell, but instinctively he felt safer not giving his true identity at this stage. There were too many peculiarities to be explored at this juncture, to be too honest. The girl disappeared through the door to the back of the cottage, closing it firmly behind her. He could hear the low exchange of conversation in the next room. Suddenly the door opened again and framed in the doorway stood a large, bald-headed man of about sixty, dressed in a green tweed suit.

'Yes, sir, can I help you? My name's Smithers.' The face was sharp-featured with darting brown eyes. His complexion was sallow and David noticed how the eyelids opened and closed much more frequently than was normal. Smithers moved jerkily forward and thrust out a hand. The man was either on guard or had an affliction. All his movements appeared to be staccato.

David shook hands, 'Thank you for seeing me.'

'Goodness, that's what I'm here for.' Smithers quickly stood to one side. 'Come into my office, please.' He shot his hand out and gestured towards the door. David found himself in a repeat of the front room. Small, bare floorboards and little furniture, other than a small desk, one filing cabinet and a couple of very ordinary wooden chairs. 'Do sit down, won't you,' Smithers shot round the desk and subsided into his seat. He waved his hands briskly around the room, apologetically.

'Afraid I only come here once a week. Not much point

spending a fortune on decoration. My main office is in Horsham and Elaine lives next door and keeps an eye on things here for me. By the way, cup of coffee?'

'No, thank you,' David shook his head. 'I've only called in about The Manor House. I've heard it's on the market.'

'Yes,' Smithers blinked at him, inquiringly. 'Are you interested? Good news travels fast. Splendid property. The contents are being auctioned Friday. The house is being sold with vacant possession.'

David looked impressed. 'When was it last occupied?' he enquired.

'Hasn't been occupied since Lady Cookson died, which was, now let me see,' Smithers drummed his fingers on the edge of the desk, 'six months ago, I'd say.'

'It's been empty all winter? No-one living in?' David tried to look surprised. 'No-one there to look after all the furniture and effects?'

Smithers' eyes narrowed fractionally, as he shook his head. 'No-one's lived there.' He cracked the joints of his right hand inside the left hand, causing David to jump slightly. 'I have called in from time to time to keep a check on things for the executors – a firm of solicitors in London. I've made sure everything's been looked after. The house is fully burglar-alarmed,' he added, by way of an afterthought.

'Who has the keys for the burglar alarm apart from, presumably, yourself?' David stared at the rapidly blinking eyes.

'I'm sorry?' Smithers sallow complexion appeared to intensify, 'What on earth has that to do with you, sir?'

'My apologies,' David put up his hands in mock defence, 'I only meant if I wanted to see round the house and you weren't around, who at your Horsham office should I contact?'

'Oh.' Smithers searched David's face intently. 'Well, Alan Russell could help you, but apart from him? No-one. I am the only other person who has the keys and no-one goes there without my knowledge. Now, sir. Would you like to see over it?' His face took on the more normal agent's encouraging smile.

'What is the asking price?' David enquired.

'Well, we are looking for offers in the order of three quarters of a million pounds.' Smithers beamed. 'It's a bargain. The usual story of executors wanting to get rid of their burden as soon as possible. A real snip. Here let me give you the details.' He darted his hands into one of the drawers of his desk and gave David a sheet of particulars.

'Well, the price is a little more than I was hoping you'd say,' David grimaced, 'the upkeep has to be taken into account, but let me think about it.'

'Fine,' Smithers waved his hands aloft. 'Our phone number here and at Horsham is on the top of the sheet. Just leave a message any time and I'd be pleased to show you around.'

David stood up and shook hands and made his way back towards his car, bathed in the warmth of Smithers reiterated invitation to not hesitate and ring at any time. The sun was still shining without a cloud in the sky and David's car was like a greenhouse, as he slid behind the wheel and drove off.

He wound down the window, thoughtfully, as he slowly followed the twisting lane, intermittently lined with trees, their branches arching over him, until he could reverse into the entrance to a field and then he drove back the way he had come. So, only Smithers had the keys and no-one had lived there at all, which meant that he, David Price was mad, or there was a perfectly reasonable explanation, or Smithers was lying. He knew that was the house that they had stayed at – he even had the invitation – no, he hadn't. Carlyle had taken that off him. No evidence. No evidence? That line of thinking seemed melodramatic, again. But he couldn't think of any obvious explanation. Smithers didn't appear to appreciate his tentative enquiries about anyone in the house. What could he find out about this Mr Smithers?'

The car park at the pub now held half-a-dozen, careworn, farm workers' cars. A snack and a pint would be respite for them from the work in the fields and barns in the neighbourhood. David pulled in, locked the car and made off back down the lane he had just left. On his right was a stile with a path the other side, leading westwards along the side of the field. The stile had been repaired recently and David took care of the rough wooden edges as he climbed over it. He didn't follow the path, however, but turned left and followed the high hawthorn hedge that tracked the field along the road. Soon the gardens of the cottages could be seen and in particular that of the first cottage and thus the one that was Smithers'.

David became more cautious and kept to the shadows thrown by the hedge. There was not a sound to be heard. The countryside was at peace. Suddenly he heard a door open near him and a voice he recognised as that of the receptionist called out, 'See you in an hour' and a door slammed. Still cautiously, David reached the boundary and checking for any obvious ways of being seen, he threaded himself through the bushes and quietly made his way to the wall of the cottage, where he had seen a downstairs window open. The garden was unkempt and overgrown. He stooped low and sat on his haunches beneath the window – with luck it should be the window of Smithers' back office. Nothing happened for some moments and he accepted that he was probably on a wild goose chase. Then he heard a door open and close inside the cottage and heavy footsteps walk across the floor and cease, as a chair's feet scraped. Then a phone was picked up and after a silence, Smithers' voice.

'Someone's been here asking about the house. Had it been used since the death? Could have been all straightforward, but thought you ought to know.' Pause. 'How the hell do I know who it was – tall, dark haired fellow.' Pause. 'No, didn't give ... yes, hold it, gave the name of Ron Smith. Yes, I know. Smith's a very common name, but that's the name he gave. Said he could be interested in the place, but I didn't buy it. I thought he was fishing.' Pause. 'OK. I'll keep my eyes open.' The phone was slammed back on the hook and David heard a very unattractive belch, as the chair was again scraped along the floor, before footsteps receded through to the front of the cottage.

Some seconds later David heard a car drive away and he guessed Smithers had driven off. Too good a chance to miss? He cautiously stood up and looked into the room. Was there anyone in the cottage? What about upstairs? Only part of it was used as offices. He stood and listened. He couldn't hear anything. Fortunately the cottage next-door was hidden by tall laurel bushes and he climbed up and into the room without any fear of being seen. Everything was as he had seen it not long before. Casting his eye round the austere room, David saw an address book on the desk and he eagerly ran through the names. There was no-one in it who meant anything to him. Disappointed, he pulled open the drawers of the desk, one by one, but they were full of the usual papers and brochures one would expect in an estate agent's office. He had to admit he didn't know what he was looking for and as this office was hardly Smithers' normal place of business there was unlikely to be anything of interest anyway. Undecided as to his next course of action he was startled by the shrill peal of the telephone. David stared at it willing it to stop, but it didn't and he couldn't resist picking it up. He pulled out his handkerchief and loudly pretended to sneeze into it as he then muffled his voice.

'Hallo?'

'Who's that?' The ploy hadn't worked. The voice was suspicious.

'Smithers,' David still talked through the handkerchief.

'Is it hell!' came the reply. 'There's someone there who shouldn't be.' The voice was clearly talking to someone else as the line went dead.

Action! Get out and away! The caller could be local and be round in a few seconds! David frantically clambered out of the window and ran and stumbled his way back to his car, watching and listening for any untoward noise as he went. Nothing. Out of breath, his heart pounding and his shirt sticking to his body from the perspiration, he quickly drove off towards London. He felt sick and it was not just from the physical exercise. Those few words on the phone. He recognised the voice, but he couldn't put a name to it. Yes, he could. It was Carlyle – he was sure of it.

* * *

That evening David was sitting in his hotel room, waiting for room service to bring him dinner. He had booked in to The Post House at Heathrow Airport under his own name in the late afternoon. He couldn't believe anyone who might be looking

212

for him would be able to check on every hotel and guest-house in England and it was necessary to pay by credit card. He certainly wasn't travelling with a fortune in cash. The room was of the usual, 'Hallo, haven't we met before?' variety. He had quickly rung June at her parents and had subconsciously absorbed the room as he had been talking. Pink and grey walls, two flower prints on the walls, a small round table with two easy chairs and a large kingsized bed. The bathroom led off from just inside the door and the TV stood at an angle by the window. It could have been Frankfurt, Chicago or even, these days, Alice Springs.

The door-bell rang and he welcomed in dinner. Before settling to eat, he turned on the television for the seven o'clock news. As he tucked in to his sirloin steak and salad, his mind half paid attention to problems of inflation, balance of trade figures, democracy in China and the latest faux pas made by the Vice President of the United States. Suddenly his hand with a fork-full of salad, was arrested on its way to his mouth, by the voice of the announcer.

'In the House of Commons this afternoon the Leader of the Opposition asked the Prime Minister what she proposed to do about the serious events that had happened around the world over the last few days, concerning the press.' Up flashed a picture of the House and the Leader of the Opposition leaning on the Despatch Box. 'It cannot have escaped the Prime Minister's attention, that not only have several press barons been associated with some untimely deaths recently, but that there would appear to be factors attached to these fatalities that question the very integrity of those involved and their right to control the media that reports to the world at large, whatever news they see fit to print. I would like to ask the Prime Minister whether the Government will be undertaking a review of the structure, control and responsibilities of the press in this country?' Mutterings of approval could be heard from Opposition Members of Parliament and from the back benches came a 'Go for her, boyo!'

'Mr Speaker,' the Prime Minister was replying, 'of course, Her Majesty's Government is aware of the unfortunate incidents,'

213

here she was interrupted by a cacophony of unintelligible shouts of derision from the Opposition, but she ploughed on relentlessly, as was her style, 'but firstly, many of these matters are obviously *sub judice*, secondly, some are nothing to do necessarily with this country and thirdly the Right Honourable Gentleman must acknowledge that this Government, cannot and will not, interfere with the freedom of the press.' Cheers from her supporters then ensued, as she sat down.

'Order. Order,' was called for by the Speaker.

'Mr Speaker!,' the Leader of the Opposition in his best Welsh deriding manner, was not letting the subject rest. 'As usual, the Prime Minister is evading the issue. All that we have heard and read over the last few days involves this country, directly and indirectly. But we are not talking just about the last few days. We are talking about the last few years.' Cheers from his supporters. 'Each of these supposed press tycoons, who exert such an unacceptable major influence on the population's knowledge and awareness, must answer to Parliament.'

At this point there were many Opposition cries of support. He continued pointing and waving across the Mace, 'I am not passing any judgement on these individuals,' cries of 'Rubbish' could be heard, 'but it is even more important, if they control their empires not from London but from Sydney, or New York, or Cape Town and nevertheless influence thinking in this country, that this Parliament introduces laws to satisfy the pent-up public demand for the media to be answerable to this House.'

At this, there was uproar that lasted for several seconds, with the Speaker's plea for order patently ignored. Finally, as the noise subsided, 'Mr Speaker, I would again ask the Prime Minister to consider legislation to satisfy the obvious concern in this country, for objective control over the newspapers we read and indeed the television we watch, which at present is manifestly, indubitably, controlled by a few, a very few, wealthy magnates around the globe, who are not in the least interested in providing objective, educative, reporting, and recent events suggest they may not be fit to run their own lives honourably, never mind their newspapers.'

214

More uproar, as he concluded, 'If this Government is not prepared to do anything, then I pledge that when we are returned to power, we will.'

Pandemonium ensued, with cries of 'Censorship' and 'Dictator' heard above the general din. Finally the Prime Minister was heard to say 'Mr Speaker, we have fought two World Wars to protect the right to freedom of expression. I have nothing further to add.'

The news moved on to an oil tanker that had sprung a leak off Canada's shores and David, his heart racing, turned off the television. His hands were trembling slightly as he continued with his dinner. His mind was in turmoil. What was going on? Now questions in Parliament! And he was sure the whole series of events stemmed from a dinner party that he had attended, but according to people he had met today couldn't have taken place. What David accepted as an obvious fact, after the events of the past few days, was that he had, unwittingly, become embroiled in something big. Very big. Incidents had happened on several continents. A cover-up was obviously involved so far as the infamous weekend dinner party was concerned and that wasn't a one man and his dog exercise. This was powerful stuff! But what the hell was it all about?

David pulled back the curtains and stood frowning out over Heathrow. He watched the lights of the planes as they came into land and then disappeared from view behind the buildings across the road. His mind however wasn't really in tune with his eyes. Carlyle? David smiled wryly. A phone call or a visit to Carlyle – wherever he was – was hardly likely to elicit any information to explain the happenings. But Carlyle had to be the pivot. Work on it – think about it. He closed the curtains as he watched a jumbo lose height sedately. 'Happy landings!' he thought grimly as he reached for his wine glass and filled it. He pulled a face. Carlyle wouldn't like this wine, but some of Carlyle's guests of that weekend couldn't try it, or indeed try anything, any more. Poor sods. Or maybe they had deserved what had happened to them. Who were they? But wait a minute, he had only been thinking about the men. The wives were still about.

Yes, the wives were still about. He hoped.

15

'A cup of tea and a nice piece of home-made fruit cake, dear?'
June's mother, Karen Campbell, looked at her daughter,
anxiously.

'No. No thank you, mother. Not just at the moment.'

June was sitting in the lounge of her parents' house in
Chesham Bois. She could see across the Chess valley to the
farms rising to the north of the hill, several miles away. A red
tractor was creating regular lines of newly turned earth in a field
to her left. Straight ahead, two cars were climbing the hill and
suddenly disappeared as the road led them through a thick
wood. The sky was a pale blue, with small pockets of cumulus
cloud drifting gently eastwards.

June's mother opened the french windows. 'Must let in some of
this lovely air. Why don't you go for a walk, dear? Get some colour
into those cheeks of yours.' She folded her arms across her ample
bosom. 'Go and visit dear old Mrs King at Rose Cottage. You know
she had a stroke in March? Poor old soul has a live-in nurse now.
Afraid she'll never be the same again. She'd love to see you.'

'I will, mother, I will, but not now,' June knew she sounded
irritable and was not being sociable, but, dammit, she didn't feel
very sociable. Where was David? What was he doing? She had
left home in such haste and he hadn't rung yet. God, could
anything have happened to him?

'Is everything all right? With you and David, I mean?' Her
mother's hand rested on her shoulder, tentatively, as though it
might affect the answer. June laughed softly and looked up at
her mother's anxious face.

'Of course, mother. Everything's fine. Don't look so upset! I told you it was just an idea that David and I had. That I should take a few days off, have a rest and come and see you and father – all rolled into one. Don't look for something that isn't there!'

June jumped up and gave her mother a firm kiss on her cheek. 'Maybe I'll have a cup of tea, after all.'

Her mother beamed contentedly. Food and drink – non-alcoholic drink – she had always felt could overcome crises. Look after your stomach and you can face most things, she was very fond of remarking. She was living proof in one sense. She weighed eleven stone and it didn't cause her one moment's concern.

'That's my girl! I'll go and put the kettle on. Be a pet and see if Dad would like one, will you?'

June's lean, grey-haired father was cutting the privet hedge in the back garden. He was on a week's holiday from his solicitor's practice in Amersham. He loved his garden more than his job and was leaving the work more and more to his younger partners. He smiled broadly as June came towards him and stopped, shears in hand.

'Yes, young lady and what can I do for you?' He adored his one and only daughter and had never seen any reason to hide it.

'Cup of tea, Dad?' June wiped the perspiration off his brow with her hand, 'One's being made.'

'I'll bet it is,' he chuckled. 'Some people can't live without it and your mother's one such person. Well, I must admit I could do with a rest.'

He tucked his arm in June's and together they walked back to the house, as a small Cessna aeroplane buzzed overhead. The family house was now far too big for June's parents alone. It was a 1930s five-bedroomed detached house, in half an acre of glorious privacy. It was built when Chesham Bois was still country and few cars were ever seen or heard down the lane. Time had changed all that. Gardens had been sub-divided and the area was now little different from the rest of London's suburbia. Fortunately their house and those immediately around

217

them were owned by those who were holding on to the original conception that had been prevalent when they had been built. A wood pigeon started to coo as they reached the house.

'June! June! Its David!'

June hadn't heard the phone ring. As she ran indoors, her mother was holding the portable phone out for her.

'David, darling. Are you all right?' June realised her mother was frowning at her words. She turned away from her and walked back into the garden. Her father watched her sit on the terrace steps deeply engrossed in listening to whatever David was saying. June didn't seem to be saying very much, but her instantaneous concern had evaporated and she was clearly now talking in a normal manner.

After a few moments he took her out her cup of tea, to save it getting cold. As he arrived June was saying, 'Yes, I understand. I'll start on it straight away. Don't worry. I'll be all right. You take care too, darling. I love you. 'Bye.'

She pressed the off button, looked up at her father and smiled.

'And what are you starting on straight away, young lady?' her father enquired innocently.

'Ask no questions, get told no lies.' June replied cheekily, taking her tea.

'Well, as long as you're not in any trouble.' He licked his upper lip, as he looked her in the eyes, searchingly.

'No, Pops,' she reassured him, with a grin. 'How could you imagine me, or David, being in any trouble? Come on, I'll race you for a piece of that fruit cake.'

*   *   *

Soft morning drizzle. Enough to obscure the windscreen, but not really enough to warrant the regular use of the wipers. June turned the knob to intermittent, as she waved out of the window and left her parents' home. Winding up the window she shuddered, involuntarily. It wasn't cold. The shiver was from fear of the unknown. She headed for Amersham, which was only two miles away and found a phone box, outside the post office.

218

There was only one Abbott listed with the initial G., G.M. in fact, and June prayed that this was George – or the late departed George. The address was 38, The Hollows. A counter clerk gave her directions to The Hollows. She realised she knew the road, just down the hill from the station on the left-hand side, but hadn't known its name. Nice, solidly respectable houses. Two women were chatting in the drive. A grey-haired, tubby lady leaning on the open door of a car was talking to – Lesley Abbott! The right address! June pulled up outside the next house and heart thumping, locked the car and made her way back to number 38. As she reached the entrance to the drive, the car swung out and Lesley Abbott waved dismissively to the grey-haired lady as she pulled away.

'Hallo, Mrs Abbot,' June called out brightly, hands clenched inside her anorak. She smiled expansively, as she approached an obviously bewildered Lesley Abbott, who had been about to shut the front door.

'Its June – er, Price. You remember? We met at that weekend down at Cordington.'

At these words, Lesley Abbott's face straightened from the previous look of enquiry and she went to shut the door.

'Hey! That's not very friendly!' June's foot jammed the door open. This wasn't going to be easy.

Lesley Abbott's firm mouth opened to retort, but before she could say anything, the phone rang behind her in the hallway. It momentarily took her off guard and she stepped back turning her head towards the ringing. This was enough for June and she pushed the door open enough to step inside and shut it, before Lesley Abbott could react.

'Hadn't you better answer it?' June leaned back against the door and resolutely folded her arms. Lesley Abbott was clearly at a loss as to what to do first, as the phone continued its persistent call for attention. Then suddenly it stopped. The intense quiet was stunning. The two women were not more than three feet away from each other.

'What do you want?' Lesley Abbott's voice was controlled, but louder than necessary.

219

'Just a few moments of your time, that's all,' June tried to smile, encouragingly. Her face couldn't quite make it.

'Well?' There was no movement, no invitation to move from their positions.

'I'm sorry about your husband,' June started quietly. 'It must have been a terrible shock. It was in the papers,' she added, unnecessarily.

Lesley Abbott merely stared back, her face unmoving. 'Who are you? What do you want?'

It was now June's turn to stare. 'What do you mean "Who am I"? We were all together at Cordington for...'

'I have never been to Cordington,' Lesley Abbott cut in, impatiently, 'and I have never met you before, so would you kindly leave before I call the police. You are trespassing.'

'Don't be ridiculous,' June waved her hands in the air with exasperation, 'of course you've been to Cordington. Ian Carlyle invited us all down...'

Lesley Abbott turned and walking to the telephone table, she picked up a telephone directory. 'I will now ring the local police station,' she said over her shoulder. 'I repeat, I do not know you and you are wasting my valuable time. If you will not go of your own accord, and I clearly cannot manhandle you out, I shall have to call for assistance.' She put down the directory and began to dial a number.

June reached over and put her hand on the receiver, cutting off the call. 'What's the matter with you? Are you frightened of something, or somebody? How can you expect me to take what you say like this?'

There was no reply. Lesley Abbott merely started dialling again.

June knew she was beaten. She couldn't force the woman to say anything. If the police came, what was her reason for being there? She was visiting her parents nearby and wanted to embarrass them? What could she prove? Nothing. Nothing at this stage. Withdraw and regroup. A grandfather clock chimed, as though bidding farewell, as she walked to the front door and let herself out. There was still a suggestion of drizzle in the air as she made her way back to the car. Everything in the road seemed so tranquil and undemanding. A milkfloat purred by and a mother and her little girl were laughing, as they crossed the road in the wake of a black cat. June couldn't help wishing bitterly that the black cat had crossed her path before she went into number 38. She needed some luck.

She didn't have any some hours later, either, when she found the impressive house where Pat Thatcher lived. Again, it hadn't been too difficult to trace and she had it confirmed that it was the right Surbiton Thatcher from a nextdoor neighbour doing some gardening. As June entered the drive, with the hazy sun that had broken through warming her back, the middle-aged auburn-haired lady called out over some small shrubs.

'Are you wanting Mrs Thatcher?'

'Mrs Pat Thatcher,' June nodded, smiling.

'I'm afraid she's gone away to stay with friends for a few weeks.' The lady was happy to stop work. She walked down her gravel path towards June, wiping her forehead. 'There's no-one there now. Terrible business. Losing her husband like that. Especially it all being in the newspapers as well. Poor Pat.' She shook her head without too much obvious sadness and smiling at June, retraced her steps and re-started her shrub clipping.

June shook her head irritably, as she climbed back into her car. 'Not doing very well, are you, June?' she spoke out loud, as she turned on the ignition.

She let in the clutch and releasing the brake, started to pull out, only to be hooted at by a car that was about to pass her.

'Shit!' June waved apologetically at the woman driver, who gesticulated back in a manner that could never have been described as ladylike. Carefully she pulled out and proceeded to Ealing. To Rita Hardy.

Her luck didn't change. She found houses listed in the local telephone directory under Hardy and after several wasted visits found the next house on the list was empty. Not even any curtains. Bare boards were all there was to be seen through the windows. As June walked back to the gate the next front door opened and a young blonde woman in tight trousers and a low-cut top, called out, 'Can I help?'

'Er. I was looking for a Rita Hardy, but I've obviously got the wrong address.'

'No, no, you haven't. She left a couple of days ago.' The young woman tottered down the path on very high heels.

'Lost her husband, poor love and her with a young family and all. Anyway, seems God felt sorry for her – some relative left her a lot of money it seems and she's put all her stuff in store and left the kids with her mother. She's asked her to get the house on the market, and meanwhile, gone on a cruise while, as she said to me, "she sorts herself out". Good luck I say. Might meet another man, mightn't she?'

'Put the house on the market?' June repeated.

'Yes,' the woman nodded, 'says she wants to live by the sea.' She shrugged her shoulders and said, smiling, 'Wouldn't we all?' Abruptly she turned on her heel and disappeared indoors, without another word.

June remembered Rita well from the weekend. What she'd just heard didn't really surprise her. Not for Rita, too much or too long the grieving widow. Chest out and move on, thought June – especially with that chest. She chuckled momentarily, as she climbed back into the car. Still, it was all pretty sudden, wasn't it? Wonder what David would make of that? Money, by coincidence? Probably Hardy had life assurance, but to change everything so quickly? Did she really have a relative or could it be ... Maybe all the wives had received some money? Excitedly, she drove off towards Sutton wishing she could talk to David. Maybe Jenny Gorman had moved too?

It was early evening before she located the Gorman home in the commuter dormitory town of Sutton. A rural area, scarred by straight, tree-lined roads of detached and semi-detached houses, as though nurtured in the countryside by a giant rake.

Jenny hadn't moved. Not if the sounds of children screaming and a barking dog were anything to go by.

'Thank God! This sounds like a normal house,' June remarked to herself as she rang the doorbell.

The screaming stopped, but the dog appeared to have been startled into even more frantic barking and June could hear it scratching at the other side of the door.

'Coming, coming,' June heard a voice calling out from somewhere at the back. Then, right behind the still barking dog, 'Ben, shut up do! Get out of the way.' The door opened and an aproned Jenny Gorman stood holding a Labrador's collar, as the dog began to quieten down.

'Oh! Have you come for the Scouts Trash 'n Treasure things for next week? I'll just go and get them!' Jenny Gorman went to turn round, letting the dog go, as it slunk back into the house, now totally uninterested in the visitor.

'No. No, I haven't.' June stretched out a hand, as if to stop the retreat. 'I'm June Campbell or rather June Price. I use my maiden name for business. I'm David Price's wife. We met recently at Cordington. I was so sorry to read about your husband.' June saw a flutter of unease cross Jenny Gorman's face, and went on, 'I was in the area and thought I would just call and offer my sincere condolences. Colin seemed such a nice man. I am so sorry.'

Jenny Gorman was obviously in two minds as to how to react. She looked at June sharply and stepping to the doorway, looked urgently left and right. Apparently satisfied at the total lack of movement in the wide tree-lined road, she muttered, almost under her breath.

'You'd better come in. Quickly.'

June needed no encouragement. She was in before Jenny Gorman could have a second thought. Two bright-eyed boys were leaning over the banisters, staring at June. 'Who is it, Mum?' one shouted.

'Boys. Vamoose upstairs. And take Ben with you.'

The dog obviously understood the wish and was already clambering up the red stair carpet, passing the boys on the way. They exchanged a few words that were inaudible to June and without any fuss disappeared with the dog. A door slammed behind them.

'They're lovely kids,' Jenny Gorman led the way to the kitchen. 'Have a seat. Sorry for the mess.'

'Thank you.' June moved a tea towel and sat at the pine table that was laden with food.

'Just come in from the supermarket. Bit late today.' Jenny Gorman suddenly seemed to realise she was not talking to an old friend and her tone became sharper.

'What do you want? Why are you here?'

'Well,' June shrugged. 'I was in the area...'

'Oh, come on!' Jenny rubbed her hands together irritably, 'I remember you live in Chiswick!'

June smiled, 'So you do remember.'

Jenny passed the back of her hand wearily across her forehead, as shrieks suddenly erupted upstairs and died away as quickly. 'Look, I, have nothing to say. Absolutely nothing. I don't know why I let you in. Please go.' She moved to the kitchen door.

'Jenny, what's going on?' June pleaded. 'Please, I'm frightened. David is the only husband still alive from that weekend!'

'Well, aren't you the lucky one.' Jenny didn't move, but her face was in agony and there were tears in her eyes. 'Go home! You've nothing to worry about so long as you just forget everything. Everything!'

The last word was almost shouted. With that Jenny stumbled out to the front door and opened it. 'Go!' she said loud enough to cause a door upstairs to open. June could hear the boys come out on the landing, whispering. She realised she would learn little more and wasn't sure she wanted to. Without another word, nor a further glance at Jenny, she left.

It was very late when she arrived back at Chesham Bois. As she quietly closed the car door she glanced at the full moon in a clear sky. The stars winked at her. She didn't wink back. It was lucky, she thought, as she let herself in quietly, that she had borrowed a key to save disturbing her parents. They had both heard her come in. Neither had gone to sleep. Parents never stop worrying about their children and June's parents couldn't fathom out what on earth was going on, which was justification enough for their worries.

16

'Honey? It's David.'

June awoke to see her mother standing over her holding out the portable phone. The curtains had been pulled back and outside the sky was cloudless. June could hear a lawnmower nearby, joined by the gentle throb of a light aircraft.

'Goodness! What's the time?' June sat up, wide awake and swung her feet down onto the rug. 'Ten o'clock? Good God!'

Her mother didn't answer as she handed over the phone. You said you came for a rest, she thought, and a rest you'll have, if I can see to it.

'Darling, where are you?' June pressed the phone closely to her ear, as though she was trying to touch him.

'I'm home, June,' was David's surprising response.

'Home? But I don't understand.' June's bewilderment was blatant.

David reminded June of his day at Cordington and his night near Heathrow, deliberating. How he was sure the whole Cordington charade had been put on for the men's benefit, but now, reflecting, he was more convinced than ever that he was not meant to have been there. The invitation was a mistake and not meant for them and as soon as it was realised who they were, they had been excluded from everything that had then happened.

'And then,' continued David, 'whilst still trying to decide how to proceed, I rang home to see if there were any messages on the answering machine, and there were several, but only one that was of any importance.'

June didn't think a comment was needed. She waited.

'It was not a voice I recognised. I guess "they" would make sure it was an unconnected voice. But the message was loud and clear. I've listened to it several times since I got back. It was simply: "Forget and nothing at all will happen. Put it all out of your mind. How is Chesham Bois?"' At this June's blood ran cold. '"Just get on with your lives and forget. The door has closed".'

'"The door has closed"?' June's mouth was dry after hearing the message.

'Yes.' David went on, excitedly, 'don't you see? That verse of Carlyle's at Cordington. "We were young, we were merry, we were very very wise, And the door stood open at our feast!" The message is "The door has closed". Finito, end, closed! No threat from us and there will be no more threats from them.'

June looked at her painted toe nails, 'How do you know you're right?' she asked.

'Well, darling, I can't prove I'm right,' David replied, 'but after hearing that I'm as sure as I can be. So I drove to the office and I have dictated on to tape everything I can remember and put it in my safe with an enveloped instruction to give it to Donald Havers, if anything happens to me.'

'Oh, that's just great,' retorted June. 'A bit bloody late then, isn't it? You can't just trust a ... a ... message!' She was aghast at the turn of events.

'I'm not, by itself, June,' said David, 'but ...' there was a pause, 'have you seen today's papers?'

'No,' June shook her head. 'I was worn out, last night, and I haven't told you how I got on yesterday, yet. Anyway your call caused mother to wake me.'

'I'm sorry, darling. How did you get on?'

June briefly summarised the weary day and David responded by saying, 'There you are! More advice to forget and never mind the papers today.'

'Yes. All right,' June was getting slightly irritated, 'but what's in the bloody papers?'

David answered, 'It's been announced that Tanya and Ian Carlyle have gone to the Soviet Union, having disclosed their

226

lifetime belief in the future of Communism, and will not be returning to the UK.'

'What?' June exclaimed.

'Yes. It's true. Apparently all his business interests are in Liechtenstein trusts, set up to help the expansion of true Communism – whatever that might be – and they've gone!' There was a pause.

'How extraordinary.' June's mind was in a whirl. 'It doesn't make sense.'

'Oh, I think it could,' said David. 'Anyway, having read this in the papers and being in a total quandary as to what to do next, that's what I've done – put everything on tape.'

June realised her mother was standing frowning at her, holding a cup of tea.

'Sorry,' she said, to all and sundry, 'but ... well, bugger me.'

'June!' Her mother firmly put down the cup of tea and stalked out of the bedroom. She was not used to even mild, bad language. Certainly not in her house.

'But June,' David said positively, 'don't you see? It could all make sense. All the people who are involved with the deaths of the guests at Cordington are capitalists. Don't you think that could be the reason? Press barons. Wealthy, influential people. All sucked in, by one means or another, and now in terrible trouble. Even the Prime Minister is answering questions on it in the House of Commons! This Carlyle man has set hares off in all directions and the hounds are now chasing around, ready to tear the portals of capitalism down!'

'Aren't you getting your metaphors all mixed up?' June asked, amused, but her mind was working. 'I suppose you could be right. Can we trust the media in the hands of a few non-Government-controlled individuals? Trust the State. But why not tell Donald all about it now? He's supposed to be in one of those MI things. If there's anything in it let him find out.'

'No,' David's voice was firm, 'I told him about our weekend at Cordington the other day and he wasn't inclined to take it very seriously. Remember also that now all traces of the visit have disappeared. If Donald wants to follow it up, good for him, but

227

I'm not mentioning it any more. I, we, are getting on with our lives.'

'I'm sure,' June was pensive, 'he could find traces of the weekend, if he's a professional.'

'June,' David exploded, 'what does it matter now – to us. Let sleeping dogs lie and let the wide-awake Prices live''

'It seem such a let down.'

'Why? We can't bring the husbands back. The wives, somehow, have been bought off or terrified out of their wits and anyway we don't know who these couples are ... were, do we? They could all have been involved, for all we know. They can hardly have been innocents, damn it! As for the murders – well, murder is murder and various police forces are dealing with all of that. No, let it be.'

June drank her tea. Why did her mother make it so strong? It didn't need the cup, it could stand up on its own. She wrinkled her nose, as she returned the cup to the saucer. It was cold now, too.

'It fits,' she nodded, 'just like this cup and saucer.'

'What?' David sounded confused.

'No, forget it darling,' June smiled, 'I'll come home this morning, then.'

'No, June,' David's voice was measured. 'Please stay for a couple of days. I'll ring you morning and afternoon. I shall go back to my normal routine and if by, say, Friday night, nothing has happened, then come home and we'll pick up the pieces and you can go back to work on Monday. You'll have had a rest for a day or two, anyway.'

'All right, darling,' June was unsure, but looking out of the window at the lush green countryside, she was prepared to accept that it was a pleasant concept. 'It is a rather nice idea. All right. Ring me tonight and I'll see you Saturday morning, all being well.'

All was well and she returned home to find David immersed in a takeover investigation. Pressure of work was forcing the recent extraordinary events from the forefront of his mind. There was no blue van in their street. No more messages by post, nor by phone. He may well be being watched in some

228

covert way to make sure he heeded the advice, but David did believe it was over for them, if they just got on with their lives, and it was so much easier if one was busy.

For June, it was time to concentrate on organising the next season's stock and the sale period was on. It took June longer, but it soon began to fade from her consciousness, too. Each day brought its business problems, but during as many evenings as work would allow, came the togetherness that they had both grown to cherish. Their lives returned to normal or as normal as any lives ever are.

17

London, November 1991

The sky was leaden and the rain was the gentle but persistent kind that Londoners know so well. It was not ferocious nor gusting, but it was of sufficient, all-embracing insidiousness, that anyone caught out in it and not protected, would be soaked through in no time at all. David had been caught out in it, without even an umbrella. It had been dry and threatening when he had left the office to go to a client on his way home, but he had not bargained for the difficulty he had had finding a parking space. He had finally found one in a back street off Hammersmith Broadway and on leaving the client an hour later, there was nothing for it, but to run with his heavy paper-laden briefcase, the half mile back to the car. He arrived home sodden and quickly ran an invigorating hot shower.

'Darling, is that you?' David heard June's light voice call out a few minutes later.

'It had better be,' he yelled, 'unless you are used to other naked men roaming about in here.' He came out of the shower, rubbing himself fiercely.

'Hi!' June had thrown off her raincoat and gave him a perfunctory kiss on his nose. 'Terrible night.'

'You don't have to tell me,' David protested and he told her of his miserable journey at the top of his voice, for she had disappeared. As David dressed, he could hear her busying herself, lighting the fire and switching on the television, before beginning to clatter things in the kitchen.

David walked into the sitting room just as the signature-tune started for the early evening news and he was aware that June must have the small television on in the kitchen, for the sound was almost stereophonic.

The announcer started, 'Good evening. The body of Robert Maxwell, the publisher and newspaper proprietor, has been recovered from the Atlantic off the coast of the Canary Islands. He had been on board his yacht, *Lady Ghislaine*, but this morning he was reported missing. After an air search lasting some hours, his body was found twenty miles south west of Gran Canaria and taken to Las Palmas. A post-mortem examination is expected to be carried out tomorrow. A local witness said the body had been found naked and it is too early to determine the cause of death.'

There then followed a brief resumé of Maxwell's career by a correspondent who ended his report with: 'It is known that Robert Maxwell had been suffering from depression, exhaustion and a heavy cold when he flew from London to Gibraltar last Thursday, and one has to wonder whether this was an accident or suicide? No doubt we will know in the fullness of time.' The announcer moved on to another atrocity in Northern Ireland, as David, his heart pounding, walked leaden footed to the television set and turned it off. His mind was in turmoil. He couldn't structure his thoughts.

'Was this an accident or was it suicide, or was it murder?' David heard June's voice mimicking the announcer. He turned to see an ashen-faced June, standing in the doorway, clutching a tea towel to her breast. He realised she must have turned off the kitchen television too. All he could hear was the ticking of the grandfather clock, as June walked towards him.

'If it is murder, I am sure no-one will ever prove it.' June whispered, looking into his eyes, searching for comfort. 'We've been here before, haven't we?'

David pulled her to him and held her in a close embrace. 'You're obviously thinking that there could be a connection,' he muttered, half to himself, 'but there doesn't have to be any connection at all. The others were, what, three years ago?

231

Nothing's happened since then. This could be just an unfortunate accident. Anyway, the other newspaper owners weren't killed.'

'No,' June looked at him, 'but the result in each case was not much different. They were all disgraced, and, or, found guilty of various crimes, including murder. So good God, David, it's not difficult to associate this with the others.'

'Not difficult, darling,' David took her troubled face in his hands, 'but not reasonable.'

'Reasonable? Of course, it's reasonable,' June pulled away and slowly returned to the kitchen, as David followed. She turned on the small portable radio which was tuned into Radio Three and Sibelius' violin concerto. She picked up the potato-peeler and assiduously concentrated on the King Edwards.

'OK,' David leant against the door frame, 'let's just calm down . . .'

'I am calm,' June sounded anything but, as she interrupted him.

'OK,' David repeated, 'let's just go down memory lane for a moment.' There was no response from June.

'Hans Hawkins in Newcastle had his dealings exposed in the tabloids and amid the outcry he accepted a management buy-out for a paltry sum then committed suicide, a beaten man. Schmidt was murdered in Johannesburg six months after our famous weekend at Cordington, when his background came out. The murder was reckoned to be the work of an Israeli hit squad, suspected to be attached to Mossad. His company was floated in South Africa and is doing very well. David Charrington was found guilty of murder in Sydney, very much on the evidence of one of his own staff and is serving a life sentence in Australia, and after plea-bargaining Frank Sorretto is serving ten years and his empire declining rapidly. An unhappy band of pilgrims,' David paused, 'But none of them was killed directly, darling. None of them.'

June's shoulders were taut. 'I know,' she shook her head, vehemently, 'but in some ways they might as well have been. Maybe "they" ran out of patience or time with Maxwell, or,' she paused and glared at David, 'maybe the post-mortem will find

232

he died by committing suicide, but is it possible, these days, to be absolutely sure? Maybe "they" had helped create such a financial crisis that, rather than face ruin, this was his way out. As successful an end as the others!'

David's arms encircled her waist. 'A lot of maybes,' he whispered, 'I...'

June wriggled away. 'Don't patronise me,' she cried, 'we've lived through the hell of this for...'

The phone's shrill tones made them both jump. David reached for it.

'Hallo? Yes, this is David Price.' There was a pause, as he listened. 'When? Where? Yes, yes, I'm sorry. What do you know?'

June by this time had stopped peeling potatoes and was watching David's frowning countenance.

'I see,' David's voice was very controlled, 'yes, thank you, John. Yes, of course, I understand. Goodbye.'

'What was all that about?' June watched David turn and look out of the window, unseeing.

'It's my cousin Douglas, he's been killed in Spain,' he said slowly. 'That was John Turner, the Police Inspector I know at the club. Apparently it was a hit and run accident. I knew DP had gone on holiday to Spain. On his own, touring, he said.'

'Oh, God, I'm sorry,' June stroked David's arm. 'Can't say I ever liked Douglas very much but... where did the police say he was killed?'

'La Linea in Spain,' David replied, watching the rain increase in intensity. Nature's tears of condolence. 'La Linea,' he repeated, slowly, turning to look at June. 'Hold on a minute! Isn't that ... Where's our atlas?' David's voice had suddenly dried in his throat, as he rushed to the bookcase.

'What do you want that for?' June turned to him, perplexed.

David didn't reply, as he found the book and frantically searched the index, before turning the pages, impatiently. June walked over to him, frowning, 'What are you looking for?' she persisted.

'June,' David looked at her, trouble written all over his face, 'La Linea is not a million light years from Gibraltar, where

233

Maxwell was last week. It's just down the coast. What if DP was involved, somehow?'

There was a prolonged silence, as June put the atlas back and joined David who had gone to the sofa and was sitting, jaw resting in his hands. After several minutes, David reflected in a low, measured voice, 'Let's go back to Cordington. We know every man who was there has died, except me. I was told to forget the weekend. I was a mistake. We both accept that. What we didn't ask ourselves was, why the mistake? Someone else should have been there. The invitation wasn't addressed to David Price. It was addressed to D. Price. It was meant for my cousin. *He* should have gone. Somehow, maybe, they – "they" caught up with him later and his assignment – God, I know, it sounds unbelievable – was Maxwell, and he achieved it and now he's gone the way of all the other guests – or would-be guests – of that weekend. As it turns out, they were all partners in death, after that weekend. And the irony of that is my cousin who is, was, a partner in our firm, has also apparently joined them. He moved from one partnership to another.'

There was stillness. June was catching up with the outpouring and her mind was racing.

'But, it's all conjecture. I know. I know,' she put up her hands, 'I'm reversing the role of doubter, now, but it's, it's ... so breathtakingly awful.' She was rubbing her hands round her neck. 'We don't know it was Douglas who was invited or that he is, was, involved in anything. Anything at all.'

'Who knew the others were?' David asked drily. 'I doubt if their families did.'

'Maybe, maybe not,' June rubbed her brow, 'I know you voiced the theory back in '88 that maybe the whole thing could have been some Communist conspiracy plot, but so much has happened since then. Gorbachev is throwing his weight behind rapprochement. Russian troops are out of Afghanistan; there were no anti-Thatcher demonstrations during her visit to Poland; Hungary is becoming more democratic and worldwide the era of the hardliners is really over.' She paused, 'What did Gorbachev say? "There are no bears in Russia to be scared of any more." With all this, it's difficult to believe that what might have been the case in '88 is still the case in '91. I just can't see that the theory you voiced then could apply now, even if it was true in the first place!'

'Rubbish!' David looked askance. 'People don't change their aims just by a few words or actions. It's easy for them to encourage relaxation by the West, which is based on relief, and then when the defences are down, the aims can be achieved by other means. No,' he shook his head, 'it's possible. Come on, you started this line of thinking.'

There was another long silence, before June commented slowly, 'OK it fits. I accept that I said it, but thinking about it it's all superficial. There's a damn sight too much conjecture in it: like, I guess, all of this Maxwell business. It's three years on, for Christ sake! Maxwell has died more than three years after the Cordington weekend! Why wait this long? If it was a connected campaign to discredit the capitalist press or whatever the real objective was, wouldn't it all have happened at the same time? If all the other men at Cordington died after something that they could have been involved in, why would Douglas get involved later, knowing the same fate would happen to him? Terrible things came out about the other newspaper proprietors. What's Maxwell done if your hypothesis is right, apart from having financial problems that many people have?'

David turned. 'Don't ask me for explanations, damn it! It'll be months, if not years, before anyone knows the truth of what I suppose will be called the Maxwell affair.' He paused. 'If ever. I'm only telling you what you've just said. It fits, and,' he added, as an afterthought, 'DP, didn't know about Cordington, because he didn't go.'

'Also,' he added positively, 'as it happens, there's no wife to worry about with Douglas or DP whatever you call him, because poor Alice died last June.'

'Wife? Oh, Yes,' June nodded, 'I see what you mean. No. What were the names of those wives?' She thought for a moment. 'Rita, Lesley...' she paused frowning.

'Jenny and Pat,' David smiled, momentarily, as he helped her out. He made a wry face and walked through to the kitchen where he collected two wine glasses and proceeded to pour two

235

glasses from the wine box in the fridge. 'Perhaps I should ring Donald Havers,' he called out.

'David,' June took one of the glasses as he reappeared, 'back in, whenever, you said leave it to the professionals and let's keep our heads down and get on with our lives. For God's sake, now is the time to take your own advice! We've put it behind us and everything has been fine. Let's keep it that way! If poor old cousin Douglas really was involved we can't bring him back to life and if he wasn't, we will look like idiots and, God, we were told to forget it! Leave it to the police and any other agencies that get involved! But, don't involve us!'

David raised his glass, looking at June severely. 'You're not just a pretty face,' he said. 'Cheers and maybe more importantly, good health. That's indeed what I said and I guess I'll live by that. Pardon the pun.'

'Don't!' June shuddered and leant her forehead on his chin. 'Cheers,' she said, 'but I don't feel very cheery.'

David kissed her hair, as she asked, 'I wonder if the truth will ever come out on this Maxwell business? To tell us whether we're raving lunatics to think like this?'

David drank his wine. He didn't have a worthwhile answer and anyway he felt it was really a rhetorical question.

18

Broome, August 1996

As the Ansett flight circled in an anticlockwise direction, June thrilled at the contrasting colours below. Vivid shades of green and blue sea to the shoreline, where rich yellow beach for miles on end gave way to intense red soil inland. Extraordinarily, distinctive. The landing wheels came down and the 146 banked and headed towards the runway.

The touchdown was perfect and in only a few seconds it seemed the door of the plane was open and June and David were the first down the steps. The warmth of the sun hit them hard. The air was not humid. It was just very hot. Their stopover in Perth had been pleasant enough with clear blue skies, but there had been little warmth in the winter sun. Here, after the two-hour flight, they were in the tropics and the short walk to the small attractive terminal building reminded June that they had indeed heeded the travel guide's advice and brought plenty of sun oil. It was clearly going to be needed. June took David's arm, as they waited for the laughing Ansett staff to unload the luggage. They all wore a smart tropical uniform of white shirts, blue shorts and long white socks.

'I know this is going to be a wonderful holiday, darling,' she said, looking for their luggage.

'All I know is that I'm very tired,' David responded bitterly. He had found it virtually impossible to sleep on the long flight from Heathrow and was, he knew, stupidly irritated that June had managed to sleep so well for so long.

'You're a pig,' she banged her head on his shoulder. 'Don't spoil it before it's begun.'

'I won't,' he laughed weakly. 'Just let me get a good night's sleep and I'll be fine.'

Their luggage found, they turned to a young man wearing the uniform of the resort where they were booked, Cable Beach Club Resort. He happily took charge and with three other couples they very quickly found themselves being driven through the lush bougainvillaea-lined roads. The driver pointed out varieties of wattle and gum trees along the way and June was entranced with the journey. The earth was brick-red and blew in gentle waves across the road in front of them. There was evidence of much new residential development, with owners endeavouring to produce attractive gardens in what were clearly harsh conditions. Sand dunes hid the sea for long stretches, until the road led them to The Resort right on the beach. It looked very welcoming.

* * *

'Too bloody true, mate!' the obese, suntanned, young Australian, dressed in no more than an old, once white T-shirt, green shorts below his pot belly, and thongs, mashed the remains of his cigarette into the already over-full ashtray.

It was surprising that any ordinary level of conversation could be maintained at all, against the noise of the colour television, hanging from the ceiling at the far end of the room. It was blaring out the horse racing taking place on the other side of Australia at Flemington racecourse in Melbourne. The hand that had tuned the colour must have belonged to someone totally colour-blind, for to look at the screen severely hurt the eyes. The greens, reds, blues were so overpowering in their intensity as to be totally unreal. It didn't really matter, for no-one was looking at them. The bar at The Jackaroo was full, and animated conversation in the early evening, after the day's work, was competing successfully with the TV commentator. There was no air-conditioning, only ceiling fans cutting through the hot evening air and sending a welcome, but slight, breeze across the smoke-hazed room. The walls were wood panelled

238

and the wooden rafters, floor and tables, suggested that no attempt had been made to soften the austere impact. In fact, the impression to the newcomer was of an intention to reflect the history of the area. Harsh and frugal with few creature comforts. Old photographs of luggers caught in cyclones and local Dutch World War Two flying boats bombed by the Japanese, assisted the impression of the starkness that had been associated with Broome's recent history. The tourist boom of the 1980s may have brought much prettying-up of roads and verges in the town, but nothing had touched The Jackaroo.

'Did you see the state of that bloody four-wheel drive Andy towed in this morning?' The same man turned to the thin, leathery-faced, grizzled, older man to his left, who without looking away from his glass of beer, merely nodded, sorrowfully.

'Driver lucky to be alive, I reckon. Stupid bastard fell asleep at the wheel, they say.' 'They' were not defined. ''Parently driving down from Katherine – yer know 'ow it is.'

The older man nodded again and this time drank some of his beer. 'Andy's a good 'un,' he replied, leaning his elbows back on the bar and scratching his stubble whilst he belched.

The young man crossed his legs as he indicated to the pretty, big-breasted blonde behind the bar to refill their glasses. Or that appeared to be the message to an outsider, but what she actually did was flip open two ice-cold cans and slide them to nestle adroitly between the two men.

'Yeh, came in from Alice five years ago. Shooting through, but stayed. Yer know 'ow it is.' Again, the nod of agreement.

'G'day mate!' Their soporific conversation was interrupted by another young man, similarly dressed but wearing an akubra pulled down on his forehead and sprouting a full black beard, who had pushed his way through the madding crowd and slapped the younger of the two men on the back.

'G'day, Brian, old son. 'Ow yer doin'?' Surprisingly, the older man smiled, animatedly, at the newcomer.

'Good' was the enthusiastic response. 'Foster's, Sue,' he nodded to the quizzical barmaid. 'Just got back,' he added, turning back to his father, who nodded at the other man.

'Steve 'ere was jus' talking "bout Andy.'

Brian took a gulp, 'Yeah?'

' 'Nother roll near Lake Eda on the Great Northern Highway,' Steve responded, by way of explanation. Andy's been and brought it back.'

'Oh,' Brian didn't seem particularly interested. 'Strewth, its been bloody hot up at the pearl farm, last couple of weeks.' He shook his head.

'Yeah, would be, I reckon. Winter's almost over,' his father nodded into his beer. There was a gale of raucous laughter from a crowd further along the bar and someone was heard to yell, 'Good on yer! When the white ants stop holding hands that house'll fall over! See yer later, if not before.' But no head turned other than those in the group, as the voice disappeared through the throng.

'Still busy?' Brian turned to Steve.

'Yeah, flat out, like a lizard drinkin'. Takin' Bessie down to Perth when it gets dark,' he replied.

'How's she?' asked Brian.

'Oh, OK,' came the reply with a gulp of beer, 'reckon she'll need some new tyres when I get there.'

June and David had been sitting at a table against the wall listening, enthralled by the conversation. They had instinctively decided that to try and talk above the hubbub was pretty pointless and anyway, the atmosphere and conversation were fascinatingly different from London.

June opened her eyes wide and smiled at David, indicating her enjoyment of their early evening visit to one of the famous pubs in Broome. This was their second evening at The Resort. They had spent the time to date acclimatising to the warm weather and recovering from the trip. Jet-lag had hit both of them and they had taken sleeping pills to try and accommodate the drastic time difference from London.

June looked out of the open window beside her. 'Look at that sunset, David!'

The Jackaroo was on the edge of the area known as Chinatown and from where they sat they happened to have an

240

uninterrupted view of the sun settling, visibly slowly, over the horizon, radiating a fierce orange glow.

'It's fantastic!' June watched, as the sun sank gently out of sight, before her eyes. There was not a cloud in the sky. No-one around them seemed at all interested in the awesome sight, but then June supposed they had the opportunity of seeing it most days of the year. She had already been told that every night, visitors congregated out at Cable Beach, with or without cameras, to watch the breathtaking colours at dusk, especially if there were clouds to paint an even more beautiful picture. She could now understand why. It was as though the horizon was on fire.

'David? One more and we'd better head back for dinner?'

David nodded and disappeared into the moving throng round the television. The colour nor the context of the broadcast had improved.

'You workin' hard too?' Brian's father asked.

'Yeah. Some days I'm so tired I couldn't go two rounds with a revolvin' door. Harvest time always bloody flat out.' Brian replied. 'Worries over security these days doesn't help. Ray's had to erect radar now to keep a bloody watch over the farm. Been the odd case of boats coming in at night.'

'So I've 'eard.' His father had lost interest and lit up a cigarette, after offering one to Steve.

'Y'know I saw old Billy Derwent lunch time, pissed out of 'is mind. 'E was yellin' at his missus outside 'ere. "Woman," 'e said, "everyone's got the right to be ugly, but you're bloody abusing it!" She 'it 'im with a new tin bucket she'd just bought and flattened him! They 'ad to get 'im up to the 'ospital! I tell you, those Abos!' He cackled with laughter and started a bout of coughing. The other two roared, as June found herself giggling into her glass of white wine.

She looked out of the window again and idly watched some cars parking and others leaving. There were a few tourists looking in the windows of the now mostly closed shops. Her attention was somehow caught by a stocky short man, climbing into a grey four-wheel drive on the other side of the road and thus with his back to her. She watched as he backed out and drove off.

241

'What are you frowning about? I haven't been that long.' David placed the drinks on the table and sank into his chair. June turned to him, the frown still written all over her face.

'I just saw someone's outline as he got into his car and drive away and I'm sure I recognised him,' she replied.

David stared at her, mockingly. 'Darling, we don't know anybody in Broome! We don't even know Broome!'

'I know,' she replied hesitatingly, 'but he looked familiar.'

'Well,' David sipped his wine, 'it's not a big place. Maybe we'll see him again.'

June nodded as she heard the threesome in front of them agree that, in Steve's words, 'Wayne was 'as tight as a banjo string. Wouldn't give you the time of day.'

'Meanest bastard I've ever met,' Brian commented. 'He's become the cocky on the biscuit tin. We buy some of our supplies off him and he needs competition to wake him up.'

'It's coming, it's coming,' his father sank his lips into his glass. 'Broome's changing by the week. Full of outsiders, who've woken up to what's happening 'ere. The pearl industry and tourism are thriving and it brings others with it.' He shook his head morosely. 'Not sure I like it – there'll be squillions of people here before long. You watch.'

June leaned forward conspiratorially, 'What on earth's "cocky on the biscuit tin" mean?' she whispered to David.

'Ah!' He grinned confidentially, 'it means he's now an outsider in this closely knit town. It derives from a tin of biscuits emblazoned with a picture of a parrot, therefore it was outside, away from the biscuits.'

'Jesus!' June stared open-mouthed. 'How on earth did you know that?'

'Well,' David's complacent smile was beginning to irritate June. 'I read an article on the plane explaining some of the Oz vernacular and that happened to be one of them!'

'God help me!' June sipped her wine in disgust. 'What other smartarse quotes can you remember – no,' she paused, 'I don't think I want to know.'

242

'Only one!' David held his hand up, as a gesture of a truce. 'Underground chicken!' June forbade to respond.

'Rabbit!' David laughed. 'Only the Australians would have to use another definition for the poor old rabbit!'

June's face became troubled again, as her mind wandered back to a few moments before.

'Who *was* that, just now?' She pondered.

'Oh, come on darling, drink up and let's go,' David set the example, and picking up her bag she followed him out into the comparative calm of downtown Broome. The shops were now all shut or shutting and the parking bays emptying, exposing the small waves of red dirt for another day. A few elderly Aboriginal men in motley attire were sitting on the grass at the roadside, engrossed in conversation, the subject of which, David couldn't begin to imagine.

'They're not very pretty people, are they?' June followed his fleeting glimpse sideways and contemplated their jet-black skin and flat facial features, topped by unruly thick hair, equally black.

'They probably don't think you're very pretty, either,' David followed the sign to The Resort.

'Impossible!' June shook her head dismissively and chuckled, holding on to David's arm. Already cars had their headlights on coming towards them, as the period between daylight and night was very short, and as David leaned forward to turn his lights on, June clapped her hands to her face.

'My God! My God!'

David braked violently, as he shot her an astonished glance. She shook her head, as she lurched forward. 'No, drive on! It's all right. Sorry about that, but ... I've just realised ... that man's silhouette ... Carlyle! Bloody Ian Carlyle!'

David found it difficult to concentrate on the road, as his hands gripped the steering wheel hard. 'Rubbish, darling!' his voice sounded dry. 'He's in Russia or somewhere.'

'Exactly,' June's voice was measured panic now, 'Or some-where. It couldn't have been him, could it?'

'No, of course not!' David bit back.

'No, of course not!' mimicked June, studiously looking out of

243

her side window. 'What did Sherlock Holmes say? "There is but one step from the grotesque to the horrible".'

They drove the rest of the way in silence, but not in peace, with their own private thoughts.

*　　*　　*

The next morning David and June had an enjoyable early swim on Cable Beach. They walked for a while and David inhaled the unique smell of wet sand as the gulls screeched above them. There were a few other early risers, but as the beautifully clean, flat beach seemed to go on forever, David felt that people at this time of the morning had an average of a mile each, if they had cared to spread out. As it was they all stayed reasonably close to The Resort that overlooked the beach and clearly all luxuriated quietly, as the gentle waves lapped the shore. Nothing else could be heard, as hand in hand they climbed the few steps back from whence they had come. David's eye was caught by the mass of lilac convolvulus growing on the slopes. Natures own contribution to the new man-made development nearby.

'So what do we do, today?' he asked, as surprised, he passed a bare-breasted young woman on her way to the beach. From the colour of her breasts this was clearly not the first time she had dressed in just bikini pants.

'I know what you're not doing!' came the reply, as June playfully kicked him behind his knee, causing him to buckle momentarily.

'OK! OK! I only looked!' He chuckled, encircling her waist, as they made their way back to their room.

'There's a talk on the history of the Broome pearling industry and a look at one of the old pearling luggers down near Streeter's Jetty at ten o'clock,' June remarked over breakfast. 'Could be interesting?'

'Really?' David looked doubtful. 'This wouldn't be leading up to looking at some Broome pearls by any chance?'

'No!' June looked mortified. 'I really think it would be fascinating to learn a little bit about the pearling industry. There can't be a better place to find out than Broome.'

David looked out over the verandah at the red and purple bougainvillaea waving in the gentle breeze, as half a dozen larrakeets flew by. His gaze continued across to the palm trees beyond. 'Wouldn't you rather sit by the pool?' he asked, hopefully.

'Yes, afterwards,' June knew she had won. 'I'll go and book it, when we've finished.'

At ten o'clock they joined about twenty other tourists who were standing quietly, awkward and subdued. They had obviously all realised or had been warned, about the strength of the sun, for not one was hatless. Hats apart, their clothes were an assortment of shorts, cotton trousers, swimming trunks, T-shirts and bikini tops, reflecting a common awareness of the gathering heat of the day.

A lean, pockmarked, middle-aged man appeared, seemingly from nowhere, dressed smartly in crisp white shirt, brown shorts and white knee-length socks with brown shoes. His face was partly hidden by large sunglasses and an akubra hat.

'Welcome, ladies and gentlemen,' he began. 'My name's Chris Mayne . . .' and after a few moments of banter and finding out where people were from, he had his audience relaxed and cheerful.

'Right,' Mayne looked around his listeners, 'Broome came into being in November 1883 when the Governor in Perth issued a pronouncement naming it as such and the Crown started selling lots at twenty pounds each. There weren't many takers at the time, as the area was mosquito-ridden from the mangrove swamps, which you can still see, and was a shanty town with a few pearlers' camps of itinerant workers. The Governor in 1883 was a certain Sir Frederick Napier Broome so there was not a lot of imagination used to find a name for the town!' Several of the audience smiled, involuntarily.

'The town developed slowly and miserably, with Aborigines stalking the area and raiding for whatever they could find, before disappearing back into the bush. The pearlers actually lived on schooners offshore and it was only the poorer workers who had to make do on land. However, because of problems with the submarine cable linking Australia with the world at large, which was laid from Darwin to Java, Broome was chosen as an alternative site and in 1897 Broome's deep-water jetty was built. Shortly thereafter, with other private investment, it became the cargo port for the north western area of Australia. It developed steadily with a customs house, hospital and, of course, the inevitable police station and jail! Over the turn of the century it came to produce eighty per cent of the world's mother of pearl shell from along this coast.'

David leaned over to whisper in to June's ear, 'How about a coffee? This is going to be as boring as hell.'

'Shut up. I'm finding it very interesting!' She replied, arms firmly folded, not even looking at him. David sighed inwardly and eased his way surreptitiously into the shade that was available under the roof of a workshop near the jetty. Mayne noticed David's move and nodded.

'Maybe you would all like to move into the shade,' he said. 'I'm sure you don't need to be reminded that if you are not used to the strength of the sun up here you will regret not taking care. I'm pleased to see you're all wearing hats of some sort.'

David found himself the centre of fleeting attention, as the group shuffled in his direction. 'Smartarse,' June whispered, as she sidled up to him. David found a seat and quietly subsided into it. One or two of the others guiltily followed suit.

Mayne continued, 'In the early days, pearls and pearl shell were fished for by skin-divers. They were a mixture of Europeans, Malays and Aborigines. Although the Aborigines disliked the white man instinctively, some of them turned out to be excellent skin-divers. They had superb physiques and were hardy people. They were harshly treated by many of the pearlers, who had to combat sharks, crocodiles, swarms of cockroaches, never mind flies and mosquitos, in their desire to become rich. The skin-divers often suffered from ruptured eardrums, and from time to time would suffer shallow-water blackout – that is, they would become unconscious from holding their breath, and many died.' He paused and looked at the pensive faces around him.

'The Aborigines' reward for this frightening work?' Mayne asked. 'Food and tobacco! The pearlers saw no point in giving them money – what would they do with it? You may well ask why they did the work. Well, if I said kidnapping and enforced labour, encouraged by whips and chains?' One or two people in the crowd shook their heads sadly and the rest looked suitably grave.

'About the time Broome officially came into existence however, skin-diving was being replaced by helmet-divers and this in itself meant the end of Aborigines in pearling proper, because they couldn't handle the intricacies of the cumbersome equipment. The Japanese then came to the fore. They were very hard-working and were prepared to put up with being fed on rice and fish as well as the cramped conditions on the luggers.'

'Is that why there is a Japanese cemetery?' interjected a little, round, middle-aged lady dressed in white shirt and shorts and exhibiting a very red, sun-scorched face.

'Yes,' Mayne nodded, 'some of you may have seen already the Japanese cemetery located on Port Drive. Over nine hundred pearl divers are buried there and it has been caringly restored. Those who haven't been, I'm sure will find it very interesting. It is a fitting tribute to those who helped bring prosperity to Broome because, of course, you must appreciate that the economy of the community here was based on pearling. The spin-off was work for the hotels, shopkeepers, gaming houses where gambling was rife, shipping companies – you name it – pearling was the life source of Broome.'

'And death,' commented the same middle-aged lady, bitterly.

'Indeed,' Mayne did not look at her, but continued, 'and, of course, the turn of the century brought civilisation, as proved by T.B. Ellis, who was reputed to be the best pearl cleaner in the industry, when he took out a pawnbroker's licence!' Mayne paused and the group looked upwards as a light aircraft swept in low, to land at the airport just down the road.

'Anyway,' Mayne continued, 'although the outbreak of the

247

First World War caused a hiatus as shell became unsaleable, the Government, God bless it, guaranteed a pearl-shell price, after a while, to save the town from ruin. After the war, the Japanese were needed because they were the best, but, being foreigners, they weren't really wanted – a subtle difference!'

'What's new?' asked an elderly white-haired man, before realising he was standing next to a Japanese couple, who just carried on smiling, inscrutably.

Mayne himself now moved into the shade, as he continued, 'With the diving suits now being used, the problem of the bends became very real because, of course, divers were going to deeper water to explore the sea bed for the pearl shell. Men were being paralysed permanently and there was no compensation. Compressors were introduced to take over from hand pumps, but all they did was to encourage divers to go to even greater depths – to as much as eighty metres, but without knowledge of the risks and ways of combating them. So the Royal Navy set out to find the answers and found that men could survive if they came up slowly and gave themselves time to allow the nitrogen in the bloodstream to dissolve rather than effervesce, as the blood bubbled.'

'Ugh!' remarked the white-dressed lady, shaking her head. 'That sounds horrible.'

'Yes,' nodded Mayne, 'however, just before the First World War C.E. Heinke presented Broome with a decompression chamber that, in time, won over all the sceptics by saving many lives and curing many cases of paralysis. The bends is still a major risk to the divers of today, but by the twenties it was no longer the life-threatening factor it had been. Through the twenties the industry had its up and downs...'

'Especially for the divers,' smirked the elderly man, causing one or two of the younger girls in the crowd to titter.

'Absolutely!' agreed Mayne, amiability writ large over his face. 'By the way, you can see one of the old 1930s diving suits at Kinneys Store here in Chinatown.'

A car backfired nearby, causing a few in the group to jump. 'Christ! I thought it was a gun!' The elderly man put his hand on his chest and laughed.

'On cue as always,' Mayne grinned. 'Just to keep you all awake.'

They all watched as the old banger, spewing blue smoke, backed out and coughed and spluttered its way off, overtaken by a dust-covered wagon being driven well over the speed limit.

'God!' the same old man cried hotly as the wagon disappeared, 'he's shooting through like a Bondi tram!'

They turned back to Mayne, who rubbed his hands together and continued, 'Well, when the Second World War came, the Japanese here were all interned and the luggers were put to rest, most of them never to sail again. The war, apart from the Japanese bombing here, which you can read all about, caused families to leave, and on their return the town was in a sorry state. It took time to build up a lugger fleet again. It was through to the fifties, in fact, before the fleet was back to its pre-war numbers, and with it the Japanese returned.'

Mayne paused to blow his nose, before continuing, 'The Japanese however, affected Broome hugely at this time, in another way. They helped set up a blister-pearl industry, which gave larger and quicker-maturing pearls than their own back home. Although pearl shell was doing OK for a while, it wasn't long before the price collapsed with the development of plastics, and interest then centred on cultured pearls. There are now, after about forty years, pearl farms all round the area and you will see many fine examples of Broome pearls in the shops in town and, of course, elsewhere.'

'Are there pearl farm tours?' A small, young Japanese woman half-bowed as she spoke haltingly.

'Indeed,' Mayne nodded. 'You can find out about them at the Broome Tourist Bureau,' he waved his hand expansively, 'A good tour is the one to Willie Creek.'

'Will'e, Wont'e,' sniggered the elderly man, 'that's the question.'

Mayne gave him a fixed smile. 'The cultured pearls today are started by the divers fishing oysters from the sea bed and the lugger crew cleaning the shell, to ensure the oyster will feed properly. Then they are placed in baskets and put back into the sea, to rest on the sea bed and recover from the disturbance. But at a pearl farm, after several months, they are brought up, checked over and seeded, which means inserting a piece of grit, which actually comes from a Mississippi clam, would you believe. They are turned every two days for forty days to encourage growth and then the white substance, the nacre, in the oyster gradually covers the grit or nuclei and after about two years, if all has gone well, a pearl is produced. The harvest is August time and after sorting, all the pearls are graded. Naturally security has to be very tight. It is now a very big business on the world stage.

'The luggers used are no longer the old wooden ones, but steel ones, being converted prawn trawlers. They can take six divers who now use different gear, which I'm sure you will all be familiar with, either personally or from television – i.e. wet suits with scuba apparatus, which gives them so much more flexibility?' Most of the group nodded. They could, at last, identify with something.

'We now train about thirty new divers a year here in Broome, usually in their early twenties. Divers now have medicals, get scuba-diving certificates and are given a hard time to determine their suitability. There is a Pearl Producers Association which employs a Training Safety Officer who runs the diving programme and is available for emergency decompression. It is all very impressive.'

'But what happens if the divers are way out at sea?' A young blonde with an earnest face, covered in freckles, looked at Mayne, anxiously.

'No worries,' Mayne reassured her. 'The skipper will radio the hospital and there are always seaplanes ready and they can make a round trip in one or two hours, depending on the weather. Mind you,' he added mischievously, 'the bends aren't the divers only worry, we lost one to a shark last year!'

'Oh, my God!' The young girl shivered inside her lilac-coloured tracksuit.

'Yes,' Mayne appeared oblivious of at least one person's unease, 'the sharks are always out there,' he nodded his head seawards, 'but they are normally shy and no trouble.'

'Ugh!' was the girl's response, eyebrows knitted together.

'Yes, well, anyway,' Mayne folded his arms, 'the only other thing to say is that the men using the wet suits today are mainly Australians, and small town though we might still be, Broome is one of the world's most important pearling centres.'

There was silence, as Mayne drew breath. Some gulls screeched their interruption as they flew low over the jetty and settled happily on the deck of the wooden lugger.

'Now,' Mayne looked round the band of tourists, 'if you'd like to follow me down the jetty, you can have a look at the last wooden lugger that is in operation.'

As he strode off, the group began to follow him, but with varying degrees of alacrity. The older tourists were happy to let the younger ones forge ahead. As it happened, David and June were the last to begin moving forward, as David had chosen the best shaded spot, which was behind the doorway to the workshop. There was the bang of a door slamming behind him, causing David to turn involuntarily and his heart missed the proverbial beat. Stepping out from another exit from the workshop into the main road, he saw a man carrying some equipment, which he proceeded to throw into the back of a four-wheel drive. Although the man had his back to David, he knew at once he was watching Ian Carlyle.

Christ Almighty! June had been right! What the hell was he doing here? Broome? Russia? David's brain was in a whirl. His stomach churned and he felt sick. So much had happened since that first meeting. Terrible things. Deaths. Murders. And yet time had passed to the point where he had begun to believe it had been a dream – no, a nightmare. Now it all came flooding back. It had been real enough. He guided June's elbow, as they followed the group towards the lugger. He heard a car start and briefly looked back to see it driven off, with a throaty roar.

'What's the matter?'

David realised June was looking at him with a mixture of surprise and concern on her face. 'Nothing, nothing,' he replied. 'It's just hot.'

'Oh, for goodness sake!' she reacted irritably, 'it won't be long now!'

He followed her, incapable of replying. Several of the tourists had been helped on board the lugger by Mayne, but as the boat was not very big, the rest of the group stood and listened, as he gave them a brief idea of life on board, as it had been years ago.

'The tides can be ten metres around here, as high as any in the world,' Mayne said, to no one in particular, 'and the luggers are brought through the mangroves in the wet season, that is November to April, for maintenance. The big boats moor off the deep-water jetty at the port, south of the town. If you see any of the old photos of about 1914, in books or at the museum located in the old Customs House, you will see the jetties around here full of luggers. No longer, I'm afraid. Well, that's about it, ladies and gentlemen,' Mayne smiled broadly, 'I hope you've found it interesting...' He was interrupted by several murmurs of 'Yes', 'You bet,' and a 'Good on yer,' as the group made their way back to the road. The white-dressed lady solemnly shook Mayne's hand, as the group dispersed in several directions.

'Coffee?' June grinned, as she took David's hand, leading him towards an open air coffee shop. They found a table in the shade, as the young waitress took their order.

'David, you haven't spoken for ages. Do you feel alright?' June wasn't looking at him. The tone of her voice told him she didn't think there was anything the matter, added to which she was watching a young couple wander by, arms round each other, joined in love. He didn't reply and quickly June turned to him, surprised. 'David?' she asked.

'I'm fine, darling,' David knew his voice betrayed him.

'David, what is it?'

As the coffee arrived, David made his decision. 'June, you were right yesterday. Carlyle is here.' He heard her sucking in her breath, but continued, as he took her hand. 'He was in that workshop over the road and I saw him as he came out and drove off. He didn't see me,' he added, unthinkingly.

'How do you know?' June asked, after a moment's pause.

David looked at her comprehendingly. 'You mean, he could have seen us before I saw him.'

June nodded, 'Of course, he could.'

'Maybe, but I don't think so,' David replied, thoughtfully. 'I was behind the open door on to the jetty and he came out of another door on to the road. He had his back to me just as he had to you, yesterday. He had no reason to look at a bunch of tourists.'

June dismissed the line of thought. 'What do we do?'

David drank his coffee slowly. 'We don't have to do anything.' He then caught June's baleful look and deliberately looked her straight in the eye as he commented, 'We could be asking for trouble, if we don't keep our heads down and just enjoy our holiday.'

'Oh, come on! That's just not on.' She angrily spilled her coffee, as she put her cup back in the saucer. 'How can we just ignore him? We've got to try and find out what he's doing here! We don't have to ride a white charger up to him. Just see if he's living here and if he's using his own name, etc.' She paused and reflected for a moment. 'We're both wearing sunglasses all the time, and hats, and we don't need to parade as Chiswick executives, for him to recognise. It shouldn't be difficult to find something out, without raising our heads over the parapet.' She finished her coffee in sullen silence.

David sucked on the froth of his cappuccino, as he tried to think sensibly. 'Where's the lecture on leaving Carlyle to the professionals and just getting on with our lives?' he asked.

'This is different,' June shook her head. 'This is a very small place and if we don't stay alert he may well come across us and recognise us, anyway. All I'm suggesting is a few low-key questions, not to launch a full-scale enquiry. We don't have to take anything on, in fact,' she looked serious, 'I'd be the first to agree to leave here if necessary and find somewhere else to stay. Australia is quite a big place!'

David looked at her. 'We've seen him twice in less than twenty-four hours,' he murmured, half to himself, 'and he's got a pick-up, not a tourist car, so that suggests he's living here.'

'We'll start by going back to the workshop,' June turned to pick up her handbag.

'Hold it, hold it,' David didn't move. *We'll* do nothing. I – repeat I – might go over there. Look,' he put his hand out, 'two people asking questions is much more likely to cause comment

253

than one man, thinking he's seen an old pal.' He knew it sounded weak, but was relieved when he saw the doubt in June's face replaced by a smile.

'Yes,' she nodded, 'you're probably right. And,' she added brightly, 'you are going to do something! I'll have another coffee, while you're gone.'

David rose, patted her shoulder and eased his way out, without another word. He felt the hot sun on his back, as he retraced his steps to the workshop and the open doorway where he had stood a few minutes ago. He could hear movement from within and stepped inside. It was clearly an engineering workshop with lathes, drilling machines, lifting gear and the pungent smell of oil and grease. In the far corner, bent over a worktop was an elderly, bald-headed man in dirty, blue denim shirt and trousers. He looked up as he heard David walk in and peered at him over his spectacles.

'Er, good morning,' David walked over.

'Mornin'.' There was no enquiry, nor animosity, in the response.

'I'm just driving through Broome,' David explained, 'and as I was parking the car a few minutes ago, I thought I saw an old friend of mine from England come out of here. Unfortunately, he drove off before I could catch up with him. I wondered if you could tell me where he lives?'

The elderly man looked at David thoughtfully. 'What's your friend's name?'

'Carlyle,' David replied. 'Ian Carlyle.'

'No, 'fraid you're out a luck,' the man turned back to his bench. 'Only bloke in 'ere this morning 'as been Brian Harmer. Owns the pearl farm way up the coast at Retreat Point.' He began to chisel a piece of wood.

David persisted. 'Old resident of Broome, Brian Harmer?'

'No.' The chisel was thrown down and another one picked up. 'Bought the farm a couple of years back. Came from the East, I think. Certainly not from the Kimberleys, around here. Comes to town occasionally – plenty of work to do up there, I reckon.' His back was now stooped over the worktop and the stance pre-empted further idle chat.

254

'Thanks. Sorry to bother you,' David turned.

'No worries, mate,' came over the shoulder, as David walked out.

*   *   *

Back at The Resort, lying on loungers by the pool an hour later, David was quenching his thirst with a beer and June hers with a spritzer.

'I'm sure I wasn't mistaken. I'm sure that was Carlyle,' David took off his sunglasses, 'Which means he's obviously living here under an alias.'

'Unless the man in the workshop was lying.'

'Why should he?'

'Well,' June lay back, 'Dr Johnson said we are inclined to believe those whom we don't know because they have never deceived us.'

'Humph,' David snorted and drank his beer.

'What's Carlyle doing running a pearl farm?' June rubbed some sun-screen on her shoulders.

'Maybe he's just doing that,' David replied drily. 'Running a pearl farm. We heard this morning there's plenty of money in it!'

June shook her head. 'Maybe, but there'll be more to it than that.'

'Why the hell should there be?' David frowned, cleaning his sunglasses.

'Because men like Carlyle either retire on their ill-gotten gains and do damn all,' said June, 'or they keep working for real money and to me that isn't just running a very hard, mean business, in the hope of profits from a successful harvest. He'd want guaranteed profits,' she commented and lay back, closing her eyes.

Two young boys ran past screaming at each other, as they bellyflopped into the pool, splattering water about and breaking David's thoughts. He watched their antics for a moment or two and then became conscious of someone standing at his side. He looked up slowly, taking in a crisp white skirt and blouse, before reaching the young, smiling face of The Resort's Guest

255

Relations Manager, partly hidden behind sunglasses and a smart straw hat.

'Hallo,' she beamed, 'Mr and Mrs Price, isn't it? I'm Sue Walters. Please,' she put out her hand, as David began to rise, 'don't get up. I was just checking to see if everything's alright. Anything we can do for you?'

'Everything's fine, thank you,' replied David.

'Well, actually,' he heard June move behind him, 'there is something,' June went on, 'we'd love to have a look at a pearl farm while we're here. We've heard so much about them. Is there any chance of going to one?'

'Why, yes,' Sue Walters closed her hands together, 'just out of town there is the Willie Creek pearl farm. It is thirty-five kilometres out and they take tours most days to give you an insight as to what it's all about. I could arrange that for you, if you'd like.'

'Ah!' June smiled, 'actually we'd heard about Retreat Point and thought that might be interesting.'

'Retreat Point pearl farm?' Sue Walters frowned. 'I'm afraid they don't welcome tours, or even individual visitors, up there. And it is a long way from here as well – about three hours' drive, most of it on unsealed roads. Willie Creek would show you what's involved.'

'Well, thanks,' June nodded, 'we'll think about it.'

'Anything else I can do?'

'No,' David shook his head and smiled, 'everything's fine, thank you.'

'Well, have a nice day.' Sue Walters bowed slightly and moved on to a couple sitting under the next palm tree.

'Smart,' David watched the two boys haul themselves out of the pool and run off laughing hysterically.

'Yes,' June mumbled, 'but not very successful.'

'I'll go and see if I can buy a map of the Kimberley area in the shop.' David rose, 'and see if Retreat Point is marked.'

June dozed off pleasantly, until David returned.

'Yes, it's marked,' David tapped the map. 'It looks quite a way. But thinking about it I don't believe we should just get up and go anyway. What are we going to do when we get there? We can't go as tourists, as they won't let us in. Even if we tried, we are sure to be recognised sooner or later, if Carlyle's there.'

June wiped some perspiration off her nose. 'So what do you suggest?' she countered.

David looked at the map, pensively. 'I think we should go to the pearl farm that is here, near Broome, to appreciate a little what it's like and then at least if we go up to Retreat Point it won't be totally foreign to us. Retreat Point I reckon is two hundred kilometres away.'

'Ye-e-es,' June dragged the word out, as she looked at David, thoughtfully. 'That can't do any harm and maybe something will help us make up our minds what to do next. See if you can fix it for tomorrow, darling.'

Sue Walters was happy to arrange for them to join the tour for the next morning and relaxed in that knowledge, June and David enjoyed the rest of the day lazing round the pool. Later, after playing an early evening game of tennis, they enjoyed a sumptuous meal in The Resort's luxurious signature restaurant.

*   *   *

Over breakfast the next morning, David announced that he wasn't coming on the visit to the pearl farm, as he had had an idea.

'What?' June was gesturing for some more coffee.

'We've seen Carlyle twice in two days and that means there is a good chance he is still here. I know,' David nodded for more coffee at the young waitress hovered at the table, pot in hand, 'he may have gone north yesterday, but it's worth a wander round to see if he's still here and I can spot him. I accept it's an outside chance, but you never know.'

'And then what?' June reached for the milk.

'I'll play it by ear,' David stirred his coffee.

'Brilliant!' June knew she sounded sarcastic. 'That man has been the focal point of the most unpleasant episode in our lives and certain others can't even talk about it any more and you are just going to "play it by ear"! Brilliant!'

'June,' David stared at her fixedly, 'you don't have to tell me what we've been through. I just want to do this my way.'

257

'Yes, Frank Sinatra,' June smiled wistfully, 'but for Christ sake be careful.' She held his hand and they gripped each other, momentarily. They both knew this day could be interesting.

An hour later, David waved June off as the minibus collected several guests who were going to the pearl farm, then he found the car they had hired and drove slowly into town. The sun was already hot enough for him to turn on the air-conditioning. As he followed the main road, the loose red earth of the verges swirled in the fresh breeze and a thin film lay on the sealed surface.

Where to start? He followed several cars, slowly wending their way down Frederick Street towards Chinatown. He found a parking space outside Sun Pictures, which he knew from The Resort's brochure, was believed to be the oldest operating open-air cinema in the world. He climbed out and looked at the advertisement on the hoarding – *Four Weddings and a Funeral.* David was vaguely surprised that such modern-day hits had found their way to this 1916-built Broome cinema. He chided himself for being so patronising in his thoughts, as he involuntarily wandered into the open foyer. It clearly had some wonderful movie memorabilia to enjoy, but he turned back resolutely to the task in hand. It was a person he was looking for, not an inanimate object.

He wandered slowly through the meandering tourists and more purposeful residents, as they dived in and out of the banks, bakers, chemists, general stores. The brilliant white-painted corrugated roofs of the buildings were bright in his eyes. He walked the square of Carnarvon Street, Napier Terrace, Dampier Terrace and Short Street, admiring the three lifelike statues erected to the memory of the pioneers of the cultured pearl industry in Broome. He smiled wryly – two were Japanese. He was certainly not looking for a Japanese.

He paid particular attention to the Streeter's Jetty area and the workshops along Dampier Terrace, but he saw no sign of Carlyle, nor his four-wheel drive. Disappointed, but not surprised, he returned to his car and looking at his local map, decided he might drive down to the shopping centre marked near the Town Beach, at the other end of town.

David drove slowly, trying to keep his eyes on the road and on the sidewalk. Not as difficult a task as he had feared, as no cars drove fast. No-one was in a hurry in Broome. He was in Broome time! He drove down Hamersley Street, past the courthouse and the police station, which David thought could almost have been mocking him in his totally incoherent endeavours. As he drove past a small bank his heart missed a beat. Coming out, in blue shorts and shirt, was Carlyle! David quickly pulled into a side road some yards further on and did a U-turn so that he was facing back to Hamersley Street. Sure enough, the four-wheel drive that Carlyle had had yesterday soon pulled out and drove past, the last of a line of cars. David pulled out so as not to lose sight of it, much to the annoyance of the driver of an oncoming car, who blasted his horn. 'Stupid!' thought David, 'I'm already drawing attention to myself.'

Carlyle, in fact, drove to the Seaview shopping centre David had been going to and, having parked, strolled casually into the covered mall. David, with sunglasses and hat firmly on, locked his car and followed. By the time he had gone inside, David realised that following people was not that easy. There were many small shops inside the mall – chemist, gift shop, health foods, baker and a large supermarket. The area was busy and David could see no sign of Carlyle. After a moment's hesitation, he plumped for the supermarket. Through the turnstile, he avoided several women who were examining the large supplies of fruit and vegetables, and traversed the aisles, searching for a familiar outline.

There! At the bread counter at the far end. Carlyle was picking up a loaf which he then handed to a woman a few yards on. Tanya Carlyle! My God, she was here too! But why not? Carlyle must have left her here, whilst he had gone to the bank nearby. She had a basket already well loaded. David's brain whirled as he turned away and made his way out, opening his hands to the cashier to show he had bought nothing. Both here!

He made his way back to the car, slid in, turned on the engine to cool the temperature down and waited. It seemed like hours, but a quick glance at his watch told him it had only been fifteen minutes, when the Carlyles emerged and carried their groceries to the four-wheel drive. She was wearing a white shirt and shorts and David was fleetingly surprised at her very thick, unshapely legs. He followed them out of the car park, with fortuitously another car between them, as they retraced their route, but David was almost caught napping. Carlyle swung left into Guy Street, as the sign proclaimed, and not more than two hundred yards on, pulled across and drove into an open gateway to a small, detached, colonial-style house. David drove on and when the opportunity arose, turned round and slowly drove back past the house. He noticed it had an agent's For Lease sign outside. Another imponderable. Was their house for lease or had they leased it? The agent's name was Murchison. David picked up speed as much as the local traffic would allow and headed for Chinatown. He had seen Murchisons on his walk round this morning.

As luck would have it, there was a space outside Murchisons in Napier Terrace. David was greeted by an attractive brunette, with long straight hair and big brown eyes, dressed in a short flowered dress, who was changing an advertisement in the window.

'Hallo,' she smiled. 'Can I help you?

'Er, yes,' David smiled, 'I've just driven down Guy Street and passed a For Lease sign outside a house there. I wondered if it was still available, as I saw a car go in the gates?'

'Guy Street?' she turned to the desk. 'Oh, yes, that's available fully furnished on a minimum of three months. It's available, in fact, from any time after this weekend. It has been let for a week, which I know sounds a contradiction, but Mr Harmer is always prepared to pay well for a short letting, when he comes to town.'

'Mr Harmer?' David asked.

'Yes. He owns Retreat Point pearl farm up the coast, and when he comes to town he never wants to stay in a pub, so he pays over the odds to stay in any furnished unit, or whatever is available.'

David realised that the conversation had stopped, whilst he was thinking. 'I see. Yes,' he smiled. 'Well, maybe I could take the particulars.'

'Sure.' The brunette found the details easily and handed a

piece of paper to David. 'Give us a ring if you want to take it further. Mr Harmer is leaving today, in fact, and we'll then just clean the place after he's gone. You know.'

David nodded, thanked her and returned to the car. So Carlyle was off today. Back up the coast? Instinctively, David was sure of it. He drove back to Guy Street and confirmation was immediate. Both Carlyles were loading boxes and parcels into the four-wheel drive, obviously prior to departure. What should he do? David looked at his watch. It was eleven o'clock. Would they drive off soon in the heat of the sun? David supposed air-conditioning didn't make that the issue it had once been. He looked at his fuel gauge. Almost full, thank God. Was he going to follow them? June would argue that there was no point. They could find the pearl farm any time. Why risk being discovered?

He pulled on to the grass verge fifty yards further on and adjusted his rear-view mirror so that he could see the house. He was almost immediately distracted by a tap on his window. He turned to see the grinning white teeth and young face of an aboriginal boy, dancing up and down on the grass. David wound down the window to see what it was all about, but the boy, about seven years of age, barefoot and dressed in a vivid orange T-shirt and psychedelic shorts, laughed and ran off, followed by a younger girl wearing the same strange outfit and giggling at his daring.

Within only a few minutes the Carlyle's four-wheel drive backed out and drove down to Hamersley Street as David quickly followed. It stopped at a garage, where Carlyle filled up, before following the route out of town. As Carlyle drove out, David drove in and quickly bought two canisters of bottled water. He had read enough about breaking down in the heat of the outback and he had no idea where he was going to finish up! He trailed them easily on the Broome Road where the traffic was light, but fortunately not so light that his presence would be noticed.

There were some smallholdings and mean-looking houses on the outskirts of town that grew less frequent and David was beginning to appreciate that the journey ahead was likely to be very boring, when he was almost taken by surprise as Carlyle swung off on to an unsealed road, signposted as Beagle Bay Road. The landscape around very quickly degenerated into sparse scrub, and spinifex and wattle copses scattered along the way. David realised that he didn't have to worry about being identified, as the car in front was spewing out red dust rising several feet into the air and creating a dust-cloud spreading sideways. His eyes wandered and he marvelled at a flock of crimson-winged parrots, their colours strong and beautiful as they flew overhead.

Suddenly, David jolted himself back to the present, realising that, of course, he must be sending out the same red dust-cloud and the tell-tale message that there was a car following which Carlyle could see at the occasional bend, if he bothered to look back. Would Carlyle notice and worry about a presence behind him? But, David reasoned, why the hell should he? Carlyle was not likely to bother about cars on the road, unless ... unless he had spotted David or June earlier. Unease sat on his shoulders for some minutes, as he passed the remains of what looked like a very recent bush fire, until suddenly he realised the road surface had deteriorated and the car was not running easily. It wasn't the bloody road! He had a burst tyre!

'Shit!' He pulled over, slowed down and stopped. He saw the dust-cloud ahead gradually disappear into the distance, as he seethed inwardly. Finally, he opened the door and the heat of the sun hit him. By the time he had changed the tyre, his shirt was soaked through and he realised how dangerous the sun was up here in the Kimberleys. Thoughtfully, he drank some of his recently acquired water and turned on the engine to enjoy the air-conditioning as quickly as possible. What now? The road was deserted. All he could see were some honeyeaters, small yellow birds, flying in a westerly direction. His enthusiasm for the chase had evaporated and he turned round and headed back for Broome. He thought of June and wondered about her morning.

*   *   *

'Now you said something which I thought was very interesting, this morning,' June flicked a broken shell over with her foot, as she caught the ripple of a wave at the water's edge.

262

'What was that?' David could still detect the controlled anger in her voice, after his summation of the morning's events. He had returned just as June was about to go for a walk along Cable Beach towards Gantheaume Point. She had read that there were footprints there, embedded in the sandstone, believed to be those of a dinosaur living 120 million years ago.

'Why, you said you'd play it by ear, my darling,' came the cool reply.

David measured his stride to hers. A forceful, long stride, her feet cutting through the water, playing at her ankles. He noticed the prints of horses and a wandering dog on the wet sand. 'Yes,' he felt the sun burning his neck and shoulders.

June suddenly stopped and swung round, staring at him, white-faced. 'You bloody idiot! You might be able to play a violin by ear, but how the bloody hell do you play a villain by ear? Follow him in a car! I mean, how stupid can you be? Just you and him on a road a few hundred yards apart, for over an hour? Where else would you be going, if he began to take an interest in you? What if he stopped on the pretext of wanting help and he happened to ask you where you were going – that is, if he didn't recognise you! Do you know the name of one teeny weeny place on the peninsula?'

She turned away and strode on, the water splashing viciously, as she veered a few feet further out into the sea.

David refrained from following her out. He believed that her agitation was not anger at him, but fear of what could have happened. He strode on at the water's edge. A kite fell just ahead of him and a young father ran past him and picked it up. 'Pull, Wayne. Pull,' the father yelled, as he let go, and uncertainly but steadily the kite sailed upwards. The tension had been broken. June came to him and pushed her face into his shoulder.

'David, I don't want to lose you. Don't go in for heroics.'

He could feel her pull in her breath and guessed she was trying to control herself. He lightly gripped a buttock affectionately. 'OK darling, OK, lesson learned. No worries, as they say out here.' He tried to sound reassuring and carefree.

263

'Well, don't give me the worries,' June took his hand and pulled him onwards towards the point. There were very few people ahead of them on the white sandy beach. The holiday makers from The Resort seldom walked the whole way. It was not just the considerable distance to reach the red craggy cliffs that deterred them, but the fact that there was only one way of getting back – the same long way and on foot.

'How was your morning?' David noticed with interest the way the white sandy beach rose to undulating sand-dunes topped by scrub in some places, whereas in others as it reached the top of the beach it was immediately replaced by the harsh red earth and rock, even starker against the clear blue sky. It was as though the scene had been painted in oils, for watercolour would have caused a coalescence and there was remarkably, none.

'It was fascinating,' June held his hand. 'We saw a film that showed how the divers work along a line connected to a weight dropped from the lugger, above. They never leave their line. They have a net bag clipped to them and when they find the oysters, which apparently are very hard to distinguish amongst the marine growth, they drop them in the bag and then transfer them to a bigger bag attached to the line. When they have filled them, they come up and the deck hands clean the shell. The divers come up very gradually...'

'Yes,' interrupted David, 'we heard about that...'

'OK. OK.' June punched her hand with his. 'Back to the oysters, then. They look for oysters a minimum of one hundred and twenty millimetres long, as they have to be young to facilitate growth, but big enough to take the nuclei – which are ground clam shell...'

'From Mississippi,' David ventured.

'Look smartarse, just shut up!' June kicked him playfully, spraying water upwards. 'It's made into a ball and comes here from Japan – don't ask me why – and examined by Customs before being allowed in.'

'Customs?' David mused.

'Customs,' June nodded. 'Apparently the luggers go as far

south as Exmouth and up to the Northern Territories and the best areas are where there are considerable tides, because oysters feed on nutrients. It's all regulated by licences...'

'What isn't?' grunted David.

'To ensure,' June ignored him, 'that the waters are not overfished, the companies have quotas.'

'What happens when the nuclei are inserted?' David winced as his foot came down on a large broken shell.

'Well,' June stopped for a moment, as David hobbled momentarily, 'they place the oysters into panels with six pockets to a panel. After the turning to get them going, the oysters are suspended and allowed to do their work. There are two panels between each buoy and there are fifty buoys to a line...'

'How the hell can you remember all this?' David was walking relaxed again.

'...and there is an anchor at the end of each line. They are all suspended two metres from the surface. How do I remember? Because, boyo, I listen and retain, that's how! And,' she added, 'everything that's done to the oyster is done quickly in the sense of getting the oysters back in the water as soon as possible, or they get stressed out.'

'Like some women I know,' David grinned.

'The pearl farm check the panels regularly, including x-raying,' June pointedly ignored the interruption. 'The Fisheries Inspectorate also check that there are not more panels than allowed under the quota and the farm is not using under-sized shells. Customs drop in too.'

'Customs, again?' David stopped. 'How about turning round? We've a hell of a walk back.' The sun was now facing them and the slight breeze was on their backs.

'Yes,' June shielded her eyes momentarily, whilst she adjusted to the glare, 'they are on the alert for many things including smuggling along the coast. Drugs etc. By the way, apparently pearls are a multi-million-dollars-a-year business here. Some business!'

'Drugs.' David stopped and stared at the whispering, gentle sea, covering his feet.

'What do you mean, "Drugs"?' June looked at him.

265

David turned to her and gazed beyond. There was nothing, all the way to the horizon, as a gull, throatily, flew overhead. 'What do we connect Carlyle with?' He folded his arms as he looked at the quizzical June and before she could volunteer an answer, 'Murder, deaths, oppression, mayhem. So why couldn't he reappear and be into drug-trafficking?'

'Oh, come on!' But June's voice didn't carry any vehemence or conviction.

David strolled on, holding out his hand. 'I think I'll go and ring that house agency and ask to have a look at the house that Carlyle rented, hopefully before they've cleaned it. You never know.'

'I think you're chasing shadows,' June gripped his hand and David suspected it was for reassurance.

*   *   *

An hour later David was standing inside the hallway of the detached residence. Built of wood, raised above the ground, it had a wide verandah all the way round. Inside as he wandered through, he was impressed with the array of rugs and cane furniture amply covered with bright-coloured cushions. There were two sizeable bedrooms and a large sitting room with a dining area, which was adjacent to the well-equipped kitchen.

The same cheerful girl had given him the keys, explaining that the usual cleaner was unwell and therefore the house had not yet been cleaned. She hoped it wouldn't put him off thinking of renting it. Looking through the window, David could see the ubiquitous swimming pool, with loungers scattered along the patio. He was not impressed to see a number of dirty towels left on them. Clearly there was nothing about the Carlyles that was prepossessing. He went into the first bedroom where the double bed was unmade – the white sheets lay crumpled and the two pillows were at right-angles to the head, suggesting the sleeper had curled round them, as if they were a human companion. Instinctively, David went to the other bedroom. Sure enough that double bed was also in an unkempt state. So, they slept apart. Nothing in that. Many couples did. The further up the social ladder the more David understood it to be

266

common. But Carlyle was not up that ladder. The only ladder David would like to associate with him was one on the way to the scaffold. In the open as in the times of the French revolution. He thought momentarily of Carlyle's head dropping into a blood-soaked basket.

Bringing himself up short, he returned to the sitting room and surveyed it carefully. Nothing remarkable. Three-piece suite, bookcase, television on a sideboard, which also displayed some old sepia photos, and a large cabin trunk of 1930s vintage. Utilitarian, rather than a pleasurable home from home, David thought. He wandered into the kitchen. Dirty crockery piled in the sink and the fridge door ajar were the first things to catch his eye. He walked across to close the door, but wrapped in thought as to what he should expect to find, he realised he had opened it further, attracted by its brightly lit interior. Nothing unusual inside. Just what he would have expected. The remains of pies, butter, bread, milk and a couple of beers. He saw a large rubbish bin in the corner by the sink and after a moment's hesitation, tentatively rummaged through it to find wrappers, tissues, orange peel, banana skins, milk cartons and other normal kitchen rubbish.

Seven milk cartons. Seven? David idly picked up one of them. He was not surprised that it was as light as a feather. It was empty. Kneeling down, however, he looked at it more closely. It appeared to be unopened. He turned it upside down and pressed inwards, and the carton's base sprang open. It had clearly been undone from the wrong end! He relaxed his grip and the bottom closed over. He picked up the others. They were all the same. Empty, but the tops untouched. He turned to the open-topped one he had seen in the fridge. Yes, that was half full of milk, nothing strange about that one. He looked inside one of the others. There was no sign of any milk on the inner sides. The interior was bone dry. Should it be? He didn't really know.

The cartons all had the same labels. David read, 'Keep refrigerated below 5°C' and below that 'For use by date, see top of pack'. He looked for the date – Jan 10. All the empty ones were stamped Jan 10. The half full carton was stamped Aug 18. The cartons were alike, but in this particular respect one was significantly different. It didn't seem as though the other six had had milk in them for months. He placed them all back in the fridge and standing up shut the door, frowning. What...

His thoughts were interrupted by a knock behind him. He went to the front door. Outside, holding the fly door open as he opened the inner door, stood a young, fair-haired, slim man with a thin, anxious, face. Neither spoke for a second.

'Oh, sorry,' said the young man stepping back, 'I think I've got the wrong house.'

'Who were you looking for?' asked David.

'No. It's OK mate. Just realised. It's the next street. New to Broome and all the streets look the bloody same.'

David watched the young man half wave, spin round and walk rapidly away, as the fly door gently closed. 'Well, he certainly didn't want me,' David remarked to himself as he closed the door.

He went from room to room, but apart from oddments of packaging and other litter lying around, found nothing out of order and set off to return the keys to the agency, saying he'd think about it.

*   *   *

June sipped her glass of Australian fizz. She scowled at the absurdity of the Australians not being able to call it champagne. She reckoned it was better than many champagnes she had drunk and a darned sight cheaper.

'Well, what do you make of it, darling?' she asked, as David returned to their table on the verandah by the pool. David had come back to find June asleep and had impatiently held back the tale of his visit to town, until they had left their suite for an early evening drink.

'Well, the cartons could have been used to carry something and it wasn't milk!' David sat down.

'Drugs?' June looked at him anxiously. 'You're thinking of drugs?'

David pursed his lips. 'I don't know how drugs are carried. Whatever it was, was clearly being hidden from normal view, otherwise, why use outdated milk cartons? And the fellow that

268

came to the door. Was that really a mistake? Or had he come to see Carlyle on some rotten mission or other and had come too late?'

June watched three gulls serenely sitting in the water in the swimming pool, as the last rays of the sun cast long shadows over the grass. 'This was going to be a holiday of a lifetime. Bloody hell!'

David reached over and stroked her cheek as he saw a tear well up. 'We can drop the whole thing,' he said. 'We don't have to do anything.'

She looked at him, unblinking. 'Of course,' she sipped her champagne, 'but you know that's garbage, as well as I do.'

'Hallo, hallo,' June and David were surprised by a woman's soft voice coming from behind them. 'No, please.' A hand on David's shoulders stayed his attempt to rise. The smiling face was that of Sue Walters. 'Have you had a good day? How was your trip to the pearl farm?' Before either of them could answer, she went on, 'I'm sorry, I'm being rude. Can I introduce you to a friend of mine, Terry James?'

David looked at the tall, dark, young man and admired his heavy build, with shoulders suggesting prizefighting. David guessed however they were probably more associated with rugby or even, perhaps, a game he had only seen on television, but had instantly enjoyed – Australian rules football. The game had struck him as a combination of rugby and basketball with a touch of soccer thrown in. A real mish-mash of a game, rather like gaelic football, requiring very fit and strong athletes. Terry James certainly seemed to be fit and strong. David rose out of his chair.

'G-day,' a strong arm shot out and gripped David's hand. David tried hard not to wince at the grip. 'Hope we're not interrupting anything?' The voice was surprisingly quiet.

'Of course, not,' June purred slowly. 'Do sit down, both of you.'

David made space as he and Terry pulled over two more chairs. He felt a slight pang of jealousy, but more of annoyance at the way he felt June was playing the attracted coy young maiden. Young? Coy? He would speak to her later.

269

'Terry's with Customs up here,' Sue explained as they ordered drinks.

'How fascinating,' June fluttered her eyes at Terry, but quickly changed her facial expression when David managed to jolt her elbow off her chair, as he leaned forward to pick up his glass.

'You live here, then?' David did not look in June's direction, as he heard her half choke back a hiss of petulant, mock annoyance.

'Yes,' Terry pulled the chair in and crossed his grey-trousered legs. 'Came up from Perth last year. It's a lovely place to live. Mind you, I miss the city from time to time, but we can't have everything.'

'No,' David nodded. 'Can't be much to do up here, after Perth, I guess.'

'Oh, you'd be surprised.' Terry acknowledged the arrival of two gin and tonics. 'We cover a vast area up here and it's not a case of sitting in an office. Far from it.' He reached out and took Sue's hand. David inwardly smirked. That will keep June under control, he thought.

'What do you have to do?' June's voice was now sober and enquiring.

'Well, we're on the look-out for pretty well everything coming in or going out of Western Australia.' Terry smiled, 'From refugees coming down from South East Asia, to birds being exported for breeding. You name it.'

'He even keeps a look out for me, from time to time,' Sue commented and turned and smiled at him, radiantly.

Snap! thought David. 'It sounds interesting and varied,' he said. 'Tell us more.'

Terry sat back, jiggling the ice in his glass. 'Well, offshore we patrol by sea and air up to two hundred miles out. We're looking for illegal fishing, say, for tuna. They can be Indonesian, Thai, Taiwanese or Japanese boats. Normally the Japanese are licensed, as they pay for a quota from the Government, but not the others. Indonesian fishing boats are a pain, as the country is so close. Only a day or two away, depending on whether they are under sail or power. There always seem to be several Indonesian fishing boats impounded at Willie Creek. We're also looking for boats smuggling wildlife for trading and breeding. There's a lot of exporting of birds, to Holland for example, and reptiles, of course, that are all drugged in boxes. Talking of drugs, of course, that's big business and I'm afraid our coastline is not helpful. Vast and under populated.'

'I suppose the Aborigines are involved?' June asked.

Terry laughed. 'Never. No, they would be too unreliable for drug operators to use them. They can't stop talking! Especially after some grog. They'd tell their whole family! No,' he shook his head, 'it's all very sophisticated.'

'What drugs do they smuggle? David sipped his drink.

'Oh, heroin and cocaine,' Terry replied. 'You'd be surprised how they try and conceal it, too. We've found cocaine paste inside bicycle frames – that was a Colombian syndicate. The Colombians are very imaginative. They also used wooden wall plaques to hide it in. Eleven and a half kilos we found in them.'

June and David were silent, as they both realised that Terry was warming to his subject.

'Then we found two and a half kilos of high-quality cocaine, disguised, scented as coffee beans.'

'My God!' June put her hand to her mouth, 'I think I'd better stick to instant coffee in future.'

Terry smiled, 'I don't think you need worry.'

June pulled a face. 'Only kidding.'

'Yes,' Terry continued. 'You'd be surprised. We found five kilos in a large table imported from the States and even two kilos in an electric guitar. That came from Bangkok.'

'Is nothing sacred?' June finished her drink.

'No,' Sue replied, 'Terry doesn't think so, do you?'

Terry shook his head and then nodded, as David called the waiter over for another round. 'Thank you,' he said. 'No, nor anywhere. We caught two men recently with three kilos of heroin near Karratha, after an overseas boat had been in the area. Yachts are one of our biggest concerns, as they don't need fuel and can carry tons of the damn stuff. Our regular fishermen know if people or boats are acting a bit odd, but they basically

271

want to get on with their job and don't give it enough thought. That it might affect their family one day.'

Neither June nor David said a word, as Terry continued. 'Our job is not your high-profile action stuff, either. We have to check boat movements and logs and it's mostly tedious as hell. The Abrolhos Islands, virtually due west of Geraldton are a headache – landing strips and deserted bays. Too bloody easy, but then the whole coast is, I'm afraid. It's like snakes and ladders, but someone lost most of the ladders. We had another big catch at Dampier a while back, where ore carriers were being used. Then at Wanneroo, just north of Perth, we found computer equipment and maps buried in the sand, giving us a lot of information on smuggling from Thailand. Burma, Laos and Thailand, known as the Golden Triangle, have a well-developed transport system for heroin. Having said that, although the remoteness of the coastline may be inviting to drug traffickers, of course, the roads, or scarcity of them, poses challenges in itself. Most of the drugs are intended for the eastern states where the population harbours the demand.'

'Why don't they fly it over?' June asked.

'Oh, some of it they do, but, of course, aircraft can be tracked, whereas road transport is pretty much undetectable. Lost in the volume. Normally there aren't any arbitrary road blocks.'

A gust of wind swept across them, causing June's hair to cover her face. She parted it briskly and asked, 'How do they carry it by road?'

Terry grimaced. 'There are so many ways, I'm afraid. Some more sophisticated than others. False tanks in the air cooling system, crates of beer – the top cans will be OK, but the others will have been filled through the bottom – aluminium is easy to use. Just in the luggage. If they see a road block, say at the state border, they'll drop their cargo over the side and come back and pick it up later.'

'Sounds pretty tough trying to catch them,' David was thinking about false beer cans and cartons of milk.

'It is,' Terry admitted, 'but if it was easy I guess the bastards would find other ways. So let's not talk about me any more. What do you two do?'

The conversation relaxed into the normal pleasant banalities, associated with people skirmishing for subjects of mutual interest. After half an hour Sue and Terry excused themselves and went off, hand in hand.

'Nice couple,' June watched them disappear round the corner of the verandah.

'Yes,' David confirmed drily, 'especially Terry!'

'Poor baby,' June smirked, 'were you jealous?'

'Go for your life,' David retorted, 'if he wants an older woman I'm sure you'll do fine!'

'You *were* jealous!' June clapped her hands together joyously and then paused, 'What do you mean "older woman"?'

'Well, darling,' he replied, 'you might have good boobs, but they aren't young any more, are they?'

'Why, you miserable...'

'Come on! Let's go and find something to eat,' David leaned over and stroked her beneath her left breast as he stood up.

'And you can leave my drooping boobs alone!' June pushed his hand away, but not too strongly, as she rose and picked up her bag. 'And tomorrow?' she asked, as they made their way to dinner.

'We'll drive to Retreat Point pearl farm, taking enough to camp out under the stars if necessary and have a good look round.' David sat her down at their reserved table after the seater had left them.

'Well, let's enjoy tonight first.' June looked at him, bringing her foot up under the table and using it to stroke his inner thighs. She could tell she was awakening a localised interest with her open-toed sandal, as she picked up the menu.

He moved his chair and looked out over the shimmering ocean, lit by a clear full moon. A thin wisp of cloud cut across its face, as he murmured, 'Yes, I do feel hungry. But I don't really want much to eat, if you get my drift.'

'Very subtle,' June smiled sweetly at the young waitress, who had come to take their order.

19

The next morning was as clear and bright as each morning had been during their stay. After borrowing sleeping bags, utensils and equipment for a day or two away, together with warnings on the heat and the rough country away from the roads, June and David drove into town to pick up provisions they had agreed over breakfast they would need.

David followed the road out of town as he had when pursuing the Carlyles and shortly thereafter swung off on to the Beagle Bay road. The road was the same ochre colour, hard-baked and corrugated, as he drove at a steady pace, affected only by the occasional rut that had been caused by flowing waters in the wet season and not repaired properly. David noticed the shimmering heat on the road ahead and wondered how hot it was in London, which was now in the middle of summer. This was the Kimberleys' winter! Or what passed for it. Occasionally a car or four-wheel drive would pass them and each time the other driver lifted his or her hand in acknowledgement.

'Reminds me of the AA men in England, who used to wave,' mused June, as a large truck passed them.

'You're not old enough to remember them,' David yawned. He hadn't had much sleep. Nor had June thinking about it.

'No,' June nodded, 'but I've seen old movies and they always waved at the passing motorist.'

'I hope we won't need an AA man out here,' David commented wryly.

'I'm going to have a ziz,' June snuggled down and tried to get comfortable. 'I'm tired.'

'Can't think why,' David said brutally. 'No staying power. I told you you weren't as young as you used to be.'

'Oh, shut up.' June leaned back and shut her eyes.

David found the driving testing. The roads were straight enough most of the time, but the unsealed surface left him with a permanent feeling of mistrust. He felt that at any time his wheels would lose their grip and he was very conscious that this was not his normal habitat. Corrugated, red, hard-baked dirt, termite mounds several feet tall, shimmering heat, clear skies – thank God for air-conditioning and sunglasses. The journey itself was pretty boring. No wildlife, no kangaroos, no dingoes. Just red terracotta-coloured earth with scrub and trees averaging fifteen feet in height. He recognised wattle, bloodwood and pockets of white gum. Everything was still. Nothing overtook him; he didn't overtake any vehicle either, but as if to reassure him that he hadn't wandered off on to some ghastly unused track, the occasional car, van, or four-wheel drive, would pass heading for Broome. The odd cars were occasionally literally odd, in that they looked like rejects from a breaker's yard and were driven by, and full of, Aborigines. It seemed to David that when one of them went anywhere they took their whole family. To keep him company he played some Tony O'Connor tapes. Elegant, dreamlike music, from a mixture of woodwind, piano and orchestra, it enhanced his awareness of this starkly beautiful and still mostly unspoilt, country.

He looked at his watch and realised he had been driving for well over an hour and had seen nothing but scrub and a few flocks of birds. Storm gutters, formed by a grader scouring the earth off the road at an angle every few hundred yards, to allow the heavy downpours to run off the road, were the only signs of planned activity along the way. He hit a rut and the car shook and slithered for a moment before he righted it.

'Where are we?' June pulled herself up from her sleep.

'Australia.' David saw a turn-off ahead and slowed down. 'Beagle Bay Mission,' he felt cheered. 'We don't go on that road but it's not far from here.'

June stretched and reached for the road map. ' "Beagle Bay Mission",' she read, ' "was established by the trappist monks in

1890 to protect the local Aborigines from alleged misuse in the pearling industry." What does it mean, "alleged"? They were misused or they weren't. Is this some form of double-speak? You don't come all the way up here, in the middle of nowhere and say "Well there are allegations of misuse, so we'll build a mission to protect you, in case its true and you need 'protecting'"." June looked at David, inquisitively.

'I don't know,' he protested. 'I don't know any more than you do.' He hit a pothole.

'Wouldn't have been much of an era of joy, would it, if they were being misused and then were saved, to find themselves being protected and comforted by austere and silent trappist monks,' June muttered, as the car lurched violently. 'I must say I'm prepared to believe anything could have happened out here, however, when we were introducing our wonderful Western civilisation.' She gnawed her lip. 'We massacred them in places like Tasmania...'

Silence brooded, before she continued. 'There's an awful lot of it, isn't there?' she was looking at the horizon.

'Yes,' David agreed, 'and I can assure you that when we climb a little and go over the next hillock there'll be even more of it. In every direction its full of ... nothingness.'

'Eloquence was never one of your strong points, darling,' June slapped his thigh and reached for some fruit gums to moisten her mouth.

Half an hour later, David saw the sign to Retreat Point and thankfully swung off what the map had classified as a minor road, on to what was now designated as a track. The only difference that he could see was that it was narrower and more rutted than the minor road had been. He stopped for a call of nature and the searing heat reminded him that they were now travelling at the hottest time of the day. He couldn't get back into the car quickly enough. He was full of apprehension at the thought of falling victim to a burst tyre or something worse, which would be anything going wrong under the bonnet. He had never been any good with cars. Well, he normally had a garage within a mile. Here there wasn't a garage within an hour ... or two ... or ... stop it! He turned on the ignition and nothing happened. The second attempt was successful and he thankfully relaxed. The tension had begun to manifest itself with a clutching feeling at the pit of his stomach.

'Better now?' June half-opened her eyes.

'Fine, thanks.' David eased the car forward and was soon heading westwards, towards the Indian ocean.

After another half an hour of travelling through the same type of terrain and vegetation, only broken by the telltale signs of an occasional bush fire – blackened tree stumps and ash-whitened soil – the road climbed and then, as it dropped down, David could see through the heat haze to what looked like sea. Were those buildings on the horizon? Like pimples on skin, but definitely buildings. He quickly pulled over and stopped.

'What's the matter?' June was alert at once, as she watched David reach for Sue Walters's binoculars.

'Nothing's the matter. I think we've arrived and I don't want to be seen and,' he looked in his rear-view mirror, 'we're sending up a dust-cloud, to announce our presence.' He scanned the horizon. 'Yes, there's the sea and that must be the pearl farm.'

June looked at him anxiously. 'Well, what now?'

'Well,' David looked at his watch, 'it's just past midday, it's bloody hot outside and I would think whoever's there will be resting or eating or preparing to eat...'

'Yes, all right,' June responded irritably, 'I've got the message!'

'Look here!' David rounded on her, 'I've been driving this bloody car for hours while you've slept. I've never been in this country, never mind the Kimberleys, before. I didn't come here on holiday to catch up with bloody Carlyle again. I'm not a secret service agent, I'm an accountant. If you ask a question, tell me whether you want me to answer it in my own idiosyncratic way, or whether I ignore it and tell you to belt up.'

June crimsoned and looked ahead at the specks on the horizon. 'Sorry, sorry, sorry,' she muttered, then paused. 'What do you think should be the next move? Do you have a plan?'

David's mood evaporated and he chuckled as he ruffled her

hair. 'Now you sound like a BBC reporter! Sorry for the outburst – just a bit weary. I think we'll approach very slowly and get off the road, wherever it looks promising. Fortunately, the scrub round here does contain some trees and maybe we can move forward unseen. I want to get off as quickly as possible, because if anyone spots us they might wonder why we are not approaching at normal speed.'

June nodded. 'The earth looks pretty hard-baked and not just loose sand. We wouldn't want to get stuck up to our axle or something.'

'What do you know about axles?' David asked, surprised.

'Nothing,' June replied, 'but I've been to the cinema.'

David grinned at her, as he eased the car on, very slowly. He reckoned he was still some miles from the coast and the settlement, but he had no wish to cause any interest at all. His luck would have to hold, as he couldn't help raising some dust behind him, although the slower he went the less it was caught by the slight breeze.

After less than five minutes, David saw what looked like a natural dried riverbed to his right and he swung slowly round on to it. As it gently eased its way towards the west, David was happy to follow its route. On either side were spiky balls of spinifex choking the earth and quite thick scrub abounded. They disturbed a flock of white cockatoos as they meandered on. At one point he came across the charred evidence of a small bushfire around the track, but he couldn't tell how long ago it had happened. After some time, he pulled up suddenly, as they were about to leave the limited protection of the landscape. Ahead of them, not more than half a mile away, was a cluster of shacks and weatherboard houses. About ten in all. Between David and the settlement was a high wire fence that stretched as far as the eye could see in both directions. That wasn't going to help. It could have intrusion sensors and could even be electrified, he guessed. Bugger it! The sea beyond, was a vast whitish-blue under the murderous sun. Nothing stirred and there was no real cover for the remaining distance. David turned off the engine and wound down the window. The coolness of the air conditioning didn't take long to be overtaken

278

by the intensive heat outside, as they both stretched their muscles.

'We're under a bit of shade, but not much,' David looked around. 'There's nothing better. We might as well have some food. Wind your window down so we don't fry.'

They were quite ravenous and enjoyed some of the food they had bought in Broome. Freshening up, with some now rather tepid water, June dried her hands. 'What now?' she asked.

'I'm going to have a good look round with the binoculars.' David reached for them, 'and when it's a little cooler maybe get a little closer. I can use the river bed as cover as much as possible.'

He climbed down from the car and made his way towards a hillock several hundred yards to his right, where he lay down amongst the grasses and propped himself on his elbows. His binoculars ranged the settlement, but there was little to excite him. He could see three cars parked under a large white awning, and equipment similar to that he'd seen in Broome, sprawled around outside what he guessed was a workshop. The houses were single-storey and nondescript. There was no sign of life. A breeze ruffled his hair. It reminded him he hadn't put a hat on. Stupid idiot. Sunstroke would not be a good idea.

'Not a lot to see,' he returned to June. 'Come and sit in the shade by this side of the car for a while. We've got to be patient now, I think. Let the afternoon move on a bit.'

They sat and chatted and June dozed off, but David wouldn't allow himself that luxury. He wanted to be alert in this even more foreign place. What were the Carlyles doing up here? Anything to do with drugs? Maybe nothing at all. Maybe they were just running a pearl farm. But why? So many questions and, as yet, no answers.

Crack! He awoke with a start. What was that? Damn it, he had been asleep. His watch said four o'clock! He turned. June wasn't there! He heard a noise behind him as he quickly stood up and swung round. It was June, wincing, as she hobbled towards him.

'I had to go where little girls have to go,' she frowned, 'and I twisted my ankle on a piece of wood that broke as I trod on it. It's

OK,' she continued, 'only a moment's inconvenience. Nothing serious.'

'I must have dropped off,' David stated the obvious.

'Yes,' June smiled, as she opened the car door and found a bottle of water, 'and you had your mouth open. Not a pretty sight.'

David found the binoculars and returned to his vantage point. The sun, although still very hot, had lost a little of its earlier intensity. There was movement at the settlement. A blue van had arrived and was parked by one of the houses and four men were carrying boxes of some sort from it, into the workshop. A dinghy was chugging its way along level with the coast, just beyond the cars, and David guessed there was a jetty hidden from view down there.

'What can you see?' June had come up and was lying beside him.

'Not a lot, but a little more activity than last time,' David briefly told her. 'I think I'll make my way a little closer.'

'You'll learn Somerset Maugham's quote is true, if you're not careful,' June said firmly.

'What?' David rolled over and stared at her.

'Man has always found it easier to sacrifice his life than to learn the multiplication tables.'

David snorted. 'I know my multiplication tables and I've no intention of sacrificing my life.'

'I'm sure men don't intend to normally,' came the response, 'but they can get overly excited.'

'Oh, don't worry,' David crawled back to the security of the car and sat in the shade, knocking the earth off his trousers. 'I'm not going down there as the cavalry. There's no-one to save, as far as I know. And I'm certainly not going to try that fence. It could be alarmed or electric or both.'

June looked at him doubtfully, as she dropped herself by his side. 'What am I supposed to do?' She picked up a twig and quickly dropped it, as it was covered in ants.

'Nothing. I shan't be long.' He grinned. 'Commune with nature. Spin a tale to the spinifex.'

She shook her hair from side to side. 'God, it's still hot.' She

280

undid the top button of her shirt, waving the collar ineffectually backwards and forwards.

'Right. I shan't be long.' David kissed her cheek and bending double started to move slowly towards the settlement. He was surprised at the sound of an aeroplane and looking up saw a small seaplane flying north along the coast. It had been so quiet since they had parked that he was not expecting such an intrusion. He watched the houses as best he could and he heard a car not far away, but he couldn't use the binoculars and make progress at the same time. The dried riverbed was littered with detritus and he had to be careful as he crawled and stumbled along slowly, keeping as low as possible.

Finally, just in front of the wire fence, there was an isolated bouhinia tree with its bright-red pods casting a welcome shadow. He dropped to the ground, pulling his binoculars up into position. There was some activity by the workshop and he saw two men dressed in singlets and shorts carrying what appeared to be large cardboard boxes out. They disappeared behind the back of the blue van parked nearby. They then returned hurriedly to the workshop and repeated the exercise, as David realised they were being watched from the nearest house doorway by ... yes ... it was Carlyle. He had his arms folded and was turning his head, obviously talking to someone behind him out of sight. David's head began to pound, as he realised that he was reaching the point of no return. Should he pick up this strand of coincidence, which had brought Carlyle back into his world, or, as he had done once before, drop it and get on with his life? There was no reason for him to take this any further. Was there anything *to* take further? How could he take anything further?

He lay there for a long time contemplating his course of action, aware of the fence spreading all the way left and right when he suddenly sensed movement away to his left. He turned his head and saw a white pick-up approaching the settlement, dust spewing out behind it. As it drew up next to the blue van, its back door was flung open and out jumped another blonde singlet-and-shorts man, but instead of leaving he turned and ... God! Oh God! They had June!

David almost cried out, but his throat had choked dry. She was pushed forward by someone behind her and she fell into the arms of the man by the pick-up. For the first time David was aware of noise, as the sound of laughter ate its way across to him. June had her hands tied! That was why she couldn't control her fall. The blonde man caught her roughly and pushed her towards the house. Carlyle, at this point, came forward, bowed and clearly said something to her. She was jostled by the others and was led to the house, where they all disappeared inside.

Christ! Christ! What was he going to do? How had they found her? Did they know she wasn't alone? David looked behind him, instinctively. There was no movement nor sign of anything untoward. He rolled back onto his front, sweat dripping down his nose, as the pain of what was occurring began to sink in. If they didn't know he was around, it wouldn't take them long to find out. They weren't going to assume June was here on a coincidental happy picnic and no doubt they would be able to persuade her to tell them what they wanted to know. What would they do to her? His heart churned, as he tried to control his frustrated anger. He couldn't just blow a bugle and rush in with his troops, to rescue her. What the hell could he do?

Again his thoughts were directed for him. Through his binoculars he saw a chair brought out and placed to face in his direction. Puzzled, he then saw June led out and pushed into it. The same blonde man then undid the rope and pulling and pushing her hands roughly behind her, retied them behind the chair back. He then just turned and went back indoors. David realised the other two men had been loading the blue van throughout this episode. They called out something he couldn't hear and climbing into the cab, drove off out of the yard. He watched as the van picked up speed and disappear behind a clump of trees, as abruptly as the white pick-up had arrived. He could hear yet another plane on its way north.

He looked back to June, who could do nothing but sit. The sun was settling westwards and the heat had lessened, but it wouldn't be fun sitting out there – no hat, back to the sun. What were they doing with her? There was now no movement, no-one in sight. It didn't make sense ... or did it? He frowned. Of course it did. Of course! They were telling him they knew he was out there, watching. They knew he had to make the next step. They obviously knew where the car was. It was hardly likely to have been left unguarded. Or if it had been, it would clearly now be undriveable. He couldn't walk anywhere. They would know there was nowhere to go, but to them. June was the bait and he had no choice but to bite. Or had he? He decided he ought to check the car, if only to prove himself right. He lowered the binoculars and began to ease himself backwards, keeping his eyes on the settlement.

'Come on, shall we go, yer Pommie bastard?' David jumped out of his skin. He hadn't heard anyone come up behind him. He rolled over and looked up into the grinning face of ...? He recognised the face, but couldn't place it for a moment. Then it came to him. Bloody hell! The young man who had called at the house Carlyle had rented in Broome. As David looked at the barrel of a gun in the young man's hand, a boot kicked him hard on the shin.

'Get to yer bloody feet!' The man spoke quietly, but there was a manic gleam in his eyes, as he pulled his foot back to do it again.

'OK, OK,' David muttered, wincing at the sharp pain. He slowly clambered to his feet and instinctively brushed the sand off his chest, as he started to walk back.

'Oh, we are the neat and tidy bloody one!' The man leered at him. 'Go on, move.' He pulled a walkie-talkie from his belt and merely muttered 'Got the bastard' before pushing David in the back. They proceeded to retrace their steps across the uneven terrain with David stumbling as he went. They reached the car and next to it was a grey van.

'Keep moving, yer bastard. We've got the keys, just get in the van and drive it to the farm.'

David had seen films where people had been made to drive vehicles under the eye of a gun and had crashed them and made good their escape. But they had June and he was probably an enormous distance from any help. Forget it. Play along for the moment. He drove the unfamiliar van carefully and with difficulty back to the main track and headed west. As they approached the high fence, he saw a security camera and a gate that swung open, obviously by remote control, and then electronically closed behind them.

Nearing the house, David only had to look at the sheer terror on June's face to accelerate the last few yards before slamming on the brakes. Without looking at his captor, he jumped out and ran to her.

'David, David! I couldn't help it! They drove up and there were two of them and . . . and . . .'

'It's all right. It's all right,' he assured her, inanely, as he knelt by her side.

'Take this bloody rope off her hands.' He turned angrily to the young man, who was grinning, but still pointing the gun unswervingly at David's midriff.

There was a moment's silence, broken only by the gentle sobbing from June who had suddenly been overcome with emotion, then David angrily got to his feet. 'Come on, you maniac, she can't do you any harm!' He glared at his captor, who was momentarily taken aback by the verbal assault.

'Oh, but she can.'

David swung round to look straight into the burning eyes of Carlyle. 'And so can you, my friend. Undo her hands, Alec. Bring them both inside.' Carlyle turned and walked into the house. Hands untied, June rubbed her wrists as she let her face fall on to David's chest and he held her close.

'It's OK,' he whispered, kissing her hair.

'Is it hell!' She smiled feebly through her tears and shaking her head, quickly wiped her face, as they were pushed towards the door.

Inside David saw Carlyle talking on a two-way radio at a desk in the far corner of the room, whilst watching a radar screen. As they entered, he finished, switched everything off and walked forward.

'So, Mr, Price, how *not* good to see you again.' The look on his face was very unpleasant. 'Everybody seems to be finding me all of a sudden.' His voice rose in fury. 'Shit! I don't need it! I don't need you! I don't need anybody! I don't want anybody, any more! Why couldn't you all leave me alone? Now, I've got to leave here! I . . .'

Carlyle spun on his heel, his forehead glistening with perspiration and walked across to stare out of the windows, ignoring them.

David looked round, quickly. The room was surprisingly large and well furnished. Dining table and chairs, two sofas and a large sideboard with a display of multicoloured plates on the shelves. The floor was wooden, covered with cotton rugs and all the windows had blinds and the inevitable fly screens.

'Alec, go and get some beers.' Carlyle's voice had returned to controlled normality. The young man hesitated, for a second. 'It's all right we don't need the melodramatic presence of a gun,' Carlyle waved him on to the green door at the end. 'They can't go anywhere, with all of us around. I'm sure they realise we are well-armed, ready for any unfortunate incidents.' He turned his eyes to June and slowly looked her body up and down. 'Do sit down at the table, both of you.' It was an order, not an invitation.

'Price, when you use binoculars,' Carlyle went to the far side of the table and sat down opposite them, 'you really should realise that when facing the sun there is a certain phenomenon, called a reflection. We watched you from here, quite happily, while you were watching us. Surprisingly, you didn't try and go back, when we sent the pick-up off to come round behind you.'

So that was the vehicle he'd heard, David realised.

Alec returned with four beers, which he threw on the table, before taking one. He moved to a wicker rocking chair, in the far corner. David watched him ostentatiously put his gun on the table by his side, his eyes never leaving them, before taking a short pull on his can. He then sat down, took a swig of beer and crossed his legs contentedly.

'Alec's done time and is a good watchdog,' Carlyle had followed David's gaze and now raised a beer can mockingly in salute, as he pushed the others in David's direction. 'Good luck – to me,' he sneered and opened the can. David and June opened theirs. The liquid was cold and welcome, as David forbore to comment, or even to look at anyone or anything, other than Carlyle's smug features.

He hadn't changed all that much over the years. Slightly slimmer, dressed in a sandy shirt and shorts, his face was brown and weatherbeaten, his hair thinner and greyer. His eyes, however, were as alert as ever and David doubted that the man had lost any of his sharpness. Events had proved that in the last ... how long? David looked at his watch. It was only half an hour since the world had fallen apart. Since he had been playing boy scout and showing June how bloody clever he was. Now what?

As if he had been reading his thoughts, Carlyle brought the palms of his hands together and asked, 'Price, why have you come here? I must say it was quite a surprise to find Alec had brought back the very attractive Mrs Price – or June, I believe it is.' He leered at June, again, as he stroked his cheeks. 'I had no idea either of you were in Australia, but then,' he spread his hands, 'why should I? I haven't been interested in you, for years. Obviously, that is not mutual.'

'Yes, it is,' David responded quickly. 'We saw you in Broome and heard you were working up here, so as we are on holiday, we thought we'd have a drive up.' There was silence. 'We've never seen a pearl farm,' David added lamely.

'Really?' Carlyle yawned. 'Well, why did you turn off when you did? The road to the pearl farm was pretty obvious, but you didn't seem to want it. We watched you deliberate and then follow the river bed. You look surprised, Price. Don't be. There's a large boab tree where you stopped, with a very useful remote-controlled camera in it, wouldn't you know. So you decided to go bush – some sort of safari trek, was it? Don't disturb the animals? Observe them from a distance, that way they won't know they're being watched? Very thoughtful. What, Price, did you expect to observe from a distance?'

'I don't know,' and, thought David miserably, that's the truth.

Carlyle shook his head wonderingly. 'Odd,' he commented blandly. 'Odd. But, as that doesn't help us, I'm afraid we come to what we are going to do with you.'

There was a snigger from the corner, as Alec took a swig of his beer.

286

'Well,' said David, trying hard to sound confident, 'I guess we shouldn't intrude on your activities any longer and we'd better drive back to Broome.'

'What?' A roar of laughter erupted from Carlyle, before his fist came crashing down on the table, causing June to flinch visibly. 'I don't think so,' Carlyle's voice had become soft and silken. 'I don't think so.'

'We're only on holiday,' June's voice cracked as she went on, 'we didn't know you were even,' she faltered, 'still alive.'

'Ah,' whispered Carlyle, curling his lip, 'but you do now. And you are both still clearly as inquisitive as you once were. And that,' he rose, 'is unfortunate. Alec will now tie you to your chairs, while I think about this a little. I'm afraid you will have to become the victims of an unfortunate accident.' David heard June gasp, as Carlyle went on, 'Cars do go off the road quite often, when they're driven by visitors who don't take enough care in these foreign parts. No,' he glared at them, 'I'm afraid you have ventured one country too far. Give me the gun, Alec, and tie them up.'

Alec threw the gun across and took some rope from a wall hook, before wrenching David's hands behind him and securing him painfully to the back of the chair. June yelped with pain, as her arms were pulled back. 'David,' she turned her head, miserably, 'David.'

'Forget it,' Carlyle put the gun on the table. 'He can't help you. Alec,' Carlyle turned, 'we'll leave them here tonight, until the operations are out of the way and deal with them at first light. Their vehicle is OK where it is until the morning, when we'll fix an accident back up the road, miles from here.'

'Right,' Alec nodded and walking past David shot his fist into David's face. 'That's for shouting at me, you bastard,' he snarled, as he followed Carlyle out of the room.

David felt the rawness, as he opened his mouth painfully and gingerly licked the blood on his lips. His helplessness hurt him as much as the punch and he wanted to believe the tears he could feel in his eyes were anger, but he wasn't very sure. He could hear voices outside the house, but inside was silence.

'What are we going to do?' June's strangled question only helped to underline her obvious fear.

David shook his head numbly. 'Wait and see, might be the best alternative.' He tried to smile, but his face hurt and the attempt at being lighthearted hadn't worked on June, who began to sob, quietly. It was hot and oppressive and for the first time David heard mosquitos buzzing around nearby. He said quietly, 'We've got to be ready to act. Be ready for any opportunity that comes. When it comes.'

June looked at him. 'David, this doesn't happen in novels, but I need to pee.' Her soft tears turned to uncontrolled crying, as she sat and writhed.

'Carlyle, Carlyle!' David roared at the top of his voice, surprised at his own stridence. After a few moments the door opened and Carlyle, looking slightly bemused, framed the doorway 'My wife needs the toilet.' David realised how ridiculous he sounded.

There was a silence, before Carlyle smiled, unpleasantly and came in shutting the door behind him. 'Does she? Does she now? And why should I worry about that?' Carlyle smirked, grotesquely.

'Carlyle,' David knew his voice was only just under control, 'please.'

There was a moment's hesitation before Carlyle slowly walked over and without a word untied June's wrists, before roughly hauling her to her feet. 'Through there, the bathroom's on the left,' he nodded behind David's back, 'and don't even begin to think of escaping, or doing anything silly on your own. You're miles from anybody who could be termed neutral, let alone friendly!'

June unsteadily left the room and Carlyle rested his right buttock on the table and looked at David for a few pregnant moments.

'You are a very stupid man, Price,' he said finally, looking almost sad. 'We gave you a chance, which you seemed to understand and take. And now where are we? Back where we were. This time I'm afraid there cannot be any second chances. My only problem is to ensure that the accident is not associated with here. I've got enough other problems, now. So you will have to travel a fairly uncomfortable distance tomorrow, which is a nuisance for us and death for you.'

Before David could think of a response, he heard a door open behind him and sensed, before he saw, June's return. She quickly sat down and Carlyle, without a word, retied her hands and walked out, shutting the door firmly behind him.

'David, David!' June whispered. She could hardly contain herself. 'There's a submarine out there!'

'What?' David turned his head and stared at her.

'It's true!' she almost shouted.

'Ssh!'

'Sorry.' She was now whispering again. 'There's a jetty that runs from behind the house quite a way out and apart from dinghies and other boats moored at the end, I'll swear there is a submarine under an awning!'

'Rubbish! It's dusk out there now.' David shook his head. 'You can't see properly in this light. It'll be a fishing boat of some sort.'

'David,' her voice grew stronger, but still quiet, 'it is a submarine. I opened the toilet window to see what was going on round us and that is what I saw! It's not the sort you see in the newspapers or films. It's small – maybe thirty feet long, but *definitely* a submarine.'

David's brain seized up. A submarine? How could there be? Why? He'd never heard of them being used for anything other than as a vehicle of destruction. What on earth would be the purpose of one up here, of all Godforsaken places?

'OK, OK,' he muttered, 'I believe you. Did you see anybody about? Anybody near it or anywhere else?'

'No,' June shook her head, 'I could hear people and there was a lot of noise, but I couldn't see anybody.'

David marvelled bitterly, ' "He who would search for pearls must dive below", John Dryden wrote, but I don't think he meant submarines and I doubt if this one is searching for pearls if it comes to that!'

'What?' June sounded bewildered now.

'Nothing. Just rambling.'

Dusk fell lazily into night, as they sat there, uncomfortably losing visibility. No-one came. They were left to while the time away. Occasionally they could hear bellows of laughter and there was a lot of activity around them outside. They became aware of shafts of light emanating from huts or buildings nearby, quickly petering out in the surrounding darkness. David dozed and was into a terrifying dream of headless people decapitating every human victim they could find, when he was abruptly woken. He was thankful the dream was over, but then he realised where he was. Not a lot better. But what had woken him? Yes, it had sounded like a gunshot not far way.

'What was that?' June whispered.

Before David could reply, there was a volley of shots from close by to their right, where the sheds were. He could hear footsteps running in all directions and orders being shouted. He heard a walkie-talkie outside screeching 'They've cut the bloody wire!'. Carlyle's voice responded, but the words were too muffled to make any sense. David's pulse quickened. Whatever was happening was clearly unexpected and uninvited. There was a roar, as vehicles were started and revved up and they could hear the screeches of tyres as they were being steered in challenging directions.

Amidst the furore there was movement and noise that David subconsciously knew should make some sense to him, but he couldn't put his finger on it. More shots rang out, some near, some far, and they both instinctively ducked as bullets ricocheted around them. Pandemonium reigned. Then lights as bright as day began to pass haphazardly across the windows and yells took over as the gunshots became more spasmodic, before dying away. After what seemed like a lifetime, the door suddenly burst open, a lightswitch clicked, illuminating the room, and David, after blinking madly, gaped at the sight of Terry James and a young, dark, tousle-headed man, both in jeans, with guns held firmly in their hands.

'Are you two all right?' Terry's eyes were attending to the door behind them.

'It's OK, there's no-one in here,' David responded.

Terry ignored him completely and made his way slowly round behind David before opening the door violently with his foot. He then disappeared from view and a few seconds later there was a woman's scream that caused David to freeze momentarily, He could hear a commotion and curses before Terry led in Tanya Carlyle by the elbow. She was dressed in a dark-blue tracksuit and her hair was unkempt, falling over her face. The young tousle-headed man who had scarcely moved from the position he'd adopted on entry, smiled. 'Not there?' he asked. 'Who's she?'

'No,' Terry shook his head. 'Tell them.'

The young man opened the door and yelled 'Not in here,' before slamming it to.

'This is Grace Harmer, wife of our dear friend Brian Harmer. She was in the spare room beyond the bathroom, cowering, if that's the right word, behind the door. No trouble.' Terry shoved her towards a chair, unceremoniously. 'Sit down,' he commanded.

'I've a terrible migraine,' she whined.

'You'll have a worse one, if you don't do as you're told,' Terry spat at her. 'Now where's your husband?'

Tanya glared at him for a moment and opened her mouth to say something, but clearly thought better of it, slumped down and shut her eyes.

'Right, I'll untie our friends, Kevin, while you watch over her.'

'Carlyle was here a while back,' David said.

'Carlyle? Who's Carlyle?' asked a puzzled Terry, who quickly untied David and June, both of whom began to rub their aching wrists.

Their names are Tanya and Ian Carlyle not Grace and Brian Harmer. We ... we knew them,' David paused and looked at Tanya who hadn't moved an inch, with her eyes still shut, 'in England some years back and ...'

'Tell us later.'

Terry nodded and Kevin left the room.

'What's happened? What's going on?' June blurted out, tears of relief in her eyes.

Terry smiled at her before resting his eyes on David. 'You

smart buggers caused us a bit of a problem. Your questions were too near the knuckle, you know. Your questions to Sue about whether you could visit this pearl farm put us on notice. It wasn't very difficult to guess that you were being a little too imaginative yesterday and I couldn't leave my worries to chance. I feared you might be going to upset the applecart and Christ, you did! We had to keep an eye on you just to see what, if anything, you might get up to. When you left town we guessed where you would finish up, so we had to pull our team in. We've been carrying out an undercover operation up here for some weeks, getting ready to pounce. We followed you, but far enough behind that you would never have been aware of us and, of course, light aircraft don't cause too much attention around here, with tourist flights all the go. We overflew you a couple of times to make sure what you were up to.'

David smiled with relief, as he stood up and flexed his legs. 'What's been going on outside?' he asked.

'There's about twenty of us out there. Customs and police, a combined drug operational unit. We had a tip-off several weeks ago, back in Broome, that someone thought Harmer was up to something because he'd been seen in Derby, which is a town two hundred kilometres away, with a man the informant happened to know was in the Sydney underworld. Envelopes passed. Anyway it helped to confirm our own suspicions. We're always interested in new residents and we keep our eyes and ears open, you know. This is a good place to run a drugs operation and we had observed that there was too much vehicular activity for a normal pearl farm, but we hadn't been able to finger how the drugs were coming ashore. If it was drugs, of course.'

They heard car doors slamming and engines revving, but now it sounded controlled and Kevin came back. 'All under way, Terry,' he nodded. 'But no sign of bloody Harmer and we're bloody sure no car got away. He could be out there on his own, but if he is he won't get far. We'll get a 'copter in at daybreak and there's not that much cover out there.'

'I don't think you'll find him out there,' David had recognised the noise that hadn't made sense to him earlier. 'I think he made his getaway in the submarine. I bet it's not out there now.'

'In the *what?*' Terry looked at him as if he had suggested a departure in a spaceship.

David had been half watching Tanya Carlyle as he had voiced his conjecture and his heart beat more positively as he saw her open her eyes and look at him with hate writ large over her face, before she quickly shut her eyes and returned to her previous posture. June blurted out her story of the bathroom. There was silence, which she herself broke by adding lamely and quietly, 'I only saw it by standing on the bowl and hanging on by my fingernails. The window's a long way up.'

'You beauty,' Terry beamed, 'you could just be right. I don't understand how they're doing it, but Christ, it could be fair dinkum. Hold on I'll get Tom, he's the Detective Superintendent in charge of this operation.'

Without further ado Terry shot out and David, realising they'd taken June's story as gospel, went to the toilet and climbing on to the pedestal saw the jetty lit by several arc lights. As he returned to the sitting room that he now loathed, Terry returned with a large, thick-set, balding man, dressed in white shirt and blue trousers. There was a revolver at his hip.

There was no preamble. 'What's this about a bloody submarine?' His disbelief was transparent. June again told her story. It didn't take many moments. Hands on hip the belligerence disappeared as if by magic and suddenly there was a big smile, revealing nicotine-stained, uneven teeth.

'I like it. I like it. Terry, you may be right. It would answer a lot. I'm Tom Rolls by the way.' He proffered a large hand and shook David and June's hands warmly.

David pointed to the radar screen in the corner. 'While that is obviously useful for security, it's also good for tracking their own transport.'

Tom Rolls nodded, 'I'll go and get on to Perth. I think we're definitely going to need reconnaissance aircraft back-up at first light. Before, I thought Harmer might be hiding in the bush, but if he's got away in a sub we'll need to spread our net wider. About thirty foot long, you say,' he looked at June, who nodded, 'yeah, it could be like one of those they've found being used off the Caribbean coast. They can carry up to three tons and can

293

travel underwater for two hours with a three-man crew. They originated with the Colombian cartels and it's reckoned they've been in use for some years, so I guess it shouldn't be too surprising if one, or even more, found their way out here.'

'Where would it go to?' David frowned.

'Oh,' Tom Rolls replied brusquely, 'my guess is that it or they emanate from a large tanker or container ship, on the way to Fremantle. They'd be starting out from Indonesia, or maybe Thailand. It would need a watertight compartment and if it made the run regularly enough it would have plotted its course by building up tide and current experience.' He smiled. 'As you now know this area is pretty inhospitable and vast, so where better to locate your port of entry? But,' he slapped Terry on the shoulder, 'it looks as though we've got the buggers! We came through OK, but three of them copped it. Alan's organising the despatch of the eleven bastards we've arrested. One's caught a bullet in the leg and another in the shoulder, but I guess they'll live. We'll move them down to Perth, pretty smartly, I think. Terry, your guys are searching the sheds to see what's there. Do you want to join them?'

Terry nodded and looking happily at David and June, said 'See yer' and left the room.

'So what now?' David realised how tired he was, now that the excitement had died down and a sense of near normality had taken over. Normal? He thought he must be mad to even think of the word, after the experience of the last few hours!

As if sensing the anticlimax, Tom Rolls, without looking at David, walked to the door and opening it a foot, yelled out, 'Pete, see if you can rustle up a couple of mugs of tea for our two voyagers in here, will you?'

David heard a positive response as Rolls shut the door and sank into the chair that so recently had been Carlyle's. 'Well, I suggest you both get your heads down for an hour or two, before we drive you back to Broome.'

June, who had been watching the goings-on without comment, suddenly asked, 'I guess you'll be interrogating Mrs Carlyle – not just about this drug smuggling, but about their other activities back in England in 1988?'

294

Rolls frowned with puzzlement and fixed his gaze on her, but David quickly commented, 'I think I'd better tell you what we know about the Harmers, or as we know them, the Carlyles.'

At that moment the door opened and a police constable entered with three steaming mugs of tea. 'Thought you'd all like one,' he muttered, looking at his superior. 'Fraid there's no sugar anywhere – plenty of other white powder though,' he grinned.

'Good on yer, Pete,' Rolls waved his hand. 'Take this woman, whatever her name is, outside and stack her with the others for now.' The constable took the glowering Tanya Carlyle with him. 'Now, perhaps if you're not too tired you'd better fill me in,' he raised his bushy eyebrows questioningly at David. Silence reigned as Rolls reached for a cigarette, 'Mind?' he asked and offered them one.

'No thanks,' David shook his head, 'I'm happy to tell you what I can.' He looked at June who signified she was too, by rubbing her eyes, smiling and nodding, before reaching out for the mug of tea.

Time slipped by, as David told the Superintendent as much as he could remember from the past, with the occasional interruption from June and finished with their holiday of the last few days.

'Well, it's quite a tale, isn't it?' Rolls had lit up the last cigarette as he tossed the empty packet on the table. 'I'll get on to London in the morning and see what they know of this bastard.'

David yawned. 'I've a friend I told some of this to, back in 1988. Donald Havers. I believe he's in MI5 or something similar. He'll corroborate what I've told you.'

Tom Rolls smiled, 'He might bear out what you've told me in the sense that you told him the same story, but from what you've said he can't corroborate anything, can he? Not,' he put up his hand, 'that I don't believe you, you understand.'

'Maybe not,' June stared angrily, 'but I can. I was bloody well there. Remember?'

'Sure, sure,' Rolls now waved his hand, carrying an arc of cigarette smoke to envelop his head. 'As I said I believe you, but this Havers can only help us if he's got any other info' on the guy.'

'You're right,' David nodded blankly. 'I'll leave it to you. Anyway, I feel like a kip, in fact I'm sure we both do.' He turned to the Superintendent. 'Mind if we find a bedroom for a short while?'

'Of course not. I'd better check on progress outside.' Rolls rose and smiled. 'I'll wake you when we're ready to leave.'

David nodded thoughtfully, 'You might get your chaps to get their wet suits and diving equipment on before they leave,' he paused and looked at Rolls. 'A pearl farm run for a good profit is OK, but,' he added slowly, 'I reckon that they're also farming some drugs in the water. By that I mean hiding them there. They may be using the palette system to store stock. Some of the markers could be a telltale method of identifying what you're looking for. A pearl farm and a drug farm?'

Tom Rolls didn't say a word, but turned and left the room, breathing heavily. Without further ado, David and June went down the corridor and passing the bathroom, found what was probably the Carlyle's guest room and happily collapsed on top of the two single, made up beds. Neither spoke as their heads hit the pillows, snared by their own turbulent thoughts. They both drifted off, surprisingly quickly.

20

'I think being shot at was better than this,' June turned her head warily, only to be stared at by the following camel, whose head was unnervingly close to her right buttock. It snarled unpleasantly, as though to order, teeth bared proudly.

'Rubbish!' David turned and grinned. 'You've paid for this, so it has to be enjoyable.'

It was five days since their return from the pearl farm and relaxation had been hard to acclimatise to after their ordeal, but with nothing and nobody to disturb the tranquillity of their existence, they had gradually unwound and eased into enjoyment of the holiday. The evening had been calm and breeze-free, as they had joined some other holidaymakers on a camel train along Cable Beach, before sunset. The tide was out and the setting sun shone and glistened on the receding water that dallied with the unmoving sand.

The undulating movement of the camel was surprisingly relaxing and pleasant as they made their way back towards The Resort. A few spectators, family and friends of the riders, were waiting at the assembly point where they had all mounted in jollity and in some cases, apprehension. Several young children ran to greet them, excitedly. They skipped and danced alongside the camels, who were all strung together and led by a weathered, smiling young man, with a soiled akubra on his head and long untidy black hair escaping from all sides.

'Isn't that Terry James over there?' David mused, as they were helped off their camel. With the setting sun on their backs it was easy to see the silhouette on the escarpment in front of The Resort. Terry had his hands up to shield the sun from his face.

'Yes,' June slapped her hand in his. 'I wonder if he has any news?'

'Not sure I want any, good or bad!' David muttered. 'Life can be quite nice without any. I haven't missed the world's news and I'm damned if I'm missing the local news, either!' As they climbed the sand-filled steps to the grassy foreshore, Terry stepped forward and held out his hand.

'G-day.'

David shook Terry's hand, albeit less warmly than he might. 'How are things?' he asked.

Terry fell in beside them as they walked towards The Resort. 'Ah, good news,' he replied enthusiastically. 'We caught Harmer yesterday. Would you believe it was an Indonesian cargo ship, twenty thousand tonnes, laden with teak, sandalwood, and other assorted timber. We let it dock in Fremantle, before we made our move.' They had reached the nearest open-air bar and without a word on the subject, all three collapsed at a vacant table, ready to order a drink.

'What happened?' David caught a waitress's eye and before Terry could reply, ordered three light beers.

'Well,' Terry was clearly enjoying himself, 'the ship docked mid-morning, having been shadowed by helicopter and radar to make sure no craft offloaded on the way down. They waited an hour to let the crew think nothing was unusual and then they raided her.'

'And?' David hardly needed to ask, the eagerness was self-evident.

'It took a bit of finding. The ship, to all intents and purposes, seemed genuine enough. But they checked the measurements and the internals and externals didn't match. There was an area towards the stern that wasn't accounted for. Internally it didn't exist. It was where number seven hold should have been. Anyway they investigated and found a gangway that didn't go anywhere. At the top of it they played with some bolts and, hey presto, a bulkhead! Inside, no living quarters, but a gangway with storage rooms, some still full of heroin and at the bottom in

298

another watertight area through another bulkhead, a small submarine in a tank and our dear friend hiding inside it! He must have heard the commotion, but there was nowhere for him to go. He couldn't fire himself off like a torpedo! He was just a jettisoned passenger! The crew of the sub were obviously part of the crew of the ship. Plenty of evidence down there that they must have been at it for a considerable time. That ship has been visiting Australia for quite a while and we've yet to know whether there were other ports of call on the way. Anyway the crew are all being questioned and some will squeal. They always do.'

'Where are the Carlyles, or Harmers?' asked David, as the drinks arrived.

'In jail in Perth,' replied Terry. 'They won't see any more of the pleasures of Australia for a while,' he added contentedly and raised his glass. 'Here's to the remainder of your hols. Bet you didn't expect it to be quite so adventurous!'

'You can say that again!' smiled June.

'Well, I won't keep you,' Terry said, 'but Tom Rolls would like you to call at the police station tomorrow, if you would, and give a statement. Maybe ring first and arrange a time? By the way, Tom said thanks. Watertight bags and containers full of heroin were found offshore, all connected by cable lines on the sea bed. Very sophisticated machinery, controlling it all, was housed with marine equipment several hundred yards away from the jetty area. That was good thinking.'

David smiled, as Terry rose and bade farewell, with a nonchalant salute.

'You're very clever and he's a good-looking man,' June observed, stroking her glass against her cheek.

'We've been through that before,' David chided her. 'Come on, let's go to dinner.'

'I'd like to sit here a bit longer,' she replied.

'OK, I'll just go to the room and get a couple of sweaters.' David rose, 'It may get a bit chilly later.'

June nodded absent-mindedly and David sauntered across the lawns towards the stairs leading to the upper floor of verandahs and rooms. He observed with pleasure the playing fountains and waterfalls, and the lush ferns and bougainvillaea borders stretching round the buildings, as he joined the path at the foot of the stairs. As he did so he saw a small green snake slither across in front of him and he jumped back, startled. He knew nothing about snakes. Which were the dangerous ones, for God's sake? As he leaped back his thoughts were suddenly and dramatically interrupted by an urn crashing down in front of him, missing him by inches.

'What the . . . ?' It was one of the very large terracotta pots, two feet in diameter and three feet in height. They were liberally displayed around The Resort and filled with native West Australian flora. They were exceedingly heavy and this one was now cracked open where it had hit the brick path. David stared at the scene in disbelief.

'You all right, mate?' He turned, as an elderly white-haired man in tennis gear, carrying a racquet, hurried across the path.

'Er, yes thanks,' David nodded, overwhelmed.

The man looked up. 'It was on that plinth on the corner of the building. There, you can see,' he pointed skyward.

David stepped back and followed the man's shaking hand. Sure enough on the upper level one pot was missing from its rightful place. And there was no sign of the guardrail.

'How the hell did it fall?'

'Well, no harm done,' David suddenly wanted to be alone. 'I'll report it. Thanks for your help.'

'No worries, mate. Sure you're OK?' The would-be tennis player looked at David, anxiously.

'Sure,' David smiled and reassuringly patted the elderly man on the arm, as he contemplated the stairs. The snake was nowhere to be seen. It was either under the urn or had disappeared into the garden. David's heart was pounding and he felt weak at the knees. He could recall now the noise of footsteps running away along the wooden verandah, as his eyes had been focused on the snake. That urn had been pushed and if he hadn't leaped backwards it could have killed him.

Oh, God! Who? Why? Wasn't that all over? David climbed wearily to the upper floor. There was no sign of anyone or anything to disturb the tranquillity. No-one else had heard the commotion. No doors had opened. He could hear low-volume television coming from several rooms as he reached their door. He opened it, his hand trembling at the lock. He hesitated for a moment before entering. There was no-one there. Of course not. Why, of course? He shook his head. Broome was becoming a place too far.

*   *   *

'But who was it?' June stared at David across the dining table.

'How the hell do I know?' David answered a question with a question.

'Well, was it a man or a woman?'

David picked up his glass of water slowly, trying hard to cast his mind back to what, after all, was only a few minutes ago. He shook his head and didn't reply.

'Think,' June's hand closed over his. 'Did the steps sound short or long? Was there a clatter of heels or the soft thud of a man's foot?'

David looked through her. 'No heels. Trainers. Plimsolls. That sort of sound. Quite long strides.'

'Right, well that makes sense. A man is more likely to have been able to push one of those heavy urns than a woman.' June picked up the menu.

'Well, that solves the problem then.' David knew he sounded unfair. 'We're only looking for a man – strong and comparatively athletic. Should be easy.'

June looked over her spectacles innocently, 'We can narrow it down further,' she commented.

'How?' David asked, truculently.

'Find someone who doesn't like you.' She went back to the menu.

Before David could reply, the waiter was at his side helping them with their decisions and it was only following his departure that David continued, 'I don't know whether to be scared, angry, or what.'

June shook her head, smiling faintly. 'Be both. Being scared will keep you alert and I know that you're angry, as you've every right to be.'

'Too bloody right,' he nodded and winced, 'and that sounds Australian!'

'What next?' June asked, softly.

There was a roar of indecent laughter from the table of eight next to them, as David pondered the question. 'No idea,' he raised his voice to be heard above the decibels nearby. 'We can't assume it's a guest or a member of staff. The place is open to the public. Could be anyone in Broome.' He thought for a moment. 'It may even be a case of mistaken identity.'

'You don't believe that,' June looked up and smiled, as the waiter arrived back with the wine.

'No, I don't,' David agreed and tasted the wine, before nodding for it to be poured.

'Whoever it was, would have watched me walking back long before I arrived at the foot of the stairs. It could not have been anything but an attempted . . .' he hesitated.

'Murder,' June completed the sentence for him and then grinned halfheartedly as she raised her glass emphatically, 'Sorry, but one has to say it, doesn't one. Good health!'

David laughed humourlessly, for he knew that otherwise he might well have cried. And so did June.

After a couple of sips of wine David started and looked at his watch. 'The maid turns the beds down about now,' he said, thoughtfully.

'Yes?'

'Well, she has to come from somewhere. If she were along the verandah, but round the corner in one of the other rooms, or moving from one to another, she may have seen someone running by.' David stood up. 'I'm just going to check. Won't be a moment. And yes,' he added, 'I'll be careful.'

June watched him make his way hurriedly through the crowd at the bar before disappearing from view. He was gone what seemed like ages, but her watch told her it was only five minutes. A grim satisfaction radiated from his demeanour, as he sat down. 'Well?' she asked impatiently.

'Yes,' he replied, 'she was round the corner and as she was going into one of the suites she does remember a man she describes as slim and below medium height, hurrying by. He

302

was dressed in a blue tracksuit and trainers and wearing sunglasses. She said "Good Evening", but he didn't reply and actually looked away, which she thought a little odd, but didn't think any more of it. She said she doesn't remember seeing him before.'

'So?' June waited.

'So?' David looked bewildered.

'So?' June waved her hand, dismissively, 'What have you discovered that you didn't know already? We knew there had to be a "he". All we know is his clothes. How are you going to find him? Have a parade of all of Broome? Don't you think the clothes might have been discarded already? You've discovered nothing of any consequence. I'm, sorry,' June suddenly realised how deflating she must sound, 'I'm sorry, but isn't that right?' she finished slowly and wearily.

David nodded, 'Yes, but ridiculous as it may seem, I feel better for knowing the "he" exists. That it wasn't some feat of nature. We're properly on our guard again, now. Against what though I don't know.'

'God,' said June, 'and that makes you feel good? Let's eat before I go mad. Then we'll call the police.'

The meal was excellent. Moreton bay bugs; salmon en croute; fresh fruit and cheese. As they sat with a coffee to finish, David saw Terry James at the entrance to the dining room, looking at the guests. As he spied them, he raised his hand in recognition and threaded his way to their table.

'Hey!' he smiled, 'Mind if I join you, for a moment?' He drew up a chair without waiting for their response.

'Coffee?' David smiled politely. He didn't really want any extra company.

Terry shook his head. 'No, thanks,' he said. 'I've only come out for a quick word.' He looked awkwardly at David and then at June. 'Not very good news, I'm afraid.'

David's heart missed a beat. 'Now what?' he enquired softly.

'In fact, bloody awful news.' Terry went on, as if David had not spoken. 'The Harmers have both been killed.'

'What?' June's hands went to her throat, as though to protect it.

303

Terry nodded moodily. ' 'Fraid so. They were being taken to court for arraignment in separate vehicles, but in convoy. They were coming from the East Perth lockup in Hay Street, when a motorcyclist dressed in police uniform accelerated alongside each vehicle and placed what can only be assumed at the moment to be a type of magnetic bomb on each vehicle, then shot off. Before anyone grasped what was happening, they both exploded. It's thought they were set off by remote control. Six of the police escort and outriders were killed and three badly injured and the Harmers were both killed outright.'

There was nothing David could think of saying. The noise in the restaurant suddenly seemed to be ten times as loud. He found himself becoming disorientated – his mind was refusing to focus. He shut his eyes and took a deep breath.

'The bogus policeman?' whispered June.

'Disappeared in the mayhem that followed,' Terry replied. 'Last seen in Barrack Street heading north. Vanished I'm afraid.' He turned to David. 'Tom Rolls asked me to come and tell you. He went down to Perth with Mrs Harmer, who steadfastly refused to say anything of any consequence the whole time. He's still there. Fortunately he was waiting for them to turn up in court or he wouldn't be showing much interest in this now.' June shuddered involuntarily. 'Apparently he's been in touch with some friend of yours in London, who has now asked that you should have a detective constable in attendance for the rest of your holiday and it's being arranged. Sorry about all this.'

David pulled his sweater around his shoulders. He had suddenly gone very cold. He told Terry of his experience earlier that evening.

304

21

London, September 1996

The room seemed airless and Donald Havers eased up the sash window, with great difficulty. The noise of the London traffic assailed his sensibilities. He thrust his hands moodily into the trouser pockets of his hand-tailored, blue pinstriped suit. He really must get the hole in his right pocket sewn up. Elegant limousines were pulling up outside La Caprice and tall, young, blonde beauties in awfully short dresses, were falling out, giggling, ready to enjoy some food, wine and company. Along to his right, the doorman was smartly saluting guests as they arrived at the Ritz. Lunch time was a busy time around St James's. And he was a busy man too. Where the hell...? Ah! A buzzer rang.

'Yes, thank you. Show him in, will you?'

Havers turned from the open windows and moved round the mahogany desk towards the door as it opened. Miss Blair, a slim woman in her middle forties, stood to one side and announced quietly, 'Mr Price, sir,' before closing the door without more ado.

'David,' Havers extended his hand.

'Donald, nice to see you,' David sat down on the low, well-worn leather sofa.

'I know it's a little late for coffee, David, but I'm afraid we don't run to anything stronger.'

Havers expression was one of profuse apology.

'Coffee will be fine, thank you.' David looked around him, as the coffee pot was wielded in an expert fashion. A rather nondescript room, David was surprised to see. The carpet was even threadbare in places and the walls looked as though they could do with a clean, if not a repaint.

'Ah,' Havers had observed David's glances, 'I'm not surprised you are looking a little askance at our quarters, David, but let me assure you Her Majesty's Government hasn't really hit such bad times.' He passed the white, bone china cup and saucer across and sat down opposite David. 'You see, these are not active offices. We only use this address for the occasional meeting and nothing of consequence happens here.'

'Thanks,' David smiled, 'that puts me in my place.'

Havers laughed. 'Touché. Not very well put. The place is secure and central. And as the offices of an Arab import export business, no eyebrows are raised. But none of us uses it permanently – just,' he finished lamely, 'to meet people.'

David nodded, 'Well, you're meeting me,' and sipped his lukewarm, bitter coffee.

'Yes,' Havers looked at David searchingly. 'You've had a fascinating holiday from all accounts. How was Broome?'

'Donald, you don't give a stuff how Broome was!' He put down his unappealing cup of coffee. 'I seem – we seem – to have fallen into a fascinating follow-up of the story I told you, how long ago ... seven years or so, I guess? Not fair really, we only went there for a bloody good holiday. And June and I had started out by discussing going to Tuscany, for Christ sake!'

Havers smiled. 'Teach you to think long and hard next time, won't it?'

David didn't feel like replying.

Havers pulled out a packet of cigarettes and slowly lit one with an elegant, thin, gold lighter. 'Well, I guess you'd like to know why I asked you to come here on your first day back?'

David nodded and tried to ignore the drifting smoke from the cigarette held in Havers' elegant hands.

'Your story, when we met for lunch all those years ago, didn't really ring any bells for me. We have profiles, as you can imagine, on many agents and double agents operating within the British Isles. But Carlyle wasn't one of them. However, your

306

story interested me and caused us to try and uncover his background. And, lo and behold, to start with, we couldn't. He had materialised out of, as it were, thin air. Before he was in business in a significant way, no one had heard of him. A British birth certificate didn't exist. Then we scoured the records of refugees who had been allowed in from Europe and found he had come from Germany. His wife had left on one of the last ships out of Rostock in 1945 and it had been strafed by Russian fighters, before docking in Lubecke. We traced a couple of women who were girls with her on that ship and they remember her as a resolute young thing even then. Tanya Schneider was her name. Settled for a time at a cousin's house in Hanover.'

David frowned, 'But her name wasn't Carlyle. How on earth did you trace her?'

'Ah!' Havers smiled and allowed some of what David had now decided was revolting coffee, to pass his lips. 'They went through a marriage ceremony before they left Germany and, of course, the records show she was Tanya Schneider before becoming Koffman, before becoming Carlyle. I'll come back to all that, don't worry.'

'Hold on! Hold on!' David put up his hand. 'You say he was born in Germany. You must have done a lot of delving.'

'A lot has happened since you and I met at L'Etoile in 1988, David.'

'You're right there!' commented David bitterly.

Havers pushed his coffee away and pulled the heavy, blue glass ashtray towards him. He slowly stubbed out the cigarette amongst the ash and silently lit another. David heard a blaring horn and a screech of tyres from below. Obviously an exasperated driver had lost his patience and had been able to pull out and get on his way. Or it could have been a woman thought David, drily. Why always assume a man? Silence returned and Havers brought him back to the subject in hand.

'In fact, a remarkable lot has happened,' Havers reflected, as he repeated himself. 'The Cold War had not thawed sufficiently, at the time we met after your weekend in the country. However, not long after – one year in fact – down came the Berlin Wall, with all its ramifications. In November 1989, Hungary opened

307

its borders with Austria and immediately crowds of East Germans flowed through. Then days later the Czech authorities violently put down demonstrations, only to launch the destruction of their own government. Then Romania rose against Ceausescu. Event after event. All very remarkable. Or was it? Was it as haphazard and uncontrolled as it seemed at the time?'

David crossed his legs.' I assume that is a rhetorical question?'

Havers blinked, 'Er, yes it is. I'm sorry. I'm not trying to give a history lesson of the recent past.'

David waved his hand, 'Not at all.'

'No,' Havers smiled, 'It probably sounds it, but I'm just...'

'Setting the scene?'

'Yes,' Havers acknowledged ruefully. 'Anyway, forgive me, I'll try and be brief which is not one of my blessings, I know. Back to the happenings of 1989. In fact, we are now satisfied that the KGB were behind the whole disorderly collapse of the Communist states as we had grown to know them. Only it wasn't so disorderly, it was almost orderly.'

'I'm not sure I follow,' David frowned.

'Why should you?' remarked Havers, 'and I'm not being rude. The Soviet economy had been in a hopeless mess for over twenty years and the top echelons of the Soviet Communist Party and the KGB knew it more than anyone else. They were acquainted with all the hard facts. They had been recognised and accepted. But what to do? Ideas for radical changes had been long discussed, planned and then finally implemented when Gorbachev took over. Don't forget that Gorbachev's mentor had been Andropov, who had been head of the KGB. The all-powerful KGB with their secret police allies in the old Communist bloc, The Stasi in East Germany, the St B in Czechoslovakia, the Securitate in Romania, etc. etc. set in motion well-orchestrated plans for radical reforms.

'But, of course, like all plans they started to have a mind and impetus of their own. Not every facet can be manipulated at the right time or at the right place. Pent-up demand for freedom and open Government took over, once it was in the hands of the masses and reformists. Now we, and I mean the Governments of the West, were well aware of what was happening, because of our contacts and agents within the Soviet Union. But, it wasn't all black and white. It was natural that some elements of the KGB who had long been disillusioned were, like most other people, looking for safety and a quick buck. Either by physically changing their country of abode or changing their allegiances ideologically. Chaos reigned for a while. However, Carlyle had been in the vanguard of all that.'

David's eyebrows rose, 'Carlyle?'

Havers nodded. 'Yes, Harmer in Australia, Koffman in Germany, then Carlyle in Germany and England, but actually a Russian agent named Uri Pushkin. He had been allowed in here in the middle seventies with his wife who, of course, had become an agent. The KGB, naturally, had provided him with a "family background" to satisfy as much as possible any questions that might be raised. The story went that his family were all killed in the Russian advance of 1945. He was picked up and put on a similar refugee boat as Tanya and then brought up in an orphanage school in Dortmund. Then he moved into a small manufacturing business there.'

David frowned. 'So when did he become a Soviet agent? No, wait a minute, you said he was Russian?'

'Right,' Havers nodded. 'The boy who grew into the young man, living in Dortmund, and who Carlyle used as his background, left when the business folded in the late sixties. He told his few friends at the firm that he was going to travel around Southern Europe, including Greece and Turkey.' Havers waved his hand. 'None of them ever saw him again. He didn't keep in touch with anyone. Always a loner, apparently. Then he turns up in England many years later.'

David was fascinated. 'Where had he been?'

Havers sighed, as another cigarette end joined the others. 'Wrong question, I'm afraid,' he replied. 'This young man I've been talking about was named Otto Koffman. He was never ever traced after he supposedly left Dortmund. But the man we know as Carlyle, after he legitimately changed the name from Koffman following his marriage to Tanya, was given his background, in case questions should be asked. Which, it so happens, they weren't.'

309

'You mean Otto, whatever, was killed to give Carlyle a history?' David stared at an unconcerned Havers. 'How do you know they are different people?'

Havers shrugged, 'Once there is a doubt, it is just a question of hard slog. Dental records here and blood-types in Germany and handwriting experts are just examples. Anyway, the real Otto Koffman hadn't any money, which was certainly not the case with the new one. All apparently emanating from Luxembourg. However, a lot of what we now know is what we've pieced together with the help of an agent who worked in Moscow KGB. That Uri Pushkin "became" Otto Koffman, a man with no family, few records of any consequence and thus with a change of name, Carlyle. A master of languages, ambitious, obviously with a good brain, funds were made available to him to cement the plans, which were,' Havers looked directly at David, 'very well orchestrated. To awaken, when directed, sleepers who had been recruited over their formative years by ideology, money, blackmail or a combination, of course. Then to pull the trigger and help the co-ordinated attack to expose the British and other countries' establishments, and particularly high-profile owners of the media as being rogues and reprobates, thus untrustworthy and unacceptable. If there was no evidence,' added Havers drily, 'it could always be invented. Anyway, the aim was to cause a crisis of confidence in the West's sociological systems. To provoke unadulterated cynicism towards law and order, as it presently existed. If,' he paused, 'and it is a very important if, they couldn't be turned to work for them.' Havers looked at his watch, 'I hope I'm not keeping you?' he asked mildly.

'For God's sake, Donald,' David said, 'even if the answer was "yes", I'm hardly likely to leave now, am I?'

Havers smiled contentedly. 'Good.' He scratched the back of his neck, 'Well, going back to the kerfuffle of 1988, with the breakdown of order in the Soviet Union imminent and its effect on the long-term Russian plans, Carlyle decided he would play his own game. He didn't wait any longer for instructions. You see, before the real world was conscious of the fundamental changes taking place, the agents involved, like Carlyle and his immediate masters, were well aware that the aims were on hold,

310

and that halfhearted play-acting, based on ideology was going nowhere. Discipline was poor and it was becoming each man for himself.'

'I think I'm with you,' David leant forward. 'Carlyle used his position and the money at his disposal to bring in the sleepers and use them for his own and not his country's purposes?'

'For his financial purposes and arguably still his country's ideological ones,' Havers corrected him. 'We checked around the world, with the FBI, with BOSS in South Africa and others, when events started to focus on the past of certain tycoons and the deaths of recent visitors of theirs who had, at best, only tenuous links with them. What was common to all the deaths was that millions of pounds and other currencies had gone missing from the estates of the tycoons and disappeared in the black hole of Switzerland and middle Europe. Never found. Carlyle's cache of gold. All thanks to the sleepers.'

'And the sleepers wouldn't have known that they were being used for the wrong reasons?'

'Why should they?' Havers looked up as a speckled pigeon landed on the ledge of the window. 'They received their instructions as they had been primed to, sometime in the past and all, I say all, they had to do was carry them out. And they would have reasoned their instructions made sense ideologically.'

David watched, as the pigeon flew up and away, apparently dissatisfied with the resting place. 'And the sleepers were all called to Cordington,' he muttered reflectively.

'That's about it,' Havers was watching him closely, 'but maybe there were others.'

'What do you mean?' David frowned.

'Well, after our lunch all those years ago, we have been linking events with that weekend quite successfully, except, of course, you two were there...'

'Here!' David exploded angrily, 'you don't think we've...'

'Steady, steady,' Havers shook his head, his hands held high. 'I'm not thinking you're involved in any way. Unfortunately, we are reasonably satisfied that your cousin Douglas Price was a

311

sleeper. He was a member of a Communist fringe group in his youth, when at university...'

'So it's true,' David said slowly, at nothing in particular.

'What?' Havers asked quietly.

'Robert Maxwell and DP ... sorry, Douglas...' he trailed off.

'Let us just say, it's pretty clear you were, as you thought at the time, an unfortunate mistake. You shouldn't have been there. The best laid plans and all that,' Havers smiled.

'So that's that, then,' David uncrossed his legs and stretched them forward.

'Well, not quite,' Havers looked serious again.

'What do you meant "not quite"?'

22

June climbed the steps from the underground station at Hyde Park Corner. Ahead of her was Knightsbridge. It was a very pleasant day. She was not sure whether she would describe it to a foreigner as a late summer or an early autumn day. But it didn't really matter, as all she knew was that it was delightful. There was a gentle breeze and the sun was shining warmly from an almost cloudless sky. It was only ten o'clock, as she looked at her watch. That was good. Her appointment was for ten-fifteen, just round the corner in Wilton Place. She almost collided with a young woman running to catch a bus and realised that she was not really paying attention. She knew Wilton Place and she was on automatic pilot.

This appointment. What on earth was it all about? She had not shown David the letter that had come to her at work the previous week in the usual dreaded buff Inland Revenue envelope, as he was so busy and fraught in the office. It had been a polite but no-nonsense letter, asking her to attend at the Inland Revenue's Special Office in Wilton Place, to discuss certain financial affairs that required examination.

'What the hell are they talking about?' June had asked herself, as she had looked at the letter. 'I haven't got anything outstanding with them. My returns are up to date. There's no problem with my allowances, that I know of. I don't think I owe them any money.' She had become petulant. 'There's no phone or fax number for me to contact, to find out what it's about. If they raise any queries that I can't answer I will burden David with it, but not unless that happens.'

313

As the crawling taxis, buses and lorries spewed out their terrible pollution, she turned the corner into Wilton Place, which was comparatively calm and clean. No blue haze of exhaust fumes. The Berkeley Hotel presented itself to her, as an admirable building promising a superabundance of the famous and rich, luxuriating in their oasis. Unfortunately it was not for her. About a hundred yards beyond on the same side of the road was the terraced building that had a small brass plate on the newly painted black door. Inland Revenue. A small wooden notice was fixed to the wall by the door and above the bell-push she was about to press. It merely read Please Enter. With heart beating faster than she wished and a slight feeling of unease in her stomach, she pushed the door-handle to find the heavy door opened surprisingly easily.

Stepping inside she found an unexpectedly well-furnished entrance hall – red carpet and pleasant cream walls with prints of wild flowers adorning them. Immediately in front of her as she closed the door, stood a tall, slim, blonde receptionist, smartly dressed in a black business suit over a white blouse.

'Good morning, Madam, May I help you?' The smile was encouraging.

'Er, yes,' June nodded, 'I have an appointment at ten-fifteen.'

The smile remained fixed, as the receptionist checked a diary on her desk behind her. 'You are...?' she enquired.

'June Campbell. Actually June Price, but my tax affairs have always been addressed to me...'

'Yes Madam,' the interruption was charming. 'Would you care to follow me?' June followed the elegant figure down the hall, until at the far end the receptionist opened a door on the left and stepped back. 'Would you care to go in? You won't be kept waiting for more than a few moments.'

June nodded and entered the large, high-ceilinged room with a large bay window revealing a small inner courtyard at the back of the building. The room reflected the furnishings of the hall, but its centrepiece was a large, circular, leather-topped table, strewn with magazines. There were tall, upright, red leather chairs round the sides.

June stood stock still as she took in the room, but not in admiration of the decor, but at the stupefying sight of a woman sitting opposite, staring at her, mouth open and by the look on her face, equally stunned. The woman crossed her shapely legs, as June noticed her pale-blue fashionable dress, over which was draped a pure-white collarless linen jacket. June's heart beat accelerated it seemed tenfold, as she made her way to a chair behind the door and sat down. It gave her a moment to try and gather her wits.

'I'm sorry,' June said, with a wan smile. 'I know we've met, but I'm afraid...'

The woman looked at her straight faced, as she clutched at her handbag and gave no encouragement.

'Ah. Yes, I remember,' June continued breathlessly. 'It was a long time ago, I guess. We met at Cordington in Sussex. Let me see now, about five years ago, would it be? No,' she shook her head, 'it was 1988. You were a guest at that weekend...'

The woman was struggling with her composure. Her features darkened, as she looked down at her hands and her posture sagged, as if her spine had lost a vertebra. There was silence, only interrupted by the slow methodical beat of a grandfather clock against the far wall.

'You are, or were, Pat Thatcher,' June said. 'I was there with my husband, David, and you were there with your husband,' she hesitated and swallowed a lump that had risen in her throat, 'Maurice, wasn't it? An awful lot has happened since then,' she added, by way of explanation.

There was a moment's silence before Pat Thatcher leaned forward and said uneasily, 'Why are you here?'

June ignored the question, but commented, 'This is the most extraordinary coincidence, isn't it? Imagine meeting here of all places!' She pulled a face. 'Not a very agreeable place to meet again though, is it?' She smiled weakly, 'I can think of better things to do on a lovely day like this, than come here and be interviewed by the Inland Revenue!'

'Oh,' Pat Thatcher's eyebrows lifted in surprise and then relief appeared on her face. 'Have you been called for an interview, too?' Before June needed to respond, she went on, 'I had this most extraordinary letter the other day making certain allegations of undeclared income and saying that they wished to discuss the matter at a personal interview. All most ridiculous, but anyway here I am,' she smiled.

June looked at Pat Thatcher and cast her mind back to Cordington all those years ago. A very attractive, easy-going woman she recalled, and remembered her slight pangs of jealousy when she had seen David engrossed in conversation with her, that first evening. June thought that if anything the intervening years had improved her. There was now added poise and the slight ageing of her face gave it more character. A woman she'd rather David did not catch up with, she thought.

As her mind tried to continue in conversation mode, the door beside her opened, which made her heart surge. The call for the interview for one of them, she supposed.

'Would you care to wait in there? We won't keep you long.' The same calm, reassuring, receptionist's voice could be heard in the corridor.

'I should hope not,' came the ill-tempered drawl of a response from a woman who then slowly strode into the room, as the door shut quietly, but firmly, behind her. 'If they think they are going to mess my day up completely by dragging this thing out, they've got another think coming.'

The woman looked neither right nor left, but walked to the window and stared out at the courtyard. She was a brunette, with shoulder-length hair, in a black and white check sleeveless dress, showing off her ample, but well-controlled figure. The woman snapped open her black leather handbag and taking out her compact examined her face. After touching up her lipstick, she closed the bag and turned to sit down. It seemed as though for the first time she realised that there were people in the room with her. She had clearly been preoccupied, for whatever reason, when she had been shown in, and that almost like a dentist's waiting room, regarded anybody there as inanimate objects and of no concern. Concern, however, was now evident.

'What . . .' the woman had stood still on seeing June, 'what are you doing here?' There was total bewilderment written all over her face now, the ill-temper having been overtaken.

316

'I'm sorry?' June couldn't think of anything more constructive to say.

'Hallo,' Pat Thatcher's quiet voice interposed and the woman spun round and stared.

'Christ!' she said, 'is this some kind of reunion?'

The response was a numb shake of the head from Pat Thatcher.

'Rita Hardy, isn't it?' June was the picture of serenity, as Rita Hardy slumped into the chair beside her. 'How nice to see you again, although I'm afraid a lot has happened to us all since we met before,' June saw Pat Thatcher's face tighten visibly.

'You can say that again.' Rita Hardy had fumbled for a cigarette in her handbag and lit it, June thought, in the time it had taken her to draw breath. 'Never mind about a lot. Too bloody much, by far. I've...'

Whatever she was about to say was lost as the door opened again. June decided that she was no longer going to be surprised by the entrant. And, of course, she wasn't. As the door closed the woman standing there looking very surprised, was Lesley Abbott. Her hair, as June remembered it, was short and un-complicated. With little make-up and wearing a fawn, unstructured jacket with matching tailored trousers, she looked every bit a smart businesswoman. Suddenly June had a thought. Maybe she was the interviewer? The thought was immediately dashed by the continuing look of surprise on Lesley Abbott's face. She hadn't moved, but had slowly looked at each of the other women, as though not believing what she was seeing.

Before a word was spoken, the door opened again and as Lesley Abbott moved further into the room to allow the movement behind her, in rushed Jenny Gorman. 'Again, I'm sorry I'm late,' she called over her shoulder, 'missed the bus and you know what its like. Never there when you want them and then they come along in threes out of schedule, and of course, two of them are empty. Ah! Well, that's life!'

'There's no problem, Madam, I assure you,' June heard the receptionist's soothing voice. 'I'm afraid we're running a little late, so no harm's done.' The door closed.

'Oh, good, good,' Jenny Gorman then took stock of her

317

surroundings and the silent assembly. She brought her handbag up to her bosom and, holding it like a shield, murmured 'Goodness, gracious!' and rushed to the nearest vacant chair. She sat down, pulled a handkerchief from a pocket of her incongruous raincoat and blew her nose.

June was now utterly shocked by the last few moments and watched, stunned. Lesley Abbott came and sat between her and the door, a scowl on her face.

'Well,' said Rita Hardy, sucking hard on her cigarette, 'I wondered before you all arrived whether this was some sort of reunion and now I'm bloody well sure of it!'

'Dear me, dear me,' Jenny Gorman blew her nose again, as she looked from face to face.

Pat Thatcher tugged her skirt down and eased her bottom in the chair.

'Did you all receive letters, as I did, asking that you attend for an interview?' Rita asked.

The others all nodded.

'What's it all about?' Jenny Gorman tucked her handkerchief away and shrugged her shoulders. 'Beats me,' she said.

'Oh come on!' Rita Hardy blew some cigarette smoke up in the air. 'Much as I'm thrown by seeing you all and trying to get my wits about me, it's bloody obvious, isn't it?'

'What do you mean?' Lesley Abbot frowned rigidly, as she sat upright in her chair.

'Well,' said Rita resignedly, as she turned and put out her cigarette in the ashtray on the window sill. 'It's money isn't it? I've never declared it, have any of you? It'll be an Al Capone job.'

There was silence. Common sense told June that she should extricate herself physically from this situation, but she didn't have the remotest intention of doing so.

'Al Capone?' Jenny rubbed her nose agitatedly.

'He didn't declare his income for tax purposes and was jailed,' Rita spoke to Jenny as though admonishing an ignorant schoolgirl.

'Oh,' Jenny looked miserable, but June felt she still wasn't appreciating the point. But what was the point? She was damned if she knew what they were talking about. But she felt they were

318

all in tune with each other. She looked at her watch and was surprised to see it was after half-past ten. She checked with the lugubrious grandfather clock. Yes, it also showed twenty-five to eleven.

Pat Thatcher had noticed June's movements and nodded to her. 'Yes, I don't know what's happened to my appointment.' She whispered and turned to the others. 'What times were you asked to be here?'

One by one they all replied that they were asked to be there for ten-fifteen.

'Are we going to be interviewed together, do you think?' Jenny wriggled uncomfortably in her raincoat.

'What's happening?' Lesley snapped, rising from her seat. 'This is intolerable' Before she could reach the door, it opened and the still-smiling receptionist entered and looking at each of the women in turn said, 'I'm awfully sorry but we are running behind this morning. We shouldn't be much longer.'

'Why have we all been asked here for the same time?' Lesley demanded. 'That can't be a coincidence.'

'I'm sorry?' the receptionist fixed her with her radiance. 'We have many interviewers and rooms here. There is nothing unusual in having several people waiting at any one time. That is why we have such a large waiting room,' she added simply and left the room.

'Clever clogs.' Rita yawned, smothering her mouth with her hand.

'But why are we all here together?' June felt she should encourage this conversation. It sounded as though she had happened upon – happened upon or been invited to join – some significant resurrection of the atmosphere of that weekend at Cordington. Only now all the men were dead. Except David.

'For Christ sake! It's because of the money we got.' Rita searched for another cigarette.

'Shut up! Forget it!' Pat shuddered and with a slight moan looked down into her lap.

'How can we?' Rita inhaled thankfully. 'I received my half a million from the unknown life policy and I guess you all did, too.

It helped me accept the things that had happened and life hasn't been too bad. And I haven't asked any questions, either.'

Jenny looked up at her with tears in her eyes. 'Some of us loved our husbands,' she whispered and dug her hands deep into the pockets of her raincoat.

'Damn and blast you,' Rita snorted. 'Do you have some sort of world rights to anguish and heartache?' she asked. 'Do you think it's been fun for any of us? Money's fine and I'd be a hypocrite if I said I haven't enjoyed it. But...' she trailed off and put the cigarette to her lips.

'No new man in your life?' sneered Lesley.

'Of course,' Rita glared at her. 'In fact there've been several, if you must know. They do seem to find me attractive. Maybe it's my big tits,' she grinned mockingly at Lesley, who turned a deep pink and looked away.

'Married?' Pat asked huskily.

Rita shook her head, 'It's not that easy, is it?' she replied. 'Secrets are easier if there's no immediate person to share them with. But,' she shrugged, 'I get by. My present boyfriend only lives in the next street. It's better than living together. Space and independence, when either of us wants it. No crowding. It's good,' she added smoulderingly.

'I'm pleased,' Pat nodded, half smiling. 'I'm sure its not been easy for any of us. Half a million pounds, but with the threat of being killed if I ever open my mouth is a damn strain. I'm sure you all agree.'

'Shut up, you stupid bitch,' Lesley spat out.

'Why?' Pat retorted. 'We're all in the same boat.'

'But are we?' Lesley turned slowly and gazed at June. 'What happened to your husband? I never read or heard of anything happening to him. Did he suffer death, as ours did?' There was a stillness in the room and all June could hear, apart from that wretched grandfather clock, was a pigeon cooing on the roof of a nearby building. 'Well?'

'Er, no,' June shook her head, slowly. 'He's had a number of narrow escapes, but he's still alive, thank God.'

'Then why are you here?' Lesley's eyes narrowed and she stared at June with undisguised belligerence.

320

'Because I had a letter asking me to come at ten-fifteen, as you did,' June replied as she began to perspire. She didn't like the way the conversation was going. Think of something. Think of something to get their trust back. 'David was badly injured, though, and is now a paraplegic,' she looked at them, sorrowfully.

'When?' Lesley asked with interest.

'Oh,' June thought frantically back to the past events. 'Six years or so back.'

'How did it happen?' Jenny leaned forward, elbows on her knees, hands clasped.

'He was knocked down . . . by a blue van, near our house,' June wanted to wipe her forehead, but didn't.

'How did you know it was a blue van?' asked Lesley.

'For Christ sake!' exploded Rita, 'Who cares? Who cares what colour the bloody van was? Or where it was? He was just luckier than our men were. Maybe she hasn't been given as much money as we have. Have you?'

Before June could think what to say, she was staring at a revolver aimed at her midriff. It had appeared as if by magic from Lesley's large handbag. It was pointing unwaveringly and June began to shake.

'Oh, God. What's going on?' she protested.

'You may well ask!' Lesley said with venom. 'Something unfortunate, that's for sure. You know too much from the conversation that's been going on here. You're not one of us.'

'What do you mean? How do you know?' Jenny gaped at Lesley. 'They were at Cordington that weekend. She says her husband has been paralysed. What are you talking about?'

'Her husband hasn't been paralysed! I saw him only the other week. There was nothing the matter with him then, unfortunately.' Lesley didn't take her eyes off June.

'Saw him? Where did you see him?' Jenny looked very puzzled.

'Broome,' replied Lesley, the gun held in an unfaltering hand.

'Broome? Where on earth is that?' Jenny looked decidedly miserable and hunched her shoulders even further.

'Australia,' Lesley glared at June. 'And he was jumping well. Just like a kangaroo, when I saw him last.'

'You were there? But what were you doing there?' Jenny gasped.

June frowned. 'What do you mean he was jumping like a ... Of course! You! You were at The Resort! The maid got it wrong. It wasn't a small, slight man. It was you who tried to kill David when you pushed that urn. Stupid, stupid,' she whispered almost to herself, as she looked at her trembling hands. 'So what now? You can hardly kill me here.'

'We've had enough killings,' Jenny wailed. 'What are you doing with a gun, anyway?'

'Shut up!' Lesley rasped. 'Yes, it was unfortunate you appeared in Broome at the same time as I did, but by chance I saw you both and made sure you didn't see me. I was staying in the town, but it was easy to get in and out of The Resort.'

'But why try and kill David?' June asked.

'Retribution!' Lesley glared at her. 'He'd wasted my journey. I'd gone to bring Carlyle back into the fold, but you caused us to waste him.'

As June heard Jenny say, 'Oh God,' she herself said. 'I don't understand.'

Lesley glowered at June, 'And you're not going to in the next few minutes.' She raised the revolver. 'You and I are leaving now. There's no reason why we shouldn't. We're here voluntarily, so we'll go the same way. My gun will be in my jacket, so don't risk doing anything stupid, or melodramatic. Get up!'

June closed her eyes and rose to her feet. As she did so, there was a noise, like a hornet whizzing past and her ears sang. They hurt momentarily, but, apart from that, she felt nothing. She heard screams and the noise of a chair falling over and opening her eyes, was just in time to see Lesley slide down the wall, against which the blast had knocked her. She left a trail of blood on the wall as she hit the floor and sat there, eyes open and face covered with an expression of surprise, redness seeping into and staining the front of her jacket. June slumped back on to her seat and held her head in her hands, as gasps and sobs came from around her. Looking up, she saw the charming, elegant receptionist standing by the open door with her legs wide apart and a solid, lethal-looking gun with a silencer held in both hands, her eyes staring fixedly at the body on the floor. She lowered the gun and turned her head as a man came in, also carrying a revolver. 'Well done, Valerie,' he nodded.

There were seemingly responsive noises from all round the room. Jenny was retching, Rita was mouthing unladylike obscenities and Pat was sobbing, hysterically.

'Maybe, ladies, you'd like to come with Valerie and have a cup of tea or a stiff drink?'

The man was calm and controlled, as he moved to June's side and helped her up from the chair. June's legs felt like jelly and she was surprised at the total lack of control she had over them. Gratefully she allowed herself to be propelled out of the room.

23

June sat down on the sofa next to David. She placed her glass on the coffee table and sat back, resting her head on David's shoulder.

'OK,' she sighed. 'I'm all ears.'

It was the evening of a day June would never forget. She hadn't seen anybody shot before, but, of course, to be literal she hadn't today. She felt, however, totally justified in describing those horrendous few moments that way. Lesley Abbott dead in front of her still seemed like a nightmare. She was still waiting to be told that they had all been playing charades. Seated opposite her was the still calm man, who had helped her out of the room in Wilton Place. It seemed a lifetime ago.

'Well, good health,' Havers nodded, raising his glass, 'and thank you for making sure it all turned out as planned.' They were back at the offices in St James's that David had visited for the first time less than a week before. They now felt like very familiar and reassuring surroundings to him.

'Planned?' June spluttered into her drink. 'What do you mean "planned"? Don't tell me you knew that Abbott woman was going to try to shoot me? What if she had pulled the trigger first?' Her hand trembled as she banged her glass noisily on the table, spilling her gin and tonic. She looked at David and then Havers, before looking away to the window and saying half to herself, 'I think I'm going to throw up.'

David put his arm round her bowed shoulders, as Havers coughed politely.

324

'We had no idea that it would work out as it did, but Valerie was not the only armed person we had there.'

'No,' June commented bitterly. 'You came in like the cavalry, but you could have been too damned late, couldn't you?'

Havers looked hurt. 'We had been listening and, of course, recording, all that was being said and special agent Valerie and I were right outside, I can assure you. Anyway, it's all history now.'

'And I nearly was,' muttered June disparagingly. 'Why the hell didn't you search her when she arrived?'

'At an Inland Revenue office? Might have put her on her guard, don't you think?' Havers pursed his lips.

'I think you diced with my death!'

'We're very grateful for your help.' Havers smiled.

'Go to hell!' June was close to tears, drained by so much playing with her emotions.

'It was extremely useful,' Havers looked at his fingernails and continued as though giving a tutorial. 'Clearly she was acting on orders to bring Carlyle back and must have had some very persuasive words for him when she found him in Broome. Remember Carlyle's comment to you about others finding him all of a sudden? Lesley Abbott. The Russians are getting their act together again in many ways and she probably threatened Carlyle if he didn't return. They wouldn't have used their resident agents out there in the first instance and risk them being exposed. She was an unknown – a mere visitor on holiday. And they knew each other.'

'Well,' David commented quietly, 'that would seem to be that.'

Havers watched June, as he nodded, 'This time I think you're right. We have established, beyond any real doubt, that the Carlyles had been acting purely for themselves in 1988, but we had to get to the bottom of the other link.'

'Other link?' June repeated, perplexed and tired.

'Yes,' Havers said quietly. 'Our KGB agent knew that Moscow's London section, was of course, controlling many operations through several cells, but he had no direct access to the information he, and we, needed.'

325

'How did he find out about the link?' David asked, chewing some nuts from the bowl on the table.

Havers half-smiled, 'Through sex, would you believe?'

June snorted, 'I'd believe anything about men and sex!' she responded.

'Ah!' Havers wagged an elegant finger, 'but this time it was a man and a woman.'

'Different,' June commented and finished her drink. She rose to refill it, but didn't offer to replenish those of the men.

'Our KGB agent – let's call him Mikhail, although his real name is...'

'Is Michael?' June returned to her seat.

'I was going to say doesn't matter,' Havers smiled. 'Anyway, he was working in the Paris section and he met a very attractive woman at one of the special sports clubs they use in Moscow. He got clearance to date her a couple of times. That came to nothing, but she introduced him to a friend of hers in the London section and that blossomed into something more serious, again with official approval. After a while, because they wanted privacy, he would meet her occasionally at a dacha about twenty kilometres east of Moscow, which a friend of his had access to. They would drink, make love and talk. However, he always made sure the serious talking was done when they were out walking, of course. He wasn't prepared to take the risk of the dacha being bugged. She believed they were deeply in love and that they trusted each other, which in itself, considering their backgrounds, was quite something.

'On one visit, Irina, that was her name, told him a little about her section that was interesting. Treasonable, of course. They had high hopes of a Russian agent they had moved from Germany. Also it turned out that her section had a woman in London, married to a sleeper, but neither he nor she knew anything about each other's interests. It was seemingly very amusing to her that the man was inactive and sleeping, unaware that his wife was working. Not often, but from time to time. Gradually, as Mikhail drew information out of Irina, he realised that the identity of this woman would be useful to us, especially if we could get two birds, one male and one female, with one

326

stone. But Irina never gave away the name. That would be expecting too much. When you put me on to Carlyle, David, and what seemed to be the awakening of sleepers, we told Mikhail to try and persuade Irina to divulge whether her section's woman was married to someone who had been woken from his sleep, as it were.'

'And did she?' asked David, doubtfully.

Havers nodded, 'Yes. She was worried enough about the destabilisation going on in Russia to let things slip out. That was at the time when Moscow had begun to lose control and discipline was breaking down. She commented that they were getting conflicting orders from above and it had begun to be chaotic – a free-for-all down the line. She said a London operation seemed to have gone independent but appeared to be producing their expected results. They appeared to be having control problems with a top agent, but were not getting instructions to deal with it. Apparently she had laughed bitterly and said that the English had an expression "When push comes to shove", which was very appropriate as she would very much like to come and shove this pushy man off the white cliffs of Dover. That evening Mikhail killed Irina, by running her over after he'd dropped her off. Regrettably he had to, for fear of being discovered, as someone asking too many questions. Apparently, the love was one-way.'

'God,' June shut her eyes. 'I don't believe I'm hearing this.'

'The interesting thing, though,' continued Havers unperturbed, 'was that Mikhail knew of Pushkin through his work at Moscow control and knew that he had gone to Germany as a top agent some time before. By her fortuitous apparent play on the word Pushkin, Mikhail painted the picture for us and with the description we had, we plugged him in as Carlyle. We then filled in the jigsaw pieces from here, from Germany and from Russia. We still have agents in Moscow, of course,' he added.

'Of course,' echoed June.

'So,' David nodded thoughtfully, 'you guessed you knew who the sleepers were after I told you my story, by their activities and you pretty well knew one of the wives was the independent agent.'

June looked from David to Havers. 'You set the whole episode up. The letters from the Revenue, then the meeting, because you didn't know which wife it was? And I was the icing on the gingerbread because one of them would know I wasn't involved? How could you? How *could* you?' she cried angrily.

Havers shook his head slowly, as his eyes bore into her. 'Not so, June,' he replied. 'We had no idea whether the wife would know anything about you, or rather David's involvement or lack of it, in the original Carlyle operation. The fact that we knew the wife was not to divulge her position to her husband didn't tell us if she knew anything about a Carlyle sleeper that had gone wrong. Different cells working on a need-to-know basis with their agents? Don't forget Carlyle's action was an extracurricular one. It wasn't part of the due process. She may well not have known, and there was a chance that there would have been no climax to our little scheme today.'

June pursed her lips and returned Havers' gaze. 'I don't buy that,' she replied slowly. 'You can paint that "might, might not" picture, but you knew something would happen, if you put us all together. I was the fuse you lit to bring it to a head. You wouldn't risk getting us together for it not to work. What would be the point? All you'd have done would be to alert a professional agent that you were suspicious of something, even via the Inland Revenue. Come on, I don't buy it,' she repeated crossly.

There was quiet in the room as David listened to the hum of the evening traffic. The windows were closed, as the evening had turned surprisingly chilly after the heat of the day, but they did not shut out the noise. His mind digressed to wondering why the offices didn't have double glazing. Government spending restrictions and red tape, he guessed. He blinked as he realised that Havers had refilled their glasses, whilst refraining from replying to June's doubts.

As he now sat down, Havers looked at David in his familiar, unblinking manner and said, 'All right.' Almost as soon as he said it, the door opened and the same middle-aged woman that David had met on the previous visit stood there.

328

'OK,' Havers nodded to her and she immediately turned and went out, shutting the door.

'What about the other wives, or widows?' David asked, wondering if there was a bell-push somewhere that had summoned the woman.

'Brushed and cleaned and sent home. They were told it was all a mistake and they wouldn't be bothered again for tax or anything else,' Havers replied dismissively.

'Bully for some,' June grimaced. 'What about the body and the offices and ... ?' she finished lamely.

'Oh,' Havers smiled complacently, 'I think you'll find the offices will be empty.' He paused, 'Fresh, clean walls and just floorboards, tomorrow. Old Government offices, unused now,' he added. 'As for the body, well many people go missing and remain unaccounted for. The police files are full of them. I don't think you need worry.'

'Worry?' June snorted. 'Of course not. Why should I worry? Nothing happened, did it.'

Silence returned for a few moments, each left with their own thoughts. Something was happening outside that room, David realised, and they were waiting for the outcome. He was surprised that June appeared content to subside into her inner self. Her face looked blank, but he was sure her mind wasn't.

Suddenly a knock on the door was followed by its opening and in walked ... David knew his mouth had dropped open, as his mind wrestled with the apparition. June had cried out, as her hand flew to her mouth. It couldn't be! But, it was. Standing motionless in front of an unknown younger man, both dressed in open-necked shirts and slacks, was Carlyle. A greyer, haggard, leaner Carlyle. But, definitely Carlyle.

'David!' June turned to him, tears in her eyes, 'What's going on?'

'God knows!' he replied and swivelled round to Havers. Before he could say any more Havers bowed his head and raised his hands momentarily.

'God may or may not know, David. But on this particular subject, I confess that I do.' He eased round addressing the

329

younger man behind Carlyle. 'All right, Bulstrode,' he nodded, 'I'll see you both in the morning.'

Carlyle looked at Havers vacantly and opened his mouth, 'I...'

'I said, I'll see you in the morning,' Havers snapped. Bulstrode took Carlyle's elbow, and Carlyle stood still for a moment, looking at all three of them through expressionless eyes, then shrugged and allowed himself to be led out. As the door shut, June sobbed and picking up her glass took a large gulp. David's mouth had gone dry and he was only a second behind her in reaching for his drink.

'I'm sorry if that was a shock to you both,' Havers mouth twitched at the edges. 'I felt that only by seeing him would you really accept that he was alive, and because you have both been partners, albeit unwilling ones, in this drama, it was only right that I trust you with that knowledge.'

It was David's turn to shake his head and mutter, 'I don't believe it! I ... we ... thought he'd died in Perth! He had been blown up. Together with her. What about her?' He asked frowning.

Havers shook his head, 'No, Tanya Carlyle died all right.' He crossed his legs and flicked the crease in his trousers into place. 'Because of what happened to you both in Broome and your telling Superintendent Tom Rolls about Carlyle, he contacted me as he told you. I might add that we didn't know where the Carlyles had gone. They disappeared very successfully. They certainly hadn't gone back to the Soviet Union.' Havers shook his head. 'We were not proud of losing them. However, we thought it sensible to let it be known that all the underlings we caught, who were just moronic criminal types, would be brought to court the day after the Carlyles, or, as they were known there of course, the Harmers. That way we established the target day if anyone was interested. Although we were prepared to allow the Harmers to be remanded and begin the due process of law, we thought it would be safer that they be taken to court in four vehicles, just in case their masters, if they still had any, or their drug associates if that was all they were involved in, didn't want them around any longer. Anyway one vehicle for each of them and two empty ones. Two runs to the Court with five minutes in between and...'

'They blew up the first convoy with her in one vehicle and nobody in the other?' David looked out of the windows at the darkening sky.

'Exactly,' Havers nodded. 'So we let the story go out, of course, that they had both been killed. We didn't take him to court after that, as you can imagine. We had been pretty sure the bomb was the work of a drug syndicate in Sydney, wanting to be sure he couldn't be linked to their network. Now, it doesn't seem like that. Anyway, somebody wanted them dead, so let them be happy in their sleep at night. Now we had the best of all possible worlds. Carlyle expunged from the memory of all his predators and in our control. Nowhere to go. Nobody to turn to. No-one to protect him.'

'Except...' June trailed off quietly.

'Us,' Havers smiled.

'God, and you want him?' David asked incredulously, still with a dry throat.

'Of course, David,' Havers' smile straightened. 'Our business never ends, you know. Just because politicians speak easy words and proclaim "peace"! We've heard it all before, haven't we? What happened to Chamberlain's "peace in our time"? Didn't bloody exist, did it? It may stutter on in a non-war mode for years but – peace? Forget it. We have to remain on the alert and active at all times. Using any means at our disposal.'

'Even shits like Carlyle,' David curled his lips.

Havers momentarily closed his eyes and then looked at David, 'Yes,' he acknowledged, 'even the Carlyles of this world.'

'But your world is the Carlyles, isn't it?' June muttered. 'You probably believe you've won a victory now by having him working for you.'

'Of course,' Havers nodded. 'We'll give him a new identity, probably plastic surgery; a new nose and jawline, and when we've trawled in his mini-fortune from all over the world, we may even let him keep some of it. If he stays a good boy.'

'Any young man trafficking in drugs should be hanged at the first opportunity,' June's eyes were piercingly cold. 'About the only thing I guess Iran is right about.' She paused and then, subdued, added, 'God has a lot to answer for, if the Carlyles among us can come out on top.'

'No,' Havers rebutted firmly. 'Carlyle is, and will remain, only sitting on a red-hot poker, but I'd rather have him working for us than anyone else.'

'Why wouldn't he just return to Russia or their agents at the first opportunity?' David asked.

'Havers smiled. 'After what he did? Used his training and their trust to compromise his country for personal gain? They are not in disarray any more. If they find him they will want to know what he's told to whom. He himself believes they only wanted to debrief him and then eradicate him. That's good enough for us, especially as he's probably right.'

'Well,' David remarked, 'at least you'll be able to round up all his cohorts in this country.'

Havers shook his head. 'Cats don't always kill the mice, David. Sometimes they just watch them and play with them. Anyway, I'm afraid when Carlyle did his own thing he not only probably paid them well, he signed their death-warrants, too.'

'Well, that's something.' June stood up and looked at Havers stonily. 'David, I'd like to go now. This isn't our world.'

Havers stood up and June and David followed him to the door and as he opened it he smiled and extended his hand. June ignored him and walked out. David went to follow but stopped and turned

'Thank you for risking my wife's life' he said, as his fist slammed into Havers' nose. He savoured the gasp and the blood on the surprised face, as he followed a now smiling June down the stairs.

As they left and crossed the road to hail a taxi opposite The Blue Posts public house, June who had not said another word, quietly linked her arm into David's.

'I think next year we'd better be more careful about where we go on holiday,' David commented drily and clasped her hand.

June climbed into the taxi, still without speaking and looked out of the window. David gave the cabbie the directions home and turned to her, 'Any ideas?' he enquired, as he sat back.

'Oh, yes,' June said after a pause, 'I shall want guaranteed sun and total, total, peace and quiet.'

'Fine by me,' David said, 'Where do you have in mind?'

June looked at him sideways, as a smile began to light up her face, 'Guess.'

'Tuscany?' he suggested, as the taxi sped through Knightsbridge and on to Kensington.

'I'd like to go there sometime, yes,' she moistened her lips. 'But I don't know where Carlyle might be by the time our holiday comes round and there is no way I'm going to come up against him two years running.' She looked at the title of one of the films displayed at the Odeon cinema, as they swept by in the taxi. *Bullets over Broadway.* 'And, I don't think I want to go to America,' she added. 'No it's obvious – the one place he can't, he won't, be allowed to go back to is ... Broome,' she sighed. 'Sometimes, darling, you can be a bit slow,' she hugged him. 'I never did get my pearls.'

David heard and smiled. His hand hurt. He looked out of the window of the taxi and saw the billboards for the evening paper. "Another Government Minister sex scandal" they raved.

'You know,' he said slowly, 'Hilaire Belloc wrote:

> We had intended you to be
> the next Prime Minister but three:
> The stocks were sold; the Press was squared;
> The Middle Class was quite prepared.
> But as it is! ... My language fails!
> Go out and govern New South Wales!

'I'm afraid there's a lot of concern, in some quarters, about the way the press and the media generally behave. There doesn't seem to be much squaring any more. Do you think we've heard the last of what Carlyle was up to all those years ago, whether or not he was doing it for his own personal gain?'

'Meaning?' June looked at David, puzzled.

'Meaning, if anything startling happens to the remaining media barons in the years to come, either physically or psychologically, might we just wonder whether it is pure coincidence, or whether it has anything to do with Carlyle's old masters, or indeed his new ones?'

There was a thought-provoking silence between them as the taxi made its way slowly round Hammersmith Broadway, then June shook her head, dismissively, her hair cascading over her face. She looked up, gazing innocently at David as she pulled her hair back, and said, 'I remember another bit of Belloc. It went:

"The chief defect of Henry King,
was chewing little bits of string."

How about going to The Spaghetti House in the Chiswick High Road for a meal tonight? You know how much I love spaghetti and we haven't had any for weeks.'

As the taxi passed the brightly lit windows of Marks and Spencer in King Street, David replied, half to himself, 'Yes, The Spaghetti House is fine by me, mind you I always find spaghetti very filling. Almost a feast in itself. A feast.' He grimaced and then laughed bitterly, as he stared at the back of the elderly, bald-headed, driver. 'We were young, we were merry, but in 1988 we weren't as wise as we are now.'

June didn't speak for a moment and then as the taxi pulled up outside their house, she remarked pointedly, 'We wouldn't have been much wiser now, darling, if I hadn't chosen Broome instead of Tuscany. And that nearly cost us our lives. Maybe next year we should ... after all ... they must eat spaghetti in Tuscany, musn't they?'

EPILOGUE

He watched the last of the four women and seven men leave the room. A variety of complex personalities from many backgrounds, but bonded by one essential factor. Total commitment. If there had been any doubts about that, he would not have had them brought to him.

His gaze momentarily focused on the one small window in the cheerless office, through which he could see the leaden sky and the heavy, unremitting snow gusting from the north-east. The visitors would leave this country of seemingly endless winter and return by various indirect routes to their own countries, there to carry on with their lives and be ready for the call. Whenever.

He was older now. His face lined, his cheeks sunken and his hair greying, but his cold eyes were as penetrating and alert as they had always been. The paradox was that he still personified calmness and remoteness in spite of everything that had happened. He had been one of those who had been unable to stem the indiscipline in Moscow during the almost anarchic leadership and ideological struggles of the past few years. Now, however, he and a hard core who could be trusted from the defunct KGB, were ensuring that order and discipline were re-established by a ruthless vetting of all the security services. Considerable re-grouping had been necessary to ensure that there would be no more mistakes.

Very few knew of the existence of his elite RVS section within

335

the new Foreign Intelligence Service and he was determined to ensure that that was how it would continue. He had been promoted and placed in command and it had been his decision to leave Moscow. Proximity to other sections was an unnecessary risk. He leant forward and switched on his VDU. The screen sprang to life, glowing a soft, cobalt blue. He keyed in some roman letters and, after a moment's pause, the screen responded: 'RVS Section. Highly Classified. Enter Password'. He duly obliged. Then the request came: 'Enter Personal ID'. He keyed it in and waited. He would record today's meeting with satisfaction. Next month, he was due to hold a similar meeting with a group chosen to operate in countries, including his own Russia, that the West had once termed 'The Eastern Bloc'. New situations demanded new agendas. A cliché, but true.

The screen had, by now, requested the number of the programme he required. He responded. Then the screen shone with the letters ICBM. Western security would assume this was Intercontinental Ballistic Missiles. But not in his private world. His initials stood for International Control By Media. Finally his personal codeword. His lips twitched, sardonically, at his little private joke, as he entered 'VARESH'. An anagram of Havers. He began to input, patiently. He acknowledged that he would have to be very patient ... maybe for many years ahead. But patience, combined with infinite planning, would be rewarded in the end. He had to believe that.